CHRIS DRESSER

PURSUIT OF TREACHERY

pagodatreebooks

To Margaret
with best wishes

Chris Dresser

First published in Great Britain in 2021 by Pagoda Tree Books
an imprint of Broomfield Books and OTR Publishing;
36 De La Warr Road, East Grinstead, West Sussex RH19 3BP

ISBN 978-1-906375-10-2

Cover design by Beyond Media, www.beyondmedia.co
from original artwork by Seb Springall, www.springzart.com

Visit www.pagodatreebooks.com to read more about Chris Dresser's titles and our
other books. You can sign up for e-newsletters
to find out about our new releases.

I would like to dedicate this novel to
my long-suffering wife, Hero,
(which is her real name and well deserved)
who, after fifty-five years of marriage,
has never once suggested that I go out and get a safe job!

Editor's Note

There is a glossary at the back of the book for Afrikaans and South African words and terms.

CHAPTER 1

As Rob drove the Jeep skilfully along the dirt road, Ed wondered whether his impulsive offer of help had been a dumb thing to do. After the long flight from Atlanta in the United States to Johannesburg, South Africa, plus a nearly two-hour drive, he had arrived at Buffalo Hills country hotel. He met the manager, Rob Schutte, as he was preparing to join the other voluntary fire-fighters in a concentrated effort to halt a massive brushfire heading down the valley. On an impulse Ed offered help. It was the year 2001 and he was interested to see how South Africa was settling into its new democratic era. Perhaps an emergency like this would reveal how well the different races were now interacting with each other.

Ed was a ruggedly good-looking young man in his mid-twenties. His eyes varied between blue and green depending upon the clothes he was wearing. He wore his blonde hair cut short. At six foot two and a hundred and eighty pounds he looked and moved like an athlete. He had been a key member of his college's basketball team in his home city of Minneapolis but had always wished he were five or six inches taller to challenge some of the giants he encountered in the game. His speed and dexterity had kept him competitive. He had also belonged to the College's fire-fighting team. They had been given some basic training but the worst fire they ever had to contend with, was some guy's bedding that had caught alight when he fell asleep with a lighted cigarette in his hand!

Now he was heading towards a fire that was already visible on the hills ahead of them. He estimated that the flames must be at least fifteen feet high. A fierce wind was blowing the fire in the direction of numerous farms and homesteads, as well as the hotel where he would be staying for the next six months. Rob glanced across at him.

'Not your usual city blaze, eh?'

'Tell me about it! Do you have plenty fires around here?'

Rob shrugged.

'Maybe two or three a year. Usually around this time, August, September after a long dry winter up here on the Highveld...'

Ed was puzzled for a moment.

'Winter?'

'Southern hemisphere, remember? Our winters are your summers and vice versa.'

Ed chuckled as he realised.

'Guess I'm still disoriented from the long flight.'

Rob sounded concerned as he asked the young American if he was really up for the encounter with the fire.

'I'm fine. The adrenaline rush has already started!'

Ed's response was more bravado than good sense. In fact, he had left the States seriously worried about his younger brother's increasing hostility towards his mother and him. He had welcomed the idea of taking a contract as a mining engineer in far-off Africa. Back home there were massive disputes over their recently deceased father's decision not to appoint Justin as successor to the head of the huge Willjohn Industries. Ed himself had made it clear some years previous that he wished to pursue his own career instead of joining the family's huge conglomerate. This had placed his father in a difficult position. The younger brother, Justin, was clearly not executive material and he had finally decided to appoint his long-serving number two, Franklin de Vos as the new CEO.

Ed had welcomed the decision. Franklin was a good man. Justin on the other hand was sly, manipulative and had a vicious streak. He would have almost certainly destroyed the corporation over time. Ed and his mother remained major shareholders, with Justin receiving about ten percent. He had predictably threatened to gain control by any means possible. Ed feared that he may be able to manipulate their mother, Jean, who, despite everything, still had a soft spot for her youngest son. Ed had refused to sell his shares to Justin but if the younger brother could persuade their mother to hand over her portion, there was a real chance that Justin could eventually gain control. Ed had nearly cancelled his contract with Premier Platinum and his much-anticipated trip to Africa but his mother had insisted that he go. Jean had assured Ed that much as she also loved Justin, she could see that he was not executive material. She and Franklin would never allow the youngster to infiltrate the Group, let alone take it over.

Rob drove fast along the winding dirt road. On either side a mix of well cultivated farms and open grazing land indicated what could be lost if the fire raged out of control. Rob seemed to be good driver and Ed's attention was drawn back to the adventure in hand as the reddish glow ahead grew stronger. A dozen or so Impala, one of Africa's most prolific species of buck, suddenly streamed across the road in front of them. Rob swore under his breath as he eased off on the pedal and with great skill avoided skidding on the dirt. He managed to squeeze past the last of the dainty little creatures as they leapt away and disappeared into the bush on the far side of the road.

'Well handled' Ed commented.

Rob grinned.

'You've gotta be ready for anything on these roads, especially when animals're running away from a fire.'

'How many guys will be coming to fight it?' Ed wanted to know.

'We get anywhere between twenty and thirty depending upon the time of day or night. Mostly local farmers trying to save their crops or cattle and their buildings. We always try to send two or three guys from the hotel as well.'

'All the grass I've seen so far is either yellow or even brown. Has it not rained for some time?'

'Here on the Highveld we get summer rains and dry but bloody cold winters being at six thousand feet above sea level. The rains usually arrive in September. Today's the eighth and no sign of them yet. Just hope we're not in for a drought. It also increases the fire hazard. Once the rains come, we seldom have a problem.'

They crested a rise and suddenly the flames could be seen, racing down the next line of hills.

'Man, that's a scary sight!' Ed spoke more with admiration than with fear. 'I guess it gives you guys a real buzz every time?'

Rob gave a wry smile.

'A buzz, yes, but I'd be a fool if I didn't admit being shit-scared on occasions.'

Ed was also beginning to feel a rising tide of excitement, tinged with the inevitable anxiety of the unknown.

'So, what do we do when we get there?'

'We'll meet up with Errol Saperstein, our co-ordinator, plus the rest of the team. Errol's farm's over there, to the right...'

Rob pointed to a sign, which read, 'Amble In,' with a narrow dirt track leading off the road.

'Sounds more like a motel than a farm,' Ed said as they flashed past.

'He has a few self-catering bungalows,' Rob acknowledged. 'Errol used to have a large engineering business in Johannesburg and a holiday cottage out here. Now he's retired but keeps himself busy growing things.'

'What kind of things?' Ed asked.

Rob chuckled. 'He's quite unique in this area. He makes kosher wines and jams!'

'Is there much of a market for that here in South Africa?'

'Ja, we have a large Jewish community, mostly in Johannesburg. I think he does quite well...Aah!'

Rob slowed down as he rounded a bend in the road and came upon a convoy of about ten other vehicles. He flashed his lights and the convoy set off in front of him. A rising cloud of dust made Rob slow right down.

He glanced across at Ed. 'Having second thoughts?'

'Nah. Looking forward to it,' Ed responded.

The convoy quickly climbed the northern slopes at the far end of the valley, close to where the Sterkstroom River rose from the hillside to feed the Buffelspoort Dam far below. Ed could now see the flames steadily marching across the dry veld. In places, the flames were at least up to 20 feet high.

'The wind's unpredictable up here, so watch out if the fire changes direction.'

The convoy stopped. Rob and Ed alighted from the SUV. Rob walked around to the back of the vehicle, opened it up and took out some wet sacks. As they joined about twenty-five other men, Ed noticed that many of them carried broad strips of old conveyor belts instead of sacking. Good idea, he thought as the men trudged up the hillside and approached the flames.

There was no time for introductions. Ed and Rob joined the line of beaters who began to methodically slap at the flames. Following the men, a Land Rover towed a large red water tank with a pump and hoses on a trailer. Where the flames were too fierce, the water pump was brought into action first, with the beaters moving in behind it to beat out any remaining sparks. Most of the time, however, the beaters went on ahead. The water pump and hoses would follow up and douse the remaining sparks. The men, who were a wide assortment of ages, sizes and colours, knew their jobs well.

As Rob had predicted, the wind was gusting fiercely and constantly changing direction as it whistled through gaps in the towering mountain slopes. Suddenly the wind blew a tongue of flame across to some dry bush behind the fire fighters. One of the farmers yelled to the others to retreat before they were cut off and surrounded by the deadly wall of flame. Ed and Rob dashed for the rapidly closing gap along with the other men.

Out of the corner of his eye Ed saw one of the farmers stumble and go down. He was a rather overweight man, probably in his late fifties. He writhed on the ground clutching his ankle.

The other firefighters including Rob were well ahead and didn't see the man fall. Ed didn't hesitate. He turned back and grabbed the man under his shoulders. Ed was a powerfully built and fit young man, but the farmer was very heavy and in agony from a twisted ankle. Ed struggled to get him onto one leg and pull his arm over Ed's shoulder to support him as he tried to hop to safety. Rob had suddenly realised that his brand-new hotel guest was not right behind him. Rob turned just as the gap in the flames closed with terrifying rapidity.

'Errol, water here, now!' Rob yelled.

Errol was already moving the water tanker towards the gap that had closed, anticipating that a straggler may not have made it through in time. In seconds a powerful jet of water fought to re-open a hole in the wall of flames. Rob moved immediately, first he ran into the jet of water, thoroughly soaking himself, and then he plunged into the flames where the water was already thinning the fire. He made it through with a few wisps of smoke and burning grass attached to his body, just as Ed and the farmer staggered towards him.

Rob's additional muscle speeded up the rescue process. A few moments later, the three men emerged on the far side of the ring of fire to be greeted with cheers and applause from the rest of the men who were only now aware of the drama they had just left behind.

The injured farmer was quickly taken off Ed and Rob's hands and carried to a nearby vehicle. Ed was surrounded by most of the firefighters, who wanted to shake his hand or clap him fiercely on the back. Ed thought he would collapse from the sheer weight of their enthusiastic congratulations. Rob grinned, hugely relieved and shooed the men away. He called out.

'Meet Ed our newest hotel guest…and by the look of it who could be our quickest departure!!'

The men, including Ed, laughed. The American gave a weary wave.

'Guess I'll stick around but no one told me that Africa was this hot!'

More laughter, then the men turned back to the task of fighting the fire. The wind was dropping making their task much more controllable.

The compact figure of Errol Saperstein roamed across the veld, yelling instructions to the men as he saw the fire either retreating or advancing. Ed had never seen a grass fire before and soon discovered that the heat from the flames was alarmingly intense. The acrid smoke made him cough and his eyes stung fiercely. Back home, he had been given a smoke mask and goggles. This was a much more basic operation, although he had to admit that it was very efficient.

He was wearing a thick sweater over a t-shirt. He stepped back momentarily to rip off both articles of clothing. He then wound the t-shirt around the lower part of his face and put the sweater back on. Rob looked around and asked the youngster if he were all right. Ed gave him a "thumbs up" sign and returned to the line.

As Ed developed a rhythm to his beating, he soon forgot his tiredness in the exhilaration of the battle against the forces of nature. His new-found skill was suddenly interrupted. In the fading light, an animal raced out of the fire and leaped straight towards Ed. With a startled yelp, he spun aside and just managed to avoid being hit by a huge and terrified Kudu bull.

The creature must have been encircled by a ring of fire and had watched in terror as the flames had approached it from all sides. Finally, the magnificent antelope had panicked and jumped over the fire at its lowest point, which happened to be the place where Rob and Ed were the beaters.

It landed between Ed and Rob and then scampered off down the hill, rapidly disappearing in the gloom. There was some ribald laughter from the other beaters as Ed stared after the retreating antelope in shock and amazement. It was at least as big as a horse. Rob looked at his young protégé with concern.

'Okay?' Rob asked.

'Sure,' he replied a little shakily. 'This place is full of surprises!'

Rob shook his head in wonder.

'The odds on that happening to you have to be thousands to one. Most of the wildlife would run away from humans but this character must've felt trapped by the fire. Remind me to turn down the next guest with pyromaniac tendencies, will you?'

'Anytime,' Ed laughed. 'I'm good, really...'

It took the team a couple of hours to completely subdue the fire. The hills were littered with diabase rocks and crumbling slate, which had slowed the beaters' progress. It was now completely dark and most of the men, including Rob, had produced a number of powerful torches, with which they combed the area for any traces of smouldering grass or sparks from burning tree branches.

Errol thanked everyone then called out a few names that he asked to remain for a while until they were certain that the fire was not going to rekindle. Rob's name had not been called. As he and Ed turned to go, Rob crossed over to Errol and introduced him to Ed. Rob had never brought a hotel guest to a fire before.

Before Errol could comment, Ed grinned and told him, 'I volunteered.'

'Thanks Ed. Every pair of hands help and you did great job of rescuing Fanie. Pop into my place for a drink sometime.'

'I'd like that. Er, would I have to drink kosher wine?'

Errol chuckled. 'My reputation's spreading, I see. We cater for all tastes so don't worry.'

Ed thanked him and promised to visit the farm once he had settled in.

On the way back to the hotel, Ed told Rob that his first and most abiding impression of the valley and its people was one of enormous friendliness. Rob nodded.

'Like any small community, you get your occasional squabble, family feuds and so on but yes, they're mostly good people around here. Quite amazing when you consider the major battles that took place in this very valley just on a hundred years ago.'

Ed suddenly realised that he was exhausted. 'I'll take a rain check on that story,' he mumbled, his voice slurring from tiredness.

They pulled up at the hotel and Rob told the young man firmly that he should shower, have a quick meal and get an early night. Ed agreed wholeheartedly. Looking down, his clothes were soot-blackened and, he suspected, his face must be too, he realised that he should have taken his bedroom key with him.

He approached the desk, hoping to avoid any other guests. A delightful young blonde, Angela, manned the reception desk. She could not restrain a look of amazement as the blackened American approached.

'Willjohn, room twenty-two please,' he said, trying to be as casual as he could and as though it were quite normal to appear in the hotel looking like a tramp.

Two smartly dressed men, one black and one white, materialised out of the bar just to the left of the reception area. They also stared at him incredulously.

'Mr. Willjohn?' one of them asked.

Ed nodded, feeling his face flush red with embarrassment under the soot. The man extended his hand.

'Martin Gericke...and this is Sam Mohale, C.E.O. of Premier Platinum. I'm the General Manager. We thought...'

Ed wanted one of those enormous convolutions of rock and molten magma that had created the mountains some 200 million years ago, to have just a little hiccup that would open the ground directly underneath him and swallow him up forever.

He gulped. 'Yessir. I don't think I should offer to shake hands with you right now.'

Sam Mohale gave a nod and wore a faint smile.

'I thought that we'd arranged transport for you from the airport but by the look of it you must have hitched a ride on a coal truck!'

'I went with...'

'Yes, we've heard about the fire' Martin chipped in. 'You must be wiped out after a long flight and now beating out the flames?'

'Nothing a good shower, meal and night's rest won't cure' Ed replied more cheerfully than he felt.

'We don't want to see you until late morning at the earliest then. Take the whole day if you want.' Sam Mohale smiled at him. 'Try not to get involved in any more local adventures before you arrive. We like our new engineers to arrive in one piece!'

As Ed trudged towards his room, he chuckled to himself. Any illusions about relaxing upon his arrival in Africa were definitely shattered. Suddenly, his crazy brother's antics seemed very far away.

CHAPTER 2

Elke Stein looked at the familiar landmarks with a growing sense of pleasure as she approached the vicinity of her parent's farm in the Kroondal district about five miles away from Buffalo Hills hotel. Her fellow students, Babs and Shirley, had pressed her to join them at a beach cottage in Plettenberg Bay for the winter vacation. She had been very tempted but the pull of her special little world amongst the predominantly German community of Kroondal, as well as her father's rapidly failing health, was too strong. Now that she would be home for a few weeks, she hoped that she could take some of the pressure off her mother both in the house and on the farm. She had been told that her father could no longer work and spent much of the day sitting on the stoep of the house gazing at the farmlands in front of him, as they spread far up the slopes of the mountain.

She was doing her Masters degree in Archaeology at Tukkies, the nickname for the University of Pretoria, and could not wait to get back home, where within a few kilometres, lay some of the most fascinating history amongst the most ancient rock formations on Earth.

Her father, Isak, had also been an enthusiastic rock-hound. He had taken Elke, as a child of nine or ten, high into the mountains and painted graphic word pictures of the unbelievable forces which had thrust the land up from the plateau to create the Magalies range. The "Bushveld complex" as it is now known, was created by the thrust of molten magma between sedimentary layers of the existing quartzite and shale.

A sixty-five thousand square kilometre reservoir of liquid rock had bubbled furiously beneath the site of an ancient lake. It had finally cooled over the next 30 million years and solidified into two enormous lobes of solid rock - the largest known intrusion of its kind in the world. Masses of igneous material had forced their way in between the bedding planes, particularly between the shale and the quartzite.

Apart from the creation of a stunningly beautiful mountain range - one of South Africa's most under-rated tourist attractions - Elke thought wryly, the norite rock structure of the area, had produced the world's largest source of platinum, as well as huge reserves of chrome, iron ore, manganese, vanadium, nickel and tin. Fortunately, most of the mining had taken place on the plateau, otherwise her little patch of paradise would have been destroyed by the rapacious forays of the mining men, intent on sucking the Earth's mineral wealth dry and destroying much of its habitat in the process.

Elke had always been passionate about the preservation of the environment and had a lifelong hatred of the mining operations which took place so perilously close to her beloved Magaliesberg.

She slowed down her old Honda Etude as she entered the village of Kroondal. She glanced at the clock on the dashboard. There was just time to pop in and say hello to the Ottermans. Rolf and his father Paul were the direct descendants of the original German missionaries who had founded the village in the 1800's.

The community was still about 800 strong. Most of its inhabitants were now Afrikaans speaking, a language adapted from the Dutch of the original settlers in the Cape of Good Hope in the 1600's. Later a smattering of French and German was added to the language by the Huguenots who fled Europe to escape religious persecution. Nearly all the Kroondal families still spoke fluent German as well. English and the local Tswana tongue came a distant third and fourth with Elke's family and neighbours, although she was quite fluent in English through her university studies.

She pulled into the parking lot in front of the delightful little restaurant on the site of the original water mill built by George Otterman in 1895. Alighting from the car, she stuck her head into the general store next door. Rolf looked up and waved. He was busy with a customer and pointed to the restaurant to indicate that he would join her there shortly.

Elke nodded and went next door where she was ushered to a table amidst a fascinating array of old mill equipment, wood panelling, copper and brass ornaments. She was seated at a simple but elegant wooden table with matching chairs. She sat down and smiled as she looked around. She was back in home territory!

*

Ed had woken up late but just in time for breakfast. Despite his exhaustion and embarrassment at meeting his new bosses looking like a chimney sweep, he had slept like the dead from nine-thirty that evening until about nine the following morning.

The previous night, Rob Schutte, who knew the mining executives well, had arrived at reception a few moments after Ed had left for his room, looking like Ed's black brother. He had praised Ed for his public-spirited insistence that he help out and suggested that the poor guy be given a chance to get cleaned up, eat and go to bed. Sam had explained that they had already done just that.

Ed stepped out of the door to his hotel room and looked out over the hotel's extensive lawns. The sky was a cloudless blue and the air crisp. The birds had already started their morning chatter. A glorious purple-backed bird was scratching for worms and bugs on the lawn. He later discovered that it was a Plum Coloured Starling. A number of Finches and Crimson Breasted Shrikes completed an exotic introduction to Ed's first morning in Africa.

After ordering a lavish breakfast in the hotel's elegant mock-Tudor dining room, he was approached by Don Watson, the second of the hotel's three directors. The third director, Elliot Standen, a retired accountant, divided his days between Johannesburg and the hotel. He was not in residence at the time.

Don was dark-haired, bearded and somewhat shorter than his partner, Rob.

'Believe the boys gave you a fiery welcome last night!'

'Yeah, it sure got my attention after a long journey.'

'Anyway, it was the buzz of the valley this morning,' Don told him.

They chatted and chuckled together for a while until Ed's breakfast of fried eggs, tomatoes, sausages, liver and onions appeared.

Premier Platinum Mine's driver, Moses, was waiting for him when he finally emerged from the hotel. Ed looked forward to his first day on the job and fully intended to make a better impression on the boss, Sam Mohale, than he had the night before.

*

Elke smiled at Rolf over the restaurant table. Although not related, he and his wife treated her like a niece, or even perhaps a daughter. On occasions, she helped out at the little restaurant, which so many friends and family regarded as the social hub of their world, in addition to the imposing Lutheran Church, that many of the community attended every Sunday morning.

Elke was a classic Nordic beauty. She had a tall, slim, athletic figure, striking blue eyes and long blonde tresses. Her hair either cascaded over her shoulders or was collected together in a ponytail and wound around at the back of her head in a typically Germanic fashion.

Either way, she was the centre of attention for virtually all the young men in the district, as well as a number of university students in Pretoria. Despite her affinity for Kroondal and its environs, she was certain that

11

she would marry out of the community one day. Right now, however, her studies came first. She was also a prominent field hockey player at university, with the probability of provincial or even national honours around the corner.

As Oom (Uncle) Rolf stared at her fondly, he wondered how such a beautiful young woman was prepared to risk a nasty injury from a ball or stick, in a game like hockey. The answer, he supposed, was that Elke was truly unaffected or not even particularly conscious of her good looks. She was one of those rare people who were actually more interested in others than trying to be interesting themselves.

Elke leaned forward, her natural smile replaced by a slight frown. 'Oom, I just wanted to ask you before I got home - how's Pa? Since the stroke.'

Rolf pursed his lips and considered his reply carefully.

'My girl, he's not too good. I know your Ma is very brave and always remains positive, but I think you should prepare yourself. His condition has deteriorated since you were last here.'

Elke tried to prevent tears from welling up. For a moment she hung her head and could not speak. Then gathering up her courage, she looked up at Rolf again. 'Is he dying?' she asked with brutal frankness.

Rolf shrugged and shook his head. 'I honestly don't know. He can still speak but he's lost nearly all the use of his left side. I'm so sorry.'

Impulsively Elke reached across and clasped his right hand in both of hers. 'You're such a good friend. I needed an honest answer. It helps me to deal with whatever's ahead.'

She stood up. Rolf followed suit. 'I'd better go and see for myself.'

They hugged briefly before Elke turned and got into her car. Rolf watched her go. He was near tears himself. Poor kid, he thought. I just hope that her mother, Marie, can keep the farm going without having to drag Elke away from her studies. That would be the greatest tragedy of all. Knowing how much Isak wanted his daughter to graduate and how close father and daughter had always been, his heart bled for the Stein family.

Marie's the strong one, Rolf thought, but she was unable to appreciate why Elke and Isak were so totally engrossed in the history and anthropology of their region. 'What's gone is gone,' she would say. 'Look to tomorrow and forget yesterday.'

To which her long-suffering husband would reply, 'Ag Marie, if only you could see the beauty that we see and how it is enhanced by knowing its origins, you would think very differently.'

Marie would sniff disdainfully and tell Isak that he was extremely fortunate that one of them was completely practical. Despite their differences, Rolf knew that the couple loved each other very much and that Isak's passing would bring great hardship to mother and daughter. Sombrely, he returned to the store and attended to Frau Weise, who wanted ten kilos of bran mash for her chickens.

CHAPTER 3

Moses drove the SUV down the hill towards the virtually flat plain at the foothills of the Magaliesberg Mountains. The predominantly quartzite hills rose at a gentle slope towards the south, in long lines, only to fall away abruptly in a series of spectacular cliff faces on the northern slopes.

The mountain range, the second oldest formation on Earth, stretched from the town of Rustenburg in the west to the city of Pretoria in the east. The ridges rose up like breaking waves of green, frozen forever in space and time, save for the erosion brought about by wind, rain, ice… and man!

A number of platinum mines were scattered over the plateau representing, in an area of no more than a couple of hundred kilometres, one of planet Earth's most fabulous concentrations of true wealth.

Ed had done his homework on the area. Ever since he had regretfully informed his ailing father that he would not be taking over the reins of the billion-dollar Willjohn Industries in Minneapolis, he had redoubled his efforts to complete his degrees in Mining Engineering and Metallurgy. He had then searched for and finally found a challenging contract in Africa. It was a continent that had always fascinated him.

South Africa and Russia possess something like seventy five percent of the world's mineral wealth. The platinum riches of South Africa's North West Province lay for many years in the shadow of the fabled gold reefs of Johannesburg and the Witwatersrand. In recent times, as the price of gold had been constantly manipulated by market forces, the value of platinum rose steadily with an ever-increasing demand for the precious metal.

Ed would be working at the Premier Platinum mine on the plateau but living in the valley deep in the nearby Magaliesberg Mountains that they were currently passing through. Some of South Africa's most turbulent recent history had been enacted in the area. In sharp contrast, the tranquil estate of Buffalo Hills Hotel now offered its guests a peaceful haven of comfort and excellence. The valley itself had something for everyone. They drove along the road overlooking the magnificent Buffelspoort dam, where a host of water sports and bass fishing were available to the tourist.

The placid waters and surrounding hills reminded Ed of the family's ranch in Wyoming. This in turn reminded him of his younger brother slyly cutting Ed's fishing lines then proudly showing their father the large brown trout, he had claimed to catch. For the sake of family harmony Ed had remained silent, even though he had seen Justin buy the trout from another fisherman earlier in the day. That was Justin for you, he thought sadly. The kid could never resist sabotaging his older brother, due to some deep-seated jealousy.

"If only Justin would apply his fertile and devious mind to positive issues, he could undoubtedly be a success in a number of fields," Ed thought, but his brother was fixated on Willjohn Industries. Fortunately, their father had realised that to give the younger son control would have been a recipe for disaster.

Ed sighed. He was travelling through magnificent countryside in the stimulating and challenging nation that had quite recently obtained a democratically elected government, after over a century of turbulence and struggles for power. He made a determined effort to push his brother's twisted ideas from his mind. Even at a distance of many thousands of miles, Justin had the ability to get under Ed's skin and spoil the moment. The American watched a hawk flying high over the dam seeking its prey. Ed made a resolution there and then that he would not spend his days worrying about what was happening back home. He would have quite enough of a challenge holding down the job in a strange new country that had an extensive history of mining. He would not be dealing with amateurs and he would have to prove his worth to them.

Ed was a newly qualified mining consultant from the FlowTech Corporation, of Minneapolis, USA. FlowTech had sent him out on a contract with Premier Platinum Mines. It was Ed's first trip to Africa and this was his first assignment. He was predictably nervous about the task which lay ahead.

He replayed scene after scene in his mind of an earlier occasion in which hard-bitten miners and on-site engineers had sneered at him as a youngster with his theoretical knowledge. Ed's uncle, Carl, ran a one-horse bauxite mine in Arizona. The lad had spent a number of vacations in the desert with the grizzled old veteran. Uncle Carl had mocked him incessantly.

'What they say in the books don' mean diddly squat when yor facing leaky hydraulics,' and again, 'if'n yew cain't loosen that stub axle, only one remedy - Coca Cola!! Pour it on and she'll work loose faster'n yew can spit, fellah!'

And he was right every time. As the SUV stopped at the security gates of Premier Platinum Mines, Ed reassured himself with the knowledge that Uncle Carl had given him more practical advice on mining than he had learned in four years at college.

Moses exchanged greetings with the gateman, a smiling young African, smartly dressed in a navy-blue jacket, grey trousers and tie. They spoke in the language of the Tswana people, who had inhabited the region for many centuries. They, along with the Ndebele people, an offshoot of the Zulus, who fled the wrath of King Shaka Zulu in the nineteenth century, occupied much of the area of the Magaliesberg Mountains and its surroundings. Both the Fokeng and the Kwena Mmatua clans of the Tswana nation were long established in the valley of Buffalo Hills.

David, the guard, handed over the register for Ed to fill in. When the young American handed it back, David checked Ed's surname and chuckled. 'So, you are three people in one Sir, Edward, William and John?'

Ed nodded resignedly. 'Yeah, the kids at school figured that one out - called me Threeperson!'

The guard laughed delightedly and ushered them through into the mine's parking ground. Ed noted the innate good humour and friendliness of the rural Africans in contrast to the surliness and pre-occupation of both blacks and whites he had briefly encountered at Johannesburg's Oliver Tambo International Airport. He presumed it was largely due to the stress of urban living, which was much the same in major cities all over the world. He had been surprised to discover that Greater Johannesburg was a sprawling metropolis of some six million people and growing all the time.

Ed was ushered into Sam Mohale's office. Sam was on the phone. His secretary pointed to a seat at a boardroom table set to one side of the spacious room. Sam signalled that he would be with Ed in a moment.

He carried on his conversation in a language that Ed presumed would also be Tswana. There are eleven official languages in the new South Africa, aside from a number of off-shoot dialects from the main groupings such as Zulu, Xhosa, Sotho and Tswana. Ed listened to the sounds but apart from the occasional English words like 'platinum', 'tonnage' and 'Jo'burg', he could not relate it to any tongue he had heard in other parts of the world.

Sam was a big man of about forty-five. A touch over-weight but his broad shoulders and graceful movements suggested his earlier involvement in some sporting activities. He wore an elegant charcoal grey suit with a colourful tie. His cufflinks were diamond encrusted and set in platinum - what else? His shaven head, strong jaw and forceful demeanour gave him a distinct "presence" and unmistakable signs of leadership qualities.

The young American felt a twinge of anxiety as Sam ended his conversation abruptly and scowled as he slapped the phone down on its cradle. He looked up at Ed as he rose from his desk, picked up a large file, then flashed a broad smile with perfect white teeth.

'How's Mr. Try-for-black this morning?' Sam said with a chuckle.

'Perfectly all-white, Sir,' Ed said with a straight face.

Sam was taken aback for a split second but then roared with laughter and slapped Ed on the shoulder as he came to sit down at the table. Still chuckling, Sam opened the file.

'Alright. Onto more important matters. The company that recommended you, FlowTech, provided most of our hydraulics when this mine was commissioned ten years ago. We've had very little trouble with the machinery but after so many years, there was bound to be some wear and tear, as your predecessor found out.'

Ed nodded. 'Yessir, Dan gave me a detailed report before he left. He's told me to watch out for the pump at number 3 shaft.'

'Ja, it's a bitch. I'm considering replacing it completely.'

'Can I have a look at it first? Dan says that, in hindsight, perhaps he should've re-sleeved the pistons.'

Sam shrugged. 'If you can save us money I'll be delighted, but only if it'll be reliable. Stoppages are more expensive, in the long run, than replacement.'

They spoke for another twenty minutes. Ed was delighted to find a senior executive who had taken the trouble to understand how his mine worked. Sam was not just a number-cruncher.

In the course of the conversation, Sam revealed that he had taken a degree in Mining Engineering at Johannesburg's University of the Witwatersrand, rated a world leader in mining technology. He had then gone on to Manchester University in Britain to obtain an MBA.

Sam called Martin Gericke into his office and asked him to show Ed where he would be working, then give him a grand tour of the mine.

Martin, a burly and rather taciturn Afrikaner, was very much a hands-on manager who had climbed the corporate ladder from the bottom rung upwards. Ed discovered that Martin came from a family who could not afford to send him to university. He had left school and spent nearly ten years on the Gold Mines in Welkom in the Northern Free State.

He had switched to platinum mining in order to be closer to Annelise, his childhood sweetheart, who was not prepared to leave the Rustenburg district. They had married a short while later and now after twenty years, Martin was regarded as one of the most knowledgeable men in the platinum industry. Ed likened him to his uncle in Arizona and thought how lucky the mine was to have a combination of both practical and academic skills at the very top.

Ed's office was small but serviceable. He would share a secretary, Miss Basson, with a trainee manager, Jason Matthews. He also had a state-of-the-art computer, e-mail and fax at his disposal.

All his earlier fears about not fitting in began to evaporate. He decided to attack the problem of the pump in number 3 shaft directly after lunch.

*

Elke rode her pony, Witblitz (White Lightning, also the name of a potent alcoholic home brew made in the Cape Province) along the trail, which led up the steep rise to the high point of her parents' farm. From the very top, she would see the rugged and magnificent bastions of the Magaliesberg range. The kloofs (cliffs) were punctuated with numerous breaks and massive spill-overs of giant boulders peeping out from between the rich and exotic foliage of the area.

It was this view that drew Elke back time and time again to the area. Numerous rivers and streams tumbled over the rocks and sometimes, in places like Eastern kloof or Retief's kloof, the water fell thirty or forty metres into crystal clear mountain pools. These pools were hidden from the casual traveller's eyes by barriers of rocky shale and a host of indigenous plants. The plants had names such as the Buffalo Thorn bush, Heartwood, the Common Coral Tree and the Peeling Plane. Exotic plants and flowers such as the remarkable Umbrella flower, wild Peach, crimson Flag or Royal Paintbrush spattered vivid colours amongst the dark greens and vari-coloured pastels of the rocks, which almost overpowered all else in that area.

Elke sighed and mentally prepared herself for the ordeal of seeing her father in his present condition. He was sleeping when she had arrived home and she took the opportunity to go for a ride and settle her thoughts before she saw him. She gently nudged Witblitz around and headed down the trail to the farmhouse.

Isak Stein had been such an active man. To be trapped in an ailing body must be doubly distressing for him. Elke just hoped that in some way, he would still be able to enjoy the splendours of his farm through her eyes and her vivid descriptions, when she returned to the house. Elke sometimes wondered if she and her father had a telepathic understanding of each other.

Isak had for much of his life sublimated his aesthetic senses, in order to carve a good income from this beautiful, but often treacherous, land. His wife Marie was a warm, loving, but severely practical, person. Elke was the one who carried forward the barely articulated hopes and dreams that Isak had for his beloved mountain range and the rich but unpredictable farmland which occupied the valley and part of its lower slopes.

Elke made a decision as she descended from the top of the cliffs that, no matter how it would be achieved, she would make sure that her Dad would visit this place again one day. In her heart, she knew that he was dying, but to bring him here once more would be the greatest gift she could conceive of giving him in exchange for being the wonderful father that he had always been.

Elke loved her mother too, but it was a different kind of no-nonsense, let's-get-the-job-done, kind of relationship. Marie was not a dreamer and she sometimes despaired that Elke had taken on so many of Isak's impractical characteristics. In the same way that Marie was inclined to treat Isak as a talented but wayward child, she viewed her daughter in a very similar light.

Marie was already planning her words for when she broke the news that Elke would not be going back to University. She would have to help her mother run the farm instead. Should that not be successful, Marie knew that they would soon have to sell the property. She also realised that if that happened, it would kill Isak as surely as if she had thrust a knife in his heart. It did not particularly occur to her that it would also shatter Elke's hopes and dreams forever!

CHAPTER 4

When Ed picked up his key from Buffalo Hills reception after work, Angela appeared from the office behind the reception desk. She smiled at the young American and handed him an e-mail printout.

'They've tracked you down already.'

'Who's they?' he asked puzzled.

Angela looked mildly shocked. 'I wouldn't dream of reading your mail, Mr Willjohn.'

'Sure … I meant where's it from? Okay, I can figure it out myself now, can't I?'

He looked down at the pages in his hand. Angela gave him another smile and disappeared back into her office.

The e-mail was from his mother. It seemed that she was missing him already and that his brother Justin was up to his tricks again.

Ed loved his mother dearly, but she was an uncomplicated, trusting sort of person. Now it seemed that his brother was already trying to work around the trust fund which was due to him at the age of 25, in four years' time.

Ed dumped the e-mail on a table and headed for the shower. Not much he could do about it from so far away, except perhaps to advise his mother as best he could. He wondered whether the laws in South Africa were similar to those in the US and whether someone could help him from this end. It all seemed to belong to another world, another time. He savagely turned on the cold tap and stepped under the icy jets of water in the vain hope that it would wash his thoughts away.

*

Elke emerged from her shower, refreshed and with a lighter heart. She had spent one glorious hour in the comforting solitude of the mountains. On the way down she had spotted a troop of vervet monkeys playing in the riverine bush surrounding the stream which tumbled down over the cliffs to her left and formed a delightful little secret haven of clear pools and splashing, sparkling water as it tumbled over the boulders at the foot of the cliffs. Vervet monkeys usually roam in troops of about twenty in number. They come down to the ground from time to time but spend most of their days in the cover of the nearest trees.

Elke had used a pair of powerful binoculars to watch them, noting how there was at least one older dominant male in the troop, possibly two.

These older males would not allow the endlessly hyperactive youngsters to tease the adults beyond the point where they would completely lose their cool. Elke noted that the strong hierarchical figure would play "bad cop" and allow the rest of the troop to be the more tolerant "good cops," which brought a lively, but nevertheless peaceful, harmony to the group. She was saddened by thoughts of how badly humans dealt with their lively enthusiastic children in the current electronic age. They were either dumped in front of a television set, yelled at or smacked for trivial misdemeanours. There was no predictability in the parents' discipline and many youngsters had all their healthy liveliness knocked out of them by the time they were ready to face the world on their own.

For the delightful little grey vervet monkeys, life was simply a matter of defending your territory if it had ample food resources, having fun but not overstepping the mark. If one ignored the predators such as the occasional leopard, life as a monkey might certainly be desirable. Elke, however, did not shirk the additional responsibilities of being part of her own family. She loved both parents dearly, even if she and her mother sometimes seemed to come from different planets.

She went through into the dining room. Her mother was at the table waiting for her. Her father was still asleep, exhausted from the brief labour of visiting the stoep and staring at the far hills, earlier in the day.

As Elke sat down and bowed her head while her mother said grace, she could not help but compare the complexity of their lives with those of the freedom-loving monkeys.

*

Marius De Wet and Rob Schutte were having a beer in the hotel's comfortable bar when Ed entered and headed for a stool on the far side. Rob, a strong believer that hotel guests should have the opportunity to meet with the locals whenever it seemed appropriate, waved to Ed and called out.

'Evening Ed, come and join us.'

Ed changed direction and headed towards them. Rob and Marius stood up. Rob introduced Marius as a local farmer and retired businessman and ordered Ed a local beer. He recommended a Windhoek Lager, which

Ed found compared very favourably with the beer he drank in the US.

'It was originally a Namibian beer but in fact it's brewed locally,' Marius commented as they settled down to enjoy the brew.

'Has it got anything to do with the prior German occupation of Namibia?' Ed asked.

Marius nodded, 'There were two breweries that appeared in the days of the German administration. One was in Windhoek, hence this lager and another in Swakopmund on the coast. The beer there is called Hansa.'

'That seems pretty German, I guess' Ed responded.

Marius nodded. 'But what was unique about the original beer when it was still brewed there, was that all the water for the town of Swakopmund was obtained from boreholes which were slightly brack, because of a seepage of sea water.'

'Doesn't sound great,' Ed commented.

'Strangely enough the beer was incredible. Trouble was that until you got used to it, you often got an upset tummy, which the locals called a Swakopmunder.'

Rob laughed, 'I must warn you, Marius is one of those people who has a wealth of trivia on almost any subject relating to Africa.'

'It's just a hobby' Marius added 'but don't trivialise it, pal. Some of it is valuable data.'

'Like I'm forewarned if I ever drink beer in Swakopmund,' Ed chuckled. Marius shook his head solemnly 'Don't worry, their water's crystal clear these days. Of course, the beer's not quite the same, but it's still pretty good!'

After a few minutes Rob excused himself to go and check on dinner in the main dining room. Marius insisted on a second round and then asked Ed a question.

'One of my hobbies is an interest in names and their origins. Your surname, Willjohn - never heard of it before. Is it English or Welsh or something?'

Ed shrugged. 'Dunno. My old man never really discussed it but I seem to recall he once told a friend that it had a Dutch origin. Not that it sounds Dutch exactly.'

Marius thought about this and rolled the name around on his tongue. 'Willjohn ......Willjan ... Viljan ...' Suddenly he looked at Ed with excitement. 'Viljoen. Ja. That's it. Viljoen!'

Ed tried to get his tongue around it 'Vil-Joen.' He pronounced it with a hard 'J' as in the English, or in this case American, style.

Marius shook his head. 'No, my friend, try 'j' as in Ya, then oo, Viljoen, Vilyoon.'

Ed nodded. 'It could fit. So that's also an Afrikaans name?' The young

American had read enough about South Africa to know that the majority of whites were of Dutch origin. Marius smiled.

It's quite common around here. Any idea when your family reached the United States?'

Ed thought about it. 'I'm not sure but I think my great-great grandfather or something like that, arrived just after the turn of the Twentieth Century.'

Marius suddenly had an idea. 'Wait a minute! As you may know, we had a war between the British and ourselves in the 1890's until 1902. Then after all kinds of political manoeuvring, the Treaty of Vereeniging ended the war in June 1902. Pretty well, anyhow.'

Marius shook his head at the thought and finished off his beer.

'But there were a few Boer Generals who refused to sign the Peace Treaty with the British.'

'Excuse me, but I'm not clear what you mean by Boer?' Ed interjected.

'Boer is the Dutch word for farmer. We were always considered to be a nation of farmers and the name Boer stuck. Today I reckon that our enemies call us Boers in an insulting way but many of us use it with pride. It was our heritage, even though not many of us are farmers today.'

'You are, I believe' Ed commented.

'After a lifetime in business and banking. Now it's a hobby for my retirement but it does dig deep into my roots. Anyway...'

'Yeah sorry I interrupted you.'

'Okay. Some of the Boer Generals who refused to sign the Treaty of Vereeniging left the country and went into voluntary exile. One of them...'

'Don't tell me' said Ed suddenly excited. 'One of them was called Viljoen!'

'Not only that,' Marius replied. 'He left South Africa to settle in the United States.'

*

Elke and her mother had a modest supper of Boerewors and Pap, which consisted of a traditional Afrikaner sausage and mealie meal (maize meal) which was called 'Pap' when cooked into a stiff porridge-like substance. It was a favourite meal amongst both the Afrikaners and many of the Highveld Africans.

Marie Stein was almost silent during her meal. Elke saw the tell-tale signs and predicted that her mother was about to make a major pronouncement. She was not wrong. As they toyed with their strong black coffee and sugar, her mother looked up at her.

'Skatjie, darling, I'm sorry to say this but I need your help on the farm. You won't be going back to 'Varsity!'

CHAPTER 5

Elke had cried herself to sleep but the following morning she woke with a curious sense of calmness. It was almost as though she had known her mother was going to take her out of 'varsity and that she had gone through the motions of being upset, simply because it was expected of her.

In fact, as she sat up in bed, stretched and bent over to open the curtains, she knew that she was even slightly relieved at the decision. Not that she didn't enjoy her studies, but she had begun to feel increasingly guilty about her mother having to cope on her own in the weeks since her father had had the stroke. Besides, she was well into her thesis and she was confident that she would get permission to finish it at home. How she would achieve that after getting up at five and spending the day on the land, she wasn't sure. Anyway, the land did require an enormous amount of attention in the sowing season and during harvest but the rest of the time, well, she would see.

Over breakfast Elke calmly told her mother that she accepted her decision.

'If we have to give up my last year of Tukkies to save the farm, then that's what we must do.'

For once Marie Stern was almost tearful.

'My Kleintjie, you never cease to amaze me. You fight me all the way over something but when you realise that it's hopeless, you stop being the dreamer and become a little more practical. More like me!'

'Never as practical as you, Ma! I still want to save the mountains from the miners and the property developers!'

They both laughed and Marie finally permitted herself a couple of tears. Elke got out of her chair and came across to hug her. Elke's thoughts were already turning to finding a way of telling her Dad that it was okay and that saving the farm was the most critical thing to achieve.

24

Ed sat at his desk in the mine offices and worked on the laborious task of extrapolating figures on ore production versus production costs. Martin had gleefully thrust the paperwork at him the day before. As he tapped away at his calculator, Ed's mind could not help wandering back to his chat with Marius De Wet the night before. Suddenly, from nowhere, he was faced with the possibility of having Afrikaner ancestry. It was far too early to really have an opinion on whether or not he liked the idea. He had only been in the country a few days and had only met a handful of these "Afrikaners." He liked the ones he had met. Martin Gericke was a rough diamond but someone who Ed trusted instinctively. Marius was amusing, urbane, a sophisticated ex-city dweller with something of the philosopher, as well as the historian, in him. Rob spoke Afrikaans but his parents were Hollanders, so he hardly counted.

Ed had read enough South African history to realise that the Afrikaners were labelled as one of the more villainous groups of the Twentieth Century. As the creators and instigators of Apartheid, the world would not easily forgive them.

However, Ed had also read a little about the earlier Afrikaners, or Cape Dutch as they were known then, about the Great Trek and their epic and heroic adventures as they spread north from the Cape in the Nineteenth Century, seeking to avoid the heavy-handed control of British Imperialism at its height. As an American, Ed could certainly relate to that.

'Damn.'

Ed glanced at the total on the calculator and realised that according to his figures, the mine had dug up half of Southern Africa! He laughed and started again. Time enough to think about his possible forebears later. Anyway, Marius had invited him to dinner the following night, at one of the restaurants in the German enclave of Kroondal. Marius had promised to try and find out more detail on the General Viljoen who had settled in the United States rather than live under any form of compromise with the British. Viljoen had been one of the hardcore Boers who were to become known as the "Bitte Eindes," or bitter-enders in English.

Martin stuck his head into the office.

'How're you doing?' he queried. Ed smiled wryly. 'OK, I guess. I'm just redoing last month's figures. Some Afrikaner got in my way.'

'Huh?' Martin responded, looking confused and mildly irritated.

'It's a joke, Martin. I'll have 'em on your desk by lunch-time.'

'Thanks, ou pal' the other man responded and closed the door.

*

Marie took her daughter around the farm. Elke had lived on the property all her life and at first she was sceptical that there was anything that she could still learn about the place. An hour later, Elke was suitably chastened. Living on a farm was one thing, farming was altogether something else. Marie explained some of the finer points of citrus farming to her as they walked along the groves of almost ripe oranges.

Harvesting would begin in the next couple of weeks and Marie felt that it would be a perfect opportunity for Elke to experience the pressures of ensuring that the fruit was picked before the first violent Highveld storms of the early spring. Elke had often helped the workers as a small child but this had consisted more of pick one, eat one, or use an orange as a ball with which to play catch with some of the little black children whose parents were carefully picking the fruit.

Now her mother was showing her which oranges were ripe for picking, which were flawed and unsuitable for packing as first grade fruit for export, as well as the number required from each picker on a daily basis. Like so much of life, Elke thought, you took things for granted. They just happened. Someone did the task and it was none of your business. Suddenly, the farm had become her business, or partly so, at any rate. Elke's initial, slightly numb acceptance of her new status was rapidly changing into a tingling feeling of excitement. She could see why her mother was so utterly determined that the farm should not fail. It was a good business provided that they both gave it their full attention. This would in turn honour her father's life's work, which he could at least observe from the silent and sombre world of his damaged body during his final months.

*

Sam Mohale called out to Ed as he walked down the corridor on his way to the Jeep SUV that Martin had provided for him that morning.

'Got a moment?'

Ed obediently turned and entered Sam's office, where the big African gestured for Ed to sit.

'Settling in okay?'

Ed smiled. 'Like I've been here all my life. The same gripes, the same problems…and…the same kinda decent people I'm used to back home.'

Sam nodded. 'There're a number of similarities between South Africa and the United States. Comfortable at the hotel?'

'Perfect' Ed replied. 'I'm getting to know some of the locals too…'

'Local whites, that is…' Sam interjected, with just a hint of a smile.

Ed grimaced. 'Oops. You got me there. I wouldn't know how…'

'I'm not being critical, my friend. South Africa's very fortunate to have come through its transition to a democracy with as few hiccups as it has. We've still got a long way to go, though.'

Ed nodded. He was interested to hear Sam's thoughts on the subject. 'Seems to me, as an outsider, that the country's got an atmosphere of cautious optimism. Maybe you see it differently.'

Sam looked at him intently. 'Because I'm black or because I'm South African?'

Ed thought fast. Was he stirring up a hornet's nest here? Just how sensitive were the South Africans of all races? Up to this point, he had not really entered into any kind of political or racial conversation. One of the things he liked best so far was that these issues had not been thrust in his face as he had half-expected they would be.

Ed replied carefully 'I would hope that you are first and foremost a South African, in the same way that I'm an American, no matter what my origins are.'

'Man, you don't know the half of it,' he added under his breath. Sam clearly accepted his answer and nodded.

'Quite right, but I do have pride in my African culture, as part of that South African-ness.'

Sam stood up and tidied a couple of papers on his desk.

'Come. I'll walk out with you.'

Ed also stood and followed Sam through the office door. Sam looked back at him.

'How'd you like to be exposed to some Tswana culture?' he asked.

Why not? Thought Ed. I'm about to get a low-down on the Afrikaners. Let's keep a balance.

'Sure. I'd like that.'

'Good, I'll set up a visit to a village near here. I don't want it to sound like a big deal but my surname, Mohale, is the name of the Royal family in this region. I'd like you to meet some interesting people.'

'We Americans have a reputation for taking a superficial look at the rest of the world, based on the certainty that the US of A is the centre of the Universe.' Sam laughed in agreement. 'I really would like to take an in-depth look around while I'm here and it looks as though I've happened upon one of the more interesting regions of the country.'

'Interesting and least known, Ed. If you Americans have heard of an African tribe or nation, ten to one, it's a Zulu warrior, to coin a phrase. When I was at varsity in Manchester they all called me Zulu. I tried explaining that I was Tswana but it was too complicated, so I remained a Zulu.'

They reached the car park and Ed left, promising to accompany Sam to the village of Mohale in the near future.

*

Elke returned to the farmhouse in the late afternoon. Her head was buzzing with data on the citrus, as well as the smaller areas of vegetables and lucerne (alfalfa) which they also cultivated. Marie would not let her off the hook. She went into the office and re-emerged with some ledgers and copies of the "Farmer's Weekly," an excellent magazine for the farming community that had been published for many years.

'Here's your homework' Marie told her cheerfully. 'Farming's not all about fields and sunshine.'

At that moment the phone rang. Marie picked it up and smiled as she heard the voice on the other end. She looked at Elke.

'It's your old boyfriend, Kurt.'

Elke took the phone with a sinking feeling in her stomach.

CHAPTER 6

Ed hit a strong backhand which made the squash ball strike the wall just above the red line and drop infuriatingly into the corner with hardly any bounce at all. Brent, a fellow guest, raced forward, lunged at the dying ball, missed it by centimetres and collapsed in a sweaty heap in the corner. Ed leaned against the wall in relief. It had been a tough game but he had finally prevailed.

'Game, set and match to the Yank,' Brent grumbled as he wearily picked himself up but the smile on his face belied his tone of voice.

'See you in the bar before dinner' Ed called out as he opened the door to his room.

Brent, unlocking a room further along the row of outside suites, raised a hand in acknowledgement.

Having worked out most of his aggression on the squash court, Ed felt more inclined to confront a long e-mail from his brother Justin in Minneapolis. He could not remember a time when Justin had sent him good news. It was invariably confrontational or just plain irritating. Mostly Justin and he communicated through their mother and only when absolutely necessary. He opened the e-mail, resisting the impulse to have a shower and dinner before addressing it.

He read the document with a growing sense of fury. Justin was suggesting that Ed, as a non-participant in the engineering and industrial conglomerate that their father, Jonathan, had built, should resign as a director and sell his shares to Justin. He added that he was going up to New York the following day, to speak to the investment bankers who controlled most of the Willjohn Group's investments.

The youngster clearly wanted control but could not achieve this without obtaining either Ed's or his mother's shares. Their father, shortly before his death, having realised that Justin was a loose cannon, had urged both his wife Jean and oldest son Ed to resist any approaches by

Justin in this respect. Hence the appointment of Franklin de Vos as his successor in both the President and CEO's chairs.

Franklin had spent most of his working life with Willjohn Engineering. He was the obvious choice of successor once Ed had made it clear that he wanted to pursue his own career.

Justin had scraped through college, obtaining a degree in English and American literature between his relentless pursuit of as many nubile young women as he could attract with his money and his rather weak "pretty boy" looks. Ed sometimes wondered whether his brother's obsessive pursuit of women did not serve to hide some other deeply repressed desires.

Ed slammed the papers down on the coffee table and headed for the shower. Justin had almost persuaded Franklin to sell off the family ranch in Wyoming. 'Over my dead body' Ed muttered as he entered the shower. The ranch was the site of some of Ed's happiest childhood memories. Justin on the other hand spent most of his time on the ranch playing computer games and watching violent movies. Ed would certainly not be giving in to any of Justin's proposals, but he knew with a dull certainty that the youngster would not give up.

Suddenly, with a shock, Ed remembered that Marius De Wet was taking him out to dinner. He rushed out of the shower and grabbed some clothing. Damn Justin, he thought bitterly. Even at long range, the little bastard could get under his skin to the extent of making him almost forget an evening he was really looking forward to.

*

'I believe you're back for good,' Kurt began when Elke reluctantly picked up the phone.

She silently cursed her mother's dedication to finding a "suitable" husband for her. Kurt von Wallenstein, on paper at least, was a great catch. He came from an illustrious, wealthy and aristocratic family. His father Ernst had developed one of the largest citrus farms in the district and Kurt was crazy about Elke. She did not return his adoration. He was tall, handsome, well-built and about as charming as a codfish. He had no sense of humour and would spend hours reeling off mindless facts and statistics about his farms, the state of the economy and the innumerable advantages of becoming Frau von Wallenstein.

Elke was about to turn down his offer of dinner when she saw her mother's disproving frown. At least he's always been a perfect gentleman she thought. If it's going to keep Mom happy, I might as well go out with him. Kurt droned on about his latest vehicle, a Volvo station wagon, and how he would pick her up at exactly 7:30 p.m., please don't be late and how they would go for dinner at the Bauernstube where they had just received a large new stock of excellent German wines.

'See you at seven thirty!'

Elke cut across the burble, put the phone down and smiled at her mother.

'If I die of boredom, I would like to be buried at the top of the mountain please,' she told Marie as she made her way to her bedroom.

*

The sun had already disappeared behind the far hills as Marius and Ed drove past the Buffelspoort Dam. In the fading light, Ed listened with fascination as Marius pointed out landmarks and described the battle of Buffelspoort.

'Have you heard of Jan Smuts?' Marius asked Ed.

'I read about him before I came out here. Sounds like quite a guy, Prime Minister of South Africa and a Field Marshall in the British Army during World War...'

Marius chuckled 'Ja, and the irony is that he was the General in charge of the Rustenburg Commando in December 1900, one of the most able of the Boer leaders in the fight against the British.'

'Is that right?' Ed responded surprised. 'How come he later fought with the British?'

Marius sighed. 'That's something to discuss another time. It's very involved. The Afrikaners have been divided on the issue, not only over Smuts but also the many other Boers who decided that to continue to fight was futile. Whereas the bitter-einders, Boers who fought to the very end, saw people like Smuts as traitors to their Volk.'

Marius's vehicle passed an African on a bicycle and Ed noticed it was David, the gateman from the hotel. He waved at the man who instantly broke into his cheery smile and waved back.

'How long did the split last?' asked Ed.

Marius replied with a touch of irritation.

'It's still there in many respects. When South Africa, as part of the British Commonwealth, agreed to join in with the Allied Forces to fight Hitler, a large number of Afrikaners refused to comply and were interned. Listen I wanted to tell you about the battle of Buffelspoort while we're driving through here. Can this other issue wait?'

'Sure.'

Ed was both amused and impressed by Marius's huge enthusiasm and knowledge of local history. Ed was to discover later that Marius's great grandfather was Kotie de Wet, brother of the famous Boer General, Christiaan de Wet.

'Boer scouts discovered that the British were about to send a convoy of two hundred and seventy-six wagons from their military base at Rietfontein, which is near the village of Koster about fifty kilometres

South East from here, to the British Garrison in Rustenburg.' Marius chuckled. 'Apparently they were running low on Christmas turkeys and other choice goodies. In fact, there were also plenty of valuable provisions, clothing and even munitions included in the convoy. The Boers were running desperately short of supplies at the time, so they decided to ambush the convoy and capture as many wagons as they could.'

As Marius chatted on, he brought the battle alive to his young American guest. He pointed out two kopjes (small hillocks) at the West end of the valley which had become a focal point of the conflict. As he spoke, Ed's vivid imagination started to hear sounds of gunfire, the shouts of men in battle as well as the screams of the wounded and dying as he was mentally transported back from Monday the 10th of September 2001 to 3rd December 1900.

*

Smuts and his Commander galloped at full speed away from the kopjes they had intended to occupy. To their consternation the British, under the command of Major J S Wolrige-Gordon, had anticipated a possible ambush in the valley and had sent men ahead to secure both kopjes.

Smuts was furious. He had intended to get there first and pour gunfire down from above as the wagons passed along the trail between the two conical hills, which rose some seven hundred feet above the floor of the valley. He rode his horse as hard as he dared on lesser known paths around the side of the valley to the hills at the eastern end, where the deputy Commandant General in charge of Western Transvaal, Koos de la Rey, was waiting to attack the British from the rear as soon as Smuts had stopped their forward progress. Now the entire plan had to be revised. It was imperative that the Boers attacked before the wagons left the valley.

General de la Rey had already altered his plans and had sent the bulk of his men after the second half of the convoy, which had been split into two. The British had turned the second batch of wagons around as soon as they heard gunfire up ahead. In the event, the Boers did not capture any of the second batch who quickly fought off the Boers and returned, exhausted to Rietfontein.

Smuts reined in his horse, dismounted and approached his Commanding Officer, who remained on a secluded rise overlooking the valley below, where the first convoy of British wagons were plodding steadily towards Rustenburg. After a quick salute Smuts explained his situation to de la Rey.

'Ja, I heard the gunfire, Jan, which is why I sent most of my force to capture the second convoy.'

'I'd still like to attack the first convoy, Oom Koos. I had hoped you would have some extra men for me but ...'

He looked around at the handful of men guarding the General. Smuts was a small, wiry and intense man with sandy hair and piercing blue-grey eyes. De la

Rey pointed to the British in the valley below them. 'I think you should eliminate those men who think they are well hidden in that donga (gully) over there. By then I should have some more men. Boshoff is on his way.'

*

Ed came out of his reverie, as Marius pulled off to the side of the road and switched off the engine. For some moments both men stared at the surrounding hills with their sparse yellow tufts of grass and a liberal sprinkling of rocks, boulders and occasional thorn trees. The sun had dropped below the horizon and the sky was producing a magnificent kaleidoscope of colours from the fading blue of the day to a succession of darkening orange and reds as the sun sped on its Westward journey. Marius seemed lost in a world of heroic memories.

'So, what happened next?'

'Smuts had a helluva fight on his hands but he managed to destroy all resistance from the men in the donga. By that stage Lieutenant Boshoff arrived and together with Smuts they took out the British rifleman on the one kopje but left the two field guns alone on the other side, as it would have resulted in too great a loss of life.'

'What happened to the wagons?' Ed asked.

Marius leaned forward to switch on the car's ignition as he replied. 'They captured 138 wagons and 1832 oxen, which kept the Boers well supplied for some time.'

Marius drove back onto the road and headed for Kroondal in the fading light.

'But I tell you this, Jan Smuts was nearly killed that day. I wonder to what extent it would've altered history, if he had been.'

'What happened?'

'Well, first of all a scout, sent by Smuts to ask for more reinforcements from de la Rey, came across the Boers in charge of the captured wagons. They gave him some beer and, not having eaten that day, he became so drunk that his message was never delivered.'

'Did the Boers have a problem with discipline?'

Marius nodded thoughtfully. 'Ja, remember these were farmers who had banded together to defend their land. They weren't really soldiers. They were wonderful horsemen and crack rifle shots from hunting wild animals but they had little idea of military discipline.'

'How was Smuts almost killed?'

Marius paused a moment as he pulled off the road into the driveway of the Bauernstube Restaurant.

'He was still deciding whether or not to try and capture the field guns at the top of the other kopje and was hiding behind a boulder, with an 18-year-old scout called Cilliers, who was lying well hidden in tall grass watching the enemy. A British sniper suddenly rose up some twenty-five metres away and took aim at Smuts, who saw the man and called to Cilliers to fire on him.

The British sniper fired first, missed Smuts and by sheer bad luck put a bullet in young Cilliers' head, killing him instantly. Smuts never forgot the young man's needless death.'

'War doesn't seem to have any sense to it' Ed commented as they left the car and headed for the entrance to the restaurant.

'But when you think of it, only eighteen British soldiers were killed in the entire battle and just a handful of Boers. How does that compare with the massive losses in the World Wars?'

'And even acts of terrorism,' Ed added as they entered the restaurant.

On their way to their table, Marius stopped briefly to say hello to Elke and Kurt who were already dining together. Elke's somewhat resigned expression lit up when she saw Marius. They hugged each other briefly, then Marius turned around to introduce Ed to the couple.

'I've been telling Ed about the battle of Buffelspoort.'

Elke and Ed's eyes met with a momentary mutual spark of interest before Marius moved on to where the Maitre d' was waiting to seat them. No one in that Restaurant or anywhere else for that matter could have foreseen how, within 12 hours of that moment, nothing would ever be quite the same again on planet Earth.

CHAPTER 7

Marius and Ed settled down to study the menu. Ed couldn't resist glancing across at the gorgeous young girl he had just met, albeit momentarily, as they had entered the restaurant. Even from a distance it was clear that she was not exactly enraptured by her partner's conversation. There is always a special kind of intensity in the eyes, face and even body language of someone in love as they listen to what the person of their dreams has to say. The eyes hungrily study the other person's face, as though to record every microsecond of the moment forever. Elke was stifling a yawn. This was clearly not one of those special moments.

As an extremely eligible bachelor back home, Ed had had no shortage of girlfriends. He had set a target long ago to remain uninvolved, but certainly not celibate, until he was thirty years old. He had seen too many of his friends attempt marriage in their early twenties, mostly with disastrous results. He was not yet desperate for female company but Elke had his juices racing. He idly wondered how he could contrive a further conversation with her. Clearly her partner wasn't cracking it.

'Beautiful, isn't she?' Marius said quietly with a chuckle. Ed, embarrassed, looked away from her and nodded at Marius.

'Sorry, I'll try the Hunter's Schnitzel' he said lamely.

'Don't be sorry, ou pal. I've known Elke since she was a baby. There isn't a man in the valley who doesn't think that the world is a more attractive place with people like her in it! Poor old Kurt, he doesn't stand a chance, for all his millions.'

The wine steward arrived at that moment. Marius suggested that they sample one of the Rhone Rieslings that had just arrived.

'May I be honest?' Ed asked.

'Of course. You don't like wine?' Marius replied.

'I do, but I really prefer red, and so far all the South African wines I've tried have been great.'

Marius smiled approvingly and ordered a Bertrams Cabernet Sauvignon 1997. As the steward left, Marius looked sternly at the young American.

'Now if you can keep your hormones in check for a few minutes, I'd like to tell you what I've found out about your possible ancestor, General Viljoen...'

At that moment, a large florid looking man in his fifties, sitting at the table to their right, shoved his chair back and tried to stand up. He was having trouble breathing and as he stood upright, he started to collapse on the floor clutching his chest. His wife, an equally large woman of about the same age let out a stifled scream and tried to get out of her chair to go to his assistance.

Ed's response was faster than anyone else's. He leapt out of his seat and knelt down beside the man, quickly loosening his tie and collar.

'Can you hear me, Sir?' Ed spoke clearly and with an unmistakable voice of authority. The older man made a gagging sound.

'Don't try to talk, just nod if you can. D'you have chest pains?' The man nodded, still gagging and choking as he fought the rising agony of a major heart attack. Ed looked up and was disconcerted to see Elke already standing over them, concern written on her face. Hell of a way to get her attention, he thought, momentarily.

'The Manager's calling an ambulance. Anything I can do? I've had some basic training.'

Ed started to loosen the man's belt. 'We don't have a doctor here, do we? The guy's having a serious heart attack. I'm also not qualified.'

Elke bent down and started to loosen the man's shoes. 'No doctor, sorry - let's do what we can. The ambulance should be here in a few minutes.' Ed and Elke used whatever limited skills they had to make the man comfortable.

Marius in the meantime was comforting the man's wife. The Manager of the restaurant arrived to assure them that the ambulance was on its way and the rest of the restaurant's customers quietly finished their meals and left as soon as they could.

Kurt, looking completely out of place, wandered over and told Elke that if the man needed to be transferred to a Johannesburg hospital, he would get the family's chopper fuelled up and ready.

Ed looked up and shook his head. 'Thanks, but if he were to be moved that far, he'd need a proper casevac chopper with life support systems.'

Half an hour later, the drama was over. The ambulance had arrived within minutes. A couple of paramedics rushed in and had the man quickly stabilised before wheeling him out of the restaurant. Marius escorted the man's wife to the ambulance where she was allowed to ride with her husband. One of the paramedics glanced back at Ed and Elke who were both now suffering from a sense of sudden anti-climax.

'I think he has a good chance,' the man said. 'You two did all you could and it may have just saved his life.'

Marius re-appeared and insisted that Elke and Kurt join them for the rest of the evening. The Manager thanked the young couple and insisted that dinner was on the house.

Ed looked around at the cosy surroundings of the restaurant. It was furnished in a typical Austrian or Tyrolean style, with wooden furniture, wood-panelled walls, any number of brass fittings and several "profound" sayings and mottos on plaques around the walls. For a moment Ed wondered whether he was dreaming but was the dream Central Europe and the reality Africa, or was it the other way around? Elke watched him looking around and smiled.

'Are you wondering what a place like this is doing in the middle of the African countryside?' she asked.

Ed nodded. 'Marius told me you have a large German community here, so I guess I shouldn't be surprised. He glanced across at Kurt who was clearly displeased that his little tête-à-tête with Elke had been disturbed.

'Your names' he nodded at both Elke and Kurt 'are German then, not Afrikaans?'

Kurt replied reluctantly, almost unwilling to be drawn into a conversation with the friendly American, whom he immediately perceived as being a serious threat to his attempts to consolidate his relationship with Elke. Kurt may have been dull, but he was no fool.

'Ja. Elke's family have been in the district since the first missionaries came out from Germany in 1898. Her great grandfather on her mother's side, Christian Muller, was the first pastor of the Lutheran Church and he founded the mission here. My family, on the other hand, only came out after the Second World War.'

'Strikes me there was more than just one New World that appealed to emigrants from an overcrowded and depressed Europe of the nineteenth century. We Americans assume that if someone wanted to leave Europe the only direction he'd be heading was to the US of A. Now, I'm not so sure.'

'What're your origins, Ed?' Elke asked. Ed glanced at Marius who grinned and shrugged. 'Funny you should ask that. Marius invited me here tonight to tell me about someone who may have been my great grandfather, a Boer War General.'

There was a stunned silence. All eyes turned to Marius, who shrugged again. 'Look, it's only a theory but when Ed told me he thought his unusual surname, Willjohn, came from a Dutch origin...'

37

'Viljoen!' Elke and Kurt exclaimed.

'I'm still doing research on the man, but he was a prominent Boer General who fought battles against the British at Ladysmith in Natal and later at Doornkop in the Transvaal. As the war was coming to an end he was strongly in favour of peace, which made him unpopular with the bitter-einders who wanted to fight to, well, the bitter end.'

'In 1904 Viljoen left his wife Lenie and in 1905 he departed South Africa for... but I'm getting ahead of myself. Ed d'you have any idea where your grandfather or great grandfather lived?'

Ed thought hard. 'I seem to remember that they came from someplace out West.'

'How about Albuquerque, New Mexico?'

Ed's eyes lit up. 'Yeah.... yeah, could be. My old man had a Mexican saddle on the Ranch in Wyoming... said his Dad had brought it East from...Albuquerque...'

'There you go!' said Marius delightedly. 'It begins to fit together.'

'What did he do there?' Ed asked.

Marius frowned. 'Listen, I've heard a few rumours and followed a few false trails. I'll let you know when I get the real story but from all accounts, he was quite a character!'

Frustratingly for Ed, as well as Elke and Kurt who were by now also intrigued by Marius' enigmatic statement, the older man refused to say more. He did however promise that the moment he had the full story, he would let all of them know.

The rest of the evening was great fun for Ed, despite the dramatic beginning and Kurt's reticence. A few drinks later, even Kurt stopped being pedantic and joined in the animated discussion over the state of Africa, the US and of course the world.

There was only one discordant moment when Elke asked Ed what he was doing in South Africa. Marius had replied for him.

'Ed's a mining consultant with Premier Platinum.'

To Ed's dismay Elke's lips compressed into a thin line. She suddenly went very quiet and took no further part in the conversation until Kurt excused himself to go to the loo and Ed had the opportunity to ask Elke.

'I get the feeling you don't like what I do?'

Elke stared at him seriously for a few moments then nodded.

'This mountain range represents so many vital elements of our ecology. It's a uniquely beautiful and unspoilt place but with a whole lot of mines on our doorstep, just how long d'you think it's going to remain unspoilt?'

Ed understood the problem. Part of his Mining degree had been devoted to a study of the environmental impact of mining around the world. If she were a serious bunny-hugger he could appreciate her reaction.

He looked directly into her impossibly beautiful eyes and knew that his response would have a profound effect on their future relationship, if such a thing could exist. Ed knew with certainty that it was vitally important to him that it should continue. He suspected that he could fall very much in love with this glorious young woman, who was quite likely to dismiss him as the "enemy" if he did not select his words very carefully.

He also sensed that anything less than his genuine feelings about the environment would be quickly perceived by Elke.

'Okay, I get you!' He replied. 'Look, my family have a ranch in Wyoming and if anything were to destroy it, it would probably destroy me too. I won't try and kid you that the mining operations in this district may not pose some threat to the environment. I haven't been here long enough to know whether they do or they don't...'

Elke was watching him carefully, but he sensed that he had her attention.

'...but what I do know is that part of my task at Premier, as a Consultant is to advise on any aspects of environmental impact.'

Elke nodded. Ed felt he was turning the corner.

'Would you do me a great favour?'

'What's that?' She was startled by the question.

'In fact, two things. First, show me around your most ecologically threatened areas so that I can do a proper assessment and secondly ...' he grinned, feeling confident again. '...suspend judgment on me and my motives until after the trip.'

Glory be! She smiled back. Ed went weak at the knees.

'Call me when you're ready.' Kurt was on his way back to the table and by tacit consent, they did not refer to it again that night.

After Marius dropped Ed back at the hotel, Ed slipped into bed and lay awake for a long time, fantasising over the prospect of Elke and him riding the range together and saving the region from the ravages of mining encroachment and the consequent pollution.

CHAPTER 8

Tuesday was a glorious spring day in the valley. Ed was still trying to get used to having spring in September, just when fall should be spreading its rich profusion of browns, yellows and reds across the countryside. Instead there was an indefinable hint of seductive scents in the air. Trees and shrubs which had been almost bare when he had arrived only a few days before, now flaunted cheeky little blossoms, with miniature green leaves thrusting out boldly from yesterday's bare branches. It reminded him immediately of Elke and her passion for the environment. As he drove along the twelve kilometre stretch from Buffalo Hills Hotel to the beginning of the road to Pretoria and the Hartbeestpoort Dam, he wondered whether there was really any danger from the platinum mines, which were all situated on the plateau well away from the mountains and the valley. He decided to meet with Sam Mohale and Martin Gericke and discuss the matter with them.

*

Elke had been awake since five o'clock helping her mother organise the labourers who were beginning to harvest the oranges. It was difficult to judge how her father had reacted to the fact of her not returning to university. She had spoken to him at length and tried to explain how she had already taken in virtually all the knowledge she had been seeking from her time there. She had no interest in becoming a teacher or following any other form of academic career. In fact, the premature end of her university life could be a blessing in disguise as she was now working on the land that she loved so much and was beginning to see, first hand, just how much attention the ecology of the place required.

Her dad had seemed to understand her as she spoke, although he said very little about it. He seldom spoke now but was content to hear what his wife and daughter had to say about the farm and its surroundings. He was not particularly interested in what was happening in the rest of the world, saying that he had never been a person who could have influenced what happened in the Middle East or any of the world's other trouble spots. As long as it did not affect his family or his friends, he would leave it to others to fret about.

Elke had wheeled her father out onto the veranda as usual but today he had reached out shakily and clung to her for a few moments. His quiet voice barely rose above the level of a whisper.

'I'm pleased to have you here, skatjie, but don't lose sight of what you have learned. We can all benefit from it. The world's a troubled place…if you can make our little district a safer environment to live in…'

He seemed to be incapable of further speech but Elke understood him. She had planted a gentle kiss on his forehead and followed her mother into the yard where the labourers congregated in the morning. It was a beautiful day, but Elke sensed that her father was disturbed over something which he quite possibly did not yet understand himself.

*

Ed was walking through the plant with Martin, checking that everything was running smoothly, when Sam hurried towards them. His face was tense and troubled.

'Ed … my wife just called and told me to switch the television to CNN. There's been a terrible accident in New York…'

Ed felt a chill seize his body and his stomach muscles tightened convulsively. Who did he know in New York and what..?

'What happened?' he verbalised to Sam.

'Looks like a plane crashed into the Twin Towers, it's a hell of a mess - the top of one of the Towers is on fire. Better come and look.'

All three men hurried towards Sam's office. Ed's anxiety was growing by the second. He did not have many friends in New York and yet something was nagging at the edge of his memory.

Suddenly he remembered. 'Oh my God!' he exclaimed. 'My brother Justin was going to see our Investment Advisors in New York!'

'Would he have gone near the Twin Towers?' Martin asked.

Ed looked at him, his face ashen. 'That's where our Advisor's offices are!'

*

Rob Schutte was working on lists of materials and food to be ordered for the hotel when Angela rushed in from the Reception area, looking shocked.

'Mr Schutte, one of the guests says that there's been a disaster in New York. They saw it on the TV in their room. Two planes have crashed into that tall building.'

Rob could only think of the Empire State. He got up and rushed over to the TV Lounge which was on the other side of the Hotel Foyer from the Reception.

He switched on the TV. Angela and a couple of other office staff who had seen the commotion stared with a growing sense of disbelief as CNN showed the second plane hit the other Twin Tower and it became obvious that this was far more serious than simply a tragic accident.

*

Sam had immediately insisted that Ed phone his mother in Minneapolis. The young American had some difficulty getting through. Clearly the international lines were overloaded with callers frantically trying to contact friends and loved ones.

As he redialled and redialled, the news on the TV set at the far end of Sam's office became grimmer and grimmer. A third plane had hit the Pentagon and a fourth was missing. It was now evident that a massive terrorist attack had occurred. Ed felt sick as he continued dialling and watched the pictures on the screen. Justin and he were hardly close but when the chips were down, Justin was still his brother. The family may have been fighting each other but he was certain that his mother would be equally desperate to know where Justin was.

As he was about to redial for the umpteenth time, he heard a ringing tone. He had to make a conscious effort to prevent his fingers from cutting off the phone again. His attention was hardly on the mechanics of dialling a number.

The phone was answered by Mrs Griffiths, his mother's companion and housekeeper.

'Willjohn Residence.'

'Mrs Griffiths, it's Ed. I've just heard the news. Is my Mom at home?'

Mrs Griffiths' voice quavered as she replied. 'Edward, I'm so pleased you called. Your mother's quite frantic...'

Ed cut in 'Was Justin in New York?'

There was a silence then Mrs Griffiths replied tersely. 'I think you'd better speak to your mother. I'm putting you through.'

*

Elke wiped the sweat from her brow. It had been a warm, but not unbearable, spring day. Nevertheless, she was looking forward to a shower when she got home. She rode her pony, Witblitz, away from the orchards and headed for home. Her mother had asked her to go into Kroondal and buy more organic fertiliser for the market garden they were developing. The vegetables were not only for the consumption of the family and staff on the farm, but they were beginning to supply a number of farm stalls and vegetable shops in the district. Marie, her mother, had talked about setting up her own farm stall on the side of the main road but they did not yet have a suitable person to run it.

Elke cantered into the yard at the back of the house. As she had ridden

42

past the front of the house, she had noticed with concern that her dad was not in his usual place on the veranda.

She dismounted and hurried inside the house.

She called out to her father as she went from room to room. There was no reply, then, as she approached the sitting room, she heard a murmur of voices. Oh no, she thought, he's had a heart attack and the doctor's been called!

She rushed into the room and for a moment she felt enormous relief as she saw her father on his own, watching CNN on television. If he heard her enter, he made no sign whatsoever but simply continued to stare at the screen, which was, at that moment, replaying the awful moments of the first Tower collapsing.

Elke's relief turned to shock as the images on the screen began to impinge on her awareness. She sat on the long sofa near her dad, who suddenly spoke without looking up.

'You know I don't like TV, but Rolf Otterman phoned and said we should watch. My girl, this is the beginning of the end!'

*

Rob Schutte quietly told everyone to get back to their posts. They still had a hotel to run. He, like tens of millions of viewers across the world, was beginning to realise the enormity of what he was seeing. Rob allowed himself to dwell momentarily on the thought that of all places in the world, his beloved valley of Buffalo Hills was probably the very best place to be at this terrible moment in time. Then, almost as quickly, his mind turned towards anyone whom he might know, who could be directly involved in the tragedy. His first thought was Ed Willjohn.

Rob returned to his desk intending to call him when another awful thought occurred to him. His good friend and neighbouring farmer Errol Saperstein had called him a couple of days ago. He had excitedly told Rob that his nephew now lived in Los Angeles. The nephew had invited Errol and his wife to fly over to LA to enjoy Rosh Hashanah, the Jewish New Year, with them. Errol had mentioned that he had been of some assistance to her nephew when he was younger and this was his way of saying "Thank you."

Errol, as far as Rob could remember, had flown out from Johannesburg International the previous night and was due to spend the next day in New York before catching a connecting flight to Los Angeles.

Even this remote and beautiful valley, Rob thought sombrely, did not necessarily escape the devastating effects of the terrible events unfolding before their eyes. He picked up the phone to dial Ed at Premier Platinum while he tried to recall how to get hold of any of Errol's relatives in Johannesburg.

'Mom, it's Ed. How're you doin'?' The traditional American greeting sounded banal under the circumstances but it was automatic and Ed regretted using the words as soon as he uttered them.

'Not too good, Honey. Justin went up to New York yesterday to see the brokers today,'

'In the Twin Towers, right?'

There was a silence. Ed thought he heard a muffled sob.

'I'm afraid so... Oh Ed... Thousands have died...'

Ed grasped at straws in trying to comfort his mother.

'But CNN says that a large number were evacuated before it collapsed...'

'If he escaped, why hasn't he phoned?' His mother was sobbing openly by now.

Ed thought fast. 'Look Mom, there're all kinds of possible reasons. It must be complete chaos down there. Maybe he can't get to a phone.'

'You know your brother' his mother replied bitterly. 'He'd make sure he'd call ahead of anyone else.'

'Maybe so, Mom, but you can't be sure. The other possibility is that he got out but...he's hurt... unconscious perhaps.'

'Darling, I know you're trying to be comforting but until I hear from him...'

'I'll be on the next plane home, Mom!'

His mother gave a strained laugh. 'Haven't you heard? They've closed every airport in the US, maybe every airport in the world. This is beyond belief. Anyway, I don't want you flying right now - even if you could!'

Ed ended off the conversation as reassuringly as he could and looked bleakly at Sam and Martin. 'Guys, I'll have to go back as soon as the planes start flying again.'

CHAPTER 9

Ed returned to Buffalo Hills Hotel just after four p.m. Sam had insisted that he leave the office and remain at the hotel until he had more data on his brother Justin.

As he entered the driveway to the hotel and parked his car, Ed reflected on how easily one's life could be turned upside down. The valley was unchanged from yesterday. As the sun headed for the horizon, the calm and serenity of the place, made the devastating news a world away, seemingly surreal.

One of the waiters gave him a cheerful greeting as he walked along the path towards the reception area. He responded distractedly. He barely noticed the raucous sound of a couple of grey Loeries searching for fruit at a nearby tree, until one of them broke from cover and flew awkwardly across to another tree. The Loerie's long tails make them poor fliers and for an instant, as Ed watched, he reverted to the horrifying picture in his mind of the second plane striking the Twin Towers in New York.

For the first time he thought of the awful last moments of the helpless passengers on board. He had been so intent on wondering and worrying about the occupants of the two vast buildings and of Justin's whereabouts that the other victims were only now brought to his attention by the surprisingly cumbersome flight of the Loerie. Not that the planes were cumbersome. Far from it. In contrast, the Loerie almost expressed an unwillingness to fly because of its tail-heavy build.

Apart from the terrorists who were undoubtedly hyped up with an insane determination to destroy themselves and many others, Ed started to create images of the passengers as they tried to will the plane to miss its target. The mental image was unconfrontable and his body was convulsed with a spasm of terrible grief, not only for his brother but for the thousands who had probably perished both in the planes and in the Towers.

Regaining control of his emotions, Ed walked on towards the hotel's main entrance. As he looked away from the bird, he saw Rob standing in the entrance, watching him with a mixture of sorrow and compassion.

Ed fought back tears and tried to smile at Rob, who instinctively reached out and put an arm around the American's shoulders.

'Sam called me. Told me about your brother. Come, my friend. Come and have a stiff drink then we'll make sure that you can be contacted by your family as soon as they have any news.'

Ed was not in the habit of having a drink when he was under stress. In fact, he normally stayed away from all alcohol in a crisis, preferring to keep a clear head. However, the uncertainty and the frustration of being unable to do anything about the situation called for enormous patience. He decided to take up Rob's offer and nodded, still unable to speak.

They went into the bar, where some fifteen people were crowded around the television in the corner.

'D'you want to see more of what's going on or shall we sit outside?' Rob asked.

Ed cleared his throat. 'Outside, please.'

Rob ordered two double Bell's on the rocks. They went outside and sat down on the veranda. The sounds of CNN's endless repetition of the disaster receded into the background.

It all began to feel like a dream as Ed sat down. He observed the glorious red glow of sunset, the leisurely movements of the garden staff as they headed homewards after a day of tending to the lawns, flower beds and the general needs of a sizeable hotel estate. Was this a dream and would he awake to find himself back in the US or was it simply a nightmare from which he would awake in his hotel bed, looking forward to the leisurely pace of a day's work at the mine and the momentarily forgotten excitement of planning how to renew his acquaintance with the beautiful Elke?

The waiter appeared with the drinks. Rob lifted his glass and proposed a sombre toast.

'To your family and to all those who have been affected by today's event. To hope!'

Ed raised his glass and murmured 'Cheers,' before taking a large gulp of the scotch. The fiery liquor seemed to physically relax him as he swallowed it and he knew that Rob's thoughtful but not overpowering attention was exactly what he needed at that moment. As they chatted, Ed found himself talking about his brother and their turbulent relationship since they were teenagers. Rob let Ed talk, knowing that it could have a cathartic effect.

Elke sat with her father watching events unfold on CNN for an hour or so, until Marie entered the room. She brusquely asked what was happening and after a few minutes of sharing the unfolding drama, she stood up and spoke to Elke.

'Whatever may be happening over there, we've still got a farm to run. Elke, did you get the fertilizer?'

Elke looked at her blankly. The events in the US had wiped everything else from her mind. Above all, she could not prevent herself wondering whether Ed was directly affected by the disaster. She had suppressed an impulse to rush to her phone and call either the mine or the hotel. It might be construed as interference in his personal life when she hardly knew him.

'Elke!' Her mother angrily demanded her attention. 'Did you get the fertilizer or not?'

Elke returned to the present with a sense of shock. She was normally a diligent and responsible person and for once she had completely forgotten to carry out her duties.

'Sorry, Mom. It went right out of my head.'

She scrambled to her feet and headed for the door.

'Better hurry' Marie called after her. 'They close in twenty minutes.' Elke nodded and left at a run.

Isak Stein looked at his wife with mixed emotions. 'Ja, Marie! You're a real tower of strength but don't be too hard on the girl. Don't forget that for her generation, this is the first time that world affairs are threatening to get out of hand.'

Marie sighed. 'I know, liefling, but I cannot let go of my emotions. This farm has to survive for all our sakes.'

Isak nodded. 'I must get well again soon. It's not fair on you and Elke.'

Marie reached out a hand and squeezed his with a firm grip.

'You concentrate on getting well but don't let anything make you over-anxious. We're doing fine. Elke's a great help, even if she forgot herself today.'

They smiled at each other with all the love and tenderness of a good twenty-four year marriage. In her heart, Marie seriously doubted if Isak would ever recover but despite her seemingly tough and practical nature, she wasn't averse to wishing for miracles.

*

Ed's mother called at 10 o'clock that night to say that there was still no news about Justin.

'I heard on CNN that a large number of people were evacuated before the buildings collapsed. D'you have anyone in New York doing a search, checking the hotels and so on?'

'Yes, Franklin's contacted our insurance brokers. They've promised to do a thorough search.'

'That's great, Mom. I feel so helpless over here.'

'Don't. There's nothing you can do. I was going to drive to New York tomorrow but I've been advised not to.'

'No, don't. If you've gotten a good team looking for Justin, it's better that you stay at home for now.'

They spoke for a few minutes, each one trying to comfort the other. Ed finally put the phone down and wondered at the irony of family relationships. A day ago, he was conjuring up images of beating his young brother to a pulp over his selfish and unfeeling attitude towards his mother and him. Now suddenly Justin was his kid brother again and he was in deep trouble. That took precedence over anything else. He could, he thought wryly, always beat him to a pulp at some future date. Just let him survive the disaster first.

Wearily Ed switched off the television in his room and tried to get to sleep.

The following morning, Ed returned to work at the usual time. Sam protested that he should have stayed at the hotel, but Ed firmly rejected the idea.

'What would I do? Sit in front of the TV hour after hour?'

'You could go on a long hike,' Sam suggested.

'Not until we know what's happened. I have to be near a phone. No, it's much better that I do my job and try to take my mind off things.'

He looked at Sam, who nodded in agreement. 'How d'you think the attack will affect the platinum industry?' he asked.

Sam frowned. 'Share prices've dropped across the board, including platinum. The only thing we've heard so far is that all forms of transport have been affected. It seems as though the whole of America is in a state of shock. There's talk of the major car manufacturers laying off thousands of staff, which means fewer cars being built and therefore fewer catalysts - and less platinum. But so far it's only rumours. Let's see what happens and meanwhile we'd better concentrate on being as cost-effective as possible.'

Ed agreed. Cost-effectiveness was a major part of his mandate as Mining Consultant.

He told Sam that he would do an immediate review of all departments for the purpose of improving productivity and reduce any wastage wherever possible.

'Good,' Sam replied. 'Perhaps you'd better start off with Martin. He's brilliant at improvising, so if we need to get anything fixed, let's see if we can do it with minimal costs.'

Sam stood up and walked with Ed to the door of his office.

'One of the biggest problems with our workforce in all sectors of the economy has been that for many years cheap Black labour made White South Africans live in a fool's paradise. It didn't matter if the workforce wasn't efficient because they were paid so little. Now that we're competing more and more in the international marketplace and our workforce is understandably demanding higher and higher wages, we're struggling to remain profitable. We don't have a legacy of high productivity as they do in the Far East. So far platinum's escaped the side-effects of all this because the prices of the metal have risen steadily but now...' he shrugged.

'I get the picture,' Ed replied. 'Let's see where we can tighten our belts without trying to return to a level of poor wages and unhappy workers. It'll be a juggling act, Sam,' he smiled wryly 'but it's the kind of challenge I'd appreciate right now!'

Two days passed. Ed and his mother were fast losing any hope that Justin would be found alive. The team from the insurance brokers had checked all the major hospitals within the Manhattan area. There were a number of smaller clinics that had taken in some of the casualties on a temporary basis and they were rapidly running out of those. However, a senior Vice President of the brokers who had been a personal friend of Ed's father called Jean Willjohn and told her to hang on in there until every last option had been exhausted. There had been numerous stories of survivors suddenly appearing, whose identities had been unknown at first for a variety of reasons.

Marius was waiting at the hotel when Ed returned from work. They had spoken on the phone the previous day.

'Just came to see how you're doing' Marius said as they settled into chairs on the veranda.

This was beginning to be Ed's evening ritual as the sunset performed yet another technicolour spectacle, laced with the most perfect billowy, fluffy masses of cumulus, with a darker, angrier tinge of solid black cloud in the background. As they watched silently for some moments, little flashes punctuated the distant storm clouds, just too far away for the night chorus of bass rumbles to begin. It was at that moment that Ed knew he had fallen in love with Africa and its people of so many different and diverse cultures.

'John Does are still turning up both dead and alive in all kinds of unexpected places' Ed said finally. 'I've even heard that some casualties have been taken as far as Canada for treatment,' he added.

'Is that possible?' Marius asked.

Ed shrugged. 'Who knows? It's chaos over there. New York's fire-fighters've performed feats of heroism with some loss of life, but the logistics...' he let the words hang in the air.

'I thought *we* lived in a big country until I visited the States,' Marius said. 'I've been to the Grand Canyon, Yosemite and all over the place but the thing that gave me the greatest feeling of size and a mass of people I'd never experienced before was the Twin Towers. My wife and I went up to the roof a couple of years ago, and then came down in rush hour as people were flooding into the concourse, heading for home.'

Marius paused as he thought about it.

'I've seen rioting here, I've seen Johannesburg Station when thousands of early morning commuters arrive and the Black taxis sprawl all over the area but nothing, nothing, even remotely compared to the mass of people we saw that day. We were truly frightened. It was just too big...'

'And now it's no more' Ed murmured quietly.

The first tiny rumbles of the approaching storm filtered through the glorious warm evening air and larger flashes of the heaven's intense energy flickered in response.

Marius sniffed the air. 'Can you smell the rain?' he asked.

Ed, surprised, took a deep breath. Yes, he could sense a change. He could feel the excitement building in the atmosphere but it was an excitement tinged with a deep sadness. Not only for his brother but for a world whose equilibrium had been shattered. Would an evening like this be possible again, without the intrusion of images of death and mayhem? Ed fervently hoped so. The valley of Buffalo Hills already held a special place in his heart. He did not want that image tarnished by torrid memories.

'By the way, I saw Elke in Kroondal village yesterday,' Marius said. 'You definitely made an impression there, pal. I told her about your brother. She said for me to tell you that her thoughts and wishes are with you.'

Ed smiled. 'That's the best news I've had in a while.'

The two men chatted for a few more minutes before Marius stood up, glancing at the sky as he did so.

'That storm's going to hit us any moment now' he said. 'I'd better head home.'

He and Ed shook hands. Ed watched the silver-haired Afrikaner stride purposefully towards the parking ground. He was hugely grateful for a good friend at that moment but he could not resist the thought of young Elke holding him comfortingly in her arms.

Suddenly the Receptionist dashed out onto the veranda.

'Mr Willjohn, America's on the phone. Will you take it in your room?'

Ed waved and raced across the lawn just as the first large drops of rain hit the warm ground all around him. A huge clap of thunder nearby startled him but he could not think of anything except the call. What would he learn? He fumbled with the key, opened the door and dived inside, reaching out for the instrument of either relief or torment.

'Ed here. That you, Mom?'

His mother's voice came through clearly over the line as the rain began to beat in earnest on the roof. The intensity of the building storm was such that it would probably all be over in half an hour.

'Yes, darling. We've got news about Justin....'

At that instant, there was a sharp electronic crack on the line followed by a bellow of thunder and a brilliant white flash outside his window. Ed stared at the phone in disbelief. It had gone dead.

CHAPTER 10

There is a certain rustic charm in the fact that the Highveld's thunderstorms frequently cut off telephone lines. It serves as a reminder that nature has not been entirely vanquished by Man's technology. However, when it's a matter of life and death, there's nothing charming about waiting to get through to the United States. Ed paced up and down in his room, fretting endlessly over what his mother was trying to say as the lightning struck the line. He replayed her few words endlessly – was she sounding relieved or devastated? Ed honestly couldn't be certain. The hotel's telephonist who was renowned for her skills at connecting people to each other, worked feverishly to make contact. The line had gone down somewhere between the nearby town of Rustenburg and the hotel. Repair teams were already onto it and Ed could do nothing except wait.

Ed did not regard himself as psychic or anything like that, but his instincts were generally good. He had a feeling that Justin was still alive.

The phone rang and Ed nearly jumped out of his skin.

'Hello.' Ed shouted as he picked up the phone. 'Hello, Hello!'

His mother's voice calmly responded as though she were in the next room. 'I'm right here, Honey. I believe you've been having a storm...'

'Yes Mom. Have they found him?' Ed was not going to go through all the social niceties of his mother's telephone conversations.

'Yes, would you believe? He's in hospital...'

'Thank God! Which one? What does he say?' Ed was impatient to hear it all.

'He was taken to a small private clinic in Brooklyn and the reason why we never heard is that he's still unconscious.

'How serious is it?' Ed asked.

'The doctors say that there aren't any major injuries. He has a broken collar bone and a couple of cracked ribs but there's no obvious damage to his head or spine. They expect him to come round soon.'

'That's incredible. So, he'll be okay?'

'The doctors are optimistic. I'm having him flown over to St. Michael's Clinic here in Minneapolis the next day or so, if the planes are allowed to fly by then.'

'Mom, should I come home?' Ed asked anxiously. He had mixed feelings about doing so but his sense of duty to his family came first. Sam had already told him that Premier Platinum would not stand in his way if it became necessary for him to return.

'I don't think so,' his mother replied. 'If there're problems when he recovers consciousness, perhaps. Let's be real, Honey, what good is it going to do for you to sit next to your brother's bed if he's still unconscious?'

'Okay,' Ed felt enormously relieved. There was no way he wanted to go home at this stage, unless duty called.

'But the moment you think that I should, just let me know.'

'Sure, Darling. Anyway, you two kids would probably be yelling at each other within minutes of his regaining consciousness. I'll keep you posted.'

They chatted for a few more minutes. Jean Willjohn gave him an overview of how her friends had reacted to the disaster. She painted a picture of a nation in shock but also a nation with a rising tide of fury over what had been done to them. As she talked, Ed got an impression that many Americans were feeling what the Japanese would describe as "loss of face." The world's greatest superpower had been paralysed with shock at the audacity and the accuracy of the terrorists who had turned one of America's most visible assets, its aircraft, against itself. How could we have been so dumb, Ed thought, as his mother spoke calmly enough but with an underlying sense of outrage.

After he said goodbye and rang off, Ed sat for a long time staring into space. He decided to throw himself wholeheartedly into everything he could find in the Valley and at the Mine. Only if Justin were seriously injured would he return. It was very late when Ed finally dozed off.

*

Elke made a decision. She looked up the telephone number for Premier Platinum and dialled it. A carefully enunciated African voice answered the phone.

'Premier Platinum, good morning. How may I help you?'

'May I speak with Mr Willjohn?' Elke replied nervously, hoping that she was going the right thing.

'One moment, please.'

Elke wondered if he would even remember who she was. She nearly put the phone down but somehow she felt that this could be an important moment for her.

'Ed Willjohn speaking.' His soft American accent instantly evoked pictures of their meeting a few nights previous.

'Morning, Ed, this is Elke Stein, the girl who...'

'Of course! How're you doing?' Ed responded.

There was no mistaking the pleasure in his tone of voice. Steady, girl, steady, Elke thought. You don't want to come across as a predatory female. Somehow, she knew that he would not appreciate a woman who was too forward in her approach.

'Fine, thanks.' She tried to keep it business-like. 'Marius told me about your brother. I'm so sorry. D'you have any news?'

'Yeah, last night my mother called. They've found him but he's still unconscious.'

'Oh!' Elke was momentarily at a loss.

'The doctors expect him to recover but they won't know until he comes round. There aren't any major physical injuries as far as they can judge.'

'That must be a great relief,' she replied lamely.

'Yeah. When I think of the thousands who didn't make it, we can be thankful for what we have so far, I guess.'

There was a pause and Elke realised that he would no doubt be wondering just why she had called him.

'Look, I don't know how you feel about this but I thought that if you want to take your mind off the whole thing for a little while, we could maybe...'

'You're asking me out on a date?' Ed's voice was teasing and held a hint of a chuckle.

'Oh...no...I...er...oops!' Elke was totally thrown. Ed laughed delightedly.

'Only kidding! I reckon you'd be waiting to take me up on the challenge you threw out about the environment the other night.'

Elke's forehead broke out in a cold sweat. Was her approach so obvious?

'Ja, that's it. I'd like to show you around the area and explain what we're up against. I was hoping that you might like to take your mind off everything else.'

There was another long pause. Elke opened her mouth to jabber on mindlessly, in order to cover her confusion. At that moment she would have given anything not to be having this conversation.

'It's a deal!' Ed finally told her. 'And by the way, I really appreciate your thoughtfulness, even though we may end up on opposite sides of the ecological fence.'

Elke felt a warm glow replace the tension of moments ago.

'Wonderful! Tomorrow's Saturday. Shall we...?'

'Tell me where and when. I'll be there.'

With a rising sense of excitement, Elke arranged to collect him from the hotel at nine the following morning.

*

That evening Ed received two phone calls. The first was from his mother, to say that Justin had not yet regained consciousness and she was engaged in a debate with various doctors as to the wisdom of moving him before he came around. Ed agreed with the medicos who felt that Justin should remain where he was for the time being. Although all his vital signs were good, there could be something hidden from their examinations which may only become apparent once he was able to speak to them. Ed rang off feeling frustrated about the situation but there was nothing he could really do and his mother remained adamant that he should remain where he was.

The second call was from Marius. His friend was amused by a telephone call he had received from Elke, who had a case of very cold feet over her arrangements with Ed the following day. She was terrified that she may have given Ed the wrong impression in one of two ways. On the one hand, she didn't want Ed to think that she was pursuing him, because in a sense of course she was. On the other hand, she assured Marius that if Ed remained stubborn about the needs of the mining giants over the environment, attractive though he was, they would have a very brief association.

'So, what in the hell's that mean?' Ed asked bemused.

'She's got it bad, ou pal! That's what it means.' Marius chuckled. 'But she's a woman of principle so be careful about this mining business. If I were you, I wouldn't promise her anything you can't deliver. You may find that your bosses are not as aware of the environment as you think.'

'Point taken, Marius. I'm just going on a sightseeing trip at this stage. I need to see what her concerns are before I find out if they can be handled...or even if they should be handled.'

Marius cleared his throat and replied 'I think you're about to step onto a tightrope and it's going to be a long, long fall, if you should lose your balance.'

'Thanks, my friend. That really inspires me with confidence' Ed replied with a wry smile. 'But it's great advice and I'll play this whole thing very cautiously.'

'Good. By the way, I meant to tell you, Errol Saperstein and wife are safe. They landed in New York on the morning of September 11th and took a ferry across the water to Manhattan. They were halfway across when the first plane hit the first Tower...I believe the ferry turned back at some stage. Anyway, we'll get the full story when he returns.'

'Unbelievable!' was all Ed could say.

*

The next morning Elke arrived at the hotel promptly at nine o'clock. She was dressed in faded but neatly pressed denims and a muted check shirt that did not entirely succeed in hiding her curves. Her hair was braided in a ponytail and Ed thought that she epitomised the sort of outdoor girl one would hope to encounter when hiking in the Austrian Tyrol. After shaking Ed's hand in a rather brisk, business-like fashion, she gave him a smile that would have melted the polar ice caps, had they been within range.

'You brought me some homework?' Ed asked, eyeing a book in her hand.

Elke nodded. 'In a way.' She handed him a copy of "The Magaliesberg" by Vincent Carruthers. He looked at the excellent photograph on its cover which showed a scenic view of the mountain range in the full greenness of summer. Ed had seen enough of the surrounding mountains to immediately identify with the area.

'Thanks, this is great. Is there some stuff I should know before we set off?'

Elke thought about it and nodded. 'There's a good map and some detail on the early origins of the range, which, you may not know, are the second oldest mountains on Earth.'

Ed told her that Rob had mentioned that fact as he steered her out onto the veranda for a cup of coffee. Once they were seated, Elke busied herself looking for a couple of specific references in the book. She was still unsure about this meeting with the young American except that her heart had definitely performed some minor gymnastics when he had stepped forward to greet her in the Reception area a few moments ago.

'Thank you,' Ed said quietly.

Elke looked up in surprise. 'For what?' she asked.

'For providing me with something to think about at just the right time.'

Elke felt herself blushing. She smiled. 'Okay, but don't think that this is only a distraction. I'm serious about getting your support for the preservation and restoration of the Magaliesberg.'

Ed laughed. 'I'll bet you are. Now before we get all technical, what did you plan for today?'

Elke glanced up at the sky momentarily before replying. 'It looks like we'll get another thunderstorm this afternoon but before then, if you don't mind some driving, I'd like us to cross over to the far side of the mountains over Olifantsnek and look at the more, er, visual side. Then if we've got time I thought we should do something touristy, like go to Retief's Kloof, Hamerkop Kloof or Castle Gorge.' She smiled disarmingly again. 'It's my intention to make you fall in love with the place before I bore you to death with facts and figures.'

'Quite a marketing campaign you've gotten planned.'

She nodded. 'But I promise you, you'll soon see what I've been raving about.'

Over coffee, Elke provided Ed with the basics of what the Magaliesberg range was all about. Despite its Afrikaans sounding name, she explained that the name Magalies was derived from the African people, who had lived in the area for generations, by the name of Mohale.

Ed replied that he worked for Sam Mohale and was aware of the significance of the name. 'But how come it's considered the second oldest mountain range on earth?' He asked. 'I mean, who measures these things?'

Elke referred him to the Carruthers book which began with a chapter on geology which explains the Transvaal Sequence, 2.3 billion years ago and the Bushveld Igneous Complex 2 billion years ago.

Ed threw up his hands in mock horror. 'Okay, okay, I'll get into that later' he told her. 'Let me ask you a basic question. Do you believe that the mountains are in immediate danger?'

Elke thought about it before replying. 'I suppose I could say that the entire planet's in danger but I just happen to know something about this region. So if we leave things like the ozone layer aside for the moment, I'd have to say that the Magaliesberg range is suffering from neglect, from inefficient and damaging farming practices, from a massive drainage of water, which has been diverted to supply the mines, shall I go on?'

Ed nodded soberly. Clearly if his beloved family ranch in Wyoming were threatened by any of these issues, he would be concerned. Very concerned. He drained his coffee cup and stood up.

'I'd like to get a visual feeling of the place before we examine all the negatives.'

Elke agreed and suggested that they drive in her car, as she knew the area. As they left Reception and headed for the car park, Angela dashed out of the hotel and called out to Ed.

'Ed, I've got the States on the line.' Ed turned to Elke. 'Sorry, I'll be as quick as I can.'

Elke nodded and watched him hurry back into the hotel. She stood aimlessly on the path and hoped that the call would not ruin their day together. Ed emerged five minutes later, shaking his head in bewilderment.

'Bad news?' Elke asked anxiously.

Ed shrugged. 'Dunno. My brother's recovered consciousness....'

'That's wonderful, isn't it?'

Elke could not understand Ed's facial expression under the circumstances. He nodded slowly.

'Sure, but the curve ball is that an hour after he woke up, he announced that he would be flying out to join his brother in Africa, just as soon as he could be released from hospital!'

'Something tells me that you may not be too excited about that,' Elke said as they reached her car.

Ed shrugged again. 'Well, it's great that he's okay, but whenever my brother gets into my space, it's trouble with a capital T.'

Ed pulled a wry face. 'So, make my day and show me your beautiful mountains!'

CHAPTER 11

'I think you're nuts,' Jean Willjohn snapped at her younger son, Justin, as he lay in his bed at St. Michael's Clinic in Minneapolis.

Justin gave her a rather sly lop-sided grin. At first glance Justin was a smaller, slimmer version of his big brother Ed. However, on closer inspection, Justin's features were a much weaker replica of Ed's. The older Willjohn had a firm square jaw but the younger brother's jaw lacked the squareness and was slightly receding. It was not enough to spoil his looks completely, but in Ed's presence Justin invariably came off second best. He was also at least 20 pounds lighter and played no sport at all. His pale skin accentuated the numerous cuts and abrasions he had suffered in his miraculous escape from the Twin Towers' disaster.

'Don't worry, Mom. If they couldn't kill me in New York, I guess I'll survive Africa!'

Jean frowned. 'I am worried that you shouldn't travel until your injuries have healed, and yes, I guess I'm worried about you flying at this time.'

Justin laughed. 'If they've got any brains, they'll try other ways of attacking us. Every plane'll be more secure than Fort Knox right now.'

'I hope you're right, honey, but what's made you decide to go and see Ed? It's not as if you guys are exactly close!'

Justin's smile faded. He nodded. 'That's right, but he and I need to discuss the Corporation...'

'Franklin's got everything well under control,' Jean responded stonily.

She was dreading any kind of a confrontation with Justin on the subject of Willjohn Industries and its shareholdings. Jean was, in her own way, quite an astute business woman but Justin did not play fair. He always had some angle, which seemed logical enough – until one worked it out. When he would present one of his ideas to her, Jean would be as mad as hell with more than a twinge of guilt over the thought that she must have misjudged her youngest boy. Eventually she would reason it through and realise that he had once again been playing on her sympathy for his own ends.

'That old fool's gonna bankrupt us if we don't do something about it,' Justin retorted. 'How old's he now, sixty-five? We need a young mind in charge. Someone capable of thinking with the times, someone who can make split second decisions, someone...'

'Just like you?' his mother asked sardonically.

To her surprise, he shook his head. 'No, I'm not ready yet but I do have someone in mind.'

Jean got up from her chair where she had been sitting for the past half hour and walked over to the window overlooking the street outside. It was a grey blustery miserable sort of day. For a moment she envied Ed in Africa and Justin for wanting to go out and join him for a while. She looked back at Justin who was watching her intently. He's hatching one of his plots again, she thought.

'If you have any ideas of replacing Franklin, you can forget it,' she said. 'Far from being a geriatric, he's just been voted Vice-President of the City's Chamber of Commerce and if you think you'll get Ed to support you, you're wasting a very long trip,' she told him.

Justin's smile returned. 'Why should Ed be the only one to enjoy the sunshine?' he asked.

Jean shrugged. Justin was an unguided missile, she had long since given up on trying to fathom out how his mind worked.

'Do what you must but give yourself a few more days to get your strength back.'

'Yes, Mommy dearest,' Justin replied with his best attempt at wide-eyed innocence.

*

As Elke drove them from the hotel in the direction of Kroondal and Rustenburg, Ed explained that his brother and he were not close. He did not tell her about Justin's horrific lies which had destroyed his first real romantic relationship. He simply said that it was apparent that his brother was jealous of anything Ed did. Travelling to Africa was symptomatic of Justin's thinking. He was coming out to see what he was missing and more than likely, he would use the opportunity to try and persuade his older brother to sell his shares in the family business.

'Would you?' Elke asked.

Ed shook his head emphatically. 'No way. I have no confidence in his ability to run the place. We've got a great guy, Franklin de Vos, as CEO right now.'

'Do you want to run it one day?' Elke wondered.

'Negative. I have no interest in running it, but it doesn't mean I'll hand over to Justin who has a proven record of incompetence.' Ed sighed. 'Tell you what. This is a beautiful day, I'm in beautiful company - can we change the subject?'

Elke blushed slightly at the compliment. 'Sorry. Anyway, it's none of my business.'

They had cut across through the back roads and now emerged onto the main Rustenburg/Magaliesburg/Johannesburg road. Elke turned left towards Magaliesburg village some 50 kilometres to the South East.

The mountains were beginning to show their rugged side even before they drove over Olifantsnek, with a large expanse of water to their left and a small but attractive mountain pass into the Moot (the Dutch word Moot means Moat in English and refers to the wide valley which separates the Magaliesberg and the Daspoortrand).

Elke pointed out various beauty spots as they drove. She explained that she had decided to drive all the way down to Hartbeespoort Dam, where they would have lunch. They would then drive back along the far side of the mountains past the wall of the dam.

'That's the way I came from the airport' Ed explained.

Elke nodded. 'Yes, you would have done but the round trip'll give you a feeling for the shape of the place. I don't know about you, but whenever I go somewhere new, I like to drive around and mark my territory, like a wild animal!'

'And what kind of wild animal are you?' Ed asked her teasingly.

Elke flashed her glorious eyes at him. 'Definitely the Cat family, probably a leopard.'

'Hey, man, I'd better watch out for your claws!' Ed said in mock alarm.

Elke laughed. 'Don't worry, we normally keep well away from Man and we live on a diet of birds, rodents and insects, mostly. Once in a while, we take a small calf, goat or even a dog, which is why the farmers like to shoot us. For many years we've been classified as vermin.'

Ed rolled his eyes. 'You sure know how to turn a guy on!' he commented.

Elke giggled but felt the conversation could get out of hand, if she were not careful. She raised her arm and pointed to the majestic cliffs of the mountain range to her left.

'See that ridge?' She pointed to a distinctive ridge sticking out from the line of cliffs. 'At the foothills there is the village of Maanhaarrand which is named after the Dutch word for Hogsback - Maanhaar. It's also a syenite dyke in geological terms, the highest point and principal watershed in the Moot. There's no other way through the mountains travelling west for about 70 kilometres before we reach Hartbeespoort. On top of the pass is a place called Breedtsnek. At the moment, there's a bad gravel road which would take you back into your valley and Buffalo Hills Hotel. It's quite a spectacular pass, so one of these days as part of your "education" we should take a four-wheel drive and cross over the pass.'

Ed looked at her as she spoke, her profile, which was classic in repose, became very animated as she talked about the land that she loved so much.

'Y'know,' he said finally, 'If we turned around right now and went back to the hotel, I would already have a picture of this area as being real special. I'm surprised we don't see more tourists around here.'

Elke nodded. 'Mmm, we could do with some tourism to give the local economy a boost, but we can do without the mess they usually bring with them. You're right, though. Somehow this area never developed as a tourist destination.'

'And yet it's stunningly beautiful. Why is that, d'you think?'

Elke shrugged. 'I think the locals like to be left alone. Don't forget, the Anglo-Boer War took place only just over 100 years ago. This was some of the richest farmland on the Highveld. After the war many Afrikaans families tried to pick up the threads of their previous pastoral lives. They had had quite enough of the uitlanders, er, foreigners. Tourism's never been encouraged but the few people who have uncovered its wonderful secrets never want to go anywhere else.'

'What about the Africans in this area? My boss, Sam Mohale's black. He keeps on threatening to show me something of his people's culture.'

Elke nodded. 'I'd take him up on that if you can. The Tswana people travelled south from Zambia and Botswana a long time ago. A sub-group known as the Kwena moved into this area, with the largest clan the Kwena Mmatau, settling in 1800 close to where Maanhaarrand is now.'

'Hey, I must have the most knowledgeable tour guide in the district!' Ed exclaimed.

'Not so much knowledgeable, but passionate - about the land, that is,' she finished lamely, realising the growing chemistry between them.

*

'Where's Elke?' Marie Stein asked her husband. She had left early to go into Rustenburg to buy some spares for the tractor. Although Saturday was not an official working day, there was still plenty to do on the farm. Marie expected Elke to be there when she was needed.

Isak took a different view. 'She's taking that young American she met to see the mountains and to get him to understand the importance of preserving this region. He's with the Mines.'

'When will that child understand that we have no time for frivolities around here?'

Marie was angry at two levels. Firstly, she expected her daughter to put the farm first, second and third. Her other interests had no place in the life of a farmer. Secondly, why was she going out with a bloody Yank when she should be thinking of settling down with Kurt?

Isak shook his head gently. 'Listen, Vrou,' he said, 'you've taken her out of University. That's a major sacrifice. In time she'll understand that farming's a fulltime occupation but remember this - if this area becomes more and more polluted, then one day our farm will no longer produce its crops. Elke's determined to change all that. That's not something to be discouraged.'

'As long as she stays away from the American,' she grumbled. 'He's probably a worthless drop-out, sent out here to keep out of his family's way. I expect he thinks Elke's a rich farmer's daughter. I tell you, he's trouble!'

*

Ed and Elke had an excellent lunch at one of the numerous restaurants surrounding Hartbeespoort Dam. Afterwards Elke drove into the little village of Kosmos, where many Johannesburgers and Pretorians had weekend cottages.

The Jacarandas were now in full bloom and as they strolled along a narrow lane between houses on the hillside, Ed momentarily thought he was somewhere in the South of France on the Cote d'Azur. He caught tantalizing glimpses of the yachts moored at the Club on the other side of the dam where it narrowed into a long funnel ending at the dam wall.

Ed's spirits soared. To hell with everything else. Here he was, walking with a beautiful, intelligent girl surrounded by the most glorious scenery. Life doesn't get much better than this, he thought contentedly.

He saw a gap between the houses with a clear view of the Yacht Club only perhaps three to four hundred metres away across the water. Almost without thinking, he took Elke's hand and led her towards the gap overlooking the dam. The effect on both of them was almost electric. It was the first time they had touched. Elke risked a sidelong glance but Ed moved forward, trying to appear as though nothing had happened. Elke returned his firm clasp and for a moment time stood still.

'If I stay here long enough, maybe I could rent a yacht. Do you sail?' he asked.

They turned to look at each other and as through in a dream they both leaned forward slowly and gently until their lips met. After a few moments of gentle exploration, Ed reached out and hugged her close to him, pressing his lips hard against hers. She responded for a few seconds before pulling away nervously and averting her face.

'Hey, I'm sorry. It just kinda happened. You okay?' Elke nodded, her face still averted.

'Was that wrong?' Ed asked softly and reached across to take both her hands. Finally, Elke looked up at him, her face troubled.

'No… not wrong… but…'

'But what? That had to be one of the most special moments of my life,' he told her earnestly.

She smiled. 'That describes it perfectly…but…oh Ed, I'm just worried that this is going too fast.'

Ed pursed his lips. 'I'm not sure that there's ever a right timing for this kinda thing.'

Elke nodded, gently released herself from his hands and walked back towards the car. They did not speak again until they were both seated in the vehicle. Elke suddenly turned to him.

'Ed, d'you realise how much I care about this area, our farm, my parents, this community? You frighten me. You live so far away and you may not be able to help me at all with my mission to improve the environment in this region. You and I could so easily end up on opposite sides of the fence. Then what?'

Ed nodded grimly. She was being severely practical and he could understand her point of view, but he simply refused to buy it.

'Okay,' he said finally, 'I'm prepared to take it slowly, but you must know this - I'm not a person who tries to date every girl he meets. I have a very clear vision of the sort of girl I want to meet and commit to. You are that vision, but don't let me frighten you more than I already have. If my job and the Mining Industry come between us, I'll be outta there immediately, so let's not make it a problem. I really want to help you regardless of our relationship.'

Elke stared at him for a long moment before replying. Then she reached out her hand. Ed took it and very gently kissed it. She smiled, nodded, started the car and began the drive back on the far side of the mountains.

CHAPTER 12

Bud McNeil was angry. For some time now, he had worked a valuable scam with stolen platinum. Then, out of the blue, a number of his connections had been arrested. He realised now that the cops had probably been working with mine management to uncover the scam. The bloody fools should have noticed that they were being watched. He had no sympathy with their predicament but he was extremely worried that the cops may trace the platinum to him.

Bud was a small terrier-like man. He had beady eyes set on either side of a prominent nose, bushy eyebrows and the greying remains of once coppery red hair, a legacy of his Celtic origins. He moved quickly, spoke quickly and even ate quickly. Life for Bud was always at the double. He had made a fortune in scrap metal some years previously and had retired to develop his own game farm some forty kilometres to the West of Buffalo Hills Hotel, in the direction of the Botswana border.

The scrap metal business was always open to wheeling and dealing. Bud had seen his parents lose everything in the East Rand town of Boksburg and had decided at an early age that no one would ever get the better of him in business or anything else in life.

He had not considered himself to be a crook but nevertheless he had cut corners wherever he could. The taxman was his prime target but he was not averse to turning a blind eye to receiving goods from dubious sources. It was not a major step for Bud, therefore, when he was approached with an irresistible deal to smuggle platinum out of the country.

The main function of his game farm was the exporting of wildlife all over the world, mostly buck, antelope, zebra and so on. Bud hoped to expand into the business of buying the Big Five in due course, where the really big money could be made. When a friend of his from his scrap metal days, Saul Fredericks, suggested that the platinum could be smuggled out in the animal cages, Bud found the idea too exciting to pass up.

Now that his supply line of platinum had virtually dried up overnight, he needed new sources of the precious metal. He might wait a short while before re-opening the business but sooner or later, he knew he would try it again.

Bud pulled into the grounds of a small Café just outside Kroondal, where he would be meeting one of the foremen of the Premier Platinum Mine. They had never tried to get platinum out of Premier in the past, but Bud had an idea for a new way of smuggling the metal out of the mine. His fertile mind, had it been used for honest means, would probably have made him a wealthy man anyway but there was some quirk in his nature which seemed to prefer the adrenaline-pumping excitement of unlawful activities.

*

Elke returned home with a sense of exhilaration which swept all her other misgivings away. She was in love! No matter that his home was 15,000 kilometres away, that he was in the Mining Industry, even that he was American and not German, or at least Afrikaans, speaking. Elke knew that this was her man. Her reservations during their brief but incredibly tender moments together, were simply the reactions of a young woman from an extremely conservative community. She was still imbued with all the values of decency and integrity that her missionary forefathers had brought out from Europe in the Nineteenth Century.

Elke was sometimes amazed that these very values were the subject of derision amongst her peer group at University. It came from young people with little or no sense of values whatsoever. She was reminded of people who drank too much, insisting that others drink with them, presumably to lessen their own guilt over their actions.

She got out of the car and crossed over to the front door, but before she could open it, her mother called her sharply from the storeroom on the other side of the yard.

'Where've you been?'

Stung by her mother's tone of voice, Elke frowned and turned towards the older woman.

'It's Saturday, Mom, I had things to do.'

Her mother approached and stood quite close to her. They were about the same height. Elke could see a growing fury in her mother's eyes. Suddenly her sense of well-being was forgotten and was replaced by a fierce feeling of resentment. How dare she be angry? I've worked hard all week. I've given up my University career to help her. These were just some of the thoughts that flashed through her mind before her mother spoke.

'Since when did you think that farming is a five day a week job?' her mother asked.

'That's not fair, Mom. There was no work planned for today.'

'It's your responsibility to be available at all times.'

'Oh! So now I'm a prisoner! I can never go anywhere in case there's an earthquake or the barn catches fire...' Elke's sarcasm triggered a furious response.

'Don't you dare speak to me like that!' her mother yelled. 'Have you no respect?'

Elke fought to control her emotions. 'I have respect, Mom, when things make sense, but you're going off like a fire-cracker over something I'll never agree to. If you want me to give up everything in my life outside of the farm, forget about it.'

'You don't make the rules,' her mother stormed.

'I'm not making the rules,' Elke replied. 'I'm just trying to arrive at rules we can agree to. I will not be trapped here. I must have a life...'

'So you can go out with a worthless Uitlander,' Marie sneered at her daughter.

Oh, so this is what it's all about, Elke suddenly realised. She knew that her mother fantasised constantly over Kurt and her getting married but that would never happen. Even thick-skinned Kurt was beginning to realise that. How could she now get through to her mother on the subject? Elke had no idea of Ed's family's social position and true wealth, but she already knew with total certainty that he was no worthless bum wandering aimlessly around the world. Elke decided to try and calm things down.

'Look, Mom, I'm sorry. I should've spoken to you before I left...'

'But you knew I would not have let you go!' her mother flashed back at her.

Elke's good intentions evaporated in an instant.

'You wouldn't've stopped me. If you think I'll be your slave, forget it. Either we work out a sensible compromise here, or I'll go and pack my things right now.'

Elke found herself shouting back, which was out of character for her but she knew that this was a defining moment. Either she and her mother sorted this out or her days at home were over.

'Just who do you think you are?' Marie could not believe that her normally obedient child would ever raise her voice to her.

At that moment a soft, rather wavering voice drifted across the yard, from the stoep.

'Stop this foolishness and come over here!'

Despite his physical weakness, there was no mistaking the hard authority behind Isak Stein's voice as he called to the two women in his life to stop fighting and to join him on the stoep.

Ed returned to Buffalo Hills Hotel in a state of terrible uncertainty. Like Elke, he had realised today that this was the woman he was going to marry, no matter how great the odds. His uncertainty lay in his measurement of these odds and his worries over Elke's reaction to his first expression of his feelings for her.

Looking ahead, he could also see all kinds of complications. Elke had made it clear that she loved her home, her family and the entire region in which she lived. Would she even consider going back to the States with him one day? Or would he be prepared to make a life for himself here in the Valley? His mind was in a whirl as he arrived at the Reception desk and asked for the key to his room.

There was an e-mail for him. It was from his brother, Justin, asking to be fetched at Johannesburg International Airport on Tuesday morning at 8.30. Typical Justin, he thought. He had no consideration whatsoever about Ed having to take time off work drive over 300 kilometres there and back and settle him into the hotel. That was assuming that this was where Justin wanted to stay. Ed also knew that Justin would expect him to drive him around as he would be unable to drive on his own for another couple of weeks at least. Only at my inconvenience Ed thought grimly.

Another thought was worrying Ed. Justin had a long track record of ruining Ed's relationships with other people. He recognised already that he would have to brief Elke very thoroughly on the subject of his brother. He also realised that he had made a number of very good friends since he had arrived in the Valley just a few weeks ago. It was the sort of place where one could make good friends easily but like any small community, elements of disharmony would quickly reverberate throughout the area and could spoil forever any thoughts Ed may have of making it his home. He scowled at the e-mail and just for an instant allowed himself to wonder whether life would not have been a whole lot easier had Justin perished in the Twin Towers disaster.

Shaking his head to try and end that idea, which he felt he should never have thought, the cheerful voice of Marius de Wet hailed him from the bar.

'How's the love life, ou pal?'

Ed looked around to see Marius waving for Ed to join him in the bar. Why not, he thought, as he headed towards his friend. Marius was not alone. His brother, Jacob, was on the bar stool next to him. Jacob, although younger, was also silver haired and in many ways similar in appearance to his brother.

The introductions were made and Ed accepted a Das Lager as he sat down with the de Wet brothers. Marius insisted on a blow-by-blow account of Ed's day with the lovely Elke and received a slightly edited version.

Marius turned to Jacob and said 'I know that Ed here looks and sounds like a regular American, but you'll never guess where we think his ancestors come from!'

Jacob admitted that he had no idea, unless perhaps Ed was a Martian in disguise! Ed assured Jacob that he might technically be an alien in South Africa but not _that_ alien! Amidst the laughter, which included Rob and Don, who had just joined the group, Marius elaborated on the mysterious Mr Willjohn's possible origins.

'It came to me when Ed told us that he thought his family had some Dutch ancestors. From there, it wasn't difficult to change Willjohn into Viljoen and it then occurred to me that the Boer War General, Ben Viljoen, had settled and died in the States.'

'Anywhere near where you come from, Ed?' Jacob asked.

Ed shook his head. 'No, it's not that simple. Marius tells me that the General settled in New Mexico. It just so happens that I believe my great grandfather came from somewhere around Albuquerque.

'Hey, that's interesting!' Jacob said. 'Tell me, do you know exactly where he was?'

'We know he lived in El Paso and Albuquerque and also that he died in Las Cruces...'

'I don't believe it!' Jacob exclaimed.

Marius smacked his forehead in exasperation. 'How could I forget?' he said apologetically to his brother.

'Las Cruces is...' The brothers spoke almost simultaneously then laughed. Marius gestured for his brother to continue.

Jacob turned to Ed. 'You won't believe this, but my daughter and her husband are both working at the University in Las Cruces. My daughter's finishing her thesis and my son-in-law's lecturing in Agriculture there!'

Ed was stunned. He had given quite a bit of thought to ways of tracking down his forebears but after the September 11th disaster and his subsequent meeting with Elke, he had barely given it another thought – until now!

'Do you think....?' He began.

Jacob ended the sentence for him. '...they would try to get some information on him? Of course. The idea that two Afrikaners are living and working where a famous Boer War General died in exile, will be exciting for them. You can count on it.'

As the group around him discussed the amazing coincidence, in their excitement frequently breaking into Afrikaans, Ed's mind explored the implications of what he might discover about his origins. He had no idea about Elke's parents' attitude towards someone like him. Perhaps an Afrikaner as a great, great grandfather would be a huge bonus. Perhaps not. They were, after all, Germans first and Afrikaners second, as far as he could understand the complicated set up.

Then what would his mother and Justin think about it? Knowing Justin, he would probably freak out altogether. He had always told friends, particularly potential girlfriends, that his family were descended from British aristocracy. To discover that his great, great grandfather had fought the British and was part of a nation who later achieved universal condemnation for their infamous Apartheid Policy, would be enough to send Justin into a fit of severe depression, he thought with a degree of malice. Ed personally found that living in a predominantly Afrikaans community, except for the more international nature of Buffalo Hills, was an enriching experience. Warm, friendly fun-loving people with somewhat old-fashioned values, which were essentially no different from those of the American Midwest, were good friends to have. If he were, in fact, descended from General Ben Viljoen, then he would readily accept both the positives and negatives of such an association and who knows, in time to come, perhaps he would change the name back to its original spelling.

*

Isak Stein's handling of the growing rift between his wife and daughter was short, sharp and to the point. 'As long as I am here, I am head of the family, and this is what I require from both of you,' Isak turned to Elke first. Despite himself, his tone softened ever so slightly as he spoke to her.

'Elke, you have made a major sacrifice for the sake of our family. We are both very grateful for this,' his tone hardened again 'but half a sacrifice is as worthless as no sacrifice. If you're going to do this for us, then you will obey your mother at all times. She is now in charge and she knows only too well what needs to be done to run a farm like ours successfully. It's a hard life but a rewarding one.'

Elke opened her mouth to reply but Isak held up his hand and turned to Marie, whose eyes had suddenly welled up with tears, as her husband had once again shown his loyalty to her.

'Marie, my beloved wife, who has taken on so many burdens over the years and has never complained, please also understand that no younger generation is ever identical to the one before it. You cannot expect Elke, in the prime of her youth, to remain on the farm, day in and day out. I want both of you to work out a realistic timetable and then stick to it.' He smiled for the first time. 'Please, ladies, if a large part of this sacrifice is for me, then at least let me feel good about it. Will you let me know what has been arranged?'

Both Elke and her mother nodded silently, having been reminded once again that that their father and husband, respectively, was a very special man! Elke also wondered how on earth she was going to develop a relationship with Ed under her present circumstances. The phrase "love will find a way" came into her mind. It'd better, she thought grimly!

CHAPTER 13

'What's going on here?' Ed asked Daniel, a grizzled old foreman whose team had stopped work an hour previously.

'The men have problems, sir!' Daniel replied. 'They not feel safe anymore.'

Ed frowned and looked at the men sitting around aimlessly in the sun. Labour relations were not normally his concern but Martin, who handled all personnel functions, was attending a conference in Johannesburg. Ed had offered to cover for him at the mine in exchange for Martin looking after Ed's responsibilities the following day when he would drive to Johannesburg to fetch his brother Justin. Ed, realising that he was on thin ice, decided to play the whole thing by ear.

'Is there some way we can make the work safer?' he asked.

Daniel replied with a long rambling dissertation which had very little to do with Ed's question. Today of all days, Ed thought, as he wondered whether or not he should call Sam Mohale. Daniel, on the other hand, was delighted that the young American was the one to deal with the situation. Daniel had deliberately created the upset by planting the idea in one of the worker's minds that the walls of the stope were not sufficiently well supported. Daniel, as a veteran of over thirty years in the platinum industry, knew that the walls were fine but he needed a diversion. The added bonus of having Ed Willjohn attend to the matter would make his first effort at creating this diversion so much easier. Martin Gericke would have been far harder to convince. The man had eyes in the back of his head and he probably knew all the safety legislation off by heart.

Daniel had only been at Premier for a few weeks. He had left his previous employer when he discovered an investigation was under way into platinum theft. He had invented a "hard luck" story about his family in Lesotho and had departed before the trail of regular thefts could be laid at his door.

The old miner had no scruples about taking platinum if he could get it. He reasoned that if the mines still ran at a huge profit, what did it matter if a few ounces of the precious metal went missing? Saul Fredericks had contacted him the previous week and a meeting had been set up with Bud McNeil.

Daniel had been impressed by the scheme and had driven a hard bargain over his profits. Bud McNeil had known that without someone like Daniel on the inside, his chances of getting hold of more platinum were negligible.

Daniel had recruited three men onto his team. As soon as he was able to hold Ed's attention and persuade him to inspect the stope, the other men would set the scheme in motion. Even though they were underground workers, the scheme involved a simple but effective way for the men to be able to get into the area where the partially processed platinum was stored. Having already made the point that they would not be working again until the dispute was resolved, they were then able to slip off without being missed for the next half an hour, which was all the time they needed.

*

Elke received a call from Ed that afternoon inviting her out to dinner. She declined regretfully, saying that her father was not very well, which was at least partially true. Elke decided that she would have to ration her time with Ed or risk a confrontation with her mother with catastrophic consequences for the entire family. She desperately hoped that Ed would understand.

The young American was disappointed but he also came from a family who felt a great sense of loyalty to each other – with the exception of Justin. He told Elke to relax about it but to make sure that she would make some time for him over the weekend. He added that he would need to spend the next few evenings with Justin. They had a few family matters to sort out. Ed nearly told Elke about the havoc wreaked by his younger brother in the past but decided that it should wait until they were together. He did not enjoy trying to explain awkward situations over the phone. Instead he warned Elke that he may not be able to wait until the weekend before he saw her again and that he would hire a hot-air balloon so that he could fly over their farm and blow kisses at her from a distance!

Elke giggled. 'Better be careful. My Mom's a crack shot with her shotgun and any strange man blowing kisses at her daughter would not be greeted with enthusiasm.'

Ed sighed theatrically and said that he would somehow contain himself. He did not fancy having a load of buckshot peppering his lower regions.

When he rang off, Elke wondered for the thousandth time how to present Ed to her mother as a suitable young man in her life. His love of the ridiculous was enough to ruin his chances with the serious-minded Marie in about thirty seconds flat.

*

Ed was early for his brother's arrival at the airport. He had been warned to avoid the rush hour traffic that snarled up the motorways in the Greater Johannesburg area, between 6.30 and 8.30 every weekday morning.

He had been given a good map and found his way to the airport easily enough.

As he sat having coffee and a croissant in one of the little restaurants above the Arrivals area, he wondered just what he was in for. Justin could be very charming when he wished. He had found to his cost that forewarning people about his younger brother sometimes backfired. Justin had an uncanny sixth sense over who had been warned about him and who had not. Invariably he would charm the pants off the forewarned and leave Ed with egg on his face. Equally, he would strike like a rattlesnake against those who had not been warned, again leaving Ed decidedly eggy.

You're getting paranoid even before he's arrived, Ed thought glumly. At that moment the Airport PA announced the arrival of the SAA flight from London. Justin had spent two days in the UK with friends, instead of making the long haul directly to Johannesburg from New York.

Ed ordered another coffee. Even though Johannesburg's new terminal certainly put the airport into the category of one of the more modern he had passed through, the unloading of luggage and the Customs area took just as long as anywhere else.

About 35 minutes later, the slim figure of his brother, with one arm still in a sling, moved briskly into the Arrivals concourse, pushing a trolley laden with a set of impeccable leather suitcases. Justin waved to his older brother, who responded with a smile, which he could not claim was entirely genuine. They met up. Ed extended his hand but Justin, rather theatrically, bounded forwarded and hugged him with his one good arm.

'How're ya doin'?' Justin asked.

'Great, and you?' Ed replied, wishing with all his heart at that moment that he and Justin could really be friends as well as brothers.

As they drove out of the airport complex, Justin looked around surprised. 'Hey, I didn't expect a city this big in Africa!' Ed suddenly found himself in the curious position of acting as a tour guide. Slightly embarrassed, he admitted that he had not yet visited the city itself but had only driven out of it, as they were doing that morning.

'Soon as I'm recovered from the trip, we must come and hit the night

74

spots,' Justin commented.

Ed murmured that they could do that sometime. He suddenly realised that in the short time he had been working at Premier Platinum and staying at Buffalo Hills, he had not once had any real inclination to visit "Joeys" as many of the locals called it.

He took the concrete highway to the William Nicol off ramp, heading for Fourways. Justin was amazed at the Montecasino Complex, built as an entire Tuscan village, housing a hotel, shops, restaurant and a Casino. Immediately beyond the complex the massive Fourways Shopping Centre, with the new Fourways Crossing across the road, prompted Justin to ask 'Hey, you sure I landed in Africa?'

Ed laughed. 'Don't worry, in a few minutes we'll be in the country. I guess the reason I haven't visited Joeys yet is that it may be a great city, but I know it'll just be a variation on all the other major cities I've visited around the world.'

Justin leaned back in the seat of the vehicle. 'That's always been the difference between us, big brother. Gimme the bright lights, the action. You're just a farm boy at heart.'

Ed could not help asking 'So, what are you doin' in Africa then?'

Justin turned, all wide-eyed innocence and stared at his brother. 'To visit you, pal!' Then he looked more serious, 'and to get away from the whole New York thing.'

He shuddered. 'It still gives me nightmares, Ed. When the first plane hit, I was on the thirtieth floor. We were told to evacuate. Everyone was running to the stairs at the same time. There were people everywhere…I don't remember much…just the heat, the smell of burning, smoke, people screaming. It seemed to go on forever, we couldn't move, people were jamming the stairways fighting to get out.'

Justin, emotional, looked out of the window, not really seeing the increasingly rural vista as they drove past Lanseria Airport, a centre for light planes and smaller commercial craft.

'I don't remember much more than that…until I woke up in hospital with Mom fussing over me.'

Suddenly the young man's shoulders shook. Ed glanced across and realised that his brother was still experiencing terrible grief and trauma. Justin sobbed quietly as Ed awkwardly reached over and put his arm across Justin's shoulders.

'Okay old buddy, let it out, just let go. You're safe now!'

*

Daniel met Bud in the same little café as before. He was very pleased with himself. His first attempt at removing some platinum from Premier had been successful. The plan Bud had outlined to him a few days previously had worked superbly well. However, Daniel had relied upon Ed Willjohn's naiveté to pull it off. He dreaded trying it again with Martin Gericke. He drank a cup of coffee with Bud. The brown paper parcel containing the partly processed platinum sat on the table between them. Bud said very little and gulped his coffee as fast as he could. He picked up the brown parcel and prepared to leave.

'Thanks for the meat' he told Daniel, in case anyone was listening, although the café only contained one other customer, a very old man, and a young African waitress who spent most of her time in the kitchen.

'When can I collect the money?' Daniel asked anxiously.

Bud had been vague about that, although the foreman was not too worried. They both knew that Bud would have to pay him before the next delivery or there would be no more platinum forthcoming.

Bud looked around the café nervously, as though Daniel had revealed a major element of their scam.

'I'll leave a message. Just need to check that it's all in order.'

He strode out of the café, leaving Daniel to ponder the risks he was taking for just a few hundred rand a time versus the thousands that Bud would undoubtedly make on the deal. I take all the chances and he makes all the money, the grizzled old miner thought darkly. Perhaps I should sell to someone else. But he knew that he did not have the connections to make the sale elsewhere. Besides, he had been warned by Saul that one did not cross Bud. People had a nasty habit of disappearing or ending up dead, if they tried to get clever with the little man. All in all, better to pocket what he could get out of the deal and be grateful for that, Daniel thought, as he finished his coffee and realised angrily that he would have to pay the bill.

*

Elke watched as bags of fertilizer were loaded into her bakkie at the Behrens supermarket in Kroondal. Her mind however was far away as she wondered how it had gone for Ed. He had promised to call her when he was back at the hotel. Although Ed had not really said much about Justin, she sensed that he was not that happy about his brother joining him in South Africa. She wondered how long Justin planned to stay and whether she would have the opportunity of meeting him. The more she knew about Ed and his family, the better, she thought. When a person enters your life without any warning, there is so much to learn. With Kurt, whom she had known since childhood, there was not much she did not know about him. She was on friendly terms with his parents and his cousins on the far side of Rustenburg. She knew that he was a rugby fanatic and could reel off the names of every Springbok (South African national rugby team players) over the past fifty years. As if she cared. She enjoyed the game but the statistics surrounding it were of little interest to her. For a bleak moment she pictured herself as a dutiful wife to the endlessly boring Kurt as he droned on about the ten best rugby "front rows" of all time over dinner. She shuddered. Ed may have many areas of his life that she knew nothing about, but she knew that she became vibrantly alive every time she saw him.

*

Ed checked his map as he drove up to the T-junction just before the tiny village of Broederstroom on the South side of Hartbeespoort Dam. Justin had recovered from his fit of depression and was enjoying the rich unfolding African terrain as they approached their first contact with the Magaliesberg mountain range.

On an impulse, Ed decided to turn right towards the Pelindaba Atomic Research Station up in the hills overlooking the dam. The map showed him how to drive around the far edge of the dam and eventually arrive at the dam wall.

They wound their way around the side of the dam, past the numerous houses on the hillside, the restaurants and fast food emporiums and the snake park, which had been established by Jack Seales in the 1960's. Justin commented that so far the countryside reminded him of parts of California. Ed reluctantly agreed. Reluctantly, because he had seen enough of the region to sense its uniqueness. He did not want to relate it to California or anywhere else. He tried to play tour guide, explaining to Justin how the Magalies River flowed into the Crocodile River in the valley just below the present village of Kosmos on the North West shores of the dam. The enlarged Crocodile River then swept through the gap in the mountains and tumbled into the valley below on its way to the mighty Limpopo hundreds of kilometres to the North East on the borders of Zimbabwe.

'The dam was started in 1916 and was only completed in 1923,' Ed told his brother, he had certainly learnt a lot from Elke!

They stood briefly on the wall of the dam with its ornate lamps and geometric parapets, combining both Art Nouveau and Art Deco architecture. He pointed north, where the land flattened out dramatically. 'It was built to irrigate the farmland in the Brits' district over there. Today there's a small town of that name,' he added but he saw that he had already lost Justin's interest when the younger Willjohn turned back to the car.

As they headed away from the dam towards the valley, which Ed was beginning to think of as home, Justin turned to him with a sly smile. Ed had learned long ago that Justin's smiles were invariably designed to hide his latest manipulative scheme.

'I think you've fallen in love with the place,' he said.

Ed nodded, knowing that Justin was undoubtedly already figuring out ways of making his brother's life unbearable once again.

CHAPTER 14

'Daniel, what were you trying to do to Mr Willjohn?'

As Daniel had predicted, Martin Gericke wasted no time on checking up on the events that had taken place while he was away.

Daniel looked suitably solemn.

'The men not happy with the new stope in Number 3 shaft. They scared!'

'Come on, Daniel... it's me you're talking to, not some American kid who doesn't know what's what around here!'

The little foreman allowed himself an embarassed smile. As long as Gericke thought they were just fooling around, the real purpose of the strategy would remain hidden.

'Agh, perhaps they want to see what Mr Willjohn would do.'

Martin nodded. That was closer to the truth, probably, but he recognised Daniel for the old campaigner that he was. Men like Daniel came and went in the mining industry. Generally, they were intelligent, good at their job and natural leaders. On the darker side, however, there was always some hidden agenda. Martin did not necessarily think that Daniel was dishonest but there was no doubt he would cut corners if the opportunity arose. He was also, undoubtedly, a drinker. Even though he had never once shown any sign of having been drinking on duty, Daniel had a reputation amongst the men for boozing steadily over the weekends. He had no family in the district and was of uncertain origin. Although he spoke Tswana, it was laced with "Tsotsi Taal," a gangster language from the urban townships. He also spoke Afrikaans fluently, lending credence to the probability that he was in fact a Coloured.

However, he was also one of the best foremen Martin had employed in many years. Rather the devil you know, Martin thought, as he weighed his options.

He nodded at Daniel. 'So, you were testing him out?'

Daniel stared back impassively, neither confirming nor denying Martin's accusation.

The Afrikaner sighed. 'If your production's down this month, I'll fine you blokes for playing the bleddy fool.'

Daniel nodded. 'Ja, Meneer, but we won't be down, we'll catch up.'

Martin headed back to his office wondering what the little charade was really all about. Daniel breathed a sigh of relief and started to work out in his mind how they would manage to extract the next parcel of platinum for Bud McNeil.

Ed was pleasantly surprised when Justin expressed his satisfaction with his room at the hotel. Justin normally disliked anything arranged for him by the rest of his family. If it were out of the city, he would usually complain about anything and everything until in desperation the family would pack him off back to civilisation.

It was approaching midday. Ed suggested that they have an early lunch at Buffalo Hills. He would then go to the Mine while Justin could rest and maybe catch up on some sleep. The younger Willjohn was definitely showing signs of jetlag.

'Sounds good' Justin agreed.

They made their way to the patio where they had a drink while Ed arranged for them to be served lunch as soon as it was ready, which was normally at 12.30 pm. Rob Schutte came out of his office and joined them for a few minutes.

'How're you doing, after your ordeal?' he asked Justin.

The young man smiled wryly. 'It's like I've arrived on a different planet here,' he said. 'I guess it was the right decision, to get away, although pictures of the event still haunt me.'

Rob nodded. 'My friend Errol, who's a local farmer, just came back...'

'Great!' Ed interjected, 'I'd like to see him. How is he?'

Rob shrugged. 'He's fine but like your brother here, he won't forget the experience in a hurry.'

'Was he in New York?' Justin asked. Rob nodded, as he discreetly insisted on signing the slip for the Willjohn's drinks. 'He was on a ferry crossing over to Manhattan...'

'That's unreal' Justin responded. 'I come all these miles, to the heart of Africa and discover that a guy from here, was right there when it happened.'

'The difference was that he saw it from the outside but you saw it from the inside,' Ed commented.

'Can I meet him?' Justin asked Rob.

'I'm sure it can be arranged' the Hotel's Director replied. 'How long are you staying?'

Justin thought for a moment. 'Dunno. At least until my shoulder's mended, er d'you have doctors in Africa?'

Rob and Ed roared with laughter. Rob turned to the older Willjohn.

'I think we have some educating to do here.'

Ed nodded and smiled at his brother. 'Justin, the first thing you have to understand about South Africa, is that it's a mix of Third World ideas and attitudes with a firm foundation of First World facilities and aspirations. I had no idea when I arrived, just how much these guys here know about the US, and just how little we know about South Africa!'

Bud McNeil watched excitedly as a line of men patiently drove three superb Kudu towards the boma made of plastic sheeting. The plastic was wide open at the side where the Kudu were being driven. It narrowed down to a tunnel no more than three metres wide and some ten metres long, which in turn led to a wooden ramp. The ramp was attached to the back of a large truck, containing the cage which would eventually transport the valuable animals overseas.

No matter how many times they captured the animals, the process was a huge adrenaline rush for Bud. The little man's integrity regarding his fellow humans may have been sadly lacking but there was no doubting his sincerity towards caring for his wildlife.

In the 1950's and 60's, an Afrikaner by the name of Jan Oelefse had worked as a game ranger in Kenya. He had worked with Game Conservationists like the Englishman Nick Carter, known as "Carter the Darter," who had pioneered the darting of Rhino at that time. Jan had returned to South Africa excited by the new techniques he had encountered in Kenya. However, he had been terribly distressed by the high injury and mortality rate incurred when netting animals. Buck and Antelope in particular, often broke their legs when they became entangled in the nets used to capture them.

Jan hit on the idea of using plastic instead of nets. He had discovered that wild animals regarded plastic as something solid and never tried to break through it. Subsequently his use of plastic sheeting instead of netting had been responsible for saving countless numbers of wildlife over the past fifty years.

Bud knew nothing about Jan Oelefse but he did care passionately about the animals that moved through his ranch. The fact that animals such as Kudu were worth tens of thousands of rand did not hurt either.

After the beautiful creatures were safely in their cage, Bud climbed onto the back of the truck, ostensibly to check on the antelopes. In fact, he was looking to see whether the platinum, which he had stored in the hollow poles of the cage, could possibly be detected. He knew he was being paranoid. Unless someone decided to break the cage open by sawing through the poles, there was no possibility of detection!

He felt reassured as it looked exactly like every other cage he had sent overseas. He would make good money from the animals but even better money from the precious ounces of platinum safely hidden in the cage.

*

Elke drove the tractor into the yard next to the barn and storeroom. Her mind was made up. She could no longer bear to wait in hope that an opportunity would arise for her to see Ed. She would have to take the initiative. She strode to the house, waved to her father sitting on the patio and entered the front door. Her mother had a tiny office just off to the right of the entrance hall. Marie was laboriously tapping away on the keyboard of the computer. Elke made a mental note to offer to teach her how to use eight fingers instead of two, one of these days.

Her mother did not look up. 'Did you have enough fertilizer?' she asked.

'Yes Ma, plenty!'

Elke sat down on the spare chair next to her mother's seat in front of the computer. After some minutes Marie looked up and stared at her daughter who was sitting patiently waiting for the right moment to speak to her.

'Did you want something?' her mother asked, her mind still on the accounts she was painstakingly working on.

'Ma, Ed's brother who survived the World Trade Center disaster arrived from the States today. I would like to invite both of them for Sunday lunch.'

Her mother stared at her contemplatively for a long time. Then she sighed. 'You're not going to leave this man alone, are you?'

Elke felt her temper bubbling just below the surface. Once her mother had a fixed idea it was never easy to dislodge it.

'Listen, Ma, I don't know Ed well enough to know what I want, but I do like him, very much. I'd like you to meet him. Just so it doesn't look as though I've invited him for you and Pa to look him over, I can use the excuse that his brother needs to meet some people while he's here.'

To her surprise, her mother nodded curtly.

'Right. You arrange everything, but don't expect me to fawn all over him. I still think he's after your inheritance.'

'What inheritance?' Elke asked bitterly. 'If I hadn't left 'Varsity, we could've lost the farm.'

'Ja, but if we sold it tomorrow, I would expect to get two or three million rand for it.'

Big deal, Elke thought. In dollar terms, that's two to three hundred thousand dollars. Ed would have to be pretty desperate to be after a small amount like that, but Elke knew when not to push things too far.

'Thanks, Ma, I'll call him tonight and don't worry, I'll do all the cooking.'

Marie nodded and turned back to the computer, with a growing sense of dismay.

*

Ed had hardly settled into his office at the mine when Martin tapped on the door.

'Come in!'

Ed smiled as Martin entered.

'How was your trip?'

'Fine thanks. Has your brother arrived safely?'

'Yeah,' Ed responded, 'His arm's still in a sling but otherwise he's okay.'

They discussed mining matters for a few minutes and Martin was about to leave when he suddenly remembered.

'Oh ja, after I read your report, I spoke to Daniel.'

Ed raised his eyes heavenwards. He knew that this was bound to come up.

'They were trying to con me, weren't they?'

Martin laughed. 'Ja, you got that right! And because you had to go through all the correct procedures, they spent an hour or two lazing in the sun.'

Ed felt himself flush. 'I guessed they suckered me, real well!'

Martin got up from his chair and headed for the door as he replied.

'They try it on with all new management staff. They like to see how you react, and how far they can push you in the future. As we say here, "moenie worrie nie"!'

After Martin left, Ed replayed the incident in his mind and comforted himself with the thought that he had followed procedures to the letter and, as a newcomer, it would have been foolish for him to have acted otherwise. His thoughts were interrupted by another tap on the door. He looked up to see Sam smiling at him.

After Sam had satisfied himself that Ed's brother had arrived safely and that Ed had found his way to the airport and back without problems, he asked, 'Ed, would you and your brother like to have dinner with my wife and I on Saturday night?'

Ed was delighted. 'Sure. We'd really like that.'

Sam chuckled. 'Just in case you think you'll be having some tribal delicacies like Mopane worm, my wife graduated from the University of the Sorbonne in Paris a few years ago. Her cooking has a distinctly Gallic flavour.'

'Sounds great' Ed replied. 'I intended bringing Justin to see the mine in a few days. Now I'll leave it till next week, so he will have already met you. I also look forward to meeting your wife,' he added, with the innate courtesy of so many Americans.

'By the way, you and I still have to make a date to visit the village of Mohale. I haven't forgotten, but the September 11th issue...' He let the words hang.

'Stopped everything else in its tracks' Ed added. 'I look forward to both events.'

Sam left and Ed wondered wryly whether it took his wayward brother's arrival to extract an invitation from Sam. There was no doubt that the local community wanted to meet a survivor of one of the greatest man-made disasters in recent memory.

*

Justin slept for a couple of hours but as so often happens, his inner time clock was thoroughly confused and he woke again just before 5 pm. He showered, changed and strolled across the hotel's lush green lawns heading for the patio where Ed and he had lunched. A pretty young Receptionist stepped out onto the patio as he settled down. She came over to him.

'Excuse me, Sir, are you Mr Willjohn's brother?'

Justin replied that he was. 'I have a phone call for you.'

Justin followed the young girl into the foyer where she indicated a telephone booth. Wondering whether it was his mother, Justin picked up the phone.

'Justin here.'

'Justin, you don't know me, but my name's Elke Stein. Firstly, I'd like to welcome you to South Africa and to our beautiful valley.'

'Thanks, but I don't...'

'Sorry, Ed probably hasn't had time to mention me. He and I...have been out a few times...'

Elke suddenly wondered if her impulsive call had been a good idea.

'Okay,' Justin replied, thinking that the girl was either of no consequence to his brother or, more likely, so important that he was keeping little brother away from her. Justin harboured the delusion that he was just as successful with women as Ed.

'Well, I couldn't get hold of Ed. He's left the Mine and his cell phone's out of range, so I thought I'd ask you.'

'Ask me what?'

Justin was enjoying the girl's hesitation. She sounded nice, although her accent was difficult to understand.

'Would Ed and you like to join us for Sunday lunch?' She asked. 'Perhaps you can speak to Ed and have him call me back.'

Justin, as usual, wondered how he could capitalise on this new development. Better play it by ear, he thought.

'That's very gracious of you' he replied. 'I'm sure we can, but I'll have Ed call you as soon as he gets back.'

Justin put the phone down and returned to the patio with a smile on his face. His favourite game of spoiling his brother's fun was going to start even sooner than he expected.

CHAPTER 15

The rhino turned towards them aggressively, as Ed brought his car to a halt. He reminded himself that the huge animals had very poor eyesight and were simply reacting to the sound of the vehicle which would appear as some large indistinct shape a few metres away. Ed left the engine running with his car in gear and his foot on the clutch, in case of a need to make an urgent getaway.

Justin watched the huge animals nervously.

'I don't think they like us, we'd better beat it!'

Ed's immediate reaction was to remain where he was, out of perversity. He knew that his brother was scared of animals but a visit to the Pilansberg Game Reserve was part of the trade-off they had agreed to, in exchange for Ed showing him Sun City and the Palace of the Lost City. You're on my turf now, Ed thought, and when we get to the casino, I'm gonna have to prise little brother out with a crowbar. Sun City and the Pilansberg Game Reserve were conveniently only half an hour's drive from Buffalo Hills Hotel.

'No need to be nervous. They won't charge unless we get too close.'

Ed found himself playing the tourist guide again. In fact, these were the first Rhino he had ever seen as well. However, he had been careful to read up on anything or any place he was about to visit, so that he could be reasonably well prepared. He did not like to be regarded as a typical tourist.

The three rhino lost interest in the car and continued foraging for grass and green leaves. It always amazed Ed that some of the most dangerous animals in the world like rhino, hippo, elephant and buffalo were all herbivores.

Justin looked at his watch. 'Come on' he said, 'You've seen 'em, what more d'you want?'

Ed relented, eased out the clutch and continued their drive around the Reserve. It was a stunningly beautiful slice of Africa. Set in the bowl of an extinct volcano, the plains were dotted with thorn bushes, buck, antelope, stately giraffe, zebra and wildebeest. They were now climbing up the steep and twisting road on the old volcano's rim, which loomed some three to four hundred metres above the valley. The rhino often gathered in groups of two or three on the edge of the road and could be very intimidating if one turned a corner to find them crossing in front of one's vehicle.

The rest of the drive passed without further incident. They saw a few elephants in the distance but there was nothing else to cause Justin further paranoia as they headed towards the world-famous casino, hotel and entertainment complex, collectively known as Sun City.

*

Bud McNeil picked up the landline phone. 'McNeil,' he barked.

Bud was on edge. His shipment of kudu plus the precious hidden cargo of platinum should have arrived at Frankfurt Airport. His agent over there, who knew nothing of the platinum, was obliged to call him the moment the cargo had passed through Customs. Bud had expected the call at least two hours ago and he feared the worst.

'Friedrich here,' a deep guttural voice spoke to him from far away in the northern hemisphere.

'What took you so long?' Bud could not keep the irritation out of his voice.

'Ach, some fool queried the immunisation papers but zey are through Customs.'

The little man felt a wave of relief wash over him. By now he was convinced that the platinum had been discovered and that the cops would be arriving at his doorstep any moment. It's all part of the rush, he rationalised, as he began to accept that his latest foray into criminality had been successful.

'Next time call me and tell me what's going on,' he grumbled, but the bite was already out of his voice.

Friedrich apologised for the delay and rang off. Bud went over to the sideboard in his lounge and poured himself a stiff whisky. The first of many such deliveries, he thought, but I'd better wait and see whether the payment reaches me as arranged before they get the next lot.

*

Sam opened his front door and greeted the Willjohn brothers. Ed had driven at high speed, arriving at the Mohale house ten minutes later than arranged. Ed hated being late and often discovered that he was more concerned than the people he was trying to reach on time. This was no exception.

86

'Nice and punctual,' Sam commented as he shook hands with Justin and ushered them inside.

Sam lived on the border of the Mine property in a large and fairly modern house. It was a single storey and easily accommodated Sam, his wife Mphala and their three young children.

Mphala, an attractive and elegantly dressed woman in her early thirties, greeted them with a warm smile.

'I'm so glad to meet you at last, Ed. And you too, Justin.'

The brothers responded warmly to her. Ed was delighted that at last he was able to experience some social contact with Sam and his family. There were another six people for dinner, another two African couples and a white couple who turned out to be French.

Ed watched Justin anxiously. The youngster had won a few hundred rand at the Casino and had had three Jack Daniels before they arrived at the Mohales'. Ed had warned Justin that at the first sign of misbehaviour he would grab him and bundle him off back to the hotel. Justin, with the bright, rather brittle, sparkle of someone who has had a buzz from a few drinks without being actually drunk; had looked at Ed with wide-eyed innocence.

'This is your boss we're talking about here, buddy. I would never dream of embarrassing you!'

Oh yeah, Ed had thought grimly, but I can't very well hide you away. The folk around here are going to have to accept Justin the way he is. With that he relaxed into the party mode and began to enjoy himself.

Of the other two Black couples, Kamogelo Maje and his wife Boitumelo were also Tswana speaking. Kamogelo was a chief of a small clan to the west of Rustenburg. Sam and he had been at University together.

The other couple, Duma and Nobesuthu, were Zulu speaking. Mphala and Nobesotho were old friends and they were staying with the Mohales for the weekend.

The French couple, Gilbert and Renée Forcaud, had booked into Buffalo Hills. They had met Mphala in Paris. When Gilbert had been transferred to Johannesburg coincidentally, they had made a point of contacting her. This was the first time they had seen each other in over five years.

Drinks and delicious snacks, prepared by Mphala, were served. Ed gravitated towards his host and the French couple. They were speaking in French when he approached but broke off and insisted on continuing in English.

'I believe you and your brother are also staying at Buffalo Hills?' Gilbert asked. Ed nodded. 'Yeah, I've been there a few weeks already. Justin's just arrived from the States. It's a great place. Almost a home from home.'

Gilbert agreed. They had arrived at the hotel in time for lunch and had thoroughly enjoyed their meal. They had spent the afternoon swimming and sunbathing at the pool and in the late afternoon had taken the horseback trail up into the mountains behind the hotel.

'Have you been up into the mountains?' Renée asked Mphala. The Tswana beauty confessed that she wasn't much of an outdoor girl.

'But you have such a beautiful country here,' Renée remonstrated with her, 'and all these wild animals. Which is your favourite? Have you seen all of them?'

There was an embarassed silence for a moment. Sam then chuckled. 'Mphala probably hasn't seen any wild animals at all!'

Even Ed was surprised. 'Why's that?' he asked.

Sam took a long swig of his beer before replying.

'I'd rather not get into any heavy political debate tonight but let me say this,' Sam chose his words carefully. 'In the Apartheid days, it wasn't possible for us Blacks to visit Game Reserves. This meant that wildlife became more of a White man's thing.'

'But that's ridiculous!' Gilbert exclaimed. 'You are the people of Africa, not the Whites. Surely you must know more about your own environment than they do?'

Sam shook his head sadly. 'Perhaps my grandfather or great grandfather would have lived in this area when lions, elephant, rhino and so on, roamed around freely. When the White farmers began to farm huge areas of land, they either hunted the wildlife and killed them off, or they drove them onto reserves like the Kruger Park.'

'That was a good thing surely' Gilbert commented.

'Good for the animals certainly, but once they were in the reserves,' he shrugged, 'that's the last most of us saw of them, until now. The result of this was that we had already lost interest in wildlife. Blacks who'd grown up in urban communities were out of touch with their environment. Not just the wildlife but also the whole ecology. It's a serious problem and it saddens me personally.'

This was the first time that Ed had heard Sam comment on ecology. He was excited by what he heard. Clearly Sam would be open to further discussions on the issue at an appropriate time. Ed leaned forward and spoke animatedly.

'Sam, I'd like to take this subject further. I'm also very concerned about ecology and I have no idea of what is being done about it in this region.'

'That makes two of us,' Sam sighed. 'I think that's a good idea. Let's talk about it next week.'

The conversation was interrupted at that point by Mphala's domestic worker who had slipped into the room to announce that dinner was ready.

Elke sat in the farm's office trying to balance the books. Her mother had gone out to a meeting of the local Agricultural Union. Her father was content to sit in the lounge and watch some television. Since September 11th, Isak had begun to watch television more and more, particularly the news. Elke and her mother had mixed feelings about it. On the one hand, it kept him occupied during the lonely days and nights when the women were busy running the farm. On the other hand, they feared that he was withdrawing further and further into his own private world. All his dreams for the future were in danger of coming tumbling down around his ears. This withdrawal was a tacit signal that he had turned his back on reality and was beginning to wallow in the misery of a life ending in failed purposes. Elke was disturbed from her calculations by an urgent banging on the kitchen door.

She hurried through to the kitchen and called out 'Who's there?' A frantic teenage voice called out 'Missus, Missus, the baby - she is coming!'

Just what I need, Elke thought worriedly as she unlocked the door. The young girl's mother was due to have the baby in two weeks' time. Marie had told Elke not to worry about it before she left for the meeting. Irene had produced five children already and every one of them had appeared within a day of her predicted time. Now suddenly, the baby was early.

Elke had very little knowledge of midwifery, but Marie had helped bring into the world as many as a dozen children in the local area. As she followed young Beauty to the workers' quarters, she wondered whether she should call her mother or not. Let's see how it goes, she thought.

Elke tapped on Irene's door and entered. The African woman was lying on her bed groaning. A fine sheen of sweat covered her forehead and face. The birth looked imminent. 'Irene, my mother is out. Should I try and call her?'

'No little Missus' Irene gasped. 'The baby come now, now! No time to call Missus.'

Elke sighed inwardly but realised that her first adventure with midwifery was about to begin.

'Don't worry,' Irene panted. 'I tell you what to do. It will be okay.'

Glad you have confidence, Elke thought as the woman gave her instructions on the basics of bringing babies into the world.

*

The meal Mphala served was a delightful mix of Cordon Bleu and traditional African foods. They had snails for hors d'oeuvres, which everyone except the Maje's were familiar with. Prepared for this possibility, Mphala did not insist that they eat the typically European delicacy. Instead, she had her domestic helper bring them some spiced chicken wings, which were more to their liking. Duma and Nobesuthu both enjoyed snails. Ed had eaten them in New Orleans and Justin, not to be outdone by anyone, cheerfully gulped them down.

The main course was rabbit stewed in red wine. This was a meat which some Africans love and others cannot tolerate. The only one who was disconcerted by the meat was Justin, who had typically bland American tastes. Snails for some reason or other worried him less than the idea of rabbit - possibly because he had kept a few as pets when he was a child.

Mphala came to the rescue once again and produced a very plain chicken dish, which was a staple diet for many Africans. She also served some local vegetables such as Moroka, an African spinach, and Mealie pap, a corn or maize based dish which many Africans, as well as Afrikaners, prefer to potatoes or rice.

Ed was thankful that Justin had not created a scene that evening. He accepted Mphala's offering of chicken with a courtesy that Ed had not ever seen his brother produce before.

Discussions over dinner ranged from the economy of the country to President Mbeki's dream of an African Renaissance, to soccer and to Gilbert's work in South Africa with an investment bank. Sam also asked Justin to give an account of his frightening experiences at the World Trade Center. The young man held their attention for some time as he gave an emotional account of his personally traumatic experience.

As the party broke up just after midnight, Sam asked if Ed and Justin would lead Gilbert and Renée back to the hotel. Ed readily agreed. He was beginning to feel like he belonged in the region!

Ed thanked his hostess warmly. 'You and Sam must join us one evening, either at the hotel or perhaps somewhere in Kroondal.' Mphala smiled and said that they would look forward to it. Ed wondered momentarily how Elke would react to an evening with the Mohales.

*

The baby's first cry was one of the most magical moments Elke had ever experienced. She had worked with Irene for over two hours, as the breaks between the mother's contractions had grown shorter and shorter. Little Beauty had also bustled around with boiling water and fetched more blankets, while Elke had squeezed Irene's hands and tried, where she could, to lessen the pain of the contractions. Then her waters had broken and half an hour later, Elke had helped to ease a lovely little girl into the world. She had turned the infant upside down and had patted her on the backside until the welcoming cry of the newborn had brought both smiles and tears to Irene and Elke. Little Beauty in the background clapped her hands delightedly and murmured 'Sharp, sharp,' as Elke had laid the baby on her mother's chest.

At that moment, the young blonde woman had felt that there was very little wrong with people from different backgrounds who could share an experience such as this.

Irene looked up tiredly and smiled at Elke. 'Thanks, little Missus. You do the job well!'

*

On the way to the hotel, Justin turned sleepily to his brother. 'I kinda like your friends out here.'

Ed smiled. 'I only knew Sam. The others were all strangers to me too. I'm not surprised though. Sam's a great guy. Glad you enjoyed it.'

'This girlfriend of yours, we're having lunch with tomorrow. Is she White or Black?'

'You'll find out tomorrow, pal!' Ed chuckled feeling more affinity for his brother than he had in very long time.

CHAPTER 16

Ed woke up bright and early on Sunday morning. Although they had returned to the hotel after midnight from dinner at the Mohales, he had awakened with his mind buzzing at the prospect of seeing Elke again. It had only been a week since he had last seen her, but it felt more like a year. Justin's arrival had helped to take his mind off her for some of the time, but certainly not all of the time.

After failing to go back to sleep, he changed into jogging shorts, t-shirt and running shoes, then slipped out of the hotel grounds and turned left along the loop road, where both Errol Saperstein and Marius de Wet lived. It was not yet half past five and he guessed that even farmers may not be up that early on a Sunday morning.

Ed jogged at a steady pace along the side of the dirt road. It was wonderfully quiet save for the normal morning clamour of birds catching up on the day's gossip. The land rose up on a gentle curve to his left, reminding him of his first day in the country, when he had gone to fight the grass fire with Rob, Errol and the local farmers.

It was time to get to know more of the locals, he thought as he jogged. At that moment, however, the only local on his mind was Elke. He was worried about taking Justin to meet her, although in fairness, his brother had behaved extremely well with everyone he had met so far. Even Sam Mohale had murmured in Ed's ear the previous night that Justin was an interesting bloke.

Ed had to consider whether he was over-reacting to Justin's past behaviour and that his brother was not as bad as he had remembered him. Ed determined to resolve judgment on that until after luncheon at the Steins' later that day.

Justin went down to breakfast, a little after eight o'clock. He tapped on Ed's door, received no response and strolled across to the dining room. No sign of Ed there either. Justin was not unduly worried. Ed was so completely reliable, that it was unthinkable that his brother had left without him. As he stood on the patio leading from the reception area, Justin saw a very pretty young girl sitting on her own at one of the tables.

She looked up as Justin stared at her. She gave him a radiant smile. Justin was immediately entranced. She had glossy black hair and slightly olive complexion, which nodded at some Mediterranean origin. Her wide set eyes had just a hint of an oriental oval shape and were a deep brown. Even sitting she revealed a seemingly trim figure.

'Did you see a guy, just a little older than me, come past here recently?'

The girl nodded and smiled again. 'There was somebody, a blonde man in jogging clothes. He came past here carrying his room key, just a moment ago.'

Justin chuckled 'That'd be him - my brother, Ed.' Justin thought frantically of something else to say. 'You also waiting for someone?'

She nodded. 'My parents. They're often a little late.'

Justin asked if she minded him sitting down and waiting for Ed. There was the slightest hesitation, but she then told Justin he was welcome to do so.

As he sat down, she looked at him carefully. 'You sound American?'

'Right on!' He extended a hand. 'Justin Willjohn, from Minneapolis.'

She shook his hand. She had a firm, warm grip. 'Persephone Georgiadis, from Nelspruit.'

In answer to his unspoken question, she carried on, 'Nelspruit is about 350 kilometres to the east of here. I was born there but my parents are from Cyprus.'

Justin chuckled. 'I'm sorry. I guess you've solved one mystery and created another. Where's Cyprus?'

Persephone shook her head sorrowfully. 'You Americans. Does no one learn geography over there?'

'Sure, but....' Justin felt himself blushing. He hated to be caught out at anything.

She put him out of his misery. 'It's okay. I normally say I'm of Greek origin when I meet Americans. Most of them have heard of Greece!'

'Hey, we're not that bad! Is Cyprus one of those Greek islands?'

Persephone laughed a deep throated laugh. She could not have been more than nineteen or twenty but she had a wonderfully mature and sexy voice.

'No, Cyprus has its own history. It hasn't been part of Greece for centuries. Both Greeks and Turks have lived there for hundreds of years, with the Greeks in the majority. For the last twenty-five years or so, the Turks have occupied a large part of the island and cut themselves off from the Greek side. They have taken the area where my father was born, Rizokarpasso, near Famagusta. My parents have just come back from visiting my mother's family outside Paphos, on the Greek side.'

Justin could have listened to her talk all day. It wasn't the words, but it was the cute way in which she said them. He saw a middle-aged couple walking towards the patio, who certainly looked as though they could be her parents.

'How long will you be staying here?' he asked.

'Until after Christmas,' Persephone replied.

'Great. We can pick this up another time.'

Again, there was just a slight hesitation, but she smiled.

'Sure.' She glanced up and saw her parents approaching.

'My parents are rather old fashioned, so please expect them to be very formal. My Dad believes he has to protect me from every single male on the planet!'

Her parents were now only yards from the table. Justin could already sense curiosity and appraisal from the mother and outright suspicion on the father's face.

Justin stood up and extended a hand. 'Good morning, Justin Willjohn. Your daughter and I were both waiting for people to join us for breakfast.'

Nick Georgiadis took Justin's hand and nearly crushed it in a vice like grip. 'Georgiadis, my wife Marina.'

Justin also shook her hand with what was left of his fingers.

'Madam, Sir,' He almost bowed at them. 'Nice to meet you. I'm sure we'll see each other again over the next few days.'

To his relief, he could see Ed also making his way towards the patio. 'My brother has arrived.'

He smiled at Persephone and then at her parents, who were watching him carefully, and moved away to join Ed. For the first time in a long while, the stern unbending figure of Mr Georgiadis had left Justin feeling quite intimidated.

*

Elke was in a total panic. As she started to prepare lunch, she realised just how little she knew about Ed. Would he be embarrassed when her father said Grace just before the meal? Was Ed religious? What kind of food does he enjoy? Would they arrive casually dressed when her father would expect some formality? And what was Justin like? If Ed's lifestyle was an unknown to her, Justin was even more of a mystery. For a terrible moment, Elke thought of calling the hotel and telling Ed that she and her family had contracted bubonic plague or something equally spectacular. Could they postpone the lunch for maybe a decade or so?

'How're things going, skatjie?' Isak had entered the kitchen quietly and stood watching her with some amusement. Elke realised that she must look as distraught as she felt. She gave her father a wan smile. 'Oh

Pa, I'll never be ready in time. I don't even know what they like to eat.'

'Tell me, are they something strange like Hari Krishna's, or serious vegetarians?'

Elke shook her head, puzzled. 'No, Pa. At least I don't think so!'

'Listen, when you invite people to lunch, they will normally tell you, I don't eat pork or whatever their preferences are. If they say nothing, you can assume that they have normal eating habits. So just relax and you'll be ready in time with another one of your delicious meals. Marie and you are the best cooks in the world.'

Isak looked at her for a long moment and smiled.

'He must be quite important for you to get yourself into such a state, hey?'

Elke dumped the bowl of vegetables she was holding on the sideboard and rushed over to her father to hug him. There were tears in her eyes. He knew her so well and he was so amazingly understanding. Isak staggered a little under her impact. His frail body could no longer manage her boisterous shows of affection. She quickly realised that and let him go gently. She stepped back with the first smile of the day on her face.

'Thanks, Pa. Now will you please get out of my kitchen, you're distracting me!'

Isak nodded and turned away. At the door he looked back. Elke was working on the food with renewed energy.

'By the way, make sure the young one sits next to me. I really want to hear about what happened in New York.'

'Okay, Pa, whatever you want. Now please go!'

Isak nodded and left, knowing he had defused a critical moment in his beloved daughter's day.

*

Justin had just finished telling Ed about his encounter with the luscious Persephone, who was still sitting with her parents on the far side of the room, when Marius and his brother Jacob entered the restaurant.

Jacob made straight for Ed's table. Introductions were made all round and the De Wet brothers joined the Willjohn brothers for coffee.

'I wanted to catch you before you went out,' Marius began. 'Jacob here's had a fax from his daughter in Las Cruces.'

'Brilliant!' Ed exclaimed. 'I was wondering how she was doing over there.'

He turned to Justin. 'You remember I was telling you about Jacob's daughter and son-in-law, who live in Las Cruces, the city where General Ben Viljoen is buried?'

'Yeah.' Justin's face mirrored his obvious disapproval.

'This is the guy you think we may be descended from?'

Marius quickly picked up on Justin's reaction.

'I'm told that you think your family comes from Britain and you could be right. All we're trying to do here is trace any of Viljoen's descendants who may have remained in the States. Then you and your brother can see if there's a connection.'

Justin nodded glumly. Ed tried to lighten the moment by saying, 'Justin probably hopes that we're directly descended from King Arthur or one of the Knights of the Round Table.'

Justin shook his head angrily. 'Whatever. We'll both do research and see where it goes.'

Ed turned to Jacob. 'What did your daughter find?'

Jacob handed over eleven pages from the New Mexico historical review of 1977. It was an article entitled, 'Boer Colonization in the South West,' by a writer called Dale C. Maldy. Ed murmured his thanks and could not resist skimming through it while the others chatted about Justin's stay in South Africa and what he had seen so far.

The gist of it was that a General William D. Snyman was the first senior Boer officer to arrive in the United States after the Boer War. He even visited President Theodore Roosevelt, who was apparently sympathetic to the Boer cause. Ed could understand Roosevelt's empathy with settlers in a far-off land who were being hounded by the might of the British Empire.

After Snyman's meeting with the US President, more Boer colonials were permitted to land in New York without detention by immigration authorities at Ellis Island. Tugs were sent to dispatch the special passengers before their ships docked.

Benjamin J. Viljoen, Lieutenant General and formerly the second highest ranking officer in the Boer forces, arrived in New York on December 1, 1902. Captured by the British on January 25 earlier that year, he had been a prisoner of war on St. Helena until his release in September. He refused to swear allegiance to King Edward VII and he was banished from British soil forever.

Ed looked up. 'Whether we're related to this Viljoen character or not, he seems to have been quite a guy.'

'What interests me is that very few South Africans, even Afrikaners, know anything about a Boer colony in the States,' Jacob said.

'Ja, there was some publicity about Boers settling in South America and most of us know that there's an Afrikaans speaking colony in Kenya, but this American thing is quite new to most of us,' Marius added.

Ed stuck his head back into the article. It was too long to read now but he did glean a few facts, such as Viljoen, his family and friends settled on farmland in the Chamberino district, on the east bank of the Rio Grande River. The group became well known in the area for their innovative and efficient farming. Viljoen also devised a method of flood control, which was necessary because the water level of the Rio Grande often rose in the rainy season and destroyed massive areas of farmland where crops had been planted.

Viljoen was invited to become a delegate to the National Irrigation Congress at Albequerque in September of 1908. Viljoen's wife, Myrtle, also held public office as Postmistress of Chamberino from July 1907 to January 1909, when she resigned.

As many as thirty Boer families were farming on both sides of the Rio Grande in 1908.

Ed turned to the end of the article to search for possible descendants, when Jacob and Marius stood up and excused themselves. Ed thanked them warmly for their on-going interest and promised to write a letter to Jacob's daughter and son-in-law over the next few days.

After they left, Justin sat prim and disapproving. Ed reluctantly put the article away to read later and suggested that they leave for a leisurely drive which would bring them to the Stein farm by midday. Justin suggested that they should stay at the hotel until it was time to leave for lunch. This puzzled Ed for a moment but then he remembered his brother's enthusiastic description of the young girl he had met that morning. At that moment, Persephone and her parents appeared in the reception area, delivered their keys to the front desk and left for the parking area. Ed looked at his brother sardonically.

'Care to change your mind buddy?' Justin nodded forlornly.

*

Elke checked on the lamb. It was cooking nicely. She had also bought a joint of beef and was now wondering whether the brothers would prefer it rare or well done. Most Afrikaans families tended towards cooking their meat to death but her father had always insisted on his beef having a pink, even red, centre.

At that moment, her mother entered the kitchen. She had been on the lands since early that morning and was clearly unwilling to participate in any of the preparations for lunch.

'What time are your visitors expected?' she asked coldly.

'I said about midday, Ma. Listen, please try and enjoy your lunch today. I know how you feel and I'm grateful that you've let me invite them, but nobody's going to enjoy themselves if you spend the day with a long face.'

Elke held her breath. She had never spoken to her mother like that before. She waited for a blast but to her surprise her mother nodded and sighed tiredly.

'Ja, my dear. I won't be a - what do they say in English? - a wet blanket. Even I am beginning to be interested in meeting the young man. I want to see what all the fuss is about!'

CHAPTER 17

As the brothers walked out of the dining room, Ed was confronted with something totally incongruous with the South African heat and sunshine.

Rob had an artist's sketch of the hotel's dining room laid out on one of tables on the verandah. He, Don Watson and a couple of the senior staff were discussing the merits of proposed Christmas decorations. Rob looked up and gestured for Ed and Justin to come over and have a look. The brothers looked at the sketch then looked at each other confused. Ed turned to Rob.

'D'you guys seriously do all the northern hemisphere trimmings for Christmas?'

Rob chuckled. 'Ja. Christmas trees, holly, fake snow, turkey, brussel sprouts - the works!'

Justin frowned 'But surely it's too darned hot for that kind of meal?'

Rob shrugged. 'Tradition dies hard.'

Ed shook his head in disbelief.

'Hope you don't have Father Christmas with a red coat and long white beard. He'd expire from the heat!'

'The kids'd be totally upset if we didn't. We draw lots for the Santa role and hope we don't get it!'

Ed and Justin drove away from the hotel, with Ed still expressing his amazement at the northern traditions imposed upon southern folk. Justin could not have been less interested. In fact, he seemed to be heavily pre-occupied. As the silence grew, Ed glanced at the young man.

'What's on your mind little brother?'

They had turned on to the road towards Kroondal and Ed wanted to visit an interesting looking curio shop and tearoom a few kilometres down the road. Justin gave one of his "sweet," enigmatic smiles.

'Just taking in the local atmosphere. Dunno why you're getting so excited about Santa and Christmas over here. He'd look just as out of place in the Middle East.'

'You've got a point there,' Ed conceded. 'I suppose one should separate Santa Klaus, who comes from northern or Germanic mythology, from the religious values of Christmas. By the way, do you plan to stay here over Christmas and New Year?'

'I'm thinking about it,' Justin replied. 'I'll let you know.'

Yeah, Ed thought irritably, you'll let us know when you're ready to reveal your plans at your convenience. Sometimes, his brother's arrogance could drive him completely nuts. He pulled into the driveway of the little curio shop, which was much like any other farmhouse in the area, except for the profusion of flowers and flowering shrubs on either side of the driveway and some intriguing, hand-crafted ornaments hanging in the windows. A charming and friendly lady welcomed them as they stepped inside into a world of make-believe statues, mobiles, ceramics and pottery.

*

Sam and Mphala were finishing a late breakfast when the telephone rang. It was Martin, who was on duty at the mine over the weekend.

'Sorry to trouble you over the weekend,' Martin began.

'As long as it's important.'

Sam washed down the last of his croissant with some black coffee.

'Ja. I'm worried, boss. Some of these figures on our stocks of processed platinum don't tie up.'

'What d'you mean?'

Martin had Sam's full attention now.

'Well, according to our November figures there were 10,843 fine ounces in stock. We delivered 5,000 ounces to Johnson Mathey at the beginning of December, but we've only got 4,843 ounces left.'

'Which means that we're a thousand ounces short,' Sam interjected.

'That's right.' There was a long silence. 'That's almost half a million dollars' worth and with the rand taking a nosedive right now, we're talking eight million rand.'

Again, a long silence.

'Bloody hell!' Sam eventually managed. 'I'll be there in fifteen minutes.'

Sam slammed down the phone. Mphala looked at him worriedly.

'Trouble?' she asked.

Sam nodded. So far, Premier Platinum had not had any trouble with platinum thefts but now it looked as though somebody was helping themselves to a hell of an early Christmas present!

*

Elke tapped softly on the door of Irene's room. The cooking, after her initial bout of nerves, was under control and she wanted to make sure that mother and child were doing well.

'Kom,'

Irene's soft voice was barely audible behind the door. Elke turned the handle and pushed the door open. Mother and child were sitting up on the bed. Irene was breast feeding the little mite, who was noisily trying to extract every drop she could from her mother's swollen breast. Irene smiled tiredly at Elke.

'How's baby?' the young woman asked.

'Fine, Missus, fine. She too much hungry!' Irene replied.

'I can see that. And how are you doing?' Elke asked.

Irene looked to be almost back to her normal, cheerful self. The African woman smiled but sighed.

'Okay, Missus, I just like to tell Alpheus that he has new daughter.'

Alpheus was her husband, who worked on one of the platinum mines. He only came back home every second week or so. As a shift-worker, he spent most of his time in the mine hostel. It was impractical to try and commute to and from the mine every day.

Elke dallied with Irene for a few minutes and made sure she had everything she needed, both for herself and the baby. As she stood up to leave, she had an afterthought.

'What're you going to call her?'

Irene lifted the baby off the breast and gently helped a burp on its way.

'I like to call her Elke, Missus.'

Elke felt a twinge of emotion. She reached forward and took the child gently from her mother. The child looked up at her with adoring brown eyes. Elke leaned forward and kissed the baby on the forehead.

'Welcome, little Elke,' she said softly. 'I'll be happy and honoured for you to carry my name.'

She handed the child back to the mother and excused herself. She had sudden visions of food burning on the stove.

*

Ed and Justin pulled into the driveway of the Stein farm at five past twelve. Ed did not want to seem either obsessively punctual or impolitely late. He pictured Elke's mother as a prim, prissy and highly regimented person. Her father he saw as more of a laid back, probably pipe-smoking type, with a philosophical bent. In the event he was only partially right.

Both brothers wore smart, casual trousers and open neck shirts. Justin had added a navy-blue blazer but Ed decided upon a stylish form of lightweight safari jacket. As the slim, rather tired figure of Isak Stein appeared in the doorway of the homestead, Ed was relieved that they had both decided on smart casual. Isak was wearing grey trousers, a white shirt and tie but without a jacket. Which makes us about even, Ed decided. They stepped out of the car and made their way over to the front door and introduced themselves.

Isak welcomed them with a quiet, old world charm but there was genuine warmth in his still firm handshake. He led them directly to the stoep, where a drinks tray was laid out on a sideboard next to the tables and chairs. Marie Stein sat in one of the chairs. She was far more attractive, in a world-weary kind of way, than Ed had expected. As he shook hands with her, she smiled cordially, but accompanied it with a piercing stare, which made Ed feel that she was examining him to the very depths of his soul. Once they had been given drinks, a glass of wine for Ed and a beer for Justin, Marie apologised for Elke's absence.

'She's in the kitchen, making sure that everything's perfect, for at least the tenth time. She'll be out in a moment.'

'I hope we haven't inconvenienced you in any way,' Ed responded.

'Not at all. The one thing I insist upon is a good Sunday lunch with the family. To have some guests only adds to the pleasure of the occasion,' Isak told him.

Ed really took a liking to Isak. He was from another time, another world, but the dryness of his tone was belied by a twinkle in his eyes as he spoke. Ed also noted that he had the appearance of a man in poor health. There was an unhealthy pallor to his skin and a hint of blue on his lips - a telltale sign that his heart was in bad shape.

'Justin, I believe that you were in the World Trade Center, the day it was attacked, and that you're very lucky to be with us today!'

Isak spoke to the younger Willjohn, with a note of real curiosity as well as compassion for his ordeal.

'That's right, I guess. I don't remember much about getting out of it. The first thing I knew was some real pretty nurse taking my pulse.'

He and Isak chatted easily together and Ed was thankful that his unpredictable brother had clearly taken a liking to the old farmer, as he had himself. Ed sat sipping his wine and hoped that Elke would stop fussing over the meal and appear. He would gladly have settled for a dry and overcooked hamburger in exchange for just five minutes of her time.

'Elke tells me you're with Premier Platinum.'

Marie's voice intruded on his thoughts.

'That's right,' Ed replied.

'My cousin's niece is married to someone there, a Martin Gericke,' she continued.

'Yeah. He and I work together. He's a good guy. He has all the years of practical experience which helps to keep some of my theories on a solid footing.'

Marie nodded but Ed had the feeling that she respected his answer.

At that moment, Elke appeared. She had obviously left the kitchen and detoured into her room or bathroom for a few moments. She looked just as stunningly beautiful as Ed had pictured her in his mind over the past week. She stepped forward and shook hands with Justin before turning the full power of her glorious eyes towards him. Ed could hardly speak as she lightly shook hands with him too.

'Thanks for coming, Ed. Lunch will be served in a few minutes.'

Ed sensed a grudging approval from Marie. What do I have to prove, Ed thought fleetingly. I know who I am, where I come from. Why do I allow myself to be judged by this decent but quite ordinary woman? Because she's Elke's mother, came the immediate inner response. That means more to me than the approval of anyone. It's as simple as that.

They chatted over drinks for about ten minutes before Elke disappeared momentarily, then returned to ask them to go into the dining room for lunch. The dining room could have been a dark and rather foreboding farmhouse room, but someone, Ed suspected Elke and possibly her father, had livened up the room by painting it a cheerful cream colour to offset the wood panelling which covered the walls about half way to the ceiling. The room was typical of the period in which the farmhouse was built in the late 1890's. Ornate lace patterns extruded from the flat surface of the pressed ceilings. In the United States they were known as tin ceilings, popular from the 1890's to 1930's as cheaper versions of the exquisite plasterwork of Victorian era ceilings in Britain in Europe. It reminded Ed of some of the older homesteads he had visited in Wyoming.

They had a huge meal, superbly prepared. Elke's nervousness disappeared as soon as she was certain that her food was being enjoyed by everyone. Even the moment when her father had cleared his throat to say Grace had passed without incident. Both Ed and Justin were clearly expecting it and bowed their heads as Isak spoke softly in Afrikaans.

'Are you also in the mining business?' Isak asked Justin.

The younger Willjohn shook his head.

'No, I run a little family business back in Minneapolis.'

Ed was chatting to Elke at the time but he overheard Justin's comment and was puzzled by it. It was unlike Justin to play down anything he could brag about. The "little" family business boasted a turnover of almost half a billion dollars so far this year. Although Ed was not involved in the running of Willjohn Industries, as a substantial shareholder he received regular trading figures and was proud of the excellent progress the company had made over the past few years. Justin's influence was minimal. The chief executive, Franklin de Vos, had managed the company well since the death of Jonathan Willjohn but Ed was surprised that Justin had not taken the opportunity to blow his own trumpet. He noticed that Marie had also overheard the comment and was looking at Justin intently, but the younger Willjohn changed the subject and the moment passed.

The meal consisted of two roasts, lamb and beef, delicious roast potatoes, carrots Julienne, creamed spinach, pumpkin and sweet potatoes. After the main course and when Ed was feeling distinctly overfed, the plates were rapidly removed by Elke and her mother, to be replaced by dishes of traditional desserts - melktert, koeksisters and brandy cake, accompanied by coffee.

Ed wondered at how both mother and daughter and even Isak kept their figures but then he noticed that none of them ate in excess. This was traditional Afrikaans hospitality at its best, with huge quantities of excellent food, which the family clearly did not place on their table every day. Ed also noted that it was ironic that the Mohales had used the help of a domestic, whereas the Steins did it all on their own.

After sampling the desserts and washing them down with strong, hot coffee, Ed felt as though he urgently needed to do some exercise. As though reading his mind, Isak looked up and spoke to his daughter.

'Elke, I'm sure our guests would like to see around the farm. You could take the horses...'

Elke stood up. 'Ja. I told Nelson to bring them around to the front by two thirty. Do both of you ride?'

Ed nodded, pleased at the prospect of getting out of the house. It had been an excellent meal but he would like to spend more time chatting with Elke. He wondered if Marie would accompany them.

'If you don't mind, I'd rather stay here,' Justin said. He pointed to his shoulder. He was still wearing a sling. 'I wouldn't like to fall off.'

Isak nodded. Maybe you should rather take the bakkie,' he told Elke.

Justin interrupted them. 'I guess I'd rather just sit on your stoep and enjoy the view. You guys carry on.'

There was an awkward pause then Marie said something rapidly in Afrikaans to Elke, who nodded.

'Ed and I'll just ride up to the top of the kloof. Do you want to come too, Ma?'

Marie shook her head. 'Thanks, but I've got a few things to do around the house,' she said.

Ed was surprised. He thought that Marie would not want her daughter to be alone with him. Obviously, Isak was in no condition to ride any more.

Elke led Ed along the trail, which would take them up to the highest point of the farm, Elke's favourite place in the whole world. She was very excited at the prospect of sharing this special place with Ed. As the horses walked sedately along the path, Ed noted that Elke handled her mount with the ease of an experienced horsewoman. He was also a good rider, having spent many hours riding around their Wyoming ranch.

Back at the homestead, Justin accepted another cup of coffee and sat chatting to Marie. Isak had excused himself to lie down for a while. Marie did not take long before she started to probe into the Willjohn's family background, as Justin had anticipated from the moment he had decided not to ride with the others.

'You said you ran a small family business,' Marie began. 'Has Ed not been involved in it?'

Justin shook his head and hesitated as though reluctant to speak about it.

'No, he's never really been interested, so I kinda took it over after our Dad died. Ed, well...'

'Was there some problem with Ed, then?' Marie asked.

Justin looked suitably downcast and did not answer.

Marie nodded. 'Sorry, I don't mean to pry.'

Justin smiled at her. 'Of course, but I don't see why you shouldn't know. Ed has a long history of depression. We were delighted when he managed to get this job over here. We hope it will do him some good. I came over just to make sure that he was okay. He seems to be doing great; I'm so pleased.'

Justin watched carefully as Marie nodded and was evidently calculating ways of keeping a mentally unbalanced young man away from her daughter at all costs!

CHAPTER 18

Elke's horse, Witblitz, led the older mare, Cinnamon, ridden by Ed, along a narrow trail just below the summit of the mountain. Ed admired both the slim figure of Elke on her magnificent white stallion and the breath-taking view of the cliffs and the valley far below. It was a perfect backdrop for the creation of a picture in his mind of the woman he now realised he had fallen in love with. He sensed it was a picture that would set a benchmark for every possible future memory of her. At that moment, as though feeling the intensity of his attention upon her, she turned around in the saddle and smiled at him. Her golden blonde hair was rim-lit by the late afternoon sun and if Ed felt that he had already seen visual perfection, her act of turning around and looking at him made him momentarily dizzy, almost outside himself, as he stared back at her in awe.

'What's wrong?'

Elke was concerned about the dazed look on the young American's face. Ed struggled to find the words.

'When you've just seen perfection and it gets better, much better, I guess you could say I'm kinda shell-shocked, is all.'

Elke smiled and looked back over the valley.

'Ja. It's quite a view isn't it?' she said, deliberately misunderstanding him.

Ed shook his head in wonder. 'You'll never know,' he murmured to himself.

They rode on in silence, both savouring the special moment. Elke suddenly looked up into the sky. Ed followed her gaze. Two magnificent birds were wheeling and soaring some thirty metres over their heads. Ed noted that they were black with white chevrons on their backs, as well as some white patches on the wings. Elke had just raised her arm to point at the birds when Ed called out softly.

'I see them. What are they?'

Elke reined in Witblitz and dismounted. Ed followed suit. They moved close together and Ed instinctively put an arm around her shoulder. She gave him a little contented sigh and snuggled up to him.

'They're black eagles,' she told him. 'We're lucky to have a nest on our property.'

She pointed to a distant cliff face. Ed could just make out a large nest comprising sticks and branches.

'There's less than twenty pairs left in the region. Each pair requires about 35 square kilometres for their own territory. They mainly hunt dassies...'

'Dassies?' Ed queried.

'Oh,' Elke chuckled. 'I'd forgotten you were an uitlander, er, foreigner.'

'Oh, that sounds unfriendly,' he said half-seriously.

Elke was immediately contrite.

'Hey, I was only teasing. A dassie is a rock rabbit. There're hundreds of them around here. They live in caves or crevices in large communities and eat almost any kind of vegetable material, ranging from fruit, vegetables, grass, leaves and even the bark off some trees. They're terrified of the black eagles so you won't see any popping their heads out while the birds are in the vicinity...'

Elke suddenly broke off and watched excitedly as the male eagle suddenly broke away from the female and started to perform a series of incredible loops, followed by a dive of at least two hundred metres then soaring up again to his companion.

'Wow!' she exclaimed. 'I've read about it but never seen it before!'

'That guy should enter the world aerobatic championships!'

'You know what's happening?'

Ed shook his head. He had seen a few American eagles but was no expert on the subject.

'This must be a new pair.'

Elke reached for notebook and pencil in her saddlebag. Ed reluctantly let go of her as she scribbled some notes in her notebook.

'That's the male's mating ritual. He's showing off to make sure that she doesn't lose interest. Once they become a pair, as far as I know, they remain together for life.'

Elke returned her notebook to her saddlebag and looked anxiously at the distant nest on the cliffside.

'I wonder if our resident pair has gone, or if they died.'

Ed returned to her side again. He reached out and gently turned her around by the shoulders until she was facing him. Her glorious blue eyes widened momentarily as she caught the intensity of his gaze.

'I'm not about to leap over the edge and dive two hundred metres to get your attention.'

'Please don't,' she murmured.

'But, I'm courting you right now, lady, and this may be the human equivalent of what those eagles are up to!'

With that he pulled her towards him. He did not have to apply any pressure at all. Elke was as hungry for his touch as he was for hers. Their lips met and pressed together with a rising passion that neither could ignore a moment longer. Ed had already noticed an indentation in the cliff face behind them. There was a thick carpet of grass below a clump of Transvaal Beeches, which reached up to the summit some five metres above them. As they kissed, Ed guided her backwards to the grass. Elke allowed herself to sink down on to the ground, despite all her earlier misgivings about taking the relationship too far. Her mind was still saying "no," but her heart was rapidly succumbing to the knowledge that Ed was a man unlike anyone else she had ever met. She wanted him desperately. The magic of their position on the edge of the cliffs, with the beautiful black eagles courting above their heads, made the situation totally irresistible.

Suddenly, there was a deep staccato bark alarmingly close to them. Both Ed and Elke looked up in shock. A troop of about twenty baboons was ambling along the path towards them.

*

When Sam returned home, the sun was already dipping down close to the horizon. Mphala and the kids had spent a lazy afternoon at home but Sam had promised to take them to lunch at Sun City followed by a swim in the tidal pool, so there was an air of gloom when Sam entered the sitting room. The kids looked up from the game they were playing on the Playstation. Sam's heart sank as they gave him a reproving glance.

'Sorry, sorry. Next week we'll do it, I promise.'

The two little faces nodded solemnly and turned back to their game. Mphala, at least, gave him a sympathetic look.

'Big trouble?' she asked.

Sam nodded. 'Look, we've been lucky so far. The other mines were targeted earlier but now they've caught the guys at their workplace, it looks as though the ringleaders are seeking new sources of supply.'

'Like Premier?'

Sam nodded again. 'We've spent the afternoon going through the records and as far as we can see, the theft took place only a week or so ago.' Sam sat down in an armchair, leaned his head back and closed his eyes.

'Sorry about our trip. I'll make it up to you and the kids, I promise.'

Mphala smiled. 'When we first got married, you worked day and night and you quickly rose to the top. We've been spoiled since you took over as manager here but I'm quite capable of surviving a few more weekends with you at the mine, if need be.'

Sam opened his eyes and murmured, 'And the little ones?'

'Time they learned that life doesn't always travel along a straight road.' She leaned across and took Sam's hand.

'I've cooked a nice supper for us, so relax. The family's okay.'

Sam squeezed her hand and looked across at the children. They were already lost in the world of virtual motor racing.

*

It was a glorious sunset. Justin sat on the stoep with Isak, who had reappeared after a rest. Marie was busy in the kitchen with some snacks. In the distance, two horses could be seen returning along the path to the farmhouse.

Justin stood up. 'Mr. Stein, I'm just going to see if you wife needs a hand.'

Isak looked at him, surprised. 'Young man, if you were to offer my wife help in the kitchen, she would never forgive you. It's not the way we do things in this country. The man stays out of the kitchen!'

Justin flushed. It was vital that he spoke to Marie before Ed and Elke returned. He decided on a more direct approach.

'Okay, I got that. I guess we're not that different in the States, particularly the farm folk. The truth is I need to ask your wife something before Ed and your daughter return. I won't offer to wash the dishes, I promise!'

Isak chuckled as the young American rapidly made his way to the kitchen but inwardly he was concerned. He had instinctively liked Ed on first meeting, but Justin worried him. There was something a touch too smooth, a little too glib for Isak's liking. He suspected that Justin was up to something. He would keep it to himself for the moment, but he would not hesitate to become involved if he felt that his beloved Elke was in any way the victim of Justin's mind games.

In the kitchen, Marie looked up as she heard a light tap on the door. Justin stood there awkwardly.

'I'm told that I dare not offer my assistance, on pain of death!'

She nodded. 'True. So, what can I do for you?'

She picked up a large tray of snacks and headed towards the door.

'I just wanted to say ...' Justin paused as though embarrassed. Marie looked at him keenly. 'You wanted to make sure that I didn't tackle Ed on the subject of his depression, didn't you?'

Justin nodded, relieved. There were no flies on this lady, he thought.

'Yeah, he's really hung up on it and I think it would slow his recovery if he were to be confronted by anyone.' He shrugged.

Marie nodded. 'Don't worry. I won't tell a soul what you've said to me. It's just between us. Anyway, it only serves to confirm what I suspected.'

They both walked back towards the stoep.

What's that?' Justin asked, noting that Ed and Elke were tethering their horses in the yard outside.

'That your brother's looking for some financial, and possibly emotional, security. It's a pity that your company doesn't appear to be large enough to help him back in America.'

Justin nodded sombrely.

'Yeah, it's one of the great disappointments of my life that I can't do more for Ed. He's basically a good guy and I couldn't wish for a more loving brother, despite everything that he's gone through!'

As the young couple approached the farmhouse, Ed noticed that Justin was joining Isak on the stoep and Marie was placing a large plate of snacks on the table. Good timing, Ed thought wryly. It was much better timing than his attempted moment of passion at the top of the mountain. The baboons had made it clear that he and Elke were on their turf and Elke had insisted that they leave.

'Some people make the fatal mistake of throwing stones at baboons,' she had said. 'The trouble is they will normally throw them back harder and more accurately than the humans. You don't mess with baboons.'

They had remounted their horses and returned down the mountain. Ed had spent the rest of the journey trying to work out whether Elke had been sorry or relieved that the baboons had broken up a moment that could have taken their relationship to a new level of commitment. Marie's probably trained those goddam critters to watch over her daughter, Ed thought darkly as they started to ascend the steps to the stoep.

Justin smiled his inevitable "sweet" smile and Isak grunted approvingly.

'Just in time for a sundowner.'

Marie gave the pair a sharp glance but said nothing. Ed immediately sensed that the shutters had gone up between him and Marie Stein. He wondered whether it was the fact of his having been alone with Elke all afternoon, or whether Justin had been spreading some of his poison once again.

*

Bud McNeil eased the throttle on his powerful speedboat and glanced behind to see whether Bonnie had timed her release of the towrope accurately and had managed to bring her slalom ski alongside the jetty. She was a good water-skier and as usual, she achieved this little feat without effort, grasping the edge of the jetty and hoisting herself up, without wetting her superb figure.

Bud waved in acknowledgement and circled around to bring the boat into the boathouse. He was at peace with the world. He had received confirmation that $400,000 had been deposited into his secret Swiss bank account on the previous Friday. With the rand doing a nosedive, it was a huge temptation to bring some of the money back into the country at an enormous profit. Bud was an old campaigner in the furtive world of money laundering and knew that this was not the time to do it. Besides, he did not really need it right now. He was doing fine. The sale of the kudu had also gone through and the proceeds he diligently transferred back into Rands, with every intention of declaring the sale to the Receiver of Revenue.

His only dilemma now was whether to risk another theft of platinum from Premier. If so, when should he do it? He had no illusions that the men working for him at the mine would eventually be caught. It was just a matter of timing the whole thing.

He had reasoned that another four or five hundred thousand dollars would give him close to a million off-shore. Bud considered himself a good gambler. He knew when to stop at the casinos. Now he had to decide when to stop with the platinum. The ease of the first operation was very seductive but he had no illusions that it wouldn't get tougher and tougher.

Bonnie was already pouring both of them double Chivas Regals in the bar to one side of the boathouse. She looked up at Bud with her cheeky, little girl smile, which belied the fact that she was nearly forty years old.

'A drink for the driver,' she cooed, handing him the Scotch.

'Thanks, babe' Bud took the drink and sipped it appreciatively.

Sometimes, he wondered whether he should marry the lady. Bud and Bonnie had an interesting ring to it but he valued his freedom still, having divorced his third wife some five years ago. He settled down on a bar stool and watched the last glorious shades of red and yellow fade from the western sky. Life couldn't get much better than this, Bud thought, as he raised his glass to Bonnie, who returned the gesture and reached out to clasp his hand.

*

Ed and Justin thanked the Stein family for a wonderful day and headed over to their car. Isak had shaken hands with both of them on the stoep and had told them sincerely that he hoped to see them again soon. Ed detected a disapproving glance from Marie but took hope in the fact that he probably had an ally in Isak, a man whom he really liked and respected.

At the car, Ed turned and shook hands with Marie.

'Thanks again for a great day and some wonderful home cooking.'

Marie nodded brusquely and said nothing. Ed knew with certainty that he had failed to win her approval. He realised that this would create real hardship for Elke. For a moment he wondered whether or not he should simply walk away from the situation and leave Elke to restore her family ties. Then he looked at the glorious young blonde as she said goodbye to his brother. He knew then, no matter what it took, he would never stop seeing Elke and that one day, against the odds, she would be Mrs Willjohn!

CHAPTER 19

Ed arrived at his office at Premier Platinum, to be told by the receptionist that Sam wanted to speak with him urgently. He hurried along to Sam's office, reviewing in his mind anything that could possibly have gone wrong in his area. All the machinery had been operating normally when he had left on Friday afternoon. If there had been a breakdown, he would have been contacted on his cell phone, so Ed knocked on Sam's door, hoping that it was nothing that he had overlooked or could have avoided.

Both Sam and Martin were waiting for him. They were grim-faced and Ed prepared himself for something serious. He was not wrong.

'Ed, we've got a major situation,' Sam began. 'About 1000 ounces of platinum are missing from the store!'

'That's terrible - but how?'

Sam held up his hand. 'We know this is outside your area of expertise, but Martin suggested that your problem-solving skills could come in handy here.'

Ed nodded at Martin, appreciating the other man's confidence in him.

'But there's a second reason.' Sam stopped and looked slightly hesitant before proceeding.

'What's that?' Ed asked him.

'Well, we think that the figures which reflect the inflow and outflow of processed platinum from the plant to and from the store to Johnson Mathey were, er, doctored somewhere between the 10th and 14th of November.'

'And that was the time you filled in for me at the plant,' Martin added.

Ed looked at the two men in shock.

'You don't think that ...' he groped for words. 'I'm not a suspect, am I?'

Sam laughed. 'No, my friend. I doubt if you'd be asked to help us with an investigation if you were a suspect!'

Ed nodded. 'But you think that they may have taken advantage of my inexperience with procedures? Oh, my God!'

Ed felt sick. He had enjoyed every minute of his time at the mine. He regarded Sam and Martin as real friends as well as business associates. He was mortified at the possibility that he was responsible for the thieves getting away with the platinum.

Martin clapped him on the shoulder. 'Relax, pal. We just think that they may have thought it easier to distract you. Not your fault.'

Ed had a sudden recall of the men complaining to him about safety in the mine and refusing to go underground on the one day. Could this have been part of it?

Ed sighed deeply. 'Okay, gentlemen. Shall I run through everything that occurred when I was on duty?'

Sam smiled for the first time. 'You see, your problem-solving skills have already kicked in, without any prompting from us.'

For the next two hours, Ed, Sam, and Martin went over and over the events at the mine on the days that Ed was deputising for Martin.

*

Justin watched appreciatively as Persephone finally undid her robe, self-consciously hitched up the straps of her bikini top and then dived into the pool. Breaking the surface, she swam strongly to the other side, turned and smiled at Justin.

'Come on in,'

Justin hesitated. His collarbone was almost healed but he still wore his arm sling. It was more for effect than anything else. He had spent a wonderful lazy morning by the pool chatting to Perse, as she was known to her friends. Her parents were mercifully otherwise occupied and it had given him an opportunity to paint a picture of Justin, the US business tycoon, Justin the unspoken hero of September 11th and other fantasies he had conjured up. Perse was an appreciative audience but she was not nearly as naïve as he had supposed. She was in her final year of Business Economics at university and more than once, her perceptive questions forced Justin to stick as closely to the truth as possible. Nevertheless, he felt he was making progress with the girl. He slowly lifted the sling off his arm and from around his neck, made a big show of putting it down slowly and gently moving his shoulders backwards and forwards.

'Swimming's probably the best exercise you can do with that shoulder,' Perse commented. 'But if you're not ready...'

Swimming was the one sport Justin had excelled in. He stepped to the edge of the pool, dived in cleanly and swam front crawl with easy economical strokes until he joined her at the edge of the far side of the pool. Hell, he thought, the goddam shoulder still hurts. Nevertheless, he forced a carefree grin, having made sure that his momentary grimace of pain had been observed by the glorious young beauty beside him. Her subtle aroma of some rich musky scent had not yet washed off in the water. Despite Justin's continued uncertainty about his sexual preferences, he had to consciously restrain himself from trying to kiss her there and then.

*

Elke and Marie headed back towards the farmhouse for lunch. They had done a quick tour of the orange groves to see if the hormone treatment was repairing the damage that the trees had sustained from the earlier harvesting and some recent hail damage. Marie had been withdrawn all morning and had been disinclined to indulge in any small talk with her daughter. Elke was determined not to ask Marie what she thought about Ed. Anyway, it was pretty clear that her mother did not approve of him. Ed's behaviour, as far as Elke could judge, had been exemplary throughout the Sunday visit. This meant that her mother either had a preconception about Ed that she could not or would not shake loose, or she had misinterpreted something that had been done or said. The vehicle entered the yard in front of the farmhouse and Elke, who was driving, brought it to a gentle halt.

'Ma, what would you like me to do this afternoon?'

'Why? Do you want to go somewhere?' Marie responded with an irritated stare at her daughter.

Elke shook her head, frustrated. 'Ma, listen, if you misunderstand my motives all the time, we're going to have a serious problem here!'

Marie sniffed, opened her door and got out of the vehicle. She then turned around and peered through the window at Elke.

'The only problem we will have is if you ever bring that American parasite here again or if you continue to see him!'

Elke opened her mouth to reply but at that moment, Irene hurried towards them, carrying Elke, her tiny baby, in her arms.

'Missus, missus,' Irene called out frantically. 'The baby is very sick, please!'

All their differences were forgotten as mother and daughter converged on Irene and the tiny bundle in her arms. The baby was having difficulty breathing and was burning hot to Marie's touch. Marie immediately took charge.

'Take them to the clinic. I'll call Doctor Vermeulen and make sure they're ready to receive the child.'

Elke nodded, and climbed back into the vehicle. Marie opened the passenger door for Irene, who quickly climbed in, clutching the baby. Elke started up and drove off as fast as she dared, towards the clinic some five kilometres down the road.

After an excellent lunch washed down by Backsberg, one of the many South African wines Justin had enjoyed during his stay at Buffalo Hills, he smiled at Persephone and decided to make his move.

'When're your parents getting back to the hotel?'

Perse looked at him mischievously.

'Does my Dad intimidate you?'

Justin was stung by the question. In his mind, no one ever intimidated him although at a lower, more sub-conscious level, he feared that the opposite was true. He shook his head.

'No ways. He's a fine gentleman. I was just wondering how much more time you and I will have together.'

Perse finished off her coffee then glanced at her watch. It was just after two.

'They said they hoped to be back by six o'clock. What did you have in mind?'

That's something you're about to find out, he thought, but I'm not about to spell it out to you, lady. Instead, he sighed and looked at her with a serious frown.

'I don't wanna break up the mood of the day, which has been great, but there's something I'd like to show you. I haven't shown it to anyone else.'

Perse was puzzled. 'That sounds very mysterious,' she replied evenly.

Justin nodded, stood up, went around and pulled her chair back. He's the perfect gentleman, Perse thought, but there's something I can't quite put my finger on. His sudden change of mood disturbed her. She liked Justin but she had no intention of becoming serious over him. What was he talking about?

Justin led her out of the dining room and down the path towards his chalet. Perse suddenly realised where they were heading.

'Hey! Where're we going?'

Justin giggled. 'I'm taking you to see my etchings.'

Perse stopped in her tracks.

'Now wait a minute!' she exclaimed. 'That's the oldest line in the book and I'm not...'

Justin turned and gently took her hands.

'Perse, I've had a wonderful day with you and I don't want to spoil a thing but, you see, after September 11th, when I was recovering in hospital and my memory was beginning to return, I did a number of sketches. I never showed them to anyone and I'm even scared to show them to you, but please, I really want to.'

Perse did not have any way of refusing him. He looked so boyish and defenceless, almost childlike. He could not possibly be harbouring any ulterior motive.

'Okay,' she said. 'I'd be honoured to see them.'

'Right on.'

Justin triumphantly led the way to his chalet.

*

Elke pulled into the parking ground of the clinic, stopped and hurried to assist Irene out of the vehicle with the infant. Baby Elke was gasping for breath now. Both her mother and Elke, her involuntary midwife, rushed her into the clinic as fast as they could.

Dr. Vermeulen was waiting for them. A plump and smiling nursing sister gently took the child from Irene and disappeared into the surgery with the doctor. Irene tearfully turned to Elke. 'Thank you, Missus. You think baby, she be alright?'

'I'm sure, Irene. You didn't have trouble with any of your other children, did you?'

Irene shook her head. The two women sat down on the hard chairs that lined the walls of the reception area.

*

'They're really good.'

Perse was genuinely impressed as she looked at the pencil sketches Justin had shown her. The sketches were in a slim drawing book. In many ways they reflected the anguish and shock of the trauma in New York. Some were repeats of the television images screened endlessly around the world, but others were remarkable faces of a cross-section of people. Perse was no artist but she had good taste and was full of admiration. She looked up at Justin who was sitting next to her on the edge of the bed. He smiled and put an arm around her shoulder. Perse stiffened momentarily then relaxed. He still looked far more vulnerable and emotional than the typical predatory male she was used to fighting off.

Even when Justin leaned forward and kissed her very gently on the lips, Perse felt no sense other than a normal desire to respond to a caring, sensitive and undoubtedly troubled young man.

Moments later, Perse's world stood on its head. Emboldened by her tentative response, Justin's tender moments quickly became passionate. As she tried to draw back, Justin held her hard and tried to force her down on the bed. Perse was strong for her size and Justin's shoulder was not yet healed. In a few moments, the young Greek girl had slipped free and stood up with her eyes blazing.

'You're a monster!' she stormed at him. 'You're a sly, manipulative, monster!' she gasped, unable to think of a better word to throw at him.

Justin looked at her with a growing sense of anger.

'Aw, come on, we both know there's a chemistry happening here. What're you worried about? Your folks're...'

'My folks have nothing to do with it,' she stormed at him. 'I'm not that kind of girl. I come from a good Greek Orthodox family and I certainly don't propose to allow any relationship to go too far before I'm married.'

Tears welled up in her eyes as she moved to the door, where she turned and looked at him with pure hatred.

'You could have been a really nice person to know and to spend time with but clearly you only have one thing in mind. It's time you learned that not all girls are like that.'

She opened the door and rushed out. Justin was stunned and mortified. He had never encountered a young, intelligent and enormously desirable woman, who was actually prepared to keep her virginity intact until marriage. Most young women he knew in the US who were prepared to go to bed with him usually said "no," initially. This easily allowed him to justify to himself that Perse had led him on unfairly. Armed with this thought he angrily threw the book of sketches (that he had bought from a friend), across the room and headed to the hotel's bar for a stiff drink. Time to get back to civilisation, he thought in a maudlin fit of self-pity, as he sank a double scotch. Ed's welcome to this place. Time to go home!

*

The doctor came out of his surgery. Irene and Elke looked up anxiously as he approached. Thankfully, he was smiling.

'Okay, you brought her to us in time,' he said. 'I believe that your baby's got some kind of chest infection, possibly pneumonia, but we will do some more tests to confirm. I've put her on intravenous antibiotics and I need to keep her here for a few days but I'm sure she'll be fine.'

Irene did not understand everything said but Elke clasped her arm and told her, 'Your baby will be fine, Irene. It's okay.'

Irene's face lit up and she gave both Elke and the doctor a glorious smile.

'Thank you, doctor. Thanks, Missus. Thanks.'

For Elke as well, it was a truly magical moment.

*

Ed came back to the hotel feeling tired but satisfied that he had played his part in the early stages of the platinum theft investigation.

There were some e-mails waiting for him at reception. The hotel had kindly printed out the pages for him. The e-mail was from Marlene Pretorius, Jacob de Wet's daughter in Las Cruces, New Mexico. It contained a whole lot more data on the life and times of Ben Viljoen, after he was released from a concentration camp on the island of St. Helena at the end of the Anglo-Boer war. Ed realised guiltily that he had not yet completed reading the previous article sent to him by Marlene. He vowed to have an early night, go to his room and study the documents in detail.

116

As he turned away from the reception desk, the first page of the write up caught his eye. It was a letter, written in 1989 by a Hal Brookham, to Judy Bennet, whose address was the Masonic Cemetery in Las Cruces. The letter thanked Judy for sending Hal an article on his uncle, Ben Viljoen. Ed looked at the letter excitedly. It was a pretty old communication but at least it was a starting point. Ed looked up to see Justin standing in front of him, his face a mask of fury.

'What's up?' Ed asked. Justin marched past him to the reception desk.

'I can't get a flight home until next week,' he replied curtly, glancing over his shoulder.

'I didn't know you wanted to go home,' Ed responded mildly.

'I do now,' Justin snarled. 'I feel it my duty to be at home with Mom for Christmas, seeing as you won't be there.'

Ed shook his head in wonder over his brother's hypocrisy. However, he did feel a slight pang of remorse over not joining their mother for the festive season, which had only crept up on him now. The combination of being in the middle of a very un-Christmas-like, hot African summer plus his worries over the recent platinum theft at the mine, had driven any thoughts of festivities from his mind. Ironically as he left the reception, he became aware for the first time that the hotel's canned music was playing one of the perennial Christmas songs, calculated to drive one crazy until the day itself.

CHAPTER 20

It had been a very long day for Elke but overall, she was satisfied with the outcome. She had received a call from her Professor at Pretoria University. He had pleaded with her to reconsider her decision not to return to university the following year. Elke had explained her family predicament and the Professor had asked her to meet with him to work out a possible way of her completing her thesis and at least getting her doctorate.

Elke had driven through to Pretoria that morning. Marie was reluctant to let her go but Isak had insisted that she be allowed to explore every opportunity to round off her academic career. The Professor had been very understanding and had obtained the Dean's agreement that Elke would have the opportunity to complete her thesis part-time over the next two years, if need be.

She had then spent a few hours visiting some close friends in Pretoria and had revealed that as compensation for leaving Varsity, she was very much in love. Her friends had made her promise to visit them, with her mysterious American beau as soon as possible.

It was dark by the time she passed the Hartbeespoort Dam. Filled with warm fantasies of herself and Ed as a married couple with at least two delightful little children, Elke, on an impulse, decided to detour via Buffalo Hills Hotel to see the man of her dreams. She could easily persuade her ever-watchful mother that she had been delayed visiting old friends, which was partially true anyway, she reasoned, as she turned off onto the twelve-kilometre road through the valley to the hotel.

*

Justin drove a hired car at a furious speed towards Sun City and angrily replayed his confrontation with Persephone that afternoon. Every time he thought through the incident, he persuaded himself with increasing certainty that she had been leading him on. She was very lucky that he was still weak from his injuries or he would have shown her a thing or two. The whole episode served to confirm in his mind that no women were to be trusted. He did not even really like them. To Justin they were simply sex objects and even then, images of beautiful young men would occasionally slip unbidden into the mental cinema of his mind. He was not yet ready to confront this alternative but every time he had a failed encounter with a woman, the possibilities of an alternative became increasingly real to him.

To hell with all of them, tonight at least, he thought. A few hours of gambling and some good whisky would soon restore his equilibrium. Besides, before he left South Africa he had to find a way to pressure Ed into selling his shares in Willjohn Industries. For the moment he saw Elke as Ed's Achilles heel but he hoped to find something even more compelling over the next few days.

*

Ed discovered that Justin had organised a hire car from Rustenburg and had gone out. The receptionist had thought he might be heading for Sun City but could not be sure.

Something had obviously gone more wrong than usual in Justin's generally chaotic world. In fact, Ed was quite surprised that it had taken this long. Justin had behaved with almost indecent "sweetness" since his arrival. His sudden outburst of temper was nothing unusual. The only question was, what had sparked it off?

Ed had no sooner asked himself that question, when Persephone approached his table in the hotel restaurant, where he had been dining alone.

Ed stood up as the beautiful young woman approached. He was aware that Justin had been making a play for her.

'If you're looking for Justin, I'm afraid he's gone out for the evening.' Ed told her.

Persephone shook her head. Ed immediately sensed that she was very agitated.

'I wondered, could you and I chat for a few minutes?' She said hesitantly.

Suddenly Ed knew that Justin's upset had something to do with the dark-haired beauty in front of him. Typical Justin, he thought angrily. She seems like a very nice person and now he's gone and ruffled her feathers. He hoped that it was nothing worse than that, but with Justin one never knew.

'Certainly. Shall we have coffee on the patio?' he suggested.

Perse nodded and they both headed out of the restaurant. Seated comfortably over some coffee and glorying in the warm scents of an African summer's night subtly intermingled with the exotic perfume of the young woman beside him, Ed decided to come straight to the point.

'Has Justin done something to upset you?'

Perse nodded. Her eyes filled with tears as she prepared her thoughts. 'That sounds like it's a common occurrence,' she said.

Ed nodded in agreement and sighed.

'I'm afraid so. I hope that you were not becoming too interested in him?'

Perse shook her head decisively. 'Fortunately not. I thought he was a very nice and interesting person but I was not becoming emotionally involved.'

'Good' Ed replied. 'I'm sorry I have to say this about my brother but the fact is that he seems to be emotionally, er, immature. How can I help you?'

Perse sat for a few moments staring into her coffee, then she looked up at Ed, and began a detailed account of what had happened between Justin and her.

Elke entered the hotel foyer and asked the receptionist whether she had seen Ed that evening.

'Yes, he went out onto the patio a few minutes ago' she replied.

Elke thanked her and went over to the door to the patio. She looked out. There were three couples at different tables. She quickly found Ed's table but stopped in her tracks as she saw that he was listening intently to an exceptionally beautiful young woman who was speaking with passionate hand gestures and who was clearly very emotional. Elke stood dead still for a few moments, with a growing sense of shock and dismay. The very last thing she would have expected was for Ed to be spending time with another woman, particularly one who was clearly speaking to him about some intimate and emotional matter. Without a further thought Elke turned, rushed back into the foyer and then out of the hotel to her car. The receptionist looked up in surprise but did not have time to ask Elke whether she had found Ed before she disappeared out of the door.

Ed listened to Perse's story of her time with Justin with growing anger. Justin was such a fool. He could just picture the girl's shock when Justin had pounced on her.

'What freaked me out was the fact that he clearly would've forced himself on me, if I hadn't been able to break free. Then I'm sure he would've claimed that I went to his room specifically for the purpose of having sex with him.' Perse shook her head sorrowfully. 'He seemed so vulnerable and so genuine in his need to share his sketches with someone.'

'I hate to be cynical, but I doubt if Justin could even draw a crooked line. He's no artist but he is a brilliant manipulator. He probably bought the sketches in New York from some street artist.'

'Unbelievable.' Perse said resignedly.

Ed thought for a moment.

'Persephone, what d'you want me to do about this?'

Perse turned her head and two large brown eyes stared hesitantly at Ed.

'I'm sure it's difficult for you,' she replied, 'but my worry is that I'm certain I would've been raped. If he tried to do it to me, he could easily do it again, and maybe he's done it before, has he?'

Ed looked at her in shock.

'Hey! There's no way I'd have let him anywhere near here if I thought he was a rapist!'

Ed drummed his fingers on the table before he spoke again.

'Look, he and I aren't very close but he is my brother and I'll try to handle him.'

'So, he has been in trouble before?'

Ed nodded. 'But not in this way, it's been, well I guess I don't need to get into that.'

'No, you don't, but to answer your question Ed, what I'd ask you to do is to talk to him and see if you can get him to realise how serious it was. If a girl says "no" that should be respected. I know we live in a troubled world and morals today are nothing like what they were in my parents' and grandparents' time, but it still doesn't mean that a girl shouldn't have a choice.'

Ed was delighted to encounter somebody with a strong set of moral beliefs. Could he say the same about American youth? Yes and no, he decided. The big cities were pretty bad but Middle America, hell, what am I thinking? What's important is that my kid brother screwed up again and this thoroughly nice person is trying to settle the issue quietly. At the same time, she's not prepared to see Justin carrying on without any restraint.

'It's not much different back home,' he said eventually. 'You get the good guys and the bad guys. What makes Justin's actions even more unforgivable is that he had a good upbringing, inculcated with all the best values.'

He was hardly the product of the ghetto Ed thought, hardly a street kid with no education and no knowledge of what society expected of him. Ed seriously began to wonder about Justin's sanity. Of one thing he was certain, there was a strong evil streak in his kid brother and it saddened him that so many others should suffer from it.

*

Justin had almost gleefully wasted over a hundred thousand rand in two hours. At one stage he was up nearly a hundred and fifty thousand but it was not in his nature to be prudent. Besides he was getting the attention he craved, even if he was losing. He made a big show of not caring about the money and reminding anyone who would listen, that he had, after all, lost less than ten thousand dollars.

Justin was also very drunk. After he had twice spilled his chips and growled at the pretty young croupier for putting them on the wrong colour, she had pushed a button under the table to alert Security that trouble could be brewing.

Two neatly dressed men watched Justin from a discreet distance for a few minutes. After he had spilled some of his drink on an angry middle-aged woman and had clumsily tried to kiss her as a crude apology, the two men moved in. They escorted him from the roulette tables. Justin was not normally a fighting drunk but on this occasion the indignity of being chucked out, coupled with his re-occurring memories of Perse's lovely face distorted with fury and hatred, triggered a momentary attempt to break free. The security men were taken by surprise as he unexpectedly pulled away and swung a roundhouse right at one of the men, catching him a glancing blow over one eyebrow. Within moments they had restrained him. This time they were neither discreet nor gentle as they frog-marched him to the security offices.

*

Ed sat in his room watching TV although his mind was elsewhere. He wondered what he could do about Justin. In a way he was relieved that his brother had decided to go back to the States as soon as possible but he also felt that this thought was a cop-out on his part. The problem would not go away. It would only be a case of out of sight, out of mind for Ed but it resolved nothing.

At that moment the phone rang. Ed sighed and picked it up. Certain it was Justin, he barked into the phone.

'So, have I gotta come and bail you out of somewhere?'

'What're you talking about, darling?'

His mother's gentle, cultured tones responded from the other side of the world.

'Oops, sorry Mom. Thought it was your youngest son. He's causing chaos as usual!'

There was a faint chuckle from his mother.

'Well, I'm glad you're not trying to bail *me* out. Is he in jail? What happened?'

Damn, Ed thought, the last thing I want is for Mom to be more worried than usual.

'No ways. I was just kidding. He went out on his own tonight and I thought I'd rattle his cage, is all.'

'Oh,' From the long pause, Ed doubted if his mother believed him. 'Anyway,' she continued 'I have some rather disturbing news from this end. Justin has contacted all the minority shareholders in the Company and told them that should a take-over bid by him prove to be successful, he will buy all of them out at a premium. Most of them have agreed in principle, which means that with his existing shares, he's only about 5% short of overriding you, Franklin and me combined.'

'What's the point?' Ed asked. 'He knows the three of us will never sell him any shares.'

'Exactly,' his mother replied. 'But Justin never does something like this for no reason. Has he spoken to you about your shares?'

'Not once.'

Ed nevertheless had a sinking feeling in his gut. This had all the hallmarks of a typical Justin build up. For the moment Ed could think of nothing which his brother could use as leverage against him. However, the trouble with people like Justin was that they never played by the rules. Others, like Ed and his mother, who tried very hard to stick to rules, never saw what was coming simply because they were incapable of thinking in the devious way that Justin had so often manipulated situations.

'I think you should be on your guard, darling' his mother told him.

'You're right. I'll watch him like a hawk. You know he intends returning to the USA next week? I wonder whether I should...'

Even though his mother did not sigh, Ed could hear the total frustration in her voice.

'Don't even think of coming back, unless you want to, Ed. Franklin's a wily old fox and can run rings around your brother. Just make sure he doesn't extract any shares out of you.'

Ed assured his mother that would be over his dead body. As he put the phone down, he wondered bleakly whether Justin might even go that far but then he remembered that in the event of his death, his entire estate was left to his mother.

Ed returned to the TV but he could not concentrate on the mediocre American sitcom that the SABC, the South African National Broadcaster, so often screened. He picked up the remote and switched it off. He looked at his watch. It was too late to call Elke, but he decided to send her a text to her cell phone. They had been doing this frequently over the past week or so. Although it was no substitute for direct contact they had delighted in sending each other affectionate expressions of their "despair" at being apart for even one minute. Ed had fun sending her a mock Shakespearian sonnet that he had written over the past few days.

Ed was about to dial Elke's number when he received a call from the

Sun City Management. Would he please come and collect his brother, whom they were holding? They would discuss with Ed when he arrived, some possible alternatives to laying a charge of assault against the young man! Ed shook his head. Might've guessed, he thought.

Before leaving for Sun City he called Sam to explain that he would be late and then he called Elke on her cell.

'Did you get my poem?' he asked. There was a long silence then Elke replied with a curt 'Yes.'

'Oops. Bad time to phone?' he asked anxiously. He had never heard her sound like that before.

'I think it's better if you don't call me again.'

Ed was stunned. 'Hey, what...?'

'I never want to see you again' Elke replied and disconnected the call.

Ed felt as though the bottom had fallen out of his world. Anguished and near tears, he raced for his car, leapt in and drove like a madman towards Elke's farm. Justin could rot in jail for all he cared at that moment.

CHAPTER 21

Ed drove at speed along the country roads between Buffalo Hills Hotel and the Stein's farm. It was just after nine o'clock and already the roads were all but deserted. Marius de Wet had once warned him always to be on the lookout for stray cattle, goats or even the occasional buck on South Africa's roads at night. In the vicinity of the hotel, most farms were well fenced and the danger was minimal but the further one travelled into the country, the greater the danger was of some creature dashing across the road at the wrong moment.

Ed defiantly ignored both warnings and common sense as he raced along the dull black ribbon stretching ahead in the beam of his headlights with the outlines of the surrounding hills rising dark and oppressive in the pale light of a full moon.

Ed's life had started to unravel over the past few weeks. First the shock of September 11th and the real possibility that Justin may be dead, then his wayward brother's arrival in South Africa and a growing feeling that he was suddenly no longer in control of his own destiny. It was a feeling that, he now recognised, seemed to occur every time Justin entered his life. Even unrelated issues, such as the theft of platinum at the mine and now Elke's sudden and inexplicable upset, all seemed to happen when Justin was in his vicinity. The fact that his brother had ended up in the custody of Sun City's security was par for the course for Justin. Ed noted with amazement that the chaos in the kid's life always seemed to spill over into the lives of those around him. As he drove, he wondered whether Justin could possibly have had anything to do with Elke's sudden refusal to speak to him.

Well, I'll find out soon enough, he thought grimly. The fact that he was going to arrive at the Stein farm at about 9.30 at night, when he knew he was already unwelcome as far as Marie was concerned, did not alter his determination to speak to Elke right away.

Ed firmly believed that the longer a dispute simmered between two people, the tougher it was to sort it out. He also knew that misunderstandings were invariably fuelled by some third party, often hidden from sight. In this case he knew with certainty who the third party would be but what in the hell had Justin said or done this time?

*

Justin sat staring angrily at the security man in front of him.

'Listen, I've given you my passport, and my credit cards. I'm a US citizen and I demand you contact my Embassy. You can't hold me like this!'

Grant Anderson was one of the senior security staff who frequently had to deal with people from all walks of life who misbehaved in one way or another at the Casino. It was always a delicate balancing act, but Grant prided himself on being able to minimise any damage to the Casino or to the guests. In Justin's case, the young man had resorted to physical violence as well as being drunk and thoroughly objectionable. They had run a credit check on him and confirmed that he was wealthy, easily capable of throwing away ten times the amount of money he had lost on the tables that night.

The fact remained however that Grant would have every right to lay a charge of assault but it was probably not the best course of action, provided the older brother arrived and gave assurances that Justin would not cause any further trouble.

Grant sighed. 'Look, Mr Willjohn, we've gone over this already. If I hand you over to the authorities or I contact your Embassy, the repercussions could be serious for you. We don't want to do that...'

'I'll bet. I'll tell them what kind of fascist thugs you employ!'

'Come now,' Grant replied, 'I've taken the names of at least four witnesses willing to testify that it was you who caused the violence. So why don't we just wait for your brother to arrive.'

Justin looked at his watch. 'He should've been here already. It doesn't take long from Buffalo Hills.'

Grant shrugged. 'You may have got him out of bed. Perhaps he'd like you to stew a bit more. Who knows? He'll get here when he gets here.'

*

The farm looked as though it had settled down for the night. Ed, expecting this, dialled Elke's cell phone but he was invited to leave a message on her voicemail. Frustrated, he switched it off without leaving a message. He then drove his car up to the front door and was relieved to see a light on in the room where Isak watched TV.

Knowing that he was about to put his head into the lion's mouth, Ed switched off his car, got out and closed the door, making as much noise as he dared, so that hopefully Isak or someone would come to the front door without him having to ring the bell. It had also occurred to him that

126

most farmers were security conscious and he didn't want to be on the receiving end of a shotgun before he could identify himself.

As he walked towards the front door, the curtains in the TV room were pulled aside slightly and someone peered out. A strong security light illuminated the yard in the area of the front door. Ed was relieved that he was already visible in the light and counted on the fact that Isak seemed to be a very fair man. Ed was confident that he would at least hear what he had to say.

As he cautiously climbed the steps to the front door, it opened and Isak stood there in his pyjamas. He certainly did not look friendly.

'Good evening, Sir,' Ed began. 'I know it's very late, but....'

'I hope this is important' Isak interrupted. 'If I hadn't recognised you, I wouldn't have opened my door at this time of night.'

Ed nodded. 'I realise that and I really appreciate your doing so. It's very important. There seems to be a misunderstanding between Elke and myself. I really need to sort it out now.'

'She went to her room half an hour ago,' Isak replied sternly.

'I suspect she was upset.' Ed stood awkwardly on the steps.

The frail but determined man in the doorway showed no sign of inviting him in.

'Yes, she was upset but...'

At that moment, Marie's voice could be heard behind the door speaking rapidly in Afrikaans. Isak nodded. He was becoming increasingly distressed and that was the last thing Ed wanted to have happen. If Isak should have a heart attack whilst dealing with him, Elke would certainly never forgive him, no matter how serious or otherwise the issue between them was. Ed realised that his emotional response to Elke's upset was not only impractical it was actually endangering this fine old man standing so resolutely in front of him.

'Excuse me, Sir. This was a mistake. I would like to speak with Elke as a matter of urgency but I was wrong to come here now. I apologise.'

There was a sudden commotion on the far side of the door. Marie's voice rose to a furious pitch and Elke's voice could be heard responding.

The next moment, Elke's hand appeared on Isak's shoulder. He turned and listened as his daughter spoke softly to him. He nodded and moved aside as Elke stepped into the doorway. Behind her Marie continued to speak sharply to her daughter. Elke ignored her and stared angrily down at Ed on the lower treads of the steps.

'You've woken up our house. You've upset my mother and father. I want you to leave now, right away, and don't come back!'

Ed felt his heart sink. In a temper, Elke was quite formidable. He could see that underneath her normally warm and friendly disposition, there was the steel that both her parents possessed. Ed suddenly realised that if he did not get through to her now, he would not get another chance.

'You never struck me as a person who condemns someone without hearing what they have to say. I realise I was wrong to come here tonight but please understand that there is nothing more important in my life than you and me. Nothing!'

'It certainly didn't look like that when I arrived at the hotel earlier this evening,' Elke replied and slammed the door in his face.

Daniel finished off his sixth brandy and Coke and smiled benignly at the world around him. He had reached that point in his drinking, where the liquor induced a few brief deceptive minutes of euphoria. In half an hour's time he would collapse and tumble forward onto the table of the shebeen, where he had cheerfully bought the last three rounds of drinks for his friends.

A raucous group of nine men were crowded around the table. Most of them were fellow miners but two were hangers-on from the township, always quick to sense when the booze was flowing.

'Hey, Daniel' one of the miners called out across the table.

He was with one of the other mines in the area but had worked with Daniel a number of times over the years.

'You got a promotion, or you up to your old tricks again?'

This was said without malice and the other men roared with laughter. If Oupa thought he would get Daniel to spill the beans, no matter how drunk he was, he had another think coming!

Daniel grinned at the older man, revealing some terribly decayed teeth.

'Hey Oupa,' he responded. 'You got a new job hey? Undercover instead of underground?'

The others roared their approval. Oupa shook his head. He did not want Daniel to open up to him but it was just part of an age-old ritual amongst the little brown man's friends, to see if the miner was sufficiently in control of his senses. Should he start gabbling away, they would quickly bundle him into a car and drive him home.

On the far side of the room, a nondescript-looking man nursed a beer and listened intently. Inspector Frank Mangose was following up on a list of suspects regarding the platinum thefts handed to his superior by Sam Mohale the previous day. Daniel was high on this list. Inspector Mangose waited in vain for Daniel to let any hint of his involvement drop, as he continued merrily to drink himself into oblivion. The only suspicious thing Frank noted was that Daniel was throwing his money around recklessly. Did his salary justify it? Frank made a note to find out the following day.

Ed stared at the closed door in dismay. The good news was that he now knew why Elke had been so upset with him. The bad news was that she had slammed the door in his face before he could explain about Perse. Here goes nothing, he thought. He stepped forward and banged hard on the door with his fist.

'Elke, listen to me,' he pleaded. 'I was speaking to a girl who had been badly treated by my brother Justin. I was trying to sort things out with her. I'd never even spoken to her before this evening. I'm no two-timer, Elke! Please come out and talk to me!'

Ed stepped back and waited. Nothing happened for an interminable moment, then the door swung open again. Ed's face fell as he saw Isak standing there. There was no sign of Elke. Isak gave him a wry smile.

'Well, you've convinced me, young man, now we need to find a way for Elke to stop being dramatic. She needs to come out of her room and listen to what you have to say.'

Ed could have hugged the man. He was so sane and seemingly unruffled after his household had undoubtedly been turned upside-down that evening.

'Perhaps I should come back tomorrow?' Ed began.

Isak should his head firmly.

'No. Something like this needs to be sorted out before bad decisions are made. It seems as though Elke's jumped to a hasty conclusion. It's not like her but her mother...' He shrugged. 'I'm afraid you didn't make a good impression there. So, the longer those two strong-willed women of mine talk about this, the worse it'll get.'

'What d'you suggest, Sir?' Ed asked.

'Come and sit inside. I'll go and try to persuade Elke to hear what you have to say.'

Ed protested that he didn't want Isak to get involved but the older man smiled tiredly at him.

'I am involved whether I like it or not. Now let me speak to them, so I can finally get some peace tonight!'

Ed sat down in the sitting-room. Although he would've preferred to plead his own case through the solidity of Elke's bedroom door if need be, he could not imagine a better negotiator on his behalf than the ailing, but still alert, citrus farmer.

*

Daniel did his predictable nosedive onto the tabletop after another couple of brandy and Cokes. The others cheered ironically. Two of them, who were close neighbours of Daniel's, lifted him up, one under either arm and hauled him out of the shebeen.

With a sigh, Frank Mangose finished his drink and wondered if he could perhaps get into conversation with the remaining men at the table. Clearly Daniel would not have anything more to say that night.

Justin paced up and down in a fury. Grant, the security man in charge of him, had grown tired of the American's whinging and had left him locked up in the detention room. It was hardly a jail cell but it also lacked any amenities other than a couple of chairs and a plain wooden table. Justin had seriously thought of bashing the window out on the top half of the door with one of the chairs, but he was now sober enough to realise that he was already in trouble. Trying to break out and damaging the place would certainly result in criminal charges being laid against him. He did not want to find that he was barred from re-entering South Africa. He foresaw that his plans to prise Ed's Willjohn shares away from him might not be accomplished on this first trip. Nor did he think that a criminal record would look good if the news reached home just as he was about to take the helm of Willjohn Industries.

His fury therefore was directed more at the ungrateful little slut who had rejected his advances and, as usual, he blamed his brother for everything else. Ed was the reason he had to travel to the wilds of Africa. If Ed had only signed over his shares before leaving the US, Justin would not have been in the World Trade Center on September 11th, and so on.

In Justin's mind, there was only one person in the world who was the root cause of all his problems and that person had left him in this dumb security office at least an hour longer than necessary. Justin hated his brother with all the intensity of someone who was desperately trying not to look at his own shortcomings.

*

It seemed like hours but in reality it was probably more like five minutes, when both Elke and Marie entered the sitting room and stared at Ed.

Marie spoke first.

'Isak has persuaded Elke to come and listen to what you have to say. I want to make it quite clear, however, that you are not welcome in this house. I will not let you return here, no matter what my daughter decides. Furthermore, I want you to know that I will do everything in my power to see that my daughter doesn't see you again. I'm sorry for the troubles you've had in the past but Elke's future happiness is my priority.'

Marie turned and abruptly left the room. Elke stood as still as a statue and stared at Ed, who was still recovering his equilibrium from Marie's outburst. First things first, he thought. I have to sort out things with Elke. The mother can wait.

Elke finally spoke. 'My dad says you explained what was happening at the hotel tonight and that it makes sense! I'm the one who needs convincing, not him!'

Ed took a deep breath and began to speak. It was the most important speech of his life.

CHAPTER 22

Ed felt as though he was standing on a tightrope over the Grand Canyon as he began his speech to Elke. The fact that she had assumed that Ed was two-timing her had shaken him to the core.

He could only assume that her mother was steadily chipping away at Elke's confidence in her relationship with him. Even though he still could not fathom why Marie had taken such a dislike to him, he realised it was a very real problem to be overcome. That was providing that he could win Elke's confidence back first.

'The girl you saw me with at the hotel wanted to talk to me about Justin's behaviour. I've never spoken to her before tonight.'

Elke nodded. Her expression was completely neutral. Ed could not decide whether he was getting through to her or not. Ed suddenly felt awkward, standing across from the girl he loved in the middle of her sitting room, late at night.

'Could we sit down?'

Elke nodded again and went over to sit in one of the single armchairs. Ed perched himself on one end of the large sofa, which faced the fireplace.

He began again. 'Look, I've never said anything to you about Justin's relationship with women because I don't believe in badmouthing anyone. I sure as hell wouldn't like anyone to badmouth me, so that's the way I play it. Unfortunately, this is a situation which requires me to be more explicit.'

Elke's calm façade was beginning to crumble but she tried very hard not to show emotion.

'Did Justin make a pass at her or something?'

Ed waved his hands around.

'Let's leave it at 'or something.' Justin's been in trouble before back in the States. I thought that he'd learned. On that occasion a girl's parents laid a charge of molestation, which was withdrawn after my old man, who was still alive, undertook to discipline him.'

'And did he?' Elke asked.

'He sure did, and Justin appeared to be sorry for what he had done. This is the first time he and I have spent any time together since then. My mother told me that Justin hasn't stepped out of line as far as women're concerned since then.'

'You're implying he's stepped out of line in other ways?' Elke picked up on Ed's carefully worded statement.

Ed shrugged. 'I don't think that's relevant here.'

He leaned forward and spoke with great intensity.

'Elke, you and I haven't known each other for long but I feel that there's a very special chemistry between us. I'm in love with you and, no matter what you think or say, that'll never change. Persephone's a beautiful young woman and I'm sure she's not the only good-looking woman that I'm going to meet over the next few years. If you're going to be jealous every time I speak to one, or even look at one, then we've got a problem.'

Elke was trying very hard not to cry as he continued remorselessly.

'Much as I do love you, I'd rather walk away right now,' he grinned wryly, 'which would sure please your mother, if you're the jealous type; because if you are, it ain't gonna work!'

Elke looked at him wide-eyed, her eyes brimming with tears, then with a little gasp she moved forward off her armchair and fell into Ed's arms. For the first time since they'd met, a few short weeks before, they were able to kiss and embrace without restraint. After a while Elke gently drew away and smiled.

'If you think a pack of baboons was a serious interruption, my mother is a whole other story!'

She giggled and Ed laughed with her.

When they had calmed down, Elke looked serious again. 'I've been such an idiot,' she began.

'Leave it alone' Ed responded. 'I've said all I have to say about it. Now maybe we can try and work out why your mother seems to think I have horns and a forked tail?'

'Oh! But I thought that they were the most interesting features of your appearance!' She teased him.

*

In the shebeen, the party was breaking up for the night. Frank Mangose had tried to keep things going by buying a few drinks but the men were tired and most had to work the following morning.

Frank turned to the man closest to him, whom he had identified as being the most likely to talk about Daniel. They spoke in Tswana.

'Does that bloke they carried home often pass out?' he asked the man, whose nickname was Boytjie.

Boytjie thought about it. 'Only when he's got enough money to drink.'

Frank took a sip of his beer which he'd been nursing for some time. 'How often's that?' he asked. 'I'd like to be around next time. He's a generous guy!'

Boytjie sniggered. 'He an old dronkie but tomorrow morning he'll be at work and no one would know.'

Frank shook his head. 'Amazing. If I drink too much I'm sick for days. I hear platinum miners earn good money. Does he save it up, then go mad once or twice a month or what?'

Boytjie sighed. 'No, it's not that easy. Daniel's always had, um, other sources of income. I don't ask questions, I just say "cheers" and drink up, when he's handing it out.'

Frank and Boytjie spoke together for another few minutes but the miner did not reveal anything more about Daniel, other than to say that the man seemed to always leave a job just before he was fired. Because he was a good worker, he soon found another job. Frank left before the other man became suspicious. Undercover police often used shebeens for their sources of information and Frank tried to use his undercover persona carefully.

In his car he called Sam Mohale on his cell phone as he had promised to do. He told the Mine Manager that Daniel showed all the signs of having more money than should be expected of him at this time of the month. Unfortunately, no one had been willing to give him any specifics.

'What about setting a trap for him?' Sam suggested.

Frank thought about it. 'Maybe, but it's also dangerous.'

He explained that if one were seen to be enticing a person into committing a crime by the courts, the case could be rejected. They discussed ways of setting traps within the law for a few minutes before Sam thanked him and rang off. Frank wearily drove home to his neat little house, his wife and three young children. Frank was not a person who enjoyed wasting his time in shebeens.

*

'Where in the hell've you been?' Justin demanded aggressively as Ed finally arrived at Sun City's security offices just after eleven o'clock.

Ed looked at his kid brother scathingly then turned to Grant Anderson.

'I think you might as well hold him overnight. He's clearly not in a fit state to come back to the hotel.'

Ed moved towards the entrance to the offices. He looked over his shoulder. 'I'll send a lawyer through tomorrow. I presume you'll want to charge him?'

'Hey, you can't do that!' Justin found his voice at last. 'Ed, please!!'

There was now real fear in the youngster's voice. Ed, who had pre-planned his entrance with Grant, just before going in to see his brother, suppressed a grin. He stopped, turned around and looked at Justin.

'You get yourself into serious trouble and then you shout at me?' Ed queried. 'You've gotta serious attitude problem, pal. If you want to come back to the hotel with me, I want an apology. Now!'

The brothers eye-balled each other. Grant watched the drama unfold with some amusement. He could see immediately that the older Willjohn was a very different proposition from his weak and dissolute brother. Although he had gone along with Ed's request to let him threaten his brother with an overnight stay at the Casino's security facility, he would be delighted to see the back of Justin Willjohn.

'Sorry. I was outta line.' Justin, the little boy lost, was speaking now. 'I'm tired, I've got a splitting headache and I just want out!'

Ed nodded and returned to the desk where Grant was sitting with Justin on the other side.

'Mr Anderson, what assurances do you need from me, to allow my brother to leave?'

Grant adopted a formal tone of voice as he replied, feeling that the whole thing really was a time-wasting charade. If the brothers Willjohn didn't hurry up and stop posturing, he'd chuck them both out anyway so that he could attend to the mass of paperwork building up on his desk.

'I need your assurance that your brother will not return to our facilities which includes the Hotel, Entertainment Centre and the Casino for the next six months.'

'I'll be gone next week anyway,' Justin mumbled.

'I also need your assurance, Mr Edward Willjohn that you make sure your brother makes good his promise to pay for damages incurred before he returns to the US. If he breaks this agreement in any way, we will take further steps. Believe me when I tell you that we are in contact with all major Casinos in the US and around the rest of the world.'

Ed nodded. He dropped a business card on Grant's desk.

'You can contact me if there's anything else. Justin will comply with your rulings and he can count himself fortunate that you've handled the situation so, er, diplomatically.'

Ed stood up. 'Let's go, little brother! I've got work in the morning.'

Justin followed Ed out of the room without a backward glance. Grant sighed with relief as they disappeared. He was delighted that his own kid brother was an angel compared with the sullen, mean-spirited misfit that had just left his office.

The two brothers walked in stony silence to Ed's car. Once they were on the road back to Buffalo Hills, Ed decided to broach the subject of Persephone.

'Let's cut to the root cause of your stupidity tonight' Ed began.

'I don't need any sanctimonious lectures from you' Justin retorted.

'This isn't a lecture, this is a statement of fact,'

Ed paused while he slowed down for a group of the much heralded stray cattle that had finally loomed out of the darkness. He shuddered to think what would have happened had he encountered the beasts earlier on his way to Elke at well over 140 kilometres an hour. He was also grateful that he had arranged with Grant to return Justin's hire car to Rustenburg the following day instead of letting the wild youngster loose on the roads. Not that my driving was any kind of example tonight, he thought grimly. Having navigated his way past the last cow intent on crossing the road right in front of his car, he continued to tell Justin exactly where he stood.

'Twice today you've committed criminal acts and twice it was decided to give you another chance.'

'Dunno what you're talking about' Justin mumbled. 'I had a few drinks and then those palookas jumped on me. I defended myself, is all.'

'Cut the crap' Ed replied. 'I'm talking about a very nice young girl called Persephone whom you tried to rape this afternoon.'

There was a moment's silence then Justin started yelling and screaming. Little flecks of spittle collected in the corners of his mouth. His eyes were totally wild and staring. For a moment Ed feared that Justin was going to have a fit of some kind, so he slowed down in case Justin turned violent. The youngster was almost incoherent with rage. Ed could only understand the occasional word or phrase as the babble spewed out of his mouth.

Finally, and with great sadness, Ed wondered if Justin was going insane. He turned his attention away from the verbal barrage which contained words like whore, slut, prostitute and manipulative, which bore no resemblance to the delightful young person Ed had met earlier that evening. Instead he wondered whether to try and get Justin on an earlier plane home, whether he should be put in a straight-jacket and sedated, with a large male nurse in attendance, or whether he should be humoured until he could get onto a plane under his own steam. The first thing he had to do, Ed decided, was to warn his mother and ask Franklin to ensure that Justin was voted off the board of Willjohn Industries. A trust fund could be set up.

Ed's thoughts were interrupted by the realisation that Justin was about to jump from the moving car. Ed stepped onto the brakes and brought the car to a skidding halt. Justin meanwhile had opened his door and was fumbling with his safety belt. Then Ed realised with relief that the youngster was crying wolf once again. Had he really intended to jump, he could have done so quite easily. Nevertheless, Justin was still weeping and wailing away. Not sure of the right thing to do, Ed suddenly swung the open palm of his hand as hard as he could and smacked Justin a stinging blow across his face. Justin shut up in mid-squeal and stared at his brother in shock as tears rolled down his cheeks.

'Now stay quiet and listen to me,' Ed commanded. 'I've gotten Perse's agreement not to press charges against you and Grant Anderson's done the same. I'm not certain that I've done the right thing. Perhaps a few weeks in a foreign jail would teach you a lesson, but I doubt it. I'm a believer in rehabilitation rather than incarceration for punishment's sake. You may be the exception to the rule. All my life our family's been bailing you out and giving you another chance. What you've done in return is kick us in the teeth, particularly me.'

'It's not like that' Justin whimpered unconvincingly.

'It is, and you know it. It's time the family recognised that you're completely out of control. Now keep quiet and try to get some sleep. We'll handle this properly in the morning.'

Justin remained mercifully silent for the rest of the trip. Ed wondered how it was possible that in a delightful rural setting such as the valley and its hotel, which he was beginning to think of as home, could be disrupted by so many dramatic situations. These ranged from Justin, to Elke and her family, and even the ongoing worry over the massive platinum theft. And he thought he might get bored when he first arrived in South Africa!

Ed pulled into Buffalo Hills' driveway and wondered wearily what further mayhem Justin could devise.

CHAPTER 23

Ed woke to the clamour of his alarm. He sat up groggily. He had had very little sleep and felt like hell. With an effort he slipped on his swim shorts, grabbed a towel and jogged over to the hotel's swimming pool some 30 metres away. It was a beautiful cool summer's morning with clear blue skies and a strong hint of a hot afternoon to follow. It would probably conclude with an exhilarating Highveld thunderstorm and a brief deluge to cool things off again. Ed dived into the pool. By his northern standards, the water was comfortably warm. He swam twenty lengths at a reasonable speed, then leapt out and dashed back to his room to change. The swim had cleared most of the cobwebs and had given him time to think about Justin as well as some delicious fantasies about himself and Elke.

He dressed rapidly and went over to Justin's room. He rapped on the door. A groan came from inside the room.

'We need to talk. Now!' he said.

'Go away' came the reply. 'Speak to you tonight!'

After a few more futile exchanges, Ed shook his head angrily and hurried in to breakfast. If Justin could find a way of putting off the inevitable, he would. On his way out to work, Ed bumped into Rob, who grinned at him sympathetically.

'Believe you had some adventures last night!' he said.

Ed shrugged. 'I think you guys hear about things before they happen around here!'

Rob chuckled. 'It's called the bush telegraph, my friend.'

Ed nodded. 'Rob, sorry, I don't wanna be late for work but would you do me a big favour?'

'Of course, if I can' Rob replied.

'I'm sure your bush telegraph told you that Justin behaved like a dumb fool last night?'

Rob gave a slight nod.

'I really need to know if he tries to leave the hotel before I get back. I don't expect you to stop him, but could you just keep me in the loop?'

Rob sighed. 'Family can make life difficult, can't they?'

'Yeah. I've gotta sort the kid out fast.'

Ed turned to go then looked back again.

'Another thing. Please make sure that any calls for me are not handed over to him. He's lethal with messages.'

'Shall do' Rob called after the tall American as he dashed for his car.

*

Ed had hardly settled into his office, when his phone rang. His heart sank. He had visions of Justin already causing havoc at the hotel.

'Yes' he answered tersely.

'Grumpy! Sounds as though you didn't get enough sleep,' a soft female voice purred.

Ed grinned so wide, he felt he was in danger of swallowing the mouthpiece of the telephone.

'Oh boy!' he exclaimed. 'You sure are music to my ears! How're you doin'?'

Elke chuckled. 'Much better now. I just wanted to say thank you.'

'For what, waking up your Mum and Dad and performing like some hysterical Prima Donna?'

'Yes for that, and much more. For making me see that I behaved like a jealous teenager, and also for proving to me that you do really care. No one else I know would have the courage to wake up hardworking farm folk in the middle of the night.'

'It wasn't quite nine o'clock!' he protested.

'Like I said, middle of the night around here.'

'Fools rush in where angels fear to tread' he replied. 'And by the way, I think your Dad is the greatest. I just wish I could get through to your mother.'

'Mmm' Elke was suddenly serious. 'If she doesn't stop interfering in my life, I'll have to leave home. If it wasn't for Dad...'

'Honey, it *is* for your Dad. That's what it's all about, and be fair to your Mom, her whole world is crumbling. Her husband, whom she adores, is a very sick man and she's had to become a father and a boss as well as a mother all rolled up into one. She's doing all this out of love, not hate. If I thought that she was malicious I'd be real worried, but she's not. She's a fine, honest, forthright and strong-minded woman, rather like someone I know.'

'Oh Ed, you're amazing. Do you not have a bad word about anyone?'

'Don't test me over my brother,' he replied.

At that moment there was a tap on the door and Martin Gericke stuck his head in. Seeing Ed on the phone he mouthed the word 'Sam' and pointed. Ed nodded. He said his goodbyes to Elke with some choice and tender phrases, then grabbed a notepad and joined the others in Sam's office.

*

Bud McNeil watched as his men drove four wildebeest into the holding pen. They would only be loaded into their cages just before the truck was ready to take them to the airport. He wondered how any buyers could bring themselves to pay good money for the species of wildlife that he saw as one of nature's misfits. Most animals had beauty and grace in their form or movement but to him wildebeest were quite disjointed creatures with large heads set into short necks and generally scrawny rather hunch-backed bodies, set on spindly legs.

At any rate, many zoos around the world needed them to complete their range of African game and Bud was certainly not averse to receiving money for something he personally did not like. The incredible symmetry of the cat family, lions, leopards, cheetahs and so on, was visual magic to Bud. A herd of giraffe in motion reminded him of the sailing ships of old. Stately, proud and remarkably fast, but the poor old wildebeest or the gnu, as some people called them, he just didn't get it.

Bud shrugged and walked back to his SUV. Perhaps one more parcel of platinum and then he could concentrate solely on the beautiful creatures of this world. He was not thinking of only four-legged beauties as he climbed aboard the vehicle. He decided there and then that he would contact Daniel. He had a shipment of two rhino coming up, which would be a perfect opportunity to store more platinum. Meanwhile he thought he would organise Bonnie for the weekend, so as to stay in practice with the beauties of the world. Bud felt very smug and satisfied as he drove off along the track back to his ranch house.

*

Detective Frank Mangose briefed Sam, Martin and Ed on his observations of Daniel and concluded by saying that the little man was undoubtedly a real pro. Even when blind drunk, he had not let down his guard for a moment. His friends were loyal or at least loyal enough so long as Daniel bought them drinks.

'So, my suggestion is that we lay a trap for him' Frank concluded.

'How d'you do that?' Ed asked immediately, mindful of all the anti-entrapment laws he had read about back home.

Sam and Martin exchanged a glance. Frank gave a brief smile and gestured towards Sam.

'Perhaps you should tell Mr Willjohn what you've got in mind'

Sam stood up from behind his desk and went over to the flipchart in a corner of the office.

'As far as we can work out, Daniel – if it was Daniel – and his team must have taken a load of precipitate...'

'Sorry' Frank interrupted. 'Just give me some basic definitions so that I can understand what's going on.'

'Yes, of course' Sam replied. 'Steps one and two of the process of obtaining pure platinum take place at the mine. The ore is mined and crushed, then in stage two it goes to the flotation or concentrator stage, where all the valuable metals are floated off with the use of chemicals. This is the precipitate. We use a reagent called Xanthate which is added to the valuable metals...'

'You say valuable metals – does that mean that you don't yet have pure platinum?'

'Right, but the smelting is done in Brakpan on the East Rand and then it goes into the base metal refinery where it's refined further, removing nickel, copper, as well as large amounts of cobalt and iron.'

'And your guess is that they took the precipitate?' Frank asked.

'More than a guess, Detective' Martin interjected. 'We measure everything and the materials missing are from that stage. Besides, it gets progressively tougher to steal from the later processes because of the very high security. In other mines thieves have gone for precipitate because it's still in the mine itself, then they do their own crude smelting with blow torches and so on.'

'And it's still valuable?' Frank queried.

'Definitely. Once it reaches its destination, which is almost certainly overseas, they re-smelt it under proper controlled conditions and the final result is pure platinum.'

Frank thought about this for some moments.

'And how did they get the precipitate out of your mine?'

Sam gave a grim chuckle. 'I wish we knew. We've been told that in other mines they've used a number of different containers. The favourite is to cut the bottom off a large gas bottle, put the precipitate inside, weld the bottom back onto the bottle and paint it to hide the weld.'

'Simple but smart,' Frank observed.

They discussed the issue for a few more minutes before Ed finally asked, 'so how d'you propose to set the trap?'

Again, there was an amused glance between Sam and Martin.

'Well, Mr Willjohn, seeing as how they thought it would be easier to get around you than our wily old Afrikaner here...'

'Not so much of the 'old' please!' Martin added, enjoying himself.

The horrible truth suddenly dawned on Ed.

'So, you want me to be in charge, so these guys can run rings around me again. Is that right?'

Sam turned to Frank with a broad grin. 'What a team I've got!'

*

Elke came off the lands for lunch, joining her father in the welcome coolness of the stoep, where a light meal had been laid out. Marie had gone into Rustenburg to look at a new truck. They could barely afford one but their old jalopy was on its last legs.

They chatted about farm matters for a few minutes. The summer rains had been good to them and the entire district was a lush green. One or two hailstorms had done some damage to the fruit trees but if one considered the roulette wheel of farming, they had been extremely lucky.

'How are you coping without 'varsity?' Isak asked his daughter.

She could see dark rings under his eyes probably due to his disturbed sleep the night before. He had not brought up the subject of Ed, and Elke would not be the first to broach it.

Elke sighed gently. 'I miss it, Pa, but I'm not bereft over it. The work I've been doing here is interesting. Ma really knows this farm and what needs to be done.'

Isak nodded. 'D'you realise that for many years, I wouldn't dream of her working at all. She would always come out onto the land, ask me how things were going and then keep quiet. After a while she would make a suggestion here and there and I was amazed at her depth of knowledge. Then one day, I came back to the house unexpectedly and found your Ma studying. She had enrolled at Unisa for a number of courses relating to agriculture. Even though Unisa is a correspondence University and not an Agricultural College, you won't believe what she has learned over the years.'

'I never knew that' Elke murmured.

'Ja, she doesn't talk about it but the whole focus of her life has been around the farm - and me, I suppose.' He grinned. 'Even before I got sick, I realised that she loved being part of managing the farm and so my old-fashioned ideas about the little woman staying at home, doing the housework and looking after the children were modified. Since then, we've become a brilliant team.'

His face fell as the reality of his present situation returned to haunt him.

'Marie knows I can't do very much these days, which is why she's looking to take you on as my replacement.'

'I don't know about that...' Elke protested, but Isak held up his hand.

'I promise you that's the way she sees it. In a perfect world she and you will run the farm while I grow old out on the stoep.'

Elke opened her mouth to protest again, but Isak cut her off. He had a point to make and was not going to be side-tracked.

'All of which is fine, except that you're a beautiful young woman who, I suspect, is very much in love with the handsome foreigner who is threatening to destroy her plans. You must understand that's why she's so anti-Ed.'

Isak sighed before continuing.

'I think he's a fantastic young man. To confront a hostile family and insist on putting the truth there for you to see, is remarkable.'

There was a silence while Isak took a long drink from a glass of orange juice. Elke looked at her father with admiration. He was such a wise and balanced person. He could see past all the histrionics and assess the reality of the situation.

'He thinks you're kind of special too, Pa,' Elke said, 'and he's right,' she added.

Isak put down the glass and stared into the distance. A few fluffy cumulus clouds on the horizon hinted at a storm for later that day.

'I don't believe that parents should ever stop their children from moving on in life. At the same time, Ma would be in a serious predicament if you were to suddenly leave us.'

Guiltily, Elke thought about her conversation with Ed earlier in the day.

'Tell me, my girl, just how serious is this relationship? Is there a possibility that you would go back to the States with Ed? Not that I would want to stop you.'

Elke felt her eyes fill with tears.

'Pa, we haven't said much about the future. Yes, we're in love and I'd like to talk to Ed about his plans. I know he's happy here.'

'Your Ma tells me that Justin owns the family business and that there's not enough money to take Ed back into it, if he should want to do that.'

'You know more than I do, Pa. We've never talked about his background. Whether he's rich or poor - I don't care. He's got a good job here. I love him very much and maybe' she said with a twinkle in her eyes 'he could be persuaded to go into farming!'

Father and daughter chuckled at the thought of how that could resolve everything, knowing rather sadly that life generally wasn't like that.

*

Ed went out onto the patio of Buffalo Hills Hotel in search of his brother and stopped in surprise. Justin was sitting at a table with Rob Schutte and Marius de Wet, as well as Rachel and Errol Saperstein, the couple who had also been in New York on that terrible day. Much as he had thought that it would be interesting for Justin and Errol to meet, he was still very angry with Justin. He dreaded to think what lies Justin could have already brought to the conversation.

CHAPTER 24

'...I guess I'd reached about the tenth floor, when everything went crazy. The bottom seemed to fall out of the stairs I was rushing down along with a mob of other guys. Y'know that feeling of falling you get in dreams sometimes? That's about how it felt.'

Justin paused for dramatic effect. Rachel Saperstein leaned forward, eagerly awaiting the next part of the youngster's story.

'And then?' She prompted.

Justin shrugged helplessly. As Ed approached the table he could see that his brother was genuinely reliving the moment.

'Then? Nothing. It all went black. Next thing I know I'm in a bright white room, drips and tubes all over me, a heart monitor beeping in the background. People, nurses mostly, running, calling for help, issuing instructions. No one was interested in me.'

Ed smiled inwardly as Justin indulged in his usual bout of self-pity. Despite his misgivings Ed did however start to get a picture of the terrible chaos and overloading that all of New York's medical facilities must have been experiencing at that moment. He quietly approached the table as Justin continued.

'Finally an exhausted looking orderly appeared with a clipboard. He went from bed to bed getting the names of anyone who was conscious. Most of 'em weren't. When he reached me, I was prepared to give him my name, a number to call my Mom, whatever but when he asked me for my name, I suddenly went blank!'

'Amnesia?' Rob asked.

Justin looked up, saw his brother and for a moment he seemed to be unsure what he should say next. Ed nodded at him.

'Carry on. I haven't heard this part of your story either.'

'Look I'd just come around moments before. Everything was scrambled. I just couldn't put thoughts into words. Anyway, he didn't press me. Said he'd come back later. I asked him to send a doctor to check me out. He looked kinda confused and said as soon as one was free. They were dealing with all the critical cases first.'

'Which is why we didn't get news of his survival for a coupla days,' Ed added.

He knew that Justin could drag out the story indefinitely. He turned to Errol Saperstein.

'I believe that you also have quite a story to tell.'

Errol chuckled.

'Nothing like as dramatic as your brother's amazing escape but it was certainly an extraordinary introduction to America. Neither of us had been there before.'

'Let's have it then' Rob chipped in. 'We'll leave Justin to recover for a moment.'

Justin hated not being the centre of attention but nodded grudgingly. Errol took up his version of the events.

'I'll keep it as short as I can. There we are arriving at JFK Airport. My nephew's son, Greg, who left these shores as a typical South African kid, is now all grown up and sporting a broad American accent. We get the big hello and hugs. He escorts us to a limo at least a mile long, loads us up and takes us to the Staten Island Ferry for the views a brief tour of Manhattan all before our connecting flight to San Diego that evening.'

As Errol got to that part of the story, Rachel reached out and clasped his hand.

'We were about halfway across to Manhattan when one of the passengers points a camera in the direction of the Twin Towers, reacts and yells out "Hey there's big fire!" We all turn to look. There's smoke pouring from the side of one of the Twin Tower buildings but none of us saw the first plane hit. I see one of the Ferry officers on a cell phone but before he can get any answers, we see the second plane hit.'

Rachel shuddered and bowed her head. Errol was also emotional.

'A minute or so later, the ferry makes a sharp turn and we head back to Staten Island. Greg is also on his cell. No one's telling us anything but by the time we return to Staten Island the news is beginning to filter through about the attack.'

A waiter approached the table. Ed ordered a beer. The others at the table still had their drinks but that didn't stop Justin from ordering another Bourbon. Errol continued.

'The driver of the Limo, Monty Strale, a friendly, gregarious man and ex New York Cabbie has as much news as is available. He tells us that downtown Manhattan is entirely blocked off and worse still, all flights in the entire United States have been grounded!'

His audience around the table are spellbound, except for an increasingly restless Justin.

'Greg's speechless. Nothing like this has ever happened before. He has been charged with the task of getting us to San Diego in time for our Jewish New Year with Michael and his family. Suddenly we're without transport, at least, the form of transport that Americans mostly take for granted - the airlines.'

'Yeah, that's what stopped me from returning to see what had happened to Justin,' Ed broke in.

Errol nodded. He was still reliving the moment.

'Furthermore, there's no way we can get into a hotel. They are either fully booked or not taking any new guests until there is some clarification as to what's happened. Greg is clearly out of his depth, as are we.'

'Monty suddenly takes charge. Bless his heart. He drives us to his home, has a quiet word with his wife and the next thing we know, we're guests of the Strale's for the night. What's more he insists that Rachel and I take the main bedroom, while he, his wife and Greg are spread around various couches in the sitting room. We protest but he says that we've been deprived of traditional warm New York hospitality as well as a tour of the city. The least they can do is to make us comfortable!'

Ed shook his head in wonder. Rob clapped his hands.

'Incredible. And the next day?'

'Well, Rachel and I are tired after our long flight from Johannesburg, so it's no great sacrifice to remain indoors. Along with the rest of the world, we watch TV in horror, amazement and a degree of fear as the drama of the aftermath of 9/11 unfolds. I don't need to retell any of that because you're all fully in possession of the details. Greg and Monty disappear into a small study where they get onto laptops and phones, to find out our options. At this point, we would have gladly hopped on the next plane home and left the Americans to mourn and recover from their unbelievable tragedy on their own. Trouble is there's no way of us returning to South Africa right away unless we drive up to Canada and fly from there.'

'It was a terrible feeling' Rachel added 'to see an entire nation in a state of collective shock. The only possible positive I could see, which became apparent over the next few days, was how Americans of all ages, sizes, colours and religions, bonded together against the common enemy. That enemy, more than anything, was the fear of the unknown. What would happen next?'

Rachel was momentarily overcome with memories of their dramatic journey. Errol took up the tale once more.

'So, the next morning Greg and Monty have a plan of action. There're still three days to the New Year. Monty has arranged a hire car for Greg. We are going to drive to San Diego! At first I tell Greg that it's far too much trouble for all concerned but on reflection I realise that there aren't any sensible alternatives. Besides which I can see that Greg is the kind of kid that is fiercely determined to succeed with any task given to him. His old man told him to go to New York and bring the Sapersteins back for New Year, so that's what he's going to do. It's one hell of a long drive. Rachel, what was the name of that nice little town where we stopped for the night in New Mexico?'

'Las Cruces, darling.'

Marius gave a gasp and then chuckled. Ed could not believe his ears. Here they were sitting comfortably on the patio of a delightful country hotel in the heart of Africa, with a huge array of tropical birds, the whistling of cicadas and general early summer sounds of a myriad of other insects and bugs, the intermittent chatter of African voices and having drinks with long-time residents of the area; all reliving the tragedy of 9/11 and now fantastically the further coincidence of two more South Africans visiting Las Cruces, an isolated town in New Mexico!

Marius briefly explained about his brother's daughter and son-in-law in the same town as well as the probability that Ed and Justin's ancestors had relocated from South Africa to Las Cruces or at least to the banks of the nearby Rio Grande. They all spent a few moments wondering what were the odds of so many South Africans and even an American of South African origin, all having been to or having a connection with Las Cruces.

Errol finished off his story by saying that they had arrived in time for the New Year. It had been a rather muted celebration because of the circumstances but it had been wonderful to have been with their nephew Michael, his wife and children. Rob thanked both Justin and Errol for their graphic accounts of the events on and around 9/11. The party broke up with Marius and the Sapersteins returning to their respective farms and Rob to his office. Ed and Justin went through to dinner.

Over the meal Ed was quiet and thoughtful but Justin, with a few drinks inside him wanted to talk. After expanding on his time in the little New York clinic where he had been treated for his injuries, Justin broached the subject of Willjohn Industries. Ed sighed. He knew that sooner or later Justin was bound to bring it up and he was quite certain that his younger brother was not going to be friendly about it. He was right.

Justin began by praising Ed's lifestyle in the delightful little valley surrounded by the Magaliesberg Mountain range.

'You've really gotten yourself a comfy situation here Ed.'

'Yeah, I like it here very much.'

'Good buddies, a beautiful girlfriend, a job you enjoy. What more could you want?'

Ed knew where this was going. He was not about to let baby brother con him into yet another situation where the only winner was one Justin Willjohn.

'I could name a few things.'

'I guess it doesn't include any involvement in Willjohn Industries, does it?'

'Depends what you mean.'

'Hey, you're not gonna fly back for regular meetings are you?'

'Of course not, but it doesn't mean I've lost all interest in the group.'

Justin shook his head frustrated and tried to bluster his way through the conversation.

'You know that Dad wanted a Willjohn to continue at the helm. Franklin will only be a temporary boss...'

Ed quickly cut him off. They were both becoming heated.

'That's not the way Dad saw it. Unfortunately, you've not shown the potential to run a large conglomerate and when I turned it down, he realised that Franklin was the ideal alternative. He's done a great job so far. Profits're up, the group is expanding...'

'Not what I hear.'

Ed had had enough. He leaned forward and spoke forcefully to his brother.

'Then you should check your sources, Justin. Just what d'you want to ask me? Stop beating around the bush.'

Justin cringed for a moment then his sly expression reappeared.

'I just want to do what is right for the family. I want to buy your shares. You won't need them here.'

'And how d'you propose to do that? Have you any idea how many million dollars they're worth?'

'Yeah I do. Of course, I'd have to pay them off, but that shouldn't be problem should it?'

Ed stared at his brother in disbelief. He was frighteningly delusional.

'How you would pay me off isn't relevant because I'm not selling you my shares. Not now, not ever! If you had my shares, you'd have a majority and the first thing you'd do is get rid of Franklin.'

'Right on and return Willjohn to family control.'

'No dice. Your shares are worth a lot of money and if you want to start up your own business, I'm sure that Mom and I between us could buy your shares. Don't even bother to ask me to sell you my shares again. It's not negotiable, so drop it!'

Justin threw down his knife and fork, ripped the napkin off his lap and stood up from the table. There was total madness in his eyes as he shouted at Ed, causing the rest of the dining room to go silent and stare at the brothers.

'You'll regret this day Ed! If you think you can hold me back and make nothing of me. You've just made the worst mistake of your life.'

As he turned to go, Ed saw the welcome figure of Elke appear at the entrance to the dining room. Justin stormed off, completely ignoring Elke. Ed stood up and greeted his beautiful girlfriend with a hug.

'What was all that about?'

Ed shook his head sadly.

'Just Justin not getting his own way and behaving like the spoilt brat that he is. D'you mind if we go out for a coffee? He's ruined my dinner for me. I don't want to be anywhere near him right now!'

Elke smiled. 'Of course. I know just the place.'

CHAPTER 25

Elke took Ed to a little coffee bar in Rustenburg. There were only three other couples in the café, and they chose a relatively quiet corner where they could chat. Once they had settled down at the table, Ed looked around and smiled at Elke.

'I think we're in a time warp!'

Elke chuckled. 'So that's what you think about our nearest metropolis!'

Ed received a menu from a friendly waitress then continued, 'I don't just mean tonight. I'm talking about our entire relationship. Or is this just the way things happen around here?'

Elke looked at him seriously. 'Ah, so Mr Big City American's becoming frustrated with the pace of life in rural Africa?'

'Hell no! I never said I didn't *like* time warps. Oh boy! Have I put both feet in it?'

Elke leaned across and clasped his arm. 'I'm just teasing, silly, although would you like to elaborate?'

Ed took a deep breath. 'Okay, here goes. I grew up in Minneapolis, a pretty big US city, but spent most of my holidays on the ranch in Wyoming. I preferred the ranch but had to live mostly in the city, which is why I chose to do a mining degree.'

The waitress returned. Ed ordered two cappuccinos and one cheesecake with two forks which was about as much as either of them could possibly manage, having already eaten.

'Now I'm a stranger in a strange land. A place where not so long ago, I experienced a summer Christmas. No snow, no holly, just bright sunshine, a swim before lunch and then a traditional turkey and all the trimmings. Amazing! But the problem is' he grimaced, 'I've fallen in love with the strange land and I've definitely fallen in love with this stranger.' Ed took her hand and kissed it gently.

'Ahh, but who's the stranger?' Elke asked gently. 'An English friend of ours became engaged to a Greek girl. As he did the rounds of her many relatives, he heard this word xenos whenever the Greek community met him. He asked his fiancée, "what's this word xenos?" "Oh, that means foreigner," she replied. He looked at her, shocked. "But I can't be a foreigner, I'm English!"'

Ed laughed delightedly. 'So, which one of us is the xenos?'

Elke nodded. 'We both are.'

'And we've got a lifetime ahead of us to find out just how different, or perhaps how alike, we both are!'

The coffees and cheesecake arrived, and they had some fun jockeying for position with their two forks attacking one cheesecake. Ed continued with his thoughts on their relationship. 'I said a time warp because we've never really been able to spend quality time alone. It's like, we've been permanently chaperoned by the entire community.'

He leaned forward and clasped both her hands. 'Could you and I arrange to spend a weekend away somewhere?'

Elke looked at him steadily for some moments before replying. 'Ed I can't think of anything I'd rather do' she paused.

'But?'

There was a definite unspoken "but" at the end of her sentence. Ed wanted it out in the open. Elke nodded and took a sip of her cappuccino before replying. The resultant cream "moustache" spoiled the seriousness of the moment. Ed picked up his table napkin and gently wiped the foam off her upper lip.

'But' she continued, 'Ma's going to be a problem and…'

She did not know how to go on. Ed took her hands again and held them firmly.

'I was waiting for a more appropriate moment but,' he swallowed and looked deep into her eyes, 'Elke, will you marry me?'

Elke gasped. Although she knew this moment must come, it still took her completely by surprise. She had been struggling to express her strong sense of moral values without wanting to put any pressure on Ed, or worse still, drive him away. Her eyes filled with tears but they were tears of such intense happiness that she had never experienced before. After making a huge effort to control her emotions, she managed a half smile.

'Before or after the weekend?' she said.

'Hey, d'you have those twenty-four-hour preachers like in Reno, Las Vegas and so on? We can do it right now.'

Elke leaned forward and they kissed, gently at first, then with such increasing intensity that the cappuccinos and remains of the cheesecake threatened to slide onto the floor. Ed pulled back with an effort. He looked at her intently.

'I get it. Marriage first, weekends afterwards.'

She nodded, the clasped his arm again. 'It's not what you would call a deal breaker, but I'd prefer it that way.'

Ed kissed her fingertips lightly. 'You got it, lady. Now, I hate to be practical but we've gotta figure out how to tackle your mother. We need to agree where we're going to live and we need to set the date!'

'Is that all?' Elke replied mildly. 'I thought you might have some serious obstacles to present!'

They spent the next hour exploring each other's thoughts and feelings about where to live and when to set the date. The subject of Marie and her disapproval of their relationship was firmly put aside for a later discussion.

*

Justin sat in the bar nursing his third Jack Daniels. He was debating sullenly with himself upon ways of getting Ed to sign over his shares in Willjohn. He was no further towards solving the problem when Sam Mohale entered the bar and with a broad smile, came over to greet him.

'Hi there, Sam. Buy you a drink?'

'Thanks, I'll have a Windhoek lager.'

Sam eased himself onto the bar stool next to Justin. In the background on TV the South African soccer team, popularly known as Bafana Bafana, were playing their best match of the African Nations Cup against Morocco. Sam watched appreciatively as Nomvete slipped past a couple of Moroccans and crossed the ball over to the centre, where Zuma missed a goal by a whisker. They were 3–0 up at the time so it was not a disaster.

'The boys're looking good tonight, at last.'

Sam picked up his glass and waved it at Justin in a "cheers" gesture.

'D'you follow soccer?'

The younger Willjohn shook his head.

'Not really. I've watched a few games. It looks pretty skilful but I'm not much into sport.'

Sam nodded and took a long swallow of the lager before asking 'Big brother around?'

Justin shook his head. 'He went out with his girlfriend. Can I give him a message?'

Sam thought about it. 'Ja, maybe you could tell him that we're going to start the operation tomorrow, so would he please be in bright and early.'

'Operation?' Justin deliberately looked confused, wanting to hear more.

'Mmmm' Sam looked around to see if he would be overheard. There was no one else within earshot in the bar.

'No harm in telling you, I suppose. We had a robbery recently. Ed's helping us set a trap.'

Suddenly Justin sensed that this could be the break he was looking for. He was a genius in the art of sounding interested, ill-informed and yet cultivating the essence of confidentiality, all at the same time. Sam, in good faith, having no reason not to trust the brother of one of his senior men, explained the basic details of the "sting" and how they hoped to catch Mr Big in the process.

'And Mr Big would be the guy who disposes of the platinum?' Justin asked.

Sam waved his glass in agreement.

'That's him. Someone who has the means of smuggling it out of the country.'

'Where do they send it?'

Sam finished his beer and stood up ready to leave.

'I'm not sure' he replied, 'but my guess would be the States. There'd be a bigger market for it there. It'll be the States or maybe the Far East. I must go. Thanks for the beer. My turn next time and don't forget to tell Ed to be in bright and early, please.'

Sam left and headed for the car park. He was feeling excited about the days ahead and the possibility of catching the platinum thieves.

Justin quickly swallowed the last of his Jack Daniels and hurried to his room. It was a hell of a long shot but it would be great if he could pull it off.

*

Ed and Elke drove back to the hotel's car park, arriving well after Sam had left the hotel. Ed escorted Elke to her car and offered to follow her back to the farm, but she declined. 'I'll be fine' she said. 'The roads are very quiet. I'll call you when I get in, if you like.'

Ed said he would like. They kissed with great tenderness before Elke got into her car and drove off into the night.

Ed walked slowly back to his room. He felt totally elated. He had not planned to ask Elke to marry him that evening, but the circumstances were right and so it had happened. And she had said yes! Life doesn't get much better than this, he thought joyfully. The light was on in Justin's room and for an instant Ed wanted to share his news with his brother. Then sanity prevailed and he knew that Justin would quickly find a way of spoiling the moment. Ed carried on to his bedroom and called his mother instead.

Meanwhile, Justin was also on the phone to the States. Although he had never been involved in any overtly dishonest activities, Justin enjoyed the company of a number of dubious characters whom he had met in bars and clubs back home. Mixing with the low-lifes but feeling superior to all of them gave Justin a vicarious thrill. One of the low-lifes he remembered particularly well was Bennie Tomassini and if he recalled correctly, Bennie had boasted about dealing in precious minerals. It had taken a few calls. Finally, Justin's close friend Karl had agreed to track Bennie down. Twenty minutes later, Karl had called back with Bennie's number. Justin was on the phone to him immediately. Bennie was easily persuaded with the promise of fifty G's if he could discover the guy who had sent a package of platinum over from South Africa some three or four weeks previously. Bennie had called back in ten minutes.

'The guy you need to speak to is one Bud McNeil' Bennie told him. 'Not a big operator, but he moved about half a million dollars' worth from a mine that's never been hit before. We think it's Premium or Premier, something like that.'

'You're a star, Bennie!' Justin cut in joyously. 'That's the one. I'll see you next week with the bucks.'

Justin lay awake for hours working out exactly how he was going to fix big brother for good. Once Ed was in a South African jail, he would easily persuade the shareholders who held 45% to insist that Ed's shares be divided up pro-rata across the Board, which would allow him to pull off a coup d'état of note, when he got home. Perhaps the South African saga was going to have a happy ending after all. First though, he had to persuade this Bud McNeil that a lot of money in the bank was infinitely better than the risk of smuggling platinum.

*

The next morning over breakfast, Justin was unusually animated. He ascribed this to the fact that he was flying back to the US in four days' time. I could get excited about him doing that too, Ed thought, as he tucked into a large and delicious breakfast of scrambled eggs, sausages, bacon and liver. However, something was nagging at him about Justin. There was that dangerous glint in his eye that so often spelt trouble.

Justin could hardly wait for Ed to leave. He had a number of things to do if he were to succeed in his plan. He considered mentioning that Sam had called into see Ed but decided against it in the hope that Sam may also forget to mention it. This was the one weak point of his plan. If Ed had any idea that he and Sam had spoken about the forthcoming trap they were setting for the platinum thieves, Ed would quickly put two and two together.

As soon as Ed left for the office, Justin rushed to his room. His first phone call was to Premier Platinum. Sam had told him previously that he liked to be in his office at seven every morning so that he could plan his day before the rest of the management team arrived. Justin was put through to Sam.

'Morning, Sam' Justin said. 'Nice seeing you last night but I have an apology to make.'

'What's that?' Sam's mind was on the forthcoming sting. He listened to Justin with half an ear. 'I totally forgot to tell Ed that you came to see him last night. He rushed through breakfast and...'

'No problem. Thanks for telling me.'

Sam was anxious to get off the phone but the younger Willjohn continued.

'Er, Sam, please will you do me a favour and not mention to Ed that you came around. He gets real mad at me when I forget things like this, and anyway, he'll be in the office in good time.'

Sam chuckled. 'Okay, my big brother would've done the same. It'll be our dark secret!'

'Of course, thanks Sam. Ed's lucky to be working with you.'

Justin put the phone down and grinned from ear to ear.

His next call was to Bud McNeil. A gruff voice answered after a couple of rings.

'McNeil!'

'Mr McNeil, my name's Mario. I'm over here for a few days and I've been told that you're preparing a parcel of goods that I might be interested in.'

There was a long silence then Bud replied 'Give me a name I recognise.'

'My contact's Bennie but he said I should mention Sean O'Driscoll.'

'Okay,' Bud sounded a bit more positive. 'Now what?'

'We need to meet this morning. I'll come to you.'

'Why should I change my existing arrangements?' Bud asked.

'Think of the number you expect to get from this deal and double it!' There was a chuckle on the other side of the phone.

'That just bought you a visit, but I'll need to know a whole lot more.' Bud told him.

'Tell me how to get there and I'll explain a deal to you that'll blow your mind!'

Bud told him.

CHAPTER 26

Ed reached the mine a few minutes earlier than usual and went straight through to Sam's office. Sam looked up from his desk and smiled at him.

'Ready to play Hercule Poirot?' he asked. 'Or maybe Mike Hammer would be more appropriate for you!'

Ed nodded. 'Whatever! So, you want me to deputise for Martin like last time, only if I see anything outta place, I look the other way!'

'Right' replied Sam. 'But be careful not to be obvious about looking the other way. They might think you're in on the scam.'

'Would that be a bad thing?' Ed wondered.

Sam thought about it.

'I'm not sure but we'd better stick to the scenario we've already worked out. Martin and his team're already in place, keeping an eye on the roads, so that we can follow the platinum when it leaves the mine.'

Ed left the offices and strolled over to the mine itself, trying to look like an eager, but ignorant, beaver about to build his first dam.

*

Justin met Bud at the roadside café where Daniel would meet the little robbery mastermind later that day. Bud and Justin had exchanged descriptions of each other over the phone. There were only a couple of other people at the café and Justin had no difficulty in identifying Bud.

They chose a table outside, where they would be completely alone. Bud had been suspicious of Justin's call at first but a quick check with Sean O'Driscoll in Chicago, who had answered from a nite club and strip joint on his cell, had confirmed that Bennie, Justin's contact, was okay. It followed therefore that Bud could at least talk to Justin with confidence. Sean had no idea of what Justin was going to propose but Bud asked if Sean knew whether the young guy could put his hands on big money if required.

'He sure can,' Sean replied.

Bud chuckled and rang off as he drove towards his rendezvous with the American.

Now sitting face to face with Justin, Bud quickly summed up the rather weak-looking and nervous young man. It would have to be simple and straightforward, Bud thought. He would not like to have too many dealings with this rich pampered kid, who obviously enjoyed flirting with the seamier side of life. As the waitress brought them coffee, Bud's opening remarks were straight to the point.

'The deal I have right now is worth half a million US. You said you could double it. Talk to me.'

Justin sipped his coffee then put the cup down.

'Some of your, er, suppliers could get hurt from this.'

'Hurt as in dead?'

Justin shook his head. 'No. Hurt as in caught and put away for a few years.'

Bud shrugged and watched appreciatively as a BMW sports screamed past them down the road at well over 180 kilometres an hour.

'Too bad. Casualties of war. They know the risks. But Daniel might identify me.'

'I don't think so' Justin replied. 'I'm told that you can get rough if people cross you. Besides, I can arrange a nice little, er, pension for him when he gets out.'

Bud nodded and looked across at the far slopes of the mountains. It would be another hot day with probably some thunderstorms in the afternoon as usual. He looked back at the kid.

'So for one million dollars, what do I have to do and how will I be assured of payment?'

Justin reached into his pocket and withdrew a slip of paper and a pen.

'To answer your second question first, write the details of an off-shore bank account where you would like to have the money deposited. It'll be deposited there at midnight our time tonight once I'm sure that our arrangement is in motion. If something goes wrong your side, Sean O'Driscoll knows how to take care of you. If I fail to perform, the very same Chicago Irishman knows how to find me. Are we okay so far?'

Bud could not find fault with Justin's reasoning so far.

'So, what do I have to do?'

Justin leaned forward and wearing his sweet angelic smile, told the man exactly what he wanted.

*

Daniel employed an entirely different tactic this time. He asked to see Ed and when the wizened little man entered his office, Ed could not resist teasing him.

'Hi Daniel. Are the guys feeling unsafe again?'

156

Daniel acknowledged the barbed remark with a wry smile.

'No sir, everything's just fine, sir. At least underground that is.'

'And so?'

'Well, sir, you know that old water tank by the canteen?' Ed nodded.

It was an eyesore. It was a large, round corrugated iron tank that had not been used for some time.

'Well, sir, the guys have been complaining that it smells and the smell's now reaching the canteen.'

Ed nodded. He had personally caught a whiff of rotting vegetation in water, when walking past the tank a couple of days ago.

'Go on.'

'Well some of the blokes thought as how we could get it out of here. We don't like eating with that smell around. A pal of mine's got a truck and we could take it away, maybe fix it up, but mostly get rid of the smell.'

Ed was impressed with Daniel. It all sounded so plausible. How in the hell were they getting the precipitate out of the store and into the water tank, or was it already there, he wondered? Anyway, that wasn't his problem. He needed to allow Daniel's men to get the platinum off the premises so that Martin could trail it and hopefully nail Mr Big who was moving it out of the country.

'When d'you want to do this, Daniel?' he asked.

'Well Sir. Me and some of the shift knock off at 4pm today. We can have it loaded and out of here by five thirty.'

Ed made a show of being reluctant and uncertain then finally agreed to let Daniel do it. The little brown man thanked him and gleefully left the office. He and his helpers had been steadily dumping kilos of precipitate into the tank over the past few days. They had managed to hide small quantities of it, as it was on its way to the storeroom. Daniel had also taken the precaution of dumping a dead cat into the tank, so that the smell was becoming unbearable, lending credence to his story.

*

Justin had hired a car for the rest of his stay in South Africa, knowing that he would need to be mobile if he were to complete all the little cycles he needed to achieve in order for his plan to work. It would be very expensive for him but he reasoned that one had to spend money in order to make money. A couple of million was nothing compared to the hundreds of millions he could soon have under his control if he could eliminate Ed from the family business.

He called in at the Stein farm on his way back to the hotel. He thought that it would be a nice touch to say goodbye before he returned to the States and it wouldn't hurt to rub a little more salt into the wounds where he could.

He was lucky. Marie was in the house working on some accounts. Isak was on the stoep as usual and greeted him courteously but without enthusiasm. The old bastard's onto me, Justin thought, but no big deal. Ed's behaviour over the next few days would be all that mattered.

Marie looked up tiredly as Justin tapped on the door of her office.

'Hallo, Justin'

She wondered what the young man had come to see her about.

'Hallo Mrs Stein. I'm leaving for the US in a few days,' he said. 'I just thought I should come over and say goodbye.'

'That's very kind of you'

She paused uncertainly then decided to open the subject of the older Willjohn.

'I am very concerned about Ed's mental state. In the light of what you've told me, I've told Elke that he will no longer be welcome at our home. I didn't give her any reason, so that your conversation with me remains confidential.'

Justin looked suitably solemn.

'I think you've made a wise decision, Mrs Stein. Sadly, I think Ed's mental health is deteriorating again. He's been mighty preoccupied over the last few days. I've got a feeling he's hung up on a lack of money, even though he's well paid at the mine. He kinda hinted that he wants to get that one big break, that'll net him a fortune. I hope he doesn't think gambling'll do it for him!'

Marie made sympathetic comments but she was clearly busy. Justin, having achieved his objective with her, said his goodbyes and left the farm confident that this would be the last time any Willjohn ever set foot on the place.

*

Ed decided on a casual stroll past the area where Daniel and his men were labouring to load the old water tank aboard an equally ramshackle lorry.

As he drew close, the smell was indeed almost unbearable. A small price to pay for a large quantity of stolen platinum, Ed thought. Daniel greeted him with a grin but Ed could see that his eyes revealed an underlying anxiety. On an impulse Ed held his nose and leaned over the tank, which was at that moment on the ground next to the truck, to peer into the round open hole on the top. He caught a brief glimpse of some foul looking water as well as some thick sludge which he presumed was mainly precipitate before Daniel's anxious voice impinged on his hearing.

'I wouldn't do that, sir. It's full of bugs, might make you sick and you'll get that nice suit dirty!'

Daniel was becoming increasingly frantic. Ed tried not to smile. He thought that it was appropriate that he should nearly become too curious, so that Daniel would have no idea that he was entering a trap.

Ed reeled away in disgust and looked back at Daniel.

'Yeah, you're right. You guys're doing a great job. Let me know when the truck's ready and I'll clear it through security.'

As he walked away, he could sense Daniel's relief. Enjoy while it lasts, pal, Ed thought. Tomorrow will be a different story altogether!

*

Justin returned to Buffalo Hills a little after four. He anxiously checked to see if Ed had arrived back early, but his vehicle was not there. Relieved, Justin hurried to the reception desk and spoke to the receptionist.

'Hi there! Say, my brother hasn't gotten back yet has he?'

'No, sir' the young blonde replied. 'He only gets here about five thirty.'

Justin paced up and down, looking irritable for a few moments, before turning back to her.

'Ed's got a phone number in his diary that I need urgently. D'you think...'

The receptionist thought about it for a moment, then said 'Will you wait a moment, sir.'

She called Rob's office but he was out and Don was nowhere to be found at that moment.

'Can't it wait until your brother gets home, sir? I'm really not allowed...'

At that moment Justin saw one of the cleaning ladies crossing the patio.

'No hassle' he said. 'I'll catch him later.'

Justin hurried outside. He had seen a way to get around the hotel's excellent security system. It was imperative that he get into Ed's room before he returned. He caught up with the cleaning lady whom he knew worked on both his and Ed's room every day.

He smiled at her. 'Afternoon, Sophie, can you help me with a problem please?'

'Yes, sir, I'll try.'

Justin scratched his head and looked really worried.

'My brother who is in room 22, has lost his car keys at work. He's got a spare set in the room and he wants me to fetch them for him. If you open his door, you can watch to see that I take nothing else.'

Sophie thought about this. She knew the two brothers and as Justin had just said, she could watch him and make sure he only touched the keys. It made sense to her. Sophie led the way and Justin was soon let into Ed's room with the master key. He quickly went to the drawer where he knew Ed kept the spare keys, took them out and thanked Sophie, as he dashed back to the car park. He realised that he had opened a potential can of worms by his actions, but he needed the keys for his plan.

He leapt into his hired car and drove at high speed into Rustenburg where he had already found a locksmith who would help him with duplicates. The trouble was that the man would close his shop at 5pm and would not wait for him. As he drove, Justin realised that he made a lousy crook. He should never have spoken to the receptionist about Ed's diary. He felt he could handle Sophie when he got back by saying that he had misunderstood his brother and was returning the keys. He thought he might try a variation of his pretended embarrassment with Sam Mohale that morning and ask Sophie not to mention anything to Ed but that would have to wait. Meanwhile he had to get to the locksmith in time and get the keys back before Ed got back.

*

Ed returned to the hotel and had in fact beaten Justin's return with the keys by a matter of minutes. Luckily for Justin, Marius was on the patio with an elderly gentleman, whom he was hoping to introduce to Ed.

'Hi Marius' Ed greeted his friend warmly.

He always enjoyed their chats and he welcomed the opportunity to take his mind off the great platinum sting, which he had found to be increasingly nerve-wracking.

Marius introduced his guest as Lionel Wulfsohn, a lifelong resident of Rustenburg who had written the definitive book on the Anglo-Boer War in the region called 'Rustenburg at War.'

'Glad to meet you, sir' Ed shook the man's hand.

At 91 years old, Lionel was an alert and sprightly gentleman from another era. Marius had told him about Ed and his growing interest in his possible Afrikaner heritage, as well as the remarkable history of the very valley in which Buffalo Hills was situated.

'I believe Marius has given you an outline of the Battle of Buffelspoort' Lionel said.

'That's right. We were going to get into more detail, but current events seem to overtake us every time we get together.'

Ed recalled the dramatic evening at Karl's Bauernstube Restaurant with Marius, where he had met Elke for the first time and had joined her in helping to save the life of the man who had had a heart attack that night. The subsequent events of September 11th and, later, Justin's arrival in South Africa had driven most thoughts of local history from his mind.

Chatting to Lionel, Ed resolved to learn more about these dynamic, often stubborn, and enormously talented people, who had fought a bitter war of survival against the might of the British Empire. This was something which many Americans readily understood. The later aberrations of the Afrikaners' Apartheid policies was something else again but now having met a number of them, he had come to the conclusion that the majority were decent human beings who had been caught up in the fanatical obsessions of the ruling party. Ed was delighted when Lionel gave him an autographed copy of his book, which he vowed to read as soon as possible.

Justin had arrived back at the hotel by then. He had found Sophie, returned the keys, played idiot younger brother who had got it all wrong and had gotten Sophie's giggling agreement to keep quiet about it. To his enormous relief, the receptionists had changed shifts so everything was on track for that night.

Justin peered out of the sitting room windows and saw Ed deep in conversation with Marius and Lionel. Talk, big brother, he thought gleefully. Pretty soon your world will turn upside-down and you'll wish you'd had the sense to hand over the Willjohn shares to me. Justin's eyes held that insane look that Ed had grown to fear over the years. Had he seen Justin at that moment, he would have known that serious trouble was coming his way.

CHAPTER 27

'You'll find the book fascinating'

Marius was referring to the copy of *Rustenburg at War* which Ed now held in his hands.

'But while you've got the author captive, so to speak' Marius grinned, 'I'd like him to tell you something about the second battle which took place at the top of this valley – the Battle of Nooitgedacht!'

Ed turned to Lionel, who nodded thoughtfully then took a sip of tea before responding.

'I believe Marius has given you the story of the Battle of Buffelspoort at the bottom end of the valley when the Boers captured 138 British supply wagons on December 3rd, 1900.'

'Yeah,' Ed replied, 'he drove me through the valley and pointed out the exact spots where the fighting took place. It was great.'

Marius smiled in acknowledgement of the compliment. Lionel continued in the measured tones of an historian trying to précis the huge mass of data at his disposal.

'Ten days later on December 13th, the Boers and the Brits were involved in one of the most intense battles of the war. After some months of virtual peace in the area, the capture of British supply wagons at Buffelspoort had stirred up a hornet's nest. This battle was called "Clements se Slag," by the Boers because of the hiding handed out to General Clements, who had left Krugersdorp with a force of 1500 men and 9 field guns, which included a 4.7-inch naval gun, also known as the cow gun, that particularly worried the Boers. Clements entered the Moot at Skeerpoort, which I believe you know is on the other side of the mountains from this valley.'

'I've been given a guided tour...' Ed began.

'...by the best-looking guide in the district, Elke Stein' Marius added mischievously.

Lionel nodded. He had been born in Rustenburg 91 years previously, the son of a Lithuanian Jewish trader who had known many of both the Boers and Brits involved in the conflict personally. He knew the Stein family well. Lionel had fought with the South African forces in North Africa in World War II, which had whetted his appetite for military history over a period of years. His interest in the first and second Anglo-Boer Wars, particularly in the Rustenburg region which had always been his home, led to the writing of the definitive book on the subject.

'I didn't know she was taking tours around here' he said mildly.

'Only very exclusive ones,' Ed chuckled. 'I was her only customer.'

Lionel smiled back. 'You're a lucky young man. She's a lovely girl. Anyway, General Clements adhered strictly to the British scorched-earth policy of the time. He captured cattle, destroyed crops and burned farmhouses as he worked his way up the valley. He finally pitched camp at a lovely farm called Nooitgedacht which literally translates as "Never thought of" at the foothills of the mountains immediately above him on the North side.'

'If you drove out of the hotel and took the road to Breedtsnek, which is still in poor condition unfortunately, you would look down on Nooitgedacht' Marius added, to give Ed a sense of geography.

'Clements chose the farm for two reasons. He planned to place a heliography station on the mountain's crest above him, which would be able to communicate with Rustenburg about 35 Kms to the North-West.'

Lionel looked at the young American questioningly for a moment.

'D'you know what a heliograph is?'

'I think so.' Ed replied 'It was a system of reflecting sunlight off mirrors to signal anyone in a direct line of sight. A darn sight cheaper than cell phones!'

'Provided you had sunlight, it was excellent.' Lionel replied. 'Anyway, the second reason for choosing Nooitgedacht was the beautifully clear stream which ran through the property directly from the mountains above, which would assure his men a good supply of fresh water.'

*

As the three men chatted together on the patio, Justin still had things to do in order to carry out his "sting" on top of the sting prepared by the Premier Platinum management.

He left the hotel again and drove to a pre-arranged rendezvous with Bud McNeil, which was well clear of the area where Daniel and his men were feverishly using welding torches to crudely process the platinum from precipitate.

*

'In fact,' Lionel told the others, 'Clements' choice of camp was disastrous, but he probably underestimated the Boers' will to attack after so many months when they had lain low as a force. The recent capture of the British supply wagons had come as a shock and was in fact the main reason for Clements' move into the area, with the intention of clearing the Magaliesberg Mountains of all Boer resistance.'

'General De la Rey and his able subordinate, Smuts, had prudently moved to the southern side of the Moot and were hidden in the next wave of mountains which separate Krugersdorp from the Moot.'

Ed, despite his concerns about the exciting operation taking place at that moment, found himself becoming more and more engrossed in Lionel's tale of past warfare. The fact that Ed could now visualise the positions of the different forces in the nearby mountains and valleys, made it all the more intriguing.

'Did De la Rey and Smuts have enough men to take on Clements?' Ed asked.

The old historian nodded. 'It was always considered that they could have taken the English on their own but as it happened General Beyers was on his way to Krugersdorp with a large force, arriving at Breedtsnek on the top of the mountain on the evening of the 12th December. Incredibly the men of the Northumberland Fusiliers, who were stationed on the crest of the mountain and who supplied heliograph communication between the British garrison in Rustenburg and General Clements, did not think it necessary to tell Clements about Beyers' arrival.'

'When Clements finally heard about Beyers later that night, he consoled himself by thinking that General Broadwood's 2nd Cavalry Brigade were nearby and would protect his northern flank. However, Beyers had cleverly told a local African chief, Koos Managalie, that he intended to defend Olifantsnek, some 25km to the west of Breedtsnek, knowing that the chief was secretly on the side of the British. This information reached General Cunningham in Rustenburg, who told Broadwood to try and intercept Beyers. Thus Broadwood made camp near to the village of Kroondal very close to Olifantsnek and nowhere near the area where Beyers had made camp for the night.'

'So much of this reminds me of the American Civil War,' Ed commented, 'with troops waiting in ambush in one place while the enemy was heading in the opposite direction.'

Lionel Wulfsohn looked up at the sky, which told him that the sun was already setting.

'Regretfully I must also head in the opposite direction and go home' he said. 'I don't drive after dark.'

'When can we get the next episode, Mr Wulfsohn?' Ed asked.

'Read the book, pal!' Marius interjected. 'It's all there.'

As the historian said his goodbyes, Ed had one more question. 'I'll read the book, I promise, but please tell me, what happened to Clements?'

Lionel sighed. 'Greed is a terrible thing. If the Boers hadn't decided to enjoy the fruits of victory after driving Clements to a nearby kopjie called Yeomanry Hill and then spend too much time looting his camp, they would very likely have either captured or killed most of his men. In the event, after defending Yeomanry Hill with the famous naval gun, which the British managed to rescue from their camp at Nooitgedacht, Clements eventually retreated East along the Moot to the British garrison at Rietfontein. The Boers failed to destroy the British forces but at least were left to loot large quantities of supplies left behind by Clements' men.'

Lionel shook Ed's hand but the old gentleman still had the last word.

'The Boers would've achieved a far greater victory if they had not stopped to enjoy the loot. You must remember though, they were mostly unpaid volunteers who knew that even if they captured the British troops, they would have to let them go again. The Boers had no facilities for prisoners of war, so there was a far greater motivation to enjoy the supplies left behind by the British than to pursue the British themselves. You can hardly blame them.'

After Lionel left, Marius stayed for a few more minutes. He could not resist asking Ed what was happening with Elke. Ed grinned at his friend.

'I've asked her to marry me!'

Marius shook Ed's hand delightedly.

'I'm really pleased for both of you, ou maat. I think you'll make a great couple!'

Marius picked up his glass of wine and toasted the future Willjohns.

'Where're you thinking of living, here or there?'

Ed shrugged. 'Look, we've talked about it, Marius. as you know, I love it here but there could be complications. What I've thought of doing is to try and provide some financial stability for their farm.'

'Could you do that?' Marius asked, unaware of Ed's actual financial status.

'I think so' Ed replied thoughtfully. 'I don't have that much ready cash but I'm working on something.'

Marius wished Ed all the best and set off home. Ed discovered from Reception that Justin had gone out again. He hoped that he would not be called out in the middle of the night to collect his young brother from another night of drunken mayhem. Other than that, Ed decided that it was a relief not to have to speak to Justin. In fact, the less he saw of him before the youngster left for the US, the better.

Ed had dinner then retired for the night, looking forward to reading the chapter on General Clements in Lionel's book.

Justin returned to the hotel about an hour after Ed had gone to bed. Justin was equally thankful that he did not have to speak with his brother. He still had the most important part of his scheme to carry out.

*

Ed was dreaming of Elke and him riding together in the mountains above the farm. Ed had just picked a glorious blossom from a tree on the hillside and was on one knee proposing to Elke all over again, when there was an insistent ringing of a telephone. Elke irritably took a cell phone out of her pocket and said 'That'll be Ma checking up on us again.'

The ringing continued and for a moment Ed lay in that strange halfway state between waking and sleeping as he began to realise that his room telephone was actually ringing. Bloody Justin, he fumed, as he stretched across and picked up the phone.

'Hello' he croaked, still half asleep.

'Is that Ed?' A strange male voice asked.

'Yes' said Ed, now fully awake.

'Martin Gericke asked me to call you.'

'Yes, and who're you?' Ed asked.

'Johnny' the man replied. 'Listen, I can't talk. Martin told me to tell you that there's a problem with the operation. He wants you down here right away!'

'Okay.' Ed replied dubiously. 'Tell me where here is and why can't Martin speak to me himself?'

'He's watching the men processing the platinum.' Johnny replied. 'He told me to get out of earshot and call you.'

'Mmmm...' Ed mumbled, already fumbling for his clothes. 'So, tell me where you are.'

*

Just before she went to bed, Elke popped her head into the TV room to see Isak. It saddened her that her father, who was until quite recently an active man, should now watch the television that he had despised for so many years. Isak was dozing but he heard Elke come in. He smiled at his daughter.

'Time for me to go to bed, hey!' he spoke tiredly.

Elke shrugged. 'That's not why I'm here, Pa. You must go when you want to go.'

'You want to talk about your young man, I suppose?'

Elke nodded and stepped forward to turn the sound of the TV down.

Elke briefly told her father about Ed's proposal. She also explained that they had spoken at length about the future. Ed had made it clear that he was quite interested in remaining in South Africa, if he could make it work. He had spoken of possibly going farming himself. He was hoping

166

for something to develop in that regard shortly.

'Where would he get the money if he doesn't have any back home?' Isak queried.

'I don't know, Pa, but I do know that Ed'll do everything he can not to upset you and Ma.'

'I hope so, for your mother's sake' Isak replied, as he prepared to get up from the TV and go to bed.

*

Ed drove his SUV slowly along the bumpy gravel road towards the point where the man called Johnny had told him that he should meet Martin. For the last few hundred yards, Ed travelled without headlights. There was a nearly full moon in the sky above and Ed found it quite easy to do once his eyes had become accustomed to the semi-dark.

Ed hoped that the sting had not gone completely wrong. Johnny had only repeated that it was important that Ed come right away. He had refused to give details. Ed was determined to play his part in the operation no matter what it took. He had enormous respect for both Sam and Martin and wanted to be fully accepted by them.

Ed stopped the vehicle at a turnoff as instructed. He got out of the vehicle and made his way quietly down to the road. He came over a rise and saw the dark shapes of a number of long low buildings in the moonlight. Johnny had told him that Martin would flash a torch three times every ten minutes from a small hill on the far side of the buildings. Ed was to make his way towards the torchlight, where Martin would meet him and brief him on what he was needed for. Johnny had also told Ed that if the torch did not flash after the American had been there for over twenty minutes, he was to return to the vehicle and await developments.

Twenty-five minutes later Ed returned disconsolately to his SUV. There had been no flashing torches, nor any sign of life.

As he stretched out his hand to open the vehicle's door, a blinding light from a number of powerful flashlights focused on his face.

Ed froze, as a guttural voice called out. 'Don't move. Put your hands up.'

Ed slowly raised his hands and tried to make out the faces of a number of men behind the lights. He could make out no details beyond the unmistakable glint of a couple of rifle barrels as some of the light spilled onto the metal.

'Who in the hell're you guys?' Ed asked then gasped as someone he knew well stepped into the light.

CHAPTER 28

The buzzer rang on the security gate. Bud had fallen asleep in front of the television set. He awoke with a start, completely disoriented. Then he remembered. With an effort he got up and went over to the gate buttons next to the front door. He cleared his throat.

'Who's that?'

'Simon' a harsh voice rasped back at him. Bud looked at his watch. 'Why in the hell are you so late? Come on in.' He pressed the buzzer, then went over to a sideboard and poured himself a shot of neat whisky before going over to the front door and opening it.

A battered old bakkie wheezed its way up the drive and stopped outside the front door. The huge bulk of Simon emerged from the driver's seat, rather like a large cork from too small a bottle.

Simon flashed a perfect set of white teeth at the little white man. Simon was a nearly two metres tall African of indeterminate origin. After a nomadic childhood in the Congo, he had wandered south and entered South Africa illegally. His great size and strength had led him to try and become a professional boxer but opportunities for black athletes of any kind were still limited in the late Apartheid years. Besides, he lacked the coordination and speed to go very far. After a couple of severe beatings by smaller and faster men, he had given up boxing and become a miner. Today he was accepted as a Zulu, but those who spoke the language well, knew that his origins were elsewhere.

Simon reached back into the bakkie and pulled out a rucksack. Bud watched him silently and then stood back to let the giant through the front door. Bud had no scruples about his double-cross on the earlier double-cross initiated by Justin, but he was anxious that no one should connect him to any of it.

Bud handed Simon a can of beer then nodded at the rucksack that the big man had dumped unceremoniously on the floor.

'How much?' Bud asked.

Simon opened the beer can and swallowed most of it in one thirsty gulp before replying.

'About two kilos.'

'Shit! You didn't take it all did you?' Bud asked, horrified.

Simon shook his head. 'No, they took a lot out. The tank they put it in was big.'

Bud nodded thoughtfully. When he had done the deal with Justin, it had occurred to him that for the American's purposes, the quantity of platinum did not matter.

Bud had arranged for Simon to get a job with Premier Platinum shortly after he had set up the first platinum theft with Daniel. Bud was a great believer in not letting the left hand know what the right hand was doing. Simon was there simply to watch Daniel and make sure that Bud's interests were looked after. Bud and Simon had done a number of deals over the years. The big man asked no questions and as long as he was well paid, he always carried out Bud's instructions to the letter.

Today's instructions had been simple. Take a quantity of platinum from the place where they were crudely refining it from the precipitate and bring it to Bud, who would then sell it as arranged. He could not resist the idea of grabbing a bonus for himself in addition to the million dollars he was due from Justin.

'Why're you so bloody late?' Bud growled as Simon swallowed the last of the beer.

Simon laughed. 'That Daniel, he tell me to help clean up afterwards. I had to stay, in case.'

Bud nodded. 'You sure no one saw you take the stuff?'

Simon nodded. 'For sure, Boss. I stop and wait, maybe half hour on the road. Nobody followed me!'

Simon eyed another beer. Bud picked up a can and lobbed it across to Simon, who caught it clumsily, opened it and started pouring the contents down his throat.

He looked up at Bud who had opened the rucksack and was eyeing the platinum appreciatively.

'I go now?' Simon asked. Bud shook his head.

'No, Simon. There'll be big trouble at the mine. You stay here for a few days. I'll get you another job soon. Anyway,' he grinned 'you may want to take a long holiday with the money you'll be getting from this.'

Bud was still weighing up the pros and cons of what to do with Simon. It all depended on the repercussions at the mine. It would be a great pity if he had to get rid of the big man permanently. He had been very useful in the past. Then again, Bud was always the supreme pragmatist.

Ed swung around in amazement as five or six Policemen, headed by Martin Gericke, walked into the light and pointed guns at him.

Martin's face reflected his fury at the discovery of Ed, of all people, in the very place and time they were expecting 'Mr Big' of the platinum heist.

'What's going down?' Ed asked nervously. 'I got your message...'

'What message?' Martin asked coldly.

Ed felt himself go numb. It was a set-up. Could Martin be involved? He doubted it. The Police Officer in charge spoke politely but firmly to him.

'Sir, we'd like to have a look in your vehicle, please?'

Ed shrugged 'Sure!'

He had nothing to hide but his mind was racing. Who had done this to him? The obvious candidate was his delightful brother but Ed could not figure out how his sibling could have found out about the platinum sting. His mind dwelled momentarily upon Marie who clearly wanted him well out of Elke's reach but he rejected that thought as fast as it occurred to him. He remained convinced that she was a decent woman fiercely protecting her family and in no way would she do something as extreme as this.

The Police were swarming all over his SUV. To his dismay he saw that they were pulling the side panels away to look inside the gap between the panels and the vehicle's body. They really meant business.

'Martin' Ed began. 'How could you think...'

'What're you doing here, Ed?' Martin interrupted bluntly.

'I told you, I got a message.'

'Who from?' Martin asked.

'I don't know. Some guy who said you couldn't talk because you were watching the platinum being processed. I guess in those sheds over there. He said you'd asked him to get me here as soon as possible and that there was a problem.'

As Ed spoke, he realised that the whole thing sounded lame, even to him. He cursed himself for not being alert enough to smell a rat.

'That's crap and you know it, Ed,' Martin spoke grimly. 'Let's see what they come up with.'

At that moment there was a triumphant shout from one of the Policemen. Ed watched in horror as the man held up a plastic bag wrapped around something that looked suspiciously like a few ounces of semi-refined platinum.

*

Justin was getting very drunk. In his travels earlier in the day, he had bought a bottle of Jack Daniel's and had left it in his room to savour in those hours when he knew he would not sleep but would be waiting anxiously for some news of Ed's arrest. He knew it would be fatal to try contacting any one of the players in the game and yet he was aching to talk to somebody, anybody - even his mother! With an unsteady hand he picked up the phone and dialled. It would still be early evening in Minneapolis.

'Hi Mom' he crooned into the mouthpiece.

There was a long pause before his mother answered.

'Justin, is that you?'

'Right on,' he answered. 'Thought I'd remind you that I'll be home in three days.'

'I don't need reminding, Justin' his mother replied irritably. 'It sounds as though you've been drinking again. I hope you're not causing your brother any more trouble. He told me about your ridiculous adventure at the Casino. Justin, when you get home, we're going to have to...'

'Yeah, yeah, I guess his version makes it sound like I was Al Capone.'

'We'll discuss it when you return, Justin. Now's not the time. How's Ed? Is he with you?'

'Ah, concern for the favourite son. None for the prodigal. All that can change, Mom!'

'What're you saying?'

Damn, he'd said too much already, Justin realised.

'No Mom, I meant to say that I'm determined to change, when I get home.'

'I hope so, honey.' his mother replied. 'I do hope so. We're all very worried about you.'

Not half as worried as you're going to be over Ed, Justin thought as he said good night and rang off. As he reached for the bottle again, it dimly occurred to Justin that he was just lousy at keeping secrets, especially when it prevented him from boasting about his little moments of genius.

*

The holding cell in the Rustenburg prison was not a nice place to be, Ed thought grimly. He knew that the following day, he would be facing charges as the prime suspect in a major platinum robbery. He had had a few sleepless hours to reflect upon his position. He was a foreigner with no knowledge of South African laws. He did not know any lawyers and although he had a number of good friends, how would they respond to the facts? Ed had watched speechless as about half a kilo of semi-refined platinum had been removed from his SUV. It had been found in a space between the side panel of the passenger door and the metal of the door itself.

How in the hell had it gotten there, he wondered? His SUV was either parked in his own parking place at the Mine or at Buffalo Hills Hotel. He always locked it and always kept the keys with him.

First things first. He had realised that he needed to find a good lawyer and, if possible, get out on bail as fast as he could. He then needed to figure out how he had been set up and by whom. The next step was to prove it. The more he thought about it, the more he was certain that Justin was the culprit, so he had to establish that Justin knew about the sting before he did anything else.

There was only one way he could think of that Justin could have learned about the operation, Sam must have told him, not realising how much Justin despised Ed. He had never mentioned to Sam that Justin was a twisted, probably psychopathic, person intent on destroying him. It was not the kind of thing that one generally told people about your brother. The only person who had any idea of how evil Justin could be was Elke. Ed had even been reluctant to tell her the full extent of Justin's aberrant behaviour.

The lawyer he needed to find would have to be really excellent. That could only be achieved through one of the people he knew well. It came down to Elke, Rob, Marius or possibly Sam himself. Even though Sam and he were on opposite sides of the fence on this issue, Ed would rather try for the help of the Premier Platinum's boss over the others. There were two reasons for this, the first being that it would keep the matter in-house and the second was that Ed was convinced that Sam was the key to connecting Justin to what was proving to be a terrible situation for himself. It was a situation that threatened everything Ed was hoping to establish in South Africa. His future wife, a growing circle of friends and his acceptance in a close-knit community would all be destroyed forever if there were even the slightest doubt that he was involved in the platinum thefts.

*

Elke called Ed's office just after 8.30am. The receptionist told her that Ed had not yet come in but she would put Elke through to Mr Gericke who may know of Ed's movements.

As she waited to be connected to Martin, Elke remembered that her mother either knew the man or was distantly related to him somehow. Elke had not actually met him, but Ed clearly thought highly of the mine's Senior Engineer.

'Gericke wat praat' Martin answered the phone in Afrikaans, which was the language spoken by the majority of whites in the area.

Elke responded in the same language. 'Mr Gericke, you don't know me but I'm Ed's fiancée. Do you know when he'll be coming in?'

There was such a long pause that Elke was about to ask whether Martin was still on the line, when Martin replied awkwardly.

'Miss Stein, there's been some trouble. Ed's down at the Rustenburg

Police Station at the moment.'

'Oh, when d'you think he'll be finished? I was hoping to see him later.'

Again, that long silence. Elke began to get an uneasy feeling.

'Look, Miss Stein, I think you should know that Ed's being questioned about the theft of platinum from our mine. It doesn't look good, I'm afraid, there's some evidence...'

'Oh no!'

Elke's mind immediately recalled Ed telling her he was working on a way to acquire a lot of money with which to buy a farm, but, no! She would not doubt him again.

'That's ridiculous,' she managed to say.

'I hope you're right' Martin responded. 'I like Ed very much, but I have to tell you that the evidence looks quite damning for him.'

There was a strangled gasp on the other end of the phone and the line went dead. Martin shook his head despondently. He was being truthful when he said that he liked Ed, but Martin did not appreciate being made a fool of. If Ed were guilty, Martin would personally see to it that he was put away for a very long time.

*

Ed was in the process of trying to get the Policeman who had delivered some very basic food and a mug of tea to him, to call an Officer to his cell, when the Captain in Charge approached with a grimfaced Sam Mohale.

Sam and Ed eyed each other for a long time, each man trying to weigh up how to approach the issue. The Captain motioned to the Constable to open the cell door. Sam stepped inside and continued to stare at Ed, who took a deep breath and began.

'Sam, I'm not going to start yelling about my innocence, although I promise you I am. I need to be represented by a good lawyer and I need to ask you an important question which will help me establish how I think I've been set up. You and I are on opposite sides here which distresses me more than you'll ever know.'

There was a pause. Sam said nothing and remained staring at Ed without emotion. Ed concluded with the question.

'Despite our situation, will you help me with these two things?'

It was not an easy decision for Sam, but finally he gave Ed the answer that would determine whether, or not, the young American could start to unravel the puzzle that threatened to change his life forever.

CHAPTER 29

Elke drove towards Rustenburg with her mind in turmoil. How could Ed have been arrested on suspicion of being involved in platinum thefts? As she asked herself that question another awful thought crossed her mind. It was an unwelcome thought and she tried to suppress it, but it would not go away. The one thing that seemed to remain a mystery with Ed, was his financial position. From what Justin had said to her mother, Ed had no assets other than his job at Premier Platinum. What if? Elke tried to shut the thought out. What if he had been so desperate to get money that he had planned to steal the platinum as a means of buying a farm for the two of them? It seemed out of character for the man she loved but she had to admit that she really did not know that much about him.

As Elke headed along the main street of Rustenburg, which could be loosely translated as the Town of Rest, she felt anything but restful but nevertheless was determined to stand by her man. Perhaps she would now think of the place as the Town of Arrest, she thought wryly, as she prepared for any surprises which might lie ahead.

*

Sam considered all his options. The sensible thing to do would be to let Ed sort out his own defense and remain neutral until the young American were found either guilty or innocent. But Sam could not ignore the fact that Ed had proved to be a valuable member of the mine's management team. They had become friends. All his instincts told him that Ed was entirely innocent, but the facts suggested otherwise. He made his decision and looked intently at Ed.

'I'll have a good lawyer contact you this morning but that's as far as I can go.'

'Thanks, Sam,' he said gratefully. 'I know that was a tough one. I won't let you down, promise!'

Sam turned to go but Ed spoke again.

'Sorry Sam, there's also the other question I need to ask.'

Sam looked back uncertainly. He hoped that Ed was not about to take too much advantage of their friendship under the circumstances.

'Sam, did my brother Justin know what was going on with the platinum theft?'

'What's that got to do with anything?' Sam queried.

Ed paced up and down the floor of the cell.

'I really need to know this, Sam!'

Sam nodded. 'The night I called to see you at the hotel, you were out with your girlfriend...'

'Called to see me? I didn't know.'

Sam frowned. He suddenly had an uneasy feeling in his stomach.

'Didn't Justin give you my message to be in the office early? You were in early anyway, so I presumed.'

'He never said a thing to me' Ed stated. 'Did you tell him anything?'

Sam nodded, looking uncomfortable. 'He's your brother. We had him round for dinner. I like him. He's different from you but he seems like a good guy!'

'That's the darned problem!' Ed responded. 'But please tell me, Sam, did you give him some idea of what we were trying to do?'

Sam looked down. He was suddenly extremely embarrassed. There had been no reason to speak so freely to Justin and in fact it was out of character for Sam who was usually a prudent and sensible businessman. He looked up again. Ed was staring at him intently. His jaw was clenching and unclenching.

'What're you trying to tell me, Ed?'

The young man let out a long sigh and made a visible effort to regain control over his emotions.

'Sam, whether you believe me or not, I've been set up. I've spent many hours in this place trying to figure it out. It comes down to this. There's only one person that I know of who hates me enough to frame me and that's Justin!'

Sam looked completely crestfallen.

'If you're right, then I've landed you in this mess. I'm very sorry.'

Ed clapped Sam on the shoulder.

'Get me a good lawyer who can arrange bail and I'll have some proof on your desk within 48 hours.'

He chuckled without humour.

'My little brother's caused me more trouble than any other person in my life and yet when I thought he was dead in New York, I was distraught. Families!'

'I'd better get onto it then. Besides, if you *are* innocent then it means we still have to catch Mr Big.'

Sam turned and signaled to the guard to let him out of the cell.

*

Elke asked the Captain in charge of the C I D if she could speak to Ed. The Captain looked at her doubtfully.

'This isn't a railway station. You're the second person here to see him. You'll have to wait until he's been formally charged.'

Elke's eyes filled with tears.

'Captain, he's American. He doesn't know many people over here. He's going to need a lawyer.'

'His boss, who was just here, said he'll be sending a lawyer through this morning' the Captain replied sternly.

Elke attempted a smile.

'That's brilliant but, please, Captain, he's my fiancée. I know he's innocent!'

'They always are,' the Captain answered curtly, but Elke's glorious eyes had begun their magic. 'Okay then, but only five minutes.'

Elke was escorted to the holding cell, where a delighted Ed could hardly wait for her to be allowed inside. They embraced briefly, before the Sergeant told them to break it up. Elke looked at her man anxiously.

'What happened?'

'It's a long story, but Sam's getting me a good lawyer.'

'But isn't he the one that's pressing charges? I don't understand.'

'Listen, sweetheart, I've been set up! And I guess it's my genius brother again.'

'Surely he wouldn't do that?'

Ed shrugged. 'One of these days I'll give you the whole story, it's ugly, real ugly.'

'The Captain's only given me five minutes. What can I do to help?'

Ed thought for a few moments.

'Could you go to the hotel and speak to Rob, he knows that I've been having hassles with Justin? Ask him if he can give you, or my lawyer, a record of any phone calls Justin's made from the hotel over the past week.'

'D'you really think?'

'Look, Sam's just told me that Justin knew about the operation that was planned to catch the platinum thieves. I got a call late last night to go to where they were refining the stolen material to meet up with Martin Gericke who was waiting to catch the guy in charge.'

'But why do they suspect you?' Elke queried.

Ed grimaced. 'I went looking for Martin, didn't find him, came back to the SUV and was surrounded by cops fronted by Martin.'

'What did they do?'

'They searched the SUV and found some stolen platinum.'

Elke gasped. 'How did it get there?'

Ed shrugged. 'No idea. The SUV was locked. It has an alarm.'

Elke grasped his arm. 'D'you keep a spare set of keys?'

'Yeah,' he replied 'but they're in my...' Ed suddenly came alive, 'Hey! That's it!'

He grabbed Elke and kissed her before the guard outside the cell could react.

'You're a genius, babe!' The spare keys're in my room and Justin knows where they are. I once told him when I thought I'd lost my keys at work. I found my set and called him back, but I never moved the spare set.'

Ed suddenly became very thoughtful.

'So how do we prove that?'

'Fingerprints?' Elke suggested.

'Maybe. Tell you what, see if you can get Rob to go with you to the room. Take a plastic bag or something and without touching too much, use a pen to stick through the ring...'

'...and bag the evidence!' Elke finished for him.

'You've been watching too many cops and robbers on TV! But, yeah, and Elke,' he paused uncertainly; 'be very careful. Justin looks like a little lost angel but I have to tell you, I'm beginning to think that he's a genuine psychopath. Don't let him see you or Rob do any of this. He could be dangerous.'

The Captain approached the holding cell and signaled to the guard to open the door. Elke glanced up and nodded at the Policeman. She snatched a quick kiss from Ed before turning to leave.

'Elke!' Ed's voice was suddenly very serious. 'Have any doubts?'

She shook her head. 'Never again! Well, to be totally honest, it crossed my mind that you were looking for money with which to buy a farm, but I didn't seriously think...'

'You should've' Ed replied. 'You must question these things, even if you think that I'm Mr Nice Guy. Anyway, when I get out, I'll tell you how I'm gonna get the money for the farm. No way will it be with platinum!'

Elke waved as she left the holding cell. Once again, she decided that life with Ed was definitely not boring, but she had better help him stay out of jail or it would certainly be a lonely existence!

*

Bud McNeil was worried. The more he thought about his deal with Justin, the more he was concerned that the youngster did not have the experience to withstand intensive investigation. Nevertheless the million dollars had been a huge incentive and Bud had received confirmation that the money was sitting in an offshore trust, waiting to be released, as soon as Ed Willjohn was arrested and charged with the theft of the platinum. Simon had left the "refinery" site before there had been any sign of the cops but Bud had received a call early that morning from a well-paid connection in Rustenburg, confirming that Ed had been taken to the town's Police Station at about four in the morning.

The moment Ed was charged with the crime, the deal would be complete from Bud's point of view. Written proof of the charge would be faxed to the US and the money would be in his offshore account an hour later regardless of whether Ed was convicted, or not. This had been a potential deal breaker with Justin, but Bud had held out and finally won the point. He had argued that it could take months for Ed to come to trial. The key thing was to destroy Ed's reputation by having him arrested and charged with a serious crime. Justin was confident that he could pull off his boardroom coup on that alone. Bud hoped so, for the youngster's sake but by then the million dollars would be safely earning Bud compound interest and would serve as his retirement fund. Bud finished breakfast and called for Simon. He wanted the big man to help him with the capture and crating of two young Rhino. With any luck the platinum they had taken would be on its way within 48 hours.

*

Justin woke up with a terrible hangover. He had drunk the entire bottle of bourbon before falling into a drunken stupor. His last vaguely coherent thought, as he began to slide into oblivion, was that he was not designed for this frontline stuff. If he did anything like this in the future, he would remain in the safety of the penthouse he intended buying in New York and have his lackeys carry out the dirty work. As he clawed his way back to semi-consciousness and staggered over to the shower, he vaguely wondered how the news would be broken to him that his brother had been arrested.

*

Elke asked for Rob at the Reception desk of Buffalo Hills Hotel. She did not know him well but was aware that he was very friendly with Marius de Wet, whom Elke had known since childhood. Ed was confident that Rob would quickly see that it was Justin who had set everything up to ensnare Ed.

Rob came out of the office area and smiled at Elke. They shook hands.

'I believe congratulations are in order. Ed told me of your engagement.'

It is always an awkward moment Elke thought, when someone begins with good news and one is the bearer of bad tidings. Elke smiled.

'Thanks, Mr Schutte.'

'Rob, please!'

'Rob, I'm afraid we've got a serious problem. Ed's asked me to speak to you. Can I see you in private for a minute?'

Rob realised that the beautiful young woman was really upset. He nodded and led the way to an office in one of the buildings just outside the main hotel structure. As soon as they were seated, he looked at Elke anxiously.

'Something's seriously wrong, isn't it?'

Elke nodded and fighting back tears, she explained about Ed's arrest, his suspicions that Justin had set him up and his need for the phone records and his spare car keys to be finger-printed.

When Elke finished Rob sat for a few moments, thinking the whole thing through. Finally, he asked a question that he realised was bound to upset her.

'Are you completely convinced in your own mind that Ed's telling you the truth?'

Elke was taken aback. She stammered back 'Yes, of course. But I, I,'

Rob leaned forward and spoke sharply.

'I don't mean to upset you further but it's a very serious matter. I have to be certain that anything I do is correct, no matter how much I like Ed. If there're any doubts at all in your mind, I must consider whether I shouldn't wait for the Police or perhaps this lawyer who will represent Ed.'

'Please, Rob, we know that this is a lot to ask but Ed said that you were already aware that Justin is a loose cannon.'

Rob nodded. 'He certainly is, and I have to say that in the time that Ed's been at our hotel, I've come to regard him as a friend, not just a guest.'

Elke stared at him, her glorious large eyes filled with tears. How could he resist her?

Rob stood up. 'Right. I'll organise everything. I think it's better if I go into Ed's room on my own. Will you wait here, please?'

'Of course' Elke replied.

'Shall I send you some coffee, breakfast perhaps?'

Elke gratefully accepted the offer of coffee.

As Rob opened the door to the little office, Justin walked past on his way to breakfast. Justin forced a smile in Rob's direction, as his head threatened to fall off his shoulders from the terrible headache from his hangover. Then he saw something that created another intense emotion, overwhelming his current discomfort. For a split second, as Rob rapidly closed the office door behind him, he clearly saw the glorious blonde hair of Elke Stein and the girl's perfect features in profile. It was in that moment that Justin knew that he had once again failed to destroy his brother. Unless, unless! Justin knew suddenly that he would have to go for broke. Desperate times required desperate measures! Miserably he continued towards the dining room as he plotted his last throw of the dice.

CHAPTER 30

Justin entered the hotel's dining room with his mind in overdrive. Even the head waiter's usual courteous greeting was ignored as he sat down over a cup of strong black coffee and tried to work out what was happening. He also hoped that the coffee would begin to clear his fuzzy head. Damn fool, he thought bitterly, you never think ahead. If you hadn't been boozing all night, you'd be able to get your mind around the situation. He noted wryly that whenever he was angry with himself, the voices in his head spoke in the third person. When he was pleased with himself, the voices used the first person! This morning he was definitely not pleased with himself.

Justin went over to the buffet display and helped himself to two fried eggs, bacon and hash browns. 'What was Ed's girl doing at Buffalo Hills?' He asked himself over and over. One of his negative "worst case scenario" inner voices grumbled on and on about Elke coming to uncover all the things he had done over the past few days.

As he thought back, he realised that there were any number of things that could point the way to his involvement in Ed's arrest. Then another, slightly calmer, voice told him that the girl had probably heard about Ed's drama and had come over to enlist Rob's help. All along he had based his confidence in getting away with everything on the fact that Ed would have no reason to believe that Justin even knew about the sting involving the platinum thefts. If the management of Premier Platinum believed Ed to be the mastermind, he could not conceive of Sam speaking to Ed, let alone telling him that Justin knew about the thefts. The concept of real friendship and trust was so alien to Justin that he immediately began to feel better, believing that no one, not even Ed, would think that he had set up the double cross.

Feeling far more cheerful, Justin ate his food with relish. All the same, he wondered how soon he would be informed that his brother had been charged with stealing platinum.

*

It seemed like an eternity for Elke as she waited for Rob to come back to the office.

Elke was very much a woman of action. Doing nothing while the man she loved was in terrible danger of losing his freedom was intolerable for her.

She was about to throw caution to the wind and leave the office in search of Rob, when the tall Manager returned with a grin on his face. He was carrying two clear plastic bags, with Ed's car keys in one, and a drinking glass in the other. He had also collected a few pages of printouts from the Hotel's telephone records.

'Thank goodness!' Elke exclaimed. 'I've been going mad in here doing nothing!'

Rob nodded sympathetically. 'Sorry it took so long' he replied.

Elke was embarrassed. 'No, no, it's all in my mind, I'm sure.'

Rob waved his hand dismissing her apologies. Then he chuckled wickedly.

'I sneaked into Justin's room and "borrowed" his toothbrush glass for purposes of comparing fingerprints!'

He picked up the phone and dialled. Elke relaxed a little, Rob was clearly a well-organised person and she was very grateful that he was willing to make things happen.

'Sam Mohale, please,'

Rob's voice cut across her thoughts. For a moment Elke wondered why Rob was calling the man who headed up the mine that Ed had allegedly just robbed. Then she remembered that Sam had promised to appoint a lawyer to handle Ed's defense.

'Hello Sam, Rob Schutte here from Buffalo Hills hotel. Yes, you too. Look, I've got Elke Stein, Ed's fiancée with me. She's explained about Ed's er predicament. Yes, yes, I don't think so either. Anyway, I believe you're finding a lawyer, excellent! Sam, I need to contact him right away. We've come up with a couple of things here that indicate that Ed's brother may have set him up. Yes, he fooled all of us. Okay.'

Rob rapidly wrote down a number on a note pad. 'Thanks Sam, you must bring your wife to the hotel for dinner. We'll all have a celebration when this mess is cleared up. Thanks. Bye.'

Rob looked up at Elke, who returned his gaze anxiously.

'Sam's not pressing charges against Ed at this stage. He and Martin both feel that he has been set up. He's sent Brian Mouton, an attorney from Rustenburg, to the Police Station, to get Ed out of there.'

Elke's eyes moistened.

'Will Ed come here?'

Rob shrugged. 'Let's find out. I've been given Mouton's cell phone number. He's on his way over to the Police Station now.'

*

Justin's momentary feeling of reassurance had evaporated again. He sat fuming in his bedroom. He should have been contacted by Bud McNeil's connection in Rustenburg, with confirmation that Ed had actually been charged with the theft of the platinum. At which point he would instruct his lawyer in the US to release the million dollars held in trust for Bud. Justin was also beginning to wonder why no one from the hotel had spoken to him. Even if someone had simply enquired whether Justin knew why Ed had not returned to the hotel last night. None of the hotel's management had spoken to him all morning. Justin's nerves had reached breaking point. Impulsively he picked up the phone and dialled Bud's number.

After a few rings a woman's voice answered, 'Bud McNeil Game Farms.'

'Can I speak to Bud, please?' Justin asked her.

'Who shall I say is calling?' the voice asked him. Justin was outraged. 'Justin Willjohn.'

He had used his real name, which he had to give Bud once the deal had been arranged. How many times in a day did they receive a call from someone with an American accent? Surely the goddam woman could tell that the call was important, he thought with the arrogance of the First World believing he was in the Third World.

'Yes.' Bud's voice was flat and unfriendly.

'Have you heard anything?'

'The instructions are quite clear. He'll call you the moment it happens!'

Bud did not appreciate Justin making unnecessary calls to him.

'Okay, sorry, I guess I'm just getting over-anxious. Dunno what the delay could be.'

'Rustenburg's a small town. Things don't move as fast as they would in New York. Believe me I've got a big stake in this too. I need to hear that it's all happened but I'm used to the pace of things around here!'

Justin rang off, wondering whether he had any Bourbon left but then immediately decided that for once his inner comforts were going to have to take a back seat if he were to steer his way successfully through the minefield, largely of his own creation.

*

Rob said goodbye to the lawyer and put down the phone. He smiled at Elke.

'Brian says that you should bring the evidence to his office. He wants you to be there in half an hour.'

182

'And Ed?'

Rob smiled mischievously. 'Brian said that Ed might pop in to see you - if he's got time!'

Elke picked up the keys and the telephone accounts.

'He'd better! Thanks for your help, Rob!' She held out her hand.

Rob clasped it in both his hands. 'Good luck! He's a good guy. I'm sure it'll work out okay.'

Then Rob had another thought.

'Hang on a second.'

He picked up the phone again and dialled the number for Reception.

'Simone, did the younger Mr Willjohn ever ask you for the keys to his brother's room when you were on duty? He did!'

Rob looked at Elke excitedly then his face fell.

'No, you did exactly the right thing. You stuck to hotel policy. No, no problem at all.'

He put the phone down and shrugged.

'I suppose I shouldn't be disappointed that she applied our strict policy and wouldn't let him into anyone else's room.'

Elke nodded, also deflated. She was so certain that Justin would have used the spare keys.

'Thanks anyway, Rob. If Justin's finger-prints are on the keys, we'll still have something important.'

As she left, Rob was staring thoughtfully out of the office window.

*

Justin watched television. It was a re-run of one of the American soaps that graced South African screens every weekday evening. He barely heard the dialogue. What was wrong? They had to have charged him by now!

The ringing of the phone made Justin jump. He leaped up and took the call. It was Bud's nameless contact.

'That Mr Justin Willjohn?' a guttural voice asked.

'That's right' Justin replied, with a sinking feeling that what he was about to hear was not at all what he was expecting to hear. He was right!

'Mr Willjohn, your brother has just been released due to lack of evidence plus the fact that Premier Platinum have declined to press charges against him.'

Justin slammed the phone down in a fury. What had gone wrong? How could they let him go when he was caught red-handed with platinum in his vehicle? He stormed out of his room. His fury was building up to a point where he was in very real danger of having a complete psychotic break. He walked blindly down the driveway in front of the Reception area, with a vague idea of getting into his hired car and driving his anger away.

Then he saw Elke getting into her car some forty metres ahead of him. Instinctively Justin stepped off the road onto a pathway where he was hidden from Elke's sight.

His mind began to focus on the problem again. Suddenly he knew that he should follow Elke. No doubt she was going to meet Ed somewhere as soon as he was released but perhaps, a number of half-formed thoughts flashed through his mind. He shook his head to clear it. It was enough for now just to follow her. Justin was confident that he would find a way to take advantage of the present situation. Somehow, he would figure out a new angle.

As soon as he saw Elke's car move through the security gates at the entrance to the hotel, he moved rapidly towards his own car.

*

Elke drove straight to Rustenburg from the hotel. She was worried about her mother's reaction to the fact that she had scribbled a hurried note for her earlier that morning. As soon as she had phoned Premier Platinum and had discovered that Ed had been arrested, Elke had looked for her mother, discovered that she was out on the lands, written the note and fled. She had considered waking her father, but it would have upset him too much and she could not have spent any time with him to calm him down.

No matter how quickly the situation with Ed was resolved, Elke knew, with a sick feeling in her stomach, that her mother would use it as additional ammunition against her fiancé. The phrase "no smoke without fire" was something Elke had heard her mother say so often. Hopefully, if Justin were thoroughly discredited, at least her mother would stop making continued references to "that nice younger brother" and implying that Justin had given her a clear picture of the real Ed Willjohn.

As Elke parked outside the offices which housed the firm of attorneys Mouton, Zwane & De Klerk in the centre of Rustenburg, Justin parked his car further down the street and waited to see what would happen.

He could see that Elke had parked outside a firm of attorneys and he guessed angrily that Ed was inside with the lawyers. Justin felt nauseous. He had done many bad things in his life. It had always been a game to him. Somehow he knew, as he watched Elke walk into the building, that he had now crossed the line. This was serious stuff and if found out, he knew that his wealth and his family's position were unlikely to help him.

*

Without words, Ed and Elke embraced for a few moments before Ed broke free to introduce Elke to his lawyer, Brian Mouton. Elke was pleased with the slim dark-haired man of about thirty-five; he had a firm handshake, a direct gaze and a distinctly no-nonsense air about him. She handed him the plastic bags containing the spare car keys, the telephone records and the glass.

'I don't know if the keys'll be much use. The receptionist told Rob...'

Ed interrupted her, 'Rob called. The cleaning lady spoke to him. She was persuaded to help Justin. He insisted that she watch to see that he didn't take anything else then told her that he'd gotten the message wrong and would she please not tell me about it.'

'Justin's prints on the key would help corroborate her story.' Brian added. 'Looks promising. Let's see what we can find out from the phone records.'

After a few minutes Ed had confirmed that there had been a number of calls to the US in the past few days, whose numbers he did not recognise. There were others like his mother's, as well as calls to Willjohn Industries, that were known to him.

There were also some calls to local numbers in the Rustenburg district. One particular number Justin had called four or five times. It was also the first of the local calls he had made.

'Where do we go from here?' Elke asked. 'Can we find out whose numbers they are?'

'Tell you what' Ed suggested. 'I can do a great imitation of Justin's voice.'

He paused for a second then continued, sounding just like his brother.

'I don't know what that brother of mine's been up to, Officer but I guess you'd better lock him up an' throw away the key!'

Elke could not help laughing, despite the seriousness of the situation. Brian put his finger on the local number that had been most frequently called.

'Try that one' he instructed. 'Just wait while I set up a recording of it.' In a couple of minutes Brian was ready. Ed dialled the number.

'Bud McNeil Game Farm,' a woman's voice answered.

CHAPTER 31

Justin sat in his car impatiently drumming his fingers on the top of the dashboard. Elke had been gone for at least twenty minutes and there was no sign of either her or Ed. Justin made plan after plan as he waited. He even thought of going into the building, finding the two of them and pretending that he had just heard of Ed's arrest. The more he thought about it, however, the more certain he was that they were already trying to prove that he had set Ed up.

In the end, the best idea he could come up with was to hope that Ed had his vehicle with him and that he and Elke would drive off separately. He would then follow Elke and see if he could get to talk to her. He would know immediately if she suspected him even if she pretended not to, then he would see what he would do after that. He knew it was a feeble plan, but he could not think of a better one.

*

The name Bud McNeil meant nothing to Ed but using Justin's voice he asked to be put through to him.

'Oh, hello Mr Willjohn. I'll put you through.'

The girl obviously knew Justin's voice by now. After a few moments, a furious Bud came on the line.

'I thought you were just a dumb kid when I first met you, but greed dulls the senses and so I listened to you. You've now destroyed a sweet little operation I had going! You've put us at risk and your bloody brother's walking around a free man!'

'I'm trying to get things back on track' Ed replied, wondering where all this would lead him.

'Ja, well, you don't exactly fill me with confidence my friend. This is going to cost you!'

'What d'you mean?' Ed asked, wondering whether his brother was going to be on the wrong end of a contract on his life.

'Exactly one quarter of that million bucks will be paid into my Swiss account by the end of US banking time today. The other 750 grand you can keep unless you can get your brother back in jail, then our original deal would stand. If I don't get confirmation by tomorrow morning our time, you'd better find a good place to hide. I'll be coming after you. You can ask my friends. Bud McNeil doesn't mess around. I'll find you wherever you are!'

'That's a lot of money for no result,' Ed whined convincingly.

'It's pocket money when you consider that my platinum pipeline's been closed down for good,' Bud responded, conveniently ignoring the fact that he would probably make almost as much as he originally planned from the platinum Simon had rescued for him the previous night.

'I'll see what I can do,' Ed mumbled.

'You'd better' Bud growled and put down the phone.

The entire conversation had been heard through a speaker phone. Brian and Elke spontaneously applauded.

'I've heard of this guy' Brian said. 'He's a retired scrap metal dealer with a dubious reputation, who recently bought a game farm in the district. I believe he buys and sells animals all over the world.'

'Sounds like the Mr Big that Sam, Martin and I were hoping to catch.'

Ed looked questioningly at the other two.

'So, where do we go from here?'

The lawyer thought for a moment.

'I've got a lot of odds and ends to sort out here. I must get the fingerprint items to forensics, speak to Sam and so on.'

He looked at Ed and Elke sympathetically.

'The best thing both of you can do is to go back to work or get some sleep. I'll keep in touch.'

'What about this Bud McNeil guy and his threats?' Ed asked.

'Don't worry. I'll speak to the cops. I think they've been trying to nail him for a while now, so they'll be delighted. As far as your brother's concerned' Brian smiled, 'we'll have a word with him sometime today. I'd like to be certain that his fingerprints are on the keys before I speak to him.'

Brian could see that Ed was still worried.

'Ed, I know you won't want your brother taken out by a hit man no matter what he's done. If necessary, I'll have him put in protective custody. Later this afternoon, I might want you to call these US numbers and see if we can pin them down as well.'

Ed agreed to stay in touch. He and Elke thanked Brian for his help and left the office together.

In the lift to the ground floor they could not resist a passionate kiss, but their moment was spoiled by a prim and disapproving elderly woman who got into the lift on the next floor down.

'Are you going back to the hotel?' Elke asked, as they got out on the ground floor.

'No, there's too much to do. I need to get to the office right away. Will you go back to the farm? We'll talk again tonight.'

They hugged briefly then left the building. Ed's SUV was to the right and Elke's car was on the left. Elke strolled to her car feeling that she had been living in some kind of movie adventure. Surely real people didn't behave like this!

Justin almost changed his mind at the last moment to go after Ed instead, but sanity prevailed. If Ed knew or even suspected that Justin had set him up, his big brother would do something drastic, like have him arrested. No, it was surely better to try and talk to Elke. At least he could use the famed Willjohn charm with her.

Elke pulled out of her parking place. Justin followed at a discreet distance. Soon they were out of town and Justin realised that she was probably heading back towards her family's farm. He didn't know exactly where it was as previously he had only visited the Stein family from the other direction, but he did know that they couldn't be too far away from the place. In which case, he knew that he should try to stop her before she got there. Justin speeded up until he was close to Elke's car. Then it was just a matter of waiting until he had the opportunity to overtake her.

*

Brian Mouton took the spare car keys as well as the toothbrush glass to the forensic laboratory attached to the police station. He was quite friendly with Detective Superintendent Frederick September who had transferred up from Cape Town the previous year. He explained that he wanted to present evidence to Captain Wilkins which would hopefully prove that his client had been set up for a crime he had not committed. Frederick took the evidence and promised to give Brian an answer after lunch.

'Has this got something to do with the platinum thefts?'

Brian nodded. 'They arrested my client last night but Premier Platinum's refused to press charges. He's a mining consultant with them and they're inclined to believe his version.'

'Which is that he was set up?'

'Ja, by his brother, would you believe!'

Frederick shook his head sadly. 'Man, that's a sick thing to do!'

'Seems like it. I'll tell you all about it at the game on Friday.'

Frederick and Brian belonged to a small group who played snooker and sometimes pool together once a week.

Ed drove towards the mine. The road from Rustenburg remained on the almost flat plateau to the North of the Magaliesburg Mountains. Ed was constantly amazed at the gentle upward slopes of the mountains on the North side, which contrasted so completely with the rugged steep cliffs of the South side which overlooked the Moot.

He was tired but in many ways exhilarated. Ed had faced a number of crises in his young life. Most, but not all, were of his brother's making. As he drove along, savouring the ever changing faces of Africa and its ebullient rainbow people, he began to understand the depth of Justin's hatred for him. For a moment he wondered what he could have done to inspire such hatred but the answer, he was convinced, lay with Justin's own demons.

From childhood Ed was regarded by the family as the steady reliable son and Justin as the erratic, but sometimes brilliant, younger brother. Not long before he died, Ed's father had called him into his palatial offices at the Head Office of Willjohn Industries. He had sat Ed down and had spoken to him for a long time. The thrust of the conversation had been to try and persuade Ed to reconsider his decision not to work for the family business. Ed had gently but firmly remained true to his own ambitions.

'At least you've got two sons, Dad.' He had added 'Let Justin take over Willjohn Industries. I'd like to remain a shareholder and put in my two cents worth from time to time but Justin's the corporate animal, and I'm not, Dad. Sorry.'

Ed's father had nodded solemnly.

'I respect your decision, son, but it does put me in a spot. Justin's definitely not Chief Executive material. He's very bright, very charming, but there's something. I don't want to bad-mouth the kid to anyone, least of all you, but if I let Justin take over the helm here, this group won't last five years.'

Ed had looked at his father emotionally. Was he letting the old guy down? Should he sublimate his own ambitions and take over Willjohn Industries for the sake of the family?

As though reading his mind his father had continued.

'Don't take on a burden you don't have to, for my sake. Franklin's been my number two for over twenty years. He'd make a great CEO. He'd keep young Justin in line and see that he never wanted for anything. He'd also value your ideas and comments from time to time. We all think so highly of you around here but I'd rather you did what you feel you need to do, than suffer in a job that you never wanted. I just hope that Justin understands.'

Two weeks later Ed's father was dead and Justin never did understand. Ed had always known that Justin would be trouble for him, his mother and the business but he had never expected anything as psychotic as the events of the last couple of days!

With any luck, it'll soon be over and then I will have to decide how to deal with the kid, Ed mused as he passed a cheerful group of African school children walking back to their village along the main road.

*

Bud McNeil was still in a fury. He drove his workers mercilessly to prepare the two Rhino for transportation. He and Simon had already placed the platinum in the hollow poles of the cage but Bud felt a growing sense of foreboding. He could not believe that his normally sound instincts had betrayed him by listening to the youngster's crazy scheme. If he could get the Rhino and the platinum out of the country in time, he was pretty confident he could obfuscate the facts and evade prosecution. He had already decided that Justin would have to be silenced permanently. He just hoped that his threats earlier in the day would scare the kid into parting with the quarter of a million dollars prior to a timely accident.

Daniel would have to go as well, he realised. He could spill the beans better than anyone else. Then with this current shipment of platinum and hopefully Justin's money, he would leave South Africa and enjoy the peace and quiet of some Caribbean island.

South Africa might just be too hot for him but he needed between 24 and 48 hours to sort everything out before he took off to the other side of the world. It would be touch and go, he thought, but there was no way he would flee empty-handed.

*

Justin followed Elke's car around a gentle bend, then seeing that there were no vehicles in sight on the long straight ahead, he pulled out onto the wrong side of the road, accelerated and came alongside Elke's car.

Elke had not noticed Justin behind her. She had been too busy arranging the adventures of the last few hours in her mind and planning what to say to her parents. When Justin drew alongside, lightly touched the hooter and grinned at her, she got a terrible fright and nearly swerved her car into his.

Justin, still pretending to be friendly, indicated that Elke should stop. He signaled with his hands that he wanted to talk to her. This was so unexpected that for once Elke was in total panic. Should she stop and talk to him or should she ignore him and drive on? Her farm was only a couple of kilometres away. She had no idea what she could or should say to him, so she decided to play dumb and carry on. She tried not to look at Justin again and steadily accelerated.

Justin's fragile plan was beginning to unravel. He started to feel a grinding pressure on the sides of his head. His anger was building to

190

a terrible crescendo and in that instant Elke became the focus of all the failures and frustrations of the past twenty-four hours. The bitch was ignoring him! How could she do that? He was the charming irresistible one. He held the fate of both Ed and Elke in his hands. He was - omnipotent! He was both strength and retribution for these fools who would not listen!

Elke suddenly felt the savage impact of Justin's car crashing into hers, forcing her off the road. She looked across in terror and saw a raving maniac at the wheel of the other car. Justin was screaming at her and the world in general as he forced her car inexorably towards a deep irrigation ditch on the side of the road. Elke screamed. The world turned upside-down for her and then went mercifully black, without sound, without sight, without feeling.

Justin's almost euphoric emotion of complete hysteria was replaced by a sense of panic as he saw Elke's car slide off the road and crash heavily into the ditch. He slowed down, stopped and then slowly reversed back to the other car. As he drew alongside, he saw with shock that Elke lay inert, drooped over her steering wheel, with blood from a gash on her forehead dripping down her face. Dammit, Justin raged to himself, now I won't even get to talk to her!

CHAPTER 32

Ed tapped on the door of Sam's office, not knowing what kind of reception he would receive.

Sam's voice called 'Come in.'

Ed entered. As he had expected, Martin was in the office with Sam. Ed and Martin looked at each other. The Afrikaner reacted first. He got out of his chair and approached Ed with his hand extended.

'Sorry ou maat,' Martin said as they shook hands. 'I couldn't believe it when I saw you last night, but...'

'But you came to capture Mr Big and I was the only prospect around!' Ed chuckled.

Martin nodded. 'Ja, man, I was praying that we wouldn't find anything on you.'

'But you did, and the cops took me away,' Ed shrugged. 'That's the way it works.'

'Ja, but I should've...' Martin began.

'Should've nothing!' Ed replied firmly. 'You did the right thing and Sam here gave me the opportunity to prove I was innocent. I've got no beef with you guys. By the way, did Brian contact you?'

'He called five minutes ago,' Sam responded. 'He told us about the phone records and how you tried the local number.'

'D'you know this Bud McNeil guy?'

'Know him by reputation,' Martin chipped in. 'He's got a game farm about ten k's from my place on the Thabazimbi road.'

'What've you heard about him?' Sam asked.

'Not much. He bought the place a couple of years ago, buys and sells game for overseas.'

'Perfect for moving the platinum,' Ed murmured.

The others nodded as Martin continued. 'I know that the cops've been asked to keep an eye on him. Seems that he's been involved in some seriously shady deals in the past but nothing they could pin on him. Something to do with scrap metal.'

Well, we've got him!' Ed announced proudly. 'We recorded my call to him. He not only implicated Justin as the guy who set me up but also mentioned that his platinum pipeline had to close down!'

Sam shook his head sadly.

'Brian doesn't think it'll get a conviction. His lawyers can argue that the recorded call was entrapment and anyway, what's a platinum pipeline? We *think* we know but can we prove it?'

Ed nodded glumly then brightened.

'Okay, what if I can get Justin to testify against him in exchange for immunity from prosecution?'

'Could work' Sam answered thoughtfully. 'But I have to say that your brother deserves to be locked away as well.'

'Agreed.' Ed responded. 'I'll make sure he pays for this. He'll be stripped of his directorships of Willjohn Industries. I'll get the lawyers to tie up his money in a trust which'll give him a living wage, no more. Believe me, there's plenty we can do - and he knows it!'

'Where's he now?' Martin queried.

'Good question.' Ed was suddenly worried. It finally made sense to him that Justin was such a loose cannon that he needed to be contained immediately.

*

Justin rapidly pulled his car onto the side of the road and leapt out, rushing towards the inert figure of Elke, at the wheel of her car. His concern was directed entirely towards the fact that Elke, dead or unconscious, could not tell him what he wanted to know. He found her attractive but in his warped mind, any girlfriend of Ed's was damaged goods.

She was still breathing but was unconscious. Her glorious blonde hair was matted with blood where her head had struck the steering wheel. Not wearing a safety belt, he noted irritably, ignoring the fact that he rarely used one. Goody-goody brother Ed would never drive anywhere without buckling up, so Justin out of perversity invariably did the opposite.

'Elke!' Justin called her name sharply as he lifted her shoulders to lean her back in her seat. Her head flopped forward. She was totally out of it.

*

Sam, Martin and Ed discussed ways of putting Bud McNeil behind bars and, if possible, recovering some of the stolen platinum. Ed had tried to contact Justin at the hotel but had been told that his brother had gone out. Ed was hardly surprised, but his worry now was that if Justin should either call Bud or visit him, they would both realise that Ed and the others were on to them.

'I think we need to get the police to raid Bud McNeil's farm as soon as possible, in case he tries to hide all the evidence,' Ed suggested to the others.

'Agreed,' Martin replied. 'Brian Mouton's already working on getting a search warrant.'

'Hope it's not too late,' Ed was suddenly really anxious. 'Maybe I could go there and play dumb, say I'm looking for Justin?'

Martin shook his head.

'He's a tough cookie. The cops think he's had a couple of guys "whacked" in the past, as the Mafia calls it!'

Ed's thoughts were in a whirl. He was not a naturally aggressive person but if pushed hard enough, he was prepared to face anything within reason. His brother was the major target of his anger but his loyalty to Premier Platinum, especially to Sam and Martin, also meant that he would do whatever it took to bring Bud McNeil to justice.

He was acutely aware that Man's personal ethics and integrity had dwindled to almost nothing in virtually every corner of the world. When the moral fibre of nations was at such a low ebb, Justice tried to wield an even mightier stick than usual. When that stick was waved too often, people failed to be intimidated by it. Ed, who had an inbuilt sense of integrity, saw it as his duty to stop the bad guys wherever possible. It was not just his own sense of outrage over what had nearly happened to him. The man had to be arrested. Ed was on the point of telling the other two that he was going to confront Bud regardless of any danger, when the telephone rang. Sam picked it up, nodded and handed the phone to Ed.

'A Mrs Stein for you.' He put his hand over the phone for a moment. 'Doesn't sound like a happy lady.'

Ed looked at the phone with a sense of foreboding. The last thing he wanted was to make matters worse between Elke's mother and him.

Ed looked at Sam. 'Sorry, I'd better take it.' He put the phone to his ear. 'Yes, Mrs Stein?'

Marie's voice quivered with anger as she spoke to Ed. 'Where is my daughter?'

Ed was speechless. Elke should have returned home within half an hour of them parting at the most.

'She left me hours ago saying she was going straight back to the farm.'

As he spoke, he had visions of car wrecks and all kinds of terrible things that could have happened to the woman he loved.

'Well, she isn't here. She has a job to do, in case you didn't know that. I've already told her that I disapprove of her association with you, and if...'

Ed cut in, speaking urgently into the phone.

'Mrs Stein, I know how you feel about me. Now's not the time. I'm real anxious about your daughter too. Unless she went to the store, I know of

194

no reason why she's not back home with you right now!'

There was a silence as Marie digested this.

'Are you telling me that something may have happened to her?'

Marie's voice was suddenly uncertain, her anger evaporating as she realised that Ed was just as confused as she was.

'Please hang on a moment' Ed said into the phone. He looked up at Sam. 'Elke's gone missing. Can I go and look for her?'

'Of course,' Sam replied. 'Need some help?'

Ed shook his head then spoke to Marie again.

'Mrs Stein, I'm sure there'll be a good reason why she hasn't returned but I'll go look for her right away. Please call me if she arrives and I'll call you if I find her.'

'Yes.' There was a pause. 'Please find her for me,' Marie pleaded with him.

'Do what I can,' Ed replied.

He put the receiver down and rushed for the door. As he opened it, he turned to the others.

'Thanks for the offer, guys. I'll call you if I need help!'

The door slammed behind him. Sam and Martin looked at each other.

'It's that bleddy brother again. I sense it in my bones!' Martin said.

Sam nodded sombrely. For them there was nothing to do but wait.

*

Justin drove along the main road heading towards the Hartbeespoort Dam wall. Elke was lying, still unconscious, on the rear seat. Justin had found some strong cord in the back of Elke's vehicle and had bound her hands with it. He had then tied her to the metal frame at the bottom of the rear seat in case she regained consciousness while he was driving. The last thing he wanted was an angry and vengeful young woman lunging herself at him when he had his hands on the steering wheel and the car doing at least 120 kilometres an hour!

As he drove, Justin reviewed his options. Should he have left her in her vehicle to be rescued as soon as the next car came along the quiet country road? Was her life in danger and would he be accused of her murder if she died? And what was he going to do with her, now that he had captured her?

For a mad moment Justin felt like accelerating as hard as he could and aiming for the nearest tree. That way, he would deprive Ed of something precious once again, in the most final and devastating way. It would also end his own life, which had somehow never seemed to work out as he had wanted it to. No, he decided, he wasn't ready to die just yet. He could still get out of this mess. The family's wealth would see to that. No matter what they thought of him, they would never leave him to rot in a remote African jail!

So, what to do with the girl then? Did he want to use her as a hostage?

Did he perhaps want to have sex with her and show her that he was the more powerful brother? He glanced back at Elke lying on the rear seat. Her face was in repose and her classical features were unmarked except for the continuous seepage of blood from the bang on the top part of her head. She was unusually beautiful, he thought, but probably lacked the fire that the stunning little Greek girl, Persephone, undoubtedly possessed, if only she'd had the courage to use it!

And where was he heading? Justin's dreams of conquest suddenly evaporated as he realised that he needed to make some plans. He had learned a few lessons from his poorly planned attempts to set up Ed as the Great Platinum Robber. Now he had to consider what his opponents, notably Ed and, by now, probably the Police, were doing. His first thoughts were that his hire car could easily be traced and they would soon be broadcasting his car's registration to every cop in the region. Up ahead was a dirt road with a few signposts proclaiming the names of farms, as well as a Cafe. There was one other sign which caught his attention. It was a picnic site.

On an impulse, he wrenched the wheel of the car and slid onto the side road. The dirt was dry and loose. For a moment it looked as though his adventure was about to end but he finally managed to correct the dry skid that had taken him a good thirty metres into the road. Somewhere he had read that one should never apply the brakes and that one should steer into the skid. To his surprise, he obeyed all the rules and ended up shaken but pointing straight down the road, in the direction of the mountains.

*

Ed approached the entrance to the Stein farm at high speed from the side away from Rustenburg. He debated whether or not to call in at the farm but decided against it. He had his cell phone with him and although the area had a number of places where the signal was low, he figured that either Marie or Elke would reach him eventually, if there was any news on that side. He raced past the Stein's entrance and carried on towards Rustenburg on the road he was certain Elke would have taken if she were on her way home.

As he rounded a bend some five kilometres from the farm, his heart sank. The flashing lights of a couple of Police cars were visible at the side of the road. Ed disregarded possible speed traps and kept his foot down until the last moment. He then braked hard and squealed to a stop. The Police were swarming all over the wreck of a vehicle that Ed realised, with shock, was Elke's. A couple of cops looked angrily in his direction, as he leapt out of his SUV and raced across the road with total disregard for the possibility of any traffic passing at that moment.

As he approached the vehicle, one of the cops, a large African, stood between him and the vehicle as he held up a warning hand for Ed to stop.

'Sorry Sir!' the man said.

Ed tried to control his emotions and enquired anxiously between gasps for breath. Extreme tension tended to make the fittest person short of breath.

'Is she all right?'

The other man's face remained infuriatingly neutral.

'Sir, we don't...' he began.

Ed in desperation forced his way past the cop and stood staring at the vehicle. The driver's door was open and the vehicle was empty. Ed looked around confused. Another cop approached him.

'D'you know whose vehicle this is Sir?'

'It's my fiancée's. Where is she?' he shouted with a rising sense of desperation.

The cops looked at each other helplessly. The second cop spoke again. This time he sounded much more sympathetic now that he knew that Ed was involved with the possible victim.

'We don't know, Sir. It was empty when we got here. My men are searching the area but we've found no-one.'

At that moment there was a shout from one of the cops inspecting tyre tracks in the dirt at the side of the road.

'Looks like another vehicle, Sarge!' the man called out. 'These tracks are fresh.'

The cops, followed by Ed, moved over the where the man was carefully inspecting the tyre marks. Enjoying his moment in the spotlight, the man picked up a twig and pointed to the markings.

'You can see that they've driven over the marks made by the crash vehicle,' he said 'which means that it had to have arrived after the crash occurred.'

The Sergeant turned to one of the men.

'Get on the radio and check if anyone's been brought into the hospital or any of the clinics around here.'

The man moved away to one of the Police cars and started to activate the radio. The Sergeant turned back to Ed, who had looked at the empty vehicle long enough to see the blood still marking the steering wheel and the front seat.

'When did you last see your fiancée?' he asked Ed.

Ed waved his hands around in frustration. 'We were in Rustenburg together at about 9.30, maybe 10 o'clock. She said she was going home. Her name's Elke Stein, her parents...'

'I know her.'

One of the other cops spoke up. He was a powerfully built, blonde Afrikaner.

'She was at school with me. Jeez, I hope she's okay!'

Then, realising, he looked at Ed sympathetically.

'Sorry, Sir' he mumbled.

The man who had spoken on the radio came back.

'No reports of any accident admissions. If someone took her, they didn't take her for medical attention.'

'Maybe he took her home. It's only a couple of k's away,' the blonde cop suggested.

Suddenly Ed knew with certainty that Justin had been there and he had Elke with him. The thought of it made his blood run very cold.

CHAPTER 33

As Justin drove on the dirt road towards the picnic site, he tried to remember what he had overheard about the various scenic spots along the Magaliesberg mountain range. Ed had been chatting to Marius de Wet about the numerous battles that had taken place in the region during the Boer War. As usual he had only been half listening but one particular comment from Marius came to mind. He had mentioned the word Kaboutermanne. Why had it stuck in his memory? Justin had no idea, but it had. Marius had explained that the word means Gnomes in English and it referred to Boers who were sick of fighting but were also unwilling to surrender. A number of them hid away for months on end in the kloofs or ravines that were scattered along the length of the mountains.

If it worked for them, it could work for me too, Justin thought grimly. He reasoned that a picnic site had to be positioned where there was some exceptional scenic beauty, otherwise no one would visit it. Therefore, it was probable that the site included one of these secluded kloofs. There was very little else visually interesting to be seen on the gently rising Northern side of the mountains. We'll know soon enough, he thought grimly, as another faded and rather crooked sign announced that the picnic site was one kilometre further down the road.

He glanced back at Elke. She was moving about restlessly on the seat but still showed no sign of regaining full consciousness. With a shock he realised that although her hands were bound together behind her back, if she were to turn over when he was entering the picnic site, the bonds would become clearly visible to anyone looking into the car. He pulled over to the side of the road, hurriedly took off the casual jacket he was wearing and laid it gently over her body. He looked at her critically for some moments and realised that he had gotten lucky with respect to the blow on the head. The way she was lying on the seat, placed the bloodied side of her head and hair downwards. To a casual observer she would look completely relaxed and fast asleep. The sooner he reached the gate and drove into the site, the better. He rapidly turned around in his seat, engaged the gears and drove as fast as he dared towards the picnic area.

*

Ed felt like a person who had returned to a parking spot to find that his car was stolen. He felt totally helpless. Elke was gone, almost certainly with Justin, and there were no clues as to where he could have taken her. They could be anywhere.

Ed felt a rising emotion of grief mixed with anger. He wanted to lash out, to yell and to attack anyone who could possibly have harmed Elke but there were not even lurking shadows to explore. Just an empty car with blood on the seat and the tyre tracks of another car next to the crashed vehicle.

He picked up his cell phone and dialed Sam, praying that he had reception where he was. The phone rang and he was quickly connected to Sam. With as few words as possible, he told his boss what he had found and his suspicions that Justin may have abducted her. Sam promised to send out every available vehicle to scour the district. He also promised that Martin would alert the Police.

'Another thing' Sam added, 'Why don't you call Rob at the hotel and find out which car hire company would have supplied your brother with a car. I'm sure they'll deal with only one or at the most two companies in Rustenburg. Get Rob to call me with the answers. I'll act as a command post and relay information as it comes in.'

'Sam, you're a pal. I've gotta find her. She's, she's my life!'

'I understand. Between us we'll get her back.' Sam reassured the young American.

However, as Sam put the phone down, he was also filled with a sense of foreboding. A beautiful young girl could be a target for all sorts of malcontents, not only Justin, he thought, but he had to agree that it seemed as though Ed's little brother had caused havoc once again.

*

Justin slowed right down as he approached the gate of the picnic site. There was a small wooden hut to one side of the gate and he could see a couple of men moving around next to the hut. He glanced back at Elke. She had hardly moved but the jacket was about to slip off her body. Justin awkwardly reached behind him and pulled the jacket back over her before he arrived at the gate. One of the men, a middle-aged African, greeted him in Afrikaans. Justin switched on the charm.

'Sorry, pal, I don't speak that language. You speak English?'

The man nodded and gave him a broad grin. 'Yes Sir, my English number one, Sir.'

'Good' Justin replied. 'We'd like to visit your picnic site.'

By now the man had noticed Elke on the back seat - who had miraculously remained in almost the same position in which Justin had placed her a couple of minutes ago.

'The Missus, she all right?' the man asked anxiously.

Justin forced a laugh. 'Yeah, we had a hell of a party last night. That's why we wanna chill out in the country today.'

'Chill, what is chill?' the man's number one English did not extend to American slang.

'Uh, relax. Can you let us in, please?'

Justin's "good humour" was wearing thin. The man shook his head regretfully.

'Sorry Sir. We closed. Come back Saturday or Sunday!'

Justin controlled himself with a real effort. All he wanted was to buy time to revive Elke, talk to her, see whether his scheme with Bud McNeil had been uncovered and then - his mind barely looked that far ahead. He would take it one step at a time.

'Listen, pal, we just want a couple of hours peace and quiet. We don't need anything else.'

Justin gave the man a knowing smile and a wink. He also took a few notes from his wallet and the gate-keeper relented.

'Okay, you go on this road' he gestured to a right-hand fork on the track which led through the gate. 'Soon you come to parking place, the river, it is close.'

At that moment Elke let out a long breath, stirred, groaned and tried to sit up.

In a flash Justin turned around and pressed her back onto the seat. 'Relax, honey. We're nearly there.' Justin hoped his voice would cover the distressed noises coming from his captive.

'Where am I, whash happened?'

She slurred her words, trying to come to terms with the complete disorientation of recovering from a blow on the head.

'Take it easy, babe!'

Justin nervously waved to the gateman and accelerated through the now open gate. The man was too dazzled by his sudden windfall to take any notice of Elke, who had turned around and was plaintively looking at him through the rear window.

*

Ed put down the phone to Rob and was delighted that his friends were rallying around him. Rob had undertaken to get the registration number of the car Justin had hired and let Sam know right away. He had also promised to call Marius de Wet and Errol Saperstein. He was certain that most members of the fire committee would help to search the district if they were available. His fellow director, Don Watson, would do a circuit up and down the valley and he would ask Elliot Standen, the hotel's senior director, who was returning from Johannesburg later in the day, to keep his eyes open on the way back to Buffalo Hills.

Ed had one more urgent thing to do and knew now that he must do it in person. He drove away from the crash site towards the Stein's farm.

*

Martin was fortunate with the Police. As soon as he explained the situation to the Captain who had helped him with the raid on the processing plant the previous night, the Policeman asked him to hold on. Martin could hear voices and the strident sounds of a radio in the background. After a couple of minutes the Captain picked up the phone again.

'We've got a couple of Flying Squad vehicles returning from Pretoria. They're just passing the Hartbeespoort Dam wall now. I've told them to set up a road-block. I can get the Brits Police to set up more blocks on the other roads. Which direction do you think he's heading in?'

As Martin was about to reply, Sam interrupted to give him the make and registration number of the car, which Martin passed onto the Police Captain.

'D'you think he might be heading West instead of East?' the Captain asked.

South was protected by the mountains and the North provided only a couple of obscure country roads other than those which went directly to the platinum mines. If Justin wanted to flee towards the cities of Johannesburg or Pretoria, he would have to travel east towards Hartbeespoort or west towards Rustenburg before turning south through Olifantsnek. The Captain then said that he would post further road-blocks on the Kroondal and Rustenburg roads as well.

Martin turned to Sam.

'I'll take a drive myself if you can spare me.'

'Of course, just keep your cell on in case.'

As Martin reached the door of Sam's office, Sam called out.

'By the way, I've asked Head Office to send the company chopper down for the rest of the day.'

'Lekker,' Martin smiled. 'I'm amazed you didn't drown in red tape achieving that!'

Sam laughed. 'A pretty girl in distress?   They're queuing up to volunteer to fly with the chopper. Besides, I told 'em that it's all part of the platinum theft investigation. They want to catch those bastards!'

'And what about Bud McNeil?' Martin asked.

Sam frowned. 'Let's find the girl first.'

Martin nodded and left the office. After an uncomfortable start to their working relationship in the first year, Martin had to acknowledge

202

that Sam and he were beginning to make one hell of a team!

*

Ed pulled up outside the Stein farmhouse. Isak was sitting on the stoep as usual, looking frailer than ever. Marie walked over to meet Ed as he got out of his SUV. She was dressed for farm work in faded jeans, a loose-fitting man's shirt and a sturdy pair of boots. Although clearly distressed, she held her emotions under control.

'The Police just phoned and told me about Elke's car. They say that it looks as though she's been driven away somewhere. What d'you know about all this?' she demanded.

'Mrs Stein, I can only guess that my brother might've found her. He was possibly following her.'

'Why should he do that?' Marie's voice cut across his like the crack of a whip. A formidable woman, Ed thought briefly as he tried to focus on the important issue of trying to find Elke.

Ed shrugged. 'Look Mrs Stein, the priority for all of us is to find Elke, so I won't get into any details but my brother's conduct is due to a vendetta against me, it's being going on for years. I had hoped that after his narrow escape on September 11th, that he may have changed and, for the first few days after he arrived out here, I truly thought he had.'

'What's that got to do with taking my daughter?'

Ed groped for a way to answer without alarming the woman more than he had to.

'I can only guess that he could be holding her to get back at me!'

'Is he that unbalanced?' Isak's soft voice intruded.

Elke's father had joined them unnoticed.

Ed nodded reluctantly. 'I'm afraid so, Sir.'

'Would he harm her?' Marie snapped at him.

Ed had a sudden mental image of a distraught Persephone, describing how Justin had tried to rape her. No harm in worrying Marie and Isak unnecessarily, Ed thought, as he controlled his reaction.

'He's basically a coward, and Elke's a strong young woman,' he replied. 'I won't pretend that he'll be pleasant but I guess his main objective would be to hurt me. I expect he'll use her as a bargaining chip.'

'Are you certain that it was Justin who took her?' Isak asked.

Ed sighed. 'I'm not certain about anything, Sir, but I can tell you that half the community are out there looking for her right now, plus the Police. We have one thing in our favour.'

Isak and Marie looked at him expectantly.

'Justin's not a hardened criminal. He's not very rational in his actions and I don't expect he's thought this through. I wouldn't be surprised if we find him quite easily.'

Ed did not fully believe it himself but he felt that he had to give Elke's parents something to cling to.

'I need to get back out there,' Ed added.

Both Marie and Isak nodded forlornly. As Ed drove away, he vowed that he would personally wring his young brother's neck for the distress he was causing so many decent people.

*

As Justin pulled away from the resort's gate Elke sat up again. Despite a blinding headache, and the shock of returning to consciousness in unfamiliar surroundings, she was beginning to realise what was happening. Justin must have taken her out of her own car. She had a vague recollection of going off the road and then nothing. Her head was throbbing badly and she tried to lift her left hand to check for any injuries. Only then did she realise that her hands were tied together.

'What're you doing?' Elke spoke with difficulty and frustration.

Justin glanced back at her, using his most cherubic smile.

'I just need to talk to you, we'll be there in a minute.'

He saw that the track was about to end in an open space that he assumed was the parking area.

They had travelled a couple of hundred metres from the gate along a rough and bumpy track which crossed over a harsh terrain consisting of long fragmented ridges of quartzite blocks, clumps of coarse grass interspersed with some huge diabase boulders.

'Why're my hands tied, if you just want to talk and where in the hell are we?'

'You were so restless when you were unconscious,' Justin used an excuse he had dreamed up some time earlier, 'so I decided to tie your hands to stop you pulling at your head wound.'

'That's bloody ridiculous! You should've either called an ambulance or taken me to the hospital, especially if I've got a head wound!'

She managed to bring both hands up to feel the side of her head. It was warm and sticky, with a large swelling just above her left cheekbone. As she brought her hands away from her head, she gasped. They were both covered with blood. Elke was by nature a courageous person but the bizarre circumstances in which she now found herself, eroded her confidence. What was Justin doing? She could tell by the brief backward glance he had just given her, that there was madness in his eyes. She was his captive in some remote place she did not recognise. His nonsense about just talking to her, she dismissed entirely. Was she being kidnapped, to be held for ransom? Would he try and rape her? Would he perhaps kill her? Elke stifled a sob. She must be strong. She must show no fear. O God, where was Ed?'

Justin stopped the car, got out of the driver's seat and opened the back door. He leaned inside and smiled his sweet smile at Elke.

'We've arrived. Can you get out on your own or do you need a hand?'

'I'm not moving until you untie my hands and tell me what we're doing here?' she snarled at him.

Justin shook his head sadly.

'You don't understand' he spoke softly, as though to a small child. 'You and I need to talk. I have to explain about Ed. He's a very dangerous guy, Elke. You've been lucky he hasn't hurt you so far. When you see the bigger picture, you'll understand everything and you'll thank me for it.'

Elke did not know whether to laugh or cry. Behind Justin she could see that the ground fell away steeply with the tops of thick groves of indigenous trees of Buffalo Thorn and Transvaal Cabbage only just visible, indicating that they were close to one of the countless number of deep kloofs in the region. They could be anywhere. Once Justin took her down into the kloof, Elke doubted very much if anyone would find her again – either alive or dead!

CHAPTER 34

Ed drove along the road between the Stein farm and Rustenburg. Not knowing what Justin might do to Elke was driving him crazy. Where were they? Could he be certain it was Justin who had taken her? And if not, was she in even greater danger in the hands of a stranger? He pounded the steering wheel in frustration then forced himself to try and think rationally.

If Justin had taken her, where would he go? Would he try to check into another hotel? He discarded that idea immediately. If Justin had Elke with him, she would certainly not keep her mouth shut – unless, of course, he had a gun or a weapon of some kind. He mentally sized the two of them up. Elke was tall and athletic. She had been a top sportswoman at school and university. Justin, on the other hand, was slightly built but Ed had to concede that little brother had a certain manic strength, especially when angry.

But was Elke badly hurt? There was blood on the seat and the steering wheel of her crashed car. Could she even be dead? That thought was totally inconceivable and for a moment his chest heaved and his throat constricted. No! He could sense that she was not dead. Besides, Justin, although undoubtedly insane, would hardly want to carry a dead body around with him. Or would he?

Ed braked angrily and pulled over to the side of the road. This was getting him nowhere. He stopped his vehicle and got out of the vehicle to look around at the scenery. The road passed through several small, somewhat conical, hills at this point. They were covered with typical sparse Highveld grass and dozens of outcroppings of diabase rocks. Here and there a lone bush or thorn tree poked its dry foliage over the top of a gully or indentation. It was beautiful in a typically African way, but his mind did not dwell on the aesthetics of his environment. He tried to picture where Justin could be hiding with Elke.

An idea had been fluttering around on the edge of his consciousness but had not become a fully-fledged thought. He concentrated hard and managed to capture the elusive mental image. Suddenly it came into focus.

The only person that Justin could regard as an ally would be the mastermind behind the platinum thefts, Bud McNeil. Perhaps he had taken Elke to Bud's farm, unaware that Bud was mad at him? Even so, it was highly likely Justin would be able to persuade Bud to help him by offering more money. It was clearly the language that Bud understood best. Ed had no illusions that Justin could access two or three million dollars quite easily. In fact, he had probably salted away a small fortune in his two years with Willjohn Industries.

Ed made up his mind, strode back to the SUV and drove off at speed towards Rustenburg. There was something he would have to do before he visited Bud McNeil.

*

Justin looked at Elke uncertainly. He did not want to use force unless he had to. He still clung to the fantasy that he could persuade her that Ed was the bad guy and he was the good guy. On the other hand, the sooner he could get the two of them out of sight somewhere in the depths of the kloof, which lay only a few tantalising metres away, the happier he would be. He needed time to convince her to cooperate with him. Then, using her as a hostage, he would take her out of the country and...

'Untie me and let me go!' Elke's voice brought him back to reality.

Elke's eyes reflected her fury and he did not doubt that she would try something foolish like attacking him, even with her hands tied together behind her back. Justin could see that she was in superb physical condition and it was quite possible that she could hurt him if he were not very careful.

'Elke, listen. I need to tell you about Ed's early life, his mental instability, the danger you've been in. I had to take desperate measures to rescue you and when you crashed,' he let some emotion creep into his voice, 'I...I thought that you could be dead. The bottom fell out of my world. By trying to save you, I had perhaps indirectly caused your death!'

Elke shook her head disbelievingly.

'You really believe in your own fantasies, don't you? You tie me up and take me to some isolated spot...'

'Only for your own safety. Elke, please believe me. We'll go down to the picnic spot. I'm sure it'll be beautiful down there, then we'll talk.'

'Untie me first!' Elke demanded.

Justin looked at her as though considering this option. Then he shook his head.

'Can't do that. You don't believe me yet. I can't have you trying

207

anything stupid until you get the bigger picture.'

'Come and get me then' Elke taunted him.

She could see the uncertainty in his eyes. Justin sighed then abruptly slid back into the driver's seat. Elke, still on the back seat, watched him carefully. What was he up to? Justin reached across and opened the glove compartment. Elke watching him caught the flash of metal as Justin reached into the compartment and withdrew a wicked looking carving knife.

'I'm sorry that you won't do it my way. Now we're gonna have to do it by - persuasion.'

He held the knife firmly as he turned in his seat to face Elke.

'I can slice you to pieces. With your hands tied, you wouldn't last two minutes. I want you outta the car now!'

They stared at each other for a few moments, measuring each other's possible strengths and weaknesses. Finally, it was Elke who gave a bitter chuckle.

'So much for your rescuing me from the dangers of your brother!'

She turned and fumbled with the rear door closest to her. Justin quickly slid out of his seat and rushed around to meet Elke who awkwardly emerged from the car and straightened up to confront him. As she stood up, she staggered for a moment - the blow on her head had weakened her more than she realised. She leaned back against the car and stared at Justin defiantly.

'And now?' she asked.

In addition to the knife, she saw that Justin held some more cord in his hands.

'Turn around and hold your hands out towards me' he commanded.

Elke looked into his eyes and saw a scary gleam in them. In her weakened state she realised that she was no match for a lunatic with a large knife. She stretched her hands out backwards as far as she could.

*

Ed emerged from a small but elegant looking hairdressing salon in the centre of Rustenburg. His blonde hair was now a glossy black colour. He carried a couple of plastic bags as he headed for his SUV parked a few metres down the street. The last sixty minutes had been busy ones for Ed. On arrival in Rustenburg he had found a sporting and safari shop where he had purchased a bush hat and Khaki Safari jacket, the kind that so many American tourists purchased for their first excursion into darkest Africa.

He had even found some baggy Khaki pants with pockets all over them and to cap it off, a pair of sturdy brown boots. To the amusement of the shop assistants, he had insisted on changing into his tourist outfit and had emerged from the store with his more usual trousers and cotton sports shirt in the plastic bags.

Another priceless forty-five minutes were taken up by having his hair dyed in the hairdressing salon. He had smiled and explained that he was due at a fancy-dress party that night. The hair was a quirky addition to his outfit with which to surprise, and probably horrify, his girlfriend.

The friendly and attractive young hairdresser had giggled and commented that she would certainly be stunned by his change of appearance from his normal golden locks to the much less striking black hair.

'Now we'll find out if she loves me for myself or my blonde hair!' Ed had joked, trying to hide the despair in his heart.

Although Bud and Justin had never met, Ed could not take a chance on the criminal mastermind associating him in any way with his brother. They did have quite a strong facial resemblance, but Ed was now confident that the black hair changed him sufficiently for Bud not to make the connection.

Ed pulled out of the parking spot and headed towards the road that would eventually branch off towards Thabazimbi and the edge of the Waterberg mountain range to the North-East of Brits.

*

Justin walked a couple of paces behind Elke as they descended along a well-worn but narrow path towards the bottom of the kloof. Thick foliage surrounded them and a chorus of bird calls served as a constant reminder that they had quickly journeyed into a virtually untouched patch of the real Africa. Even in her perilous state Elke found herself hoping that the owners of the picnic site had not built some monstrous haven for boozers and sunbathers.

Elke had to tread carefully. It was amazing how much one relied on one's arms for balance over uneven terrain. Having her hands tied behind her back made her feel as though she would fall flat on her face at any moment. She doubted whether Justin would even try to hold her up. He had attached a cord to the bonds that bound her hands together and made her walk in front of him. She felt like she was a dog on a leash. Suddenly she slipped. A stone came loose under her foot and she felt herself falling forwards down the path, which was particularly steep at that part leading down to the banks of a stream some ten metres below her.

In desperation she threw herself sideways and fell heavily into a bush to the left of the path. Only as she hit the bush did she feel any restraining tension on the line held by Justin. It did little more than wrench her arms backwards as she hit the bush, which fortunately gave way under her weight. She could feel sharp spikes and some smaller thorns pierce her clothing.

'You okay?' Justin's voice asked from behind her.

She painfully tried to roll off the bush back onto the path but some of the branches snagged in her clothing. She was unable to get up on her own.

'What does it look like?' Elke retorted.

Justin leaned over and rather roughly yanked her upright again by gripping both her upper arms tightly. Instinctively, just as she felt her feet were firmly back on the path, she lifted one foot and kicked backwards with all her strength. The blow caught Justin on the shin. He howled and spun away onto the far side of the path, stumbling then falling over two large boulders, which were on the lip of an almost sheer slope running all the way down to the river. Justin screamed as he slid down the slope and finally landed with a loud splash into a pool surrounded by a huge fragmented cathedral of high quartzite rocks.

Elke did not even try to see where Justin had fallen. Still shaking herself, she started to climb back up the path towards the parking ground. It was no easier climbing up than down with her arms still tied behind her back but her only thought was to reach the guards at the gate to the resort before Justin recovered and recaptured her.

*

Ed turned off onto the Thabazimbi road. As he did so, he realised that since Justin had arrived in the country, he had spent most of his time driving at reckless speeds trying to cope with one crisis after another. Perhaps when this is over, Elke and I can buy an ox-wagon, he thought sardonically.

Then his thoughts were crowded once more with images of Elke. Smiling, breathtakingly lovely Elke, juxtaposed with images of a torn and bleeding Elke calling for his help. Without realising it, in his torment he picked up the speed of his vehicle to 170 kph. Then he saw the speedometer and guiltily brought it down to a manageable 130, just 10 kph over the limit for the area.

Up ahead he saw a small garage with a store. He stopped at the garage and asked if they knew where Bud McNeil's farm was. One of the attendants told him it was another 10 kilometres down the road. He added that there was a big gate and Bud's name was written above the gate in large letters.

Ed thanked the man and drove on towards his destination. He was unsure of what he would do once he met Bud but at least he would make every effort to look around the place. It would be too much to expect to find Justin and Elke sitting on the stoep having coffee together, but Ed would also see if he could find any clues to link Bud with the platinum theft. He would then use that to pressure Bud into revealing where Justin was – if indeed Bud knew anything about his moves. Earlier on Ed had called Sam at the Mine to say that he was on his way to Bud's farm. Sam had been in a meeting, but his secretary had promised to let Ed know the moment he was available.

Ed wondered whether he was doing something very stupid by trying to get into Bud's farm on his own, but anything was better than sitting and waiting whilst others were looking for Elke.

*

Elke was almost blinded by sweat and dust as she continued to make her way towards the summit. Time and again she had fallen and every time she lay on the ground, she wondered if she had the strength to get up again. Then an image of Justin running after her with his carving knife would intrude on her mind and she would force herself up and carry on with little gasping mewls of fear and exhaustion.

At last the top of the path was in sight. With a final effort Elke forced her weary legs to take her to the top and a very real chance of safety.

*

Ed turned into the entrance to the Bud McNeil game ranch and stopped in front of the gates as a uniformed guard approached him with an Arrivals Book in his hand.

'Good afternoon, Sir' the man greeted him. 'Do you have an appointment with Mr McNeil?'

'Gee, ah'm sorry,' Ed began already practising his Texas twang. 'Ah wus jus' drivin' along this here bootiful valley an' I saw the sign "Game for sale." I gotta little spread in Texas...'

The African was clearly having difficulty with Ed's accent. He nodded politely and asked Ed to wait while he made a phone call. He came back in a few moments. 'Mr McNeil would be happy to see you,' the man advised. 'Please sign the book.'

Ed filled in the required details, giving himself the name Hank McCauley. One detribalised Celt to another, he thought wryly. He was ushered through the gate and told to follow the road for five kilometres, where he would find the ranch house. Mr McNeil would meet him there.

*

Elke's feet touched level ground at the top of the path. Almost crying with relief she straightened up from the nearly bent double posture she had adopted for the terrible climb with her hands bound behind her. As she straightened up, she jumped and reeled back in shock. A very wet but implacable Justin stood before her with his carving knife held in his right hand.

'Goin' someplace?' he enquired mildly.

211

CHAPTER 35

Ed drove his SUV along the road to Bud McNeil's ranch house. A number of flat-topped thorn bushes and long grass covered the land on his right, which fell away gently to a distant line of dense foliage. Ed presumed that there was a river somewhere beyond the far trees and dense bush. To his left the land rose steeply, with the typical Highveld scattering of rocks and boulders.

Bud's ranch was situated at the foothills of the Waterberg mountain range, which was fast becoming a major haven for private game ranches, as well as tourist lodges. Ed had been told by Marius some time ago that the Waterberg had the advantages of being more scenically beautiful than much of the Lowveld, as well as being malaria-free.

South Africa, Ed thought, had the appearance of being a highly developed First World country, but it did not take long to uncover the real unspoilt Africa, no more than a couple of hour's drive from the major centres of Johannesburg and Pretoria.

Ed drove over the crest of the incline and looked down on the McNeil ranch nestled in a delightful valley, some five hundred metres away. He could see small herds of buck, zebra, wildebeest and the occasional giraffe grazing peacefully on the gently rolling hills around the ranch. The thought of such a beautiful spread being owned by a gangster of note, sickened him. As he approached the ranch he kept his eyes open for any sign of the car that Justin had hired a couple of days ago. He doubted whether Justin would have swapped vehicles since then.

As he drove into the parking area in front of the ranch house, Ed saw a couple of SUV's, an ancient and battered Land Rover, a small panel van and a tractor that looked as though it had not moved for ten years or more.

As Ed stopped his vehicle, a huge African came out of the front door and strolled over to meet the American.

'Good Morning, Mr McCauley,' Simon said, extending his hand. Ed gingerly offered his hand, half expecting it to be crushed in the other's huge paw. To his surprise, Simon's grip was firm but not excessive, with the result that Ed's attempt at a boisterous Texan handshake was probably far more uncomfortable for the other man, although he showed no sign of being disturbed by it.

'Hi there, fellah,' Ed twanged, hating himself for impersonating the kind of tourist that gave Americans a bad name all over the world.

Simon courteously led Ed towards the house explaining that Mr McNeil would join him on the patio in a moment. They entered the house, walked across an entrance hall filled with African curios, bric-a-brac and mounted trophies then out again into a courtyard with a large swimming pool in the centre. Surrounding the pool was a superbly manicured lawn, with a couple of ancient Mopani bushes and an awning providing shade for the table and chairs towards which he was ushered. A tray with an ice bucket, fruit juice, beers and various liqueurs was already awaiting him on the low table.

'Do you prefer some coffee, Mr McCauley?' Simon asked as a manservant silently appeared to take his order if required. Ed, who would have loved a coffee, preferred to maintain his "good ole boy" image and asked for Bourbon. He was mildly surprised that Bud only had Scotch.

*

Sam came out of his meeting with the accountants which had dragged on endlessly. His regular secretary was on leave and the temp he had employed had left early. As soon as he said goodbye to the accountants, he went over to her desk and looked for any message from Ed. She had diligently put everything away and Sam could not find any sign of any messages. Sam's anxiety increased by the second. Presumably Martin was still out on the roads looking for the girl and Justin, but where the hell was Ed?

Sam picked up his cell phone and called Ed's number. As he feared, it was out of range. He cursed the fact that there were still so many areas of the country without cell phone signals despite the South Africans high per capita use of cell phones.

Frustrated, Sam then called Martin who was thankfully in range. Electronic Russian roulette, Sam thought grimly.

'Any luck?' he asked his Senior Engineer.

'Ag, sorry man. I've been driving around for hours now. The cops had no luck at the roadblocks just a number of unroadworthy vehicles, a couple of drunks, and a stash of dagga.'

'What about the Buffalo Hills guys and the fire committee?' Sam asked.

'Errol Saperstein found a garage where a car answering to the description of Justin's hire car, stopped for petrol. It was heading towards the dam, but the roadblocks saw nothing.'

'Which means he's probably lying low,' Sam commented.

'Ja. We doubt if he'd try to book into a hotel. The cops gave us a list of Bed and Breakfast places in the area but no luck there.'

'What about a pleasure resort?' Sam queried.

'We're checking these out now but hell, man, it's like finding a needle in a...' Martin's English failed him for a moment, 'a hay pile.'

'Haystack' the African added gently. He could also get a mental blockage on certain English phrases. This was not one of them.

Martin chuckled. 'Ja, ja. It's bloody crazy. You and I having to speak to each other in English.'

'Okay, Martin. If you promise to learn Tswana, I'll learn Afrikaans!'

Sam smiled as he said it, knowing that his Afrikaans was already fair and Martin's Tswana was non-existent.

'Would you settle for a little Sotho?' Martin asked. They both laughed. It was an ongoing debate they had had over the years. In a way it drew them closer together, both being at the mercy of the universal language, English.

'Keep looking for them. You haven't heard from Ed, have you?'

'Sorry, no. You neither?'

Martin's signal was beginning to break up.

'No. I just hope he hasn't done something foolish' Sam added into a dead phone. The signal was broken.

*

As strong as she was both in body and mind, Elke burst into tears. Justin stared at her sardonically, all pretences gone.

'You wanna play rough, bitch?' he said. 'That's the way we'll play it but you're gonna be mine. Ed doesn't deserve a thing, least of all a pretty creature like you!'

Elke switched off mentally. Listening to Justin was like hearing a broken record. Somewhere deep inside, her fierce courage welled up again. On an impulse she lashed out with her left foot, catching him on the shin. Justin reared back with a stifled yell. For a moment she thought that she had gone too far. The mad gleam reappeared. He raised his arm and the blade of the carving knife glittered in the sun. It blinded her momentarily as she tensed, preparing to dodge the thrust of the knife. When she could see again Justin had lowered his arm but the tip of the blade was now almost touching her throat. When he spoke, his voice was quiet but the intent was unmistakeable.

'Turn around and go back down the path or I'll slit you from ear to ear.'

214

Elke looked at him and saw that behind his bravado there was uncertainty in his eyes. She shook her head. Justin looked at her disbelievingly. He moved the knife forward and its point actually touched her skin. Elke was determined to wring some kind of concession from him.

'I'll only go down there if you untie my hands' she said, 'otherwise just slit my throat and be done with it, but I'd hate to be in your shoes when Ed catches up with you!'

'Don't you dictate terms to me!' he yelled at her.

She could see that he was losing control of his emotions.

Elke abruptly sat down and swung around and held out her hands behind her.

'There's no way I'll get down there again tied up like this!'

She tried not to flinch as there was a long silence, then suddenly she felt the steel of the blade next to her skin, as the knife cut through her bonds. Her hands were free. She brought them around the front of her and started shaking them to restore some circulation into numb hands and fingers. She noticed that the knife had gashed her left hand but that was the least of her worries. For a moment she considered trying to overpower Justin but he anticipated this. The knife blade jabbed her behind her shoulder blades as Justin issued instructions.

'Stand up and remain where you are. Now I'm gonna put a noose around your neck and you're gonna go down that path. I reckon you should make very, very sure you don't fall!'

*

Ed sat in the passenger seat of the old Land Rover as Bud dutifully and with surprising patience herded the two rhino, a male and a female, towards the opening of an avenue created by two long strips of thick white plastic two metres high by some fifty metres long. The opening was some thirty metres wide but narrowed down to about three metres where it was joined onto the open doors of a large truck. Inside the truck was a large animal cage constructed of steel poles with a solid roof. As they neared the plastic funnel the rhino became more and more aggressive. Even with their poor eyesight, they sensed that they were being driven into some kind of trap.

The male suddenly turned and, snorting ferociously, charged the Land Rover. The second rhino dutifully followed its mate.

Bud managed to evade the main thrust of the attack and the huge animal only clipped the rear end of the vehicle. To Ed it felt as though they had been involved in a major fender bender in a crowded New York street. Bud laughed gleefully as he swung the "Landy" around in a vicious turn, causing the outside wheels to lift momentarily as the cumbersome vehicle threatened to overturn.

Ed hung on grimly and glanced at his host. This was the Bud McNeil he had originally expected to meet – a wild cowboy who gloried in living on the edge. Half an hour ago they had sat in his magnificent courtyard, drinking Scotch and vying with each other for the title of the most ostentatious business tycoon. Ed, as Hank McCauley, had played the Texas millionaire to the hilt. Loud, brash, boastful but supremely sure of himself. He had told Bud about his 200,000 acres of prime cattle country and the little corner he had just bought, only some 80,000 acres, in the hills of Montana where he was setting up an African game ranch.

Bud had been suspicious at first but Ed knew a few names in the cattle business. He dropped the names easily and Bud, who had obviously dealt with Texans before, recognised one or two. Suddenly they were pals. After Ed had mentioned that he was prepared to spend between five and ten million dollars on African wildlife, they were bosom buddies for life!

As Ed held on tightly, Bud circled around and edged both errant rhino back towards the plastic funnel. This time it worked and Bud slowed down to a sedate 20 kph as the huge beasts lumbered along the avenue to the cage that was Ed's major centre of interest, with the exception of finding Elke.

*

Isak sat on the stoep of the farmhouse staring bleakly out over the lands. He reviewed the events of the past year starting with his first heart attack and now with the kidnapping of his only child. As a young father, he had secretly grieved over the fact that his only child, was a girl.

Isak had dreamed endlessly of the days he would spend with a son who would one day proudly take over the reins of managing the farm, and Isak would sit on the stoep, smoking a pipe and watching in wonder as his handsome and strongly built young son took the farm to new levels of prosperity.

Then Marie had given birth to a daughter, Elke, and was told that she would not be able to have more children. Isak had wept silently and alone. He had then reorganised his dreams to include his daughter. She had not disappointed him but the dream had gone terribly wrong once again when his health prevented him from working until Elke, or better still, Elke and some fine young man she would marry, would take over the farm. Marie had been extraordinary in her single-minded ability to manage the farm and indeed, Isak had to admit, she had made some improvements. Now the final piece in the jigsaw puzzle of life was missing. His beloved daughter had been taken and who knew if she were even still alive.

Isak felt Marie's rather rough worker's hands steal into his. He clasped her hand and looked round at his wife. They stared deep into each other's eyes. Twenty-five years of toil and tribulation now rested on a knife's edge. Overcome with emotion they reached out and embraced each other. Marie, the ever strong, wept in her man's arms.

'Where is she?' Marie sobbed.

'Don't give up hope, Skatjie. She's strong and resourceful and if you saw the look in the American's eyes, he will do anything to find her.'

'It's all his fault that she's gone' she wailed, 'letting his brother loose when he has mental problems.'

'He could never have foreseen this, Marie. Please be positive and have faith. It's all we've got left.'

Marie nodded and clung to her husband. Frail as he was, he was still her rock.

*

Elke leaned forward and cupped some water from the stream in her hands. She lifted them up and splashed the water over her face. It was chilly and refreshing. Justin allowed her to use the water to rinse her face then remove some of the dried blood from her forehead and her hair. Elke worked carefully on her wounds as she did not want to re-open them and lose even more blood. She had last eaten early that morning and she was feeling the effects of a growing hunger. She sipped some of the water and felt marginally better. Justin sat on the grassy bank next to her, still holding the cord, which ended in a noose around her neck.

She had managed to climb down the path without falling, knowing that if she did, she would probably strangle herself as the noose tightened. She did not have much faith in Justin letting go of his end, just to save her life. She feared that he would finally kill her anyway unless she could escape. Now that her hands were free, she just hoped that she could lull him into believing that her spirit was finally broken.

Justin spoke for the first time in minutes.

'As soon as the sun goes down, we'll get out of here. I'm gonna book us into a motel and we'll have some fun before I call my brother and tell him how it's gonna go down.'

Elke tried to keep her voice even as she asked 'What d'you mean by fun?'

'Honey, you and I are gonna get acquainted, real close like!'

Elke ignored him and continued trying to clean herself up. She knew that she would have to look out for the slightest opportunity to overpower Justin and escape. She noticed a large rock on the edge of the stream, just within her reach. Moving with infinite care, she edged herself towards the rock and concentrated on how she would pick it up before the deranged young man beside her realised what she was doing.

CHAPTER 36

Bud nudged the angry rhino forward very gently. They were now at the edge of the ramp which led up to the back of the truck and the large cage, which stood open, awaiting the huge creatures.

Bud spoke quietly to Ed. 'I try not to dart them if I can avoid it. I don't think it does them too much harm but it must leave some toxins in the system. This is the tricky part.'

As he spoke the male turned again, snorted and butted the front of the Landy! It was not as violent as the previous contact with the already battered vehicle. Bud signalled Ed to remain quiet and still. The rhino sniffed at the radiator then lost interest. Ed noticed that there was not quite enough space on either side of the vehicle for the creatures to slip past but if they tried to squeeze through, the plastic would never hold them. Fortunately, animals saw the plastic sheeting as a solid barrier and did not attempt to challenge it. Ed had never been close to a rhino and for the first time he really had a sense of the incredible strength of the animal.

There was water and fodder in the cage. The female sniffed in that direction and then cautiously ascended the ramp, entering the cage and bending her massive head down to grab some of the fodder between her leathery lips.

Ed watched Bud. The little man's eyes were sparkling. He turned to Ed and held up his hand with his fingers crossed. He then looked back at the male who was deciding whether or not to follow the female up the ramp. For a few moments Ed's worries about Elke and his knowledge that Bud was the mastermind behind the platinum thefts, faded from his mind. He watched, spellbound, as the male dithered for a few moments then slowly climbed up the ramp to join its mate.

As soon as the male was fully inside the cage, Bud let out a low whistle. A man emerged from either side of the ramp. They had been hiding underneath the structure. They swiftly swung the doors of the cage closed as a third man leapt up onto the ramp and slotted a rod into steel eyes, which were mounted one underneath the other when the two sides of the door were closed. Ed could think of more practical ways of enclosing the rhino, but he had to admit that Bud's team moved with great efficiency.

Bud leaped out of the vehicle and dashed up the ramp to confirm that the rod had been secured with a pin through a hole in the bottom of it. The top had been flattened out to prevent it slipping through the metal eyes.

Ed followed him up the ramp. After a few moments of irritation, the rhino had settled down and were munching their fodder contentedly. It crossed Ed's mind that if the platinum was somewhere inside the cage, Bud could not have found more intimidating guards.

'I hate to see them caged like this, but we don't have any option' Bud said quietly. 'They'll be leaving for the airport in about an hour, they'll fly out tonight and they'll be in their new home in Kentucky by tomorrow afternoon.'

Ed nodded, wondering who was buying the platinum and whether there was some way he could still check out the cage. A moment later, Ed got his first real break of a long and frustrating day. A small bakkie approached the truck at speed and stopped in a cloud of dust. One of Bud's staff leapt out of the car and called out to his boss.

'I've got America on the phone, sir. They say it's urgent!'

Bud looked at Ed apologetically. 'Take your time. Simon'll drive you up to the ranch when you're ready. Excuse me.'

Ed nodded, wondering whether the urgency was over the animals or platinum. He had a sudden worry that someone was warning Bud that Ed was not who he seemed to be, but he dismissed that as ridiculous.

Bud drove away and Ed turned back to the cage. On the pretext of watching the rhino, he started to visually examine every inch of the cage for possible hiding places. As he looked around the steel prison that held the rhino, his mind started to focus on Elke and Justin. So far there had been no sign of either of them at Bud's farm but he remained convinced that sooner or later his crazy brother would appear, seeking the help of the Mr Big of the platinum heist. He had no other leads whatsoever so he forced himself to concentrate on the hidden platinum in the hope that if he uncovered it, he could force McNeil to help him find Justin and the woman that Ed had pledged to protect.

*

'How d'you think you're going to get out of this mess?' Elke asked Justin.

She had the satisfaction of seeing the left side of his face twitch slightly as he considered the question. When he spoke, his voice had an edge of uncertainty that he tried to cover with a show of bravado.

'It's real simple, sweetheart' he replied. 'It's called the barter system. I've got something that Ed wants very much - you - and he's got something I want very much - shares in the family business.'

'But I thought' she began, 'that he was broke?'

Justin chuckled. 'I lied. He's worth millions right now but I aim to make sure that if he wants his girl, I get the money. Then he'll be just as broke as I said he was.' He smiled his manic smile. 'So, I wasn't telling a real lie. I just kinda pre-empted the truth.'

He leaned forward and peered into Elke's face. 'But you won't hold that against him will ya now, even if I do return his goods a little shop-soiled?'

Elke tried to move away to avoid his evil face almost touching hers.

As she moved away, she leaned towards the rock she had been eyeing, putting her hand down on top of it. She fervently hoped that it was not heavily imbedded in the surrounding soil. Keeping her eyes unwaveringly on Justin, her fingers crept around the sides of the rock. Tightening her grip she pulled at it. It moved slightly and with a sense of exultation, she knew that she had finally found a weapon.

*

Sam searched his secretary's office. He was certain that Ed would have left some message to say where he was. They had all agreed to keep in regular contact with each other. Sam cursed that he had not cancelled his meeting with the auditors. Because the temp who was filling in for his secretary had not worked at Premier Platinum before, Sam had no idea how her mind worked. She was meticulously tidy. Nothing remained on the desk or on top of the cupboards and filing cabinets along the wall. Sam had checked all the drawers in the desk and had opened most of the cupboards without seeing any sign of a message pad or diary.

As soon as he opened the last cupboard, he knew he had struck pay dirt. His appointment book, a number of current files and a notepad were neatly placed on the top shelf. He grabbed his appointment book and opened it, looking for that day's date. Opposite the 3pm section she had written Ed's name and cell number, nothing else. Refusing to give up, Sam grabbed the note pad again and saw a hastily scribbled line which read 'Mr Willjohn seeing O'Neil this afternoon.'

Sam looked at the words blankly. O'Neil – who in the hell was that and why would he visit someone when his future wife's life may be in danger? Then he made the connection. Of course, McNeil, Bud McNeil! Ed must have decided to see whether Justin had taken the girl there.

It seemed like a pretty stupid move too, but Sam knew only too well that love could be completely blind. He grabbed his cell phone and dialled Martin.

'Gericke here' Martin replied after a couple of rings.

'Thank God you still in range' Sam replied. 'Where are you now?'

'I'm close to the dam. I've been checking out a few resorts. Nothing so far. What's up, Sam?'

'Listen, Ed left a message when I was in the meeting. He's checking out Bud McNeil's place.'

'On his own? He's crazy!' Martin exploded.

'But he's also desperate. How soon could you get there and what about asking the cops to help?'

'Ja, will do. I'm on my way and I'll get the Rustenburg cops to call the Police in Brits. They're the closest.' Martin replied.

'Good luck. Shall I come along as well?' Sam asked.

'Don't think so, Boss. Better keep your central communication port open. Speak to you later.'

Martin's phone clicked off before Sam could argue.

He was right, Sam decided, but he did feel rather left out of things. Male testosterone doesn't disappear after forty, he decided.

*

Elke feverishly worked the rock loose with one hand whilst at the same time trying to maintain eye contact with the lunatic. She realised that something must have snapped inside Justin's head. When she first met him on the day that he and Ed had come to the farm for lunch, he had seemed normal enough. Now, in retrospect she was certain that he was the one who had poisoned her mother's mind against Ed.

She realised that Justin had now slipped into a fantasy world of his own making. In his desperation to destroy his brother, he was no longer dealing with reality. No matter what he did with her, Justin's position was hopeless, but he would not confront it.

All of this flashed through her mind as she prepared to lift up the rock and strike him with it. Elke was not a violent person and she had to psych herself up to even consider striking someone else, no matter how mad he was.

Justin leaned across and leered at her.

'After you've been with me for a night you probably won't want to go back to him. We'll see!'

He lifted up a hand and gently stroked her cheek. Elke forced herself to remain calm. His touch made her squirm and she knew that she had to strike him now before it was too late. Using every scrap of strength she could muster, she lifted the rock with her left hand and swung it towards his face. To her dismay, at that moment he lunged forward to kiss her. In her mind she had calculated that the rock would strike him either between the eyes or on the temple, but suddenly her target had moved. At the end of the swing she felt the momentum of the rock continue. Her fingers were unable to hold onto it. The rock slipped away, flew through the air and landed with a splash in the stream behind them.

Justin, realising that he was under attack, watched as the rock fell harmlessly into the water. He shook his head and looked back at Elke as she tried to scramble to her feet. Almost lazily he reached out and pulled on the rope that was still around her neck in a noose. As she found her feet and straightened up, the noose tightened and began to strangle her. Gasping and clutching at the noose, she was forced to step towards Justin rather than away from him. He pulled in the cord to maintain pressure, rather like a fisherman playing a trout on the end of the line. As Elke fought to breathe, she could dimly see that Justin was enjoying her struggles. She made a huge effort to stop resisting and to kneel down in front of him.

'That's better, sweetheart,' Justin murmured softly. 'Are we gonna have fun tonight, or what?'

*

Simon and the rest of Bud's team were busy rolling up the plastic sheeting. Ed had said that he would enjoy watching the rhino until Simon was ready to take him back to the ranch.

As the men moved away from the truck Ed was able to inspect the cage more closely. There did not appear to be any place either on the floor or ceiling of the cage which could contain the hidden platinum. This left the poles forming the walls of the structure. Most of the poles looked to be solid steel bars but the corner posts were much thicker in circumference.

Ed saw a spanner lying on the floor of the truck, outside the cage. Deciding that Bud's men were some distance away, Ed stepped across, picked up the spanner and started tapping one of the corner poles. It definitely sounded hollow. As he tapped it methodically up and down its entire length, he was disappointed to find that the hollow sound was consistent along the length of the pole.

There was a sudden snort followed by a tremendous thud as one of the rhino, alarmed by the tapping, crashed into the wall of the cage. Ed, already nervous about being discovered, nearly had a heart attack. The tip of the rhino's fibrous horn protruded through two of the bars close to his hands. The power and savagery of the beast was awesome. Ed took a deep breath, looked around to ensure that no one had noticed the commotion in the cage, and moved over to the next corner pole. Could he have been wrong in his certainty that Bud was using the cage as his means of transporting the platinum?

Ed was tapping the next corner pole, keeping an eye on the rhino, who inevitably turned angrily towards the noise. In the moments before the animal struck again, Ed managed to ascertain that the lower half the pole had a different sound to it when tapped. There was a deadness to the sound which told him clearly that this pole was at least half full of some substance or other.

Despite the unwelcome attention of the rhino, which he presumed was the male, he managed to check the remaining two corner poles. Like the second pole they were also either completely or partially filled. He could only presume that it had to be the platinum.

The rhino had been particularly savage and had attacked the corner three or four times before finally losing interest and going over to join its mate, who was placidly chewing on the fodder.

Ed was about to turn away when he noticed something on the floor of the cage, at the foot of the corner pole. The Rhino's onslaught had moved the pole marginally off its base. Ed shuddered to think what would happen if the creature had hit him. He bent down and carefully slipped his hand in-between the bars of the cage. The Rhino was nearby but was now disinterested in his activities. Ed supposed that there was a limit to the number of times even a belligerent beast like a rhino would bang its head against a solid object.

Ed ran his fingers around the base of the pole then withdrew his hand from the cage. He looked closely at the dark smudge on his fingers. His training as a metallurgist quickly confirmed what he already suspected. They were grains of platinum precipitate. Ed presumed that in a makeshift refinery such as the one the thieves had set up on the farm, it would be a messy operation. They may even have included some precipitate to wedge the semi-refined platinum more tightly into the poles. At last Ed had some leverage with which to pressure Bud to help him find Justin and Elke. He was much more concerned over the welfare of his fiancée than the outcome of proving Bud's possession of the platinum.

Ed straightened up and turned away from the cage, only to stare into the angry face of Simon, the giant African, who had returned whilst Ed's attention had been on avoiding the wrath of the rhino.

Ed knew with certainty that Simon was not in a friendly mood!

CHAPTER 37

Justin approached the security gate. Elke and he had left the picnic site as the sun moved close to the horizon. Elke had only just made it to the car. The combination of hunger, loss of blood and the experience of nearly choking on the noose had taken its toll. Someone less athletic than Elke would probably not have survived the day. She sat numb and dizzy in the front seat, with the point of Justin's carving knife touching her ribs. Justin had used his jacket to cover the space between himself and Elke, with his left hand keeping a steady pressure on the knife under the jacket.

The guards were already cooking some meat and mealie pap. They were clearly relieved to see Justin reappear and leave the property. Justin knew that the money he had paid was a nice bonus for them. They gave him a thumbs up with a broad smile as he went through the gate. Elke decided against any brave moves. In Justin's present condition he could easily stab her purely as a reflex action.

She gave the two men a wan smile as Justin eased through the gate and awkwardly drove away along the dirt road using only one hand.

*

'What you doing?' Simon asked belligerently, as Ed tried not to look guilty.

'Oh, jus' trying to see if this little bitty ol' cage is gonna hold those there animals,' he replied lamely.

Simon looked at the grains of precipitate on Ed's fingers, which the mining man was trying to hide without being obvious about it.

'Why're you looking at the dust?'

Simon was clearly suspicious about Ed's actions and motives.

Ed shrugged. 'Jus' wondered whether you guys keep your cages clean, is all.'

Simon was no fool and Ed was no great actor. The African was not sure whether Ed had found any trace of platinum but he was not about to take any chances. Ed told Simon that he had seen enough and had to hurry back to his hotel for a meeting. He asked Simon to thank Bud and he would be on his way immediately.

Simon shook his head. 'Sorry, Mr McCauley, I need to take you back to the ranch. Mr McNeil will want...'

On an impulse Ed decided to make a dash for it. Simon stood about six foot six tall and must have weighed at least 250 pounds. Ed was confident that he could outrun the far bigger man.

Unfortunately, Simon had anticipated Ed's moves. As the smaller man turned and jumped from the ramp, Simon pulled a large homemade catapult from his pocket. He normally used it to hunt birds, which he often cooked for his evening meal. He kept a few suitable stones in his other pocket. Ed hit the ground hard, stumbled and started to run in the direction of his SUV, which stood outside the ranch over a mile away. Simon calmly loaded his catapult, took careful aim then released a stone, which sped with remarkable accuracy straight towards Ed, hitting him hard behind his right ear! Ed collapsed in a heap on the ground. Simon strolled towards his victim, secretly quite amazed at the success of his weapon. He had never shot his catapult at anything larger than a guinea fowl before. Bringing Ed down brought a broad grin to his face as he approached the inert body of the American.

*

It was almost dark by the time Justin reached the main road and turned off the dirt in the direction of Hartbeestpoort Dam. He knew that there were a number of small hotels and hopefully a motel in the vicinity of the dam.

'How d'you expect to get me into a hotel, without my giving the game away?' Elke asked.

Truthfully, she was almost beyond resistance at that stage. All she cared about was to get some food inside her and then to sleep for a very long time. The mad machinations of Justin were a worry, but food and sleep had assumed a huge importance in her life at that moment.

'Don't worry your pretty head about that,' Justin replied.

He was also exhausted and in fact he was dreading the next step of their adventure almost as much as Elke.

A neon sign loomed up ahead. Justin caught the word "motel" and breathed a sigh of relief. He slowed the car down and pulled off onto the side of the road some hundred yards away from the entrance. Elke looked at him in alarm. Justin had already retied her hands in addition to sticking the knife in her ribs but for the past few minutes he had removed the knife and relied on the fact that if she attacked him while he was driving at high speed, they would both probably be killed.

'Why're you stopping here?'

Justin gave her one of his beatific smiles, which somehow managed to increase rather than decrease her certainty that something unpleasant lay ahead.

'I'm gonna put you in the trunk.'

Elke did not need to know much of American terminology to translate "trunk" into "boot." Either way, it was not something to look forward to!

*

As Simon approached, Ed was regaining conscious and trying to work out a strategy. The blow had only stunned him for a few seconds but he was certainly in no shape to leap up and run away. He intuitively lay completely still, as though still unconscious. He had no illusions that Simon would make mincemeat of him if it came to a straight fight.

Ed was very fit and had been an exceptional athlete but he was not a street fighter which is what he realised he would need to be, to compete with Simon. His only possible advantage lay in his speed, although Simon had overcome his first attempt to flee with contemptuous ease. Ed heard Simon's footsteps on the hard ground. Like so many big men, Simon also breathed heavily. Ed resisted an impulse to leap up and run. In fact, he waited until Simon grabbed him by the shoulders and rolled him onto his back.

As he was moved, Ed opened his eyes fractionally, and saw Simon standing over him. Ed put every ounce of strength into kicking upwards, catching the giant a glancing blow in his crotch. Simon gasped, started to buckle, then with a bellow of rage he reached down, grabbed the front of Ed's sports shirt and yanked him upright with one hand as his other hand came thundering across to hit Ed on the chin. Ed managed to swivel his head away slightly and the blow landed more on the side of the chin. Even so, Ed felt as though he had just run full tilt into one of the newly captured rhino. Fortunately for the American, Simon was also in agony and having delivered a purely reflex response to Ed's kick, he was now doubled over, clutching at the searing pain in his genitals.

Ed reeled back from the blow, nearly fell but managed somehow to remain on his feet. He turned to run but failed to see a large boulder in the darkness and fell headlong onto the ground.

The scene was reminiscent of some ancient Roman gladiatorial battle. Both men were stunned and in agony but they were also both physically, as well as mentally, determined. As Ed scrambled up once again, Simon charged him like a wounded buffalo. For a few moments they stood toe to toe slugging at each other. One of Ed's blows caught Simon a hard shot on the nose. This enraged the giant even more and his next blow finally caught Ed on the right temple, felling him like a slaughtered animal.

There was no way that Ed was going to recover this time. Simon took a few deep breaths then picked Ed up like a sack of coal, put him over one shoulder and carried him off to a nearby vehicle.

*

Justin opened the door to his chalet, switched on the lights and checked that the curtains were closed. He hurried back to the car, where Elke, whom he had both bound and gagged, was beginning to kick at the sides of the trunk. He opened it up and dragged Elke upwards until he could lever her onto his shoulders.

After a glance around to make sure no one was watching, he carried the struggling girl over to the chalet and dumped her unceremoniously onto the large double bed against the far wall. Elke's eyes blazed at him as he stared down at her. After he had closed the chalet door, he returned to the bedside and spoke to her softly. His voice was quiet but had an edge to it, which indicated to Elke that Justin was still perilously close to completely losing control.

'I'm gonna to remove your gag' he told her, 'but if I hear any noise from you, like a scream or something to attract the neighbours, I'll hurt you real bad. Then I'll gag you again until we leave. It's your choice. Nod if you agree to behave.'

Elke continued to glare at him but finally nodded. He leaned over her and untied the cord with which he had wedged a handkerchief into her mouth.

For a few moments Elke lay there gasping for breath. Since he had put the gag into her mouth, she feared she was going to choke on more than one occasion. The relief was enormous. She looked up at her captor, willing herself not to succumb into apathy and total self-pity.

'You're the last of the true romantics, aren't you?' She snarled at him.

Justin giggled. 'Now that's what's great about you, kiddo - you don't give up!'

He strode over to the telephone, picked it up, dialled 9 as instructed and waited for a response.

'Hi there, listen, I'm real tired. D'you have room service?'

He nodded as the person responded on the other end of the line.

'Yeah. I don't mind, whatever you got, but hey, I ain't eaten since this morning. Bring me two steaks will ya? Oh, and you have any Bourbon? OK, Scotch'll do. Soon as you can. Great!'

He put down the phone and grinned at Elke.

'Guess you're hungry too. Tell you what...' he left the sentence hanging as he crossed over to the bathroom and looked inside, noticing that there was only a small window with burglar bars across it; 'you take a shower now and stay in there until the food's been delivered.'

As he spoke, he removed the key from inside the bathroom door and moved across to untie Elke's bonds. Elke could think of nothing better than a hot shower at that moment, but the thought of leaving the door unlocked with Justin in the next room did not amuse her.

'How do I know you won't come in while I'm showering?' she queried.

Justin shook his head sorrowfully.

'Just when I thought we were about to start a beautiful friendship. Trouble is I can't leave the key with you, 'cos you're likely to lock yourself in and stay there.'

'I won't, I promise!' Elke implored him.

Right now, she wanted that shower more than anything else, even more than food and sleep.

'Sorry, babe, your promises ain't what they used to be, but because it suits me to have you nice and clean an' sweet smelling, as well as out of the way when the food arrives, I promise you I won't come in.'

'And your promises are more reliable than mine?' she flashed at him.

He chuckled. 'Guess not but here's what we'll do - I'll lock you into the bathroom. There's a glass cubicle inside and plenty of towels. Once you hear me lock the door you can get inside the cubicle. If I unlock the door, you'll hear me an' you'll have time to wrap a towel around you.'

Elke looked at him doubtfully as he freed the last of her bonds.

'Best offer I can make' Justin said, 'otherwise, it's the bonds and gag back on.'

Elke nodded glumly as she sat up rubbing her wrists.

'Okay, but for once don't be a pig. Just let me shower in peace, will you?'

Justin made an elaborate bow in her direction and affected an English accent.

'Certainly m'dear.'

As she entered the bathroom Justin began to close the door then stopped for a moment. He looked at her severely.

'Last thing. When the food arrives, I want you to switch off the shower and stay quiet. If you make any noise, I'll have to kill the waiter and you – don't want that on your conscience, do ya now?'

Elke sighed. 'Close the door. I'll behave if you behave.'

Justin gave her a last mischievous grin as he closed the door and locked it.

*

Ed regained consciousness for the second time in half an hour. On the first occasion his head had cleared almost immediately but this time he awoke with a blinding headache and a feeling of nausea. As he opened his eyes, he saw he was in an armchair in the sitting room of the McNeil ranch. Bud and Simon sat looking at him as he struggled to speak. Bud beat him to it.

228

'Welcome back to the real world, Ed Willjohn!'

The little man spoke softly with a crooked smile. As Ed groggily tried to work out what had given him away, Bud leaned forward and dropped Ed's wallet onto the coffee table between them. Ed also noticed a heavy duty automatic in Bud's other hand. Bud had clearly prepared himself for Ed's return to consciousness. Ed opened his mouth to speak but Bud continued.

'You won't find anything missing from your wallet. Petty larceny isn't my style.'

'Great,' Ed croaked, 'and I won't have to put on that lousy Texas twang anymore. So where do we go from here?'

Bud shrugged. 'Up to you, pal. Why're you snooping around my place in a disguise?'

Ed wished he could think more clearly as he forced himself to sound reasonably rational.

'Okay, cards on the table. My brother Justin's abducted my fiancée. Right now, I don't care about anything else except getting her back unharmed. If you know where...'

Bud grimaced and interrupted him.

'Sorry. I was hoping you could tell me where that little bastard is. I want to wring his bloody neck.'

Ed tried to smile. 'At least we've got one thing in common!'

'Why were you looking for the platinum if you're so worried about your girl?' Simon chipped in.

Ed looked at him, choosing his words carefully.

'I figured that if you knew where he is, I could use some leverage to make you hand him over to me.'

Bud snorted derisively. 'So now we're both screwed. I want my money from Justin, you want the girl and neither of us knows where he is. Your problem is that now you've figured out where the platinum is, you're a serious threat to me. I always eliminate threats.'

Bud waved his automatic meaningfully.

Ed sighed. 'That won't do you much good. You don't think I'd come here on my own without some back up, do you?'

Bud looked at him reflectively.

'Normally no, but now I know that your girl's missing in the hands of your crazy brother, I wouldn't mind betting that you just came rushing out here without a real plan.'

Which is frighteningly close to the facts, Ed thought miserably, as he tried to work out some way of stalling his execution until Sam and the Police finally figured out where he was, provided of course that Sam even got his message earlier in the day.

Justin left the key in the lock of the bathroom. He leaned his ear against the door and was relieved to hear Elke open the shower cubicle and turn on the taps. Justin was too pre-occupied with his next move to indulge in any voyeurism, even though a couple of quick mental pictures of what Elke's superb body must look like had intruded on his thoughts in the past couple of minutes. Resolutely, Justin went over to his jacket, took out his cell phone, and dialled Ed's number.

*

Bud stood up and pointed his automatic at Ed. He spoke curtly and with deadly intention.

'Give me one good reason not to finish it here and now.'

Ed felt a rising sense of unreality over the prospect of dying in the new few seconds.

'Money,' he managed to say. 'I can give you more than Justin owes you.'

'Interesting,' Bud replied 'but I think I can get that anyway, I'll...'

At that moment, Ed's cell phone rang. Everyone, including Bud, jumped at the sound.

'Let it ring.'

Ed had already taken the phone out of his pocket and glanced at who was calling him.

'I don't think so' Ed replied. 'It's the one guy we both need to talk to!'

CHAPTER 38

Bud looked at Ed, momentarily unsure of what he should do. Ed covered the mouthpiece of the phone and spoke urgently to his captor.

'Let me listen to what Justin has to say. I know how he thinks. I'll negotiate for your money as well as Elke's release.'

Bud thought, then nodded slowly as Justin's voice could be faintly heard squawking on the phone. Ed took his hand off the mouthpiece and spoke urgently to his brother.

'How's Elke?'

'She's fine,' Justin replied. 'Now this is what...'

'Let me talk to her!' Ed demanded.

'When we've finished' Justin replied irritably.

'I'm not saying anything to you until I know Elke's okay. Put her on!'

Justin smiled. He had expected Ed's demand but had decided not to give in too quickly.

'Don't you believe me?' Justin asked, tongue firmly in cheek.

'Oh sure, if you were Pinocchio your nose'd stretch from here to the moon! PUT HER ON!!!'

Ed's voice reflected the tension of his experience of both his brother's madness and the very real threat of the cold-eyed and ruthless Bud with a gun pointed at him.

'Boy, you sure are pissed!' Justin spoke reprovingly to him. 'Here she is.'

Justin had waited until Elke had finished showering and they had both eaten the steaks room service had provided for them. She had not tried to escape or attract attention, realising that her body desperately needed some sustenance if she were to stand any chance of overcoming Justin. He handed the phone to Elke and hissed at her.

'Say you're fine and nothing else. Otherwise!'

Justin raised his carving knife threateningly. Elke nodded tiredly.

'I'm okay, darling, just a bit shaken up from the crash.'

Ed let out a long breath. 'Thank God. Has he harmed you in any way?'

'Not really, I'm just tired and I...'

Justin grabbed the phone out of her hand and spoke into it.

'Satisfied?'

'Okay, so where do we go from here?' Ed asked.

'We barter, big brother. Your shares in Willjohn for Elke!'

Ed paused for a moment then replied.

'What you're asking affects a whole lot of people, not just me and you. How about if...'

'You heard my terms. It depends on how much you want her, I guess.'

Ed knew he was trapped. He'd give everything he possessed to get Elke back. He hoped his mother and his many good friends at Willjohn Industries would understand.

'Okay, how d'you suggest we do this?'

Justin chuckled contentedly. His gamble had paid off and there was still time to have some fun with the girl.

'As soon as my lawyer confirms that the share certificates are in his hands, I'll have Elke delivered to you but' he let the words hang dramatically 'how're you gonna get your signature on the transfer?'

Ed had already thought this through. 'Mom has my Power of Attorney. I'll have the shares transferred right away, but how do I know you'll deliver Elke?'

'That's your problem, Ed' Justin replied.

Ed deliberated, then responded,

'Okay, I'll have the shares put in trust to be released on condition that Elke is returned unharmed. We can have a lawyer appointed by your lawyer to confirm this, so you won't have to take my word for it, one way or the other.

'Sounds good. I'll call you in two hours to...'

At that moment Bud, who had been listening to the exchange with growing frustration, grabbed the phone out of Ed's hand.

'Hi Justin! Remember me? It's Bud. There's a small matter of money owed to me and, by the way, the bill just went up again - back to a million bucks, seeing as how you're going to inherit big time!'

There was a long silence on the other side of the phone. Bud spoke again.

'Cat got your tongue? Listen, I'll make sure Ed does the share transfer, but I want my money now, like in the next half hour. Otherwise I shoot Ed, which normally wouldn't worry you except that your mother'll get his shares, not you, but then you get to keep the girl!'

*

Marie brought two plates of food to the dining room table. She had cooked a couple of chicken breasts, pumpkin and potatoes. Isak had said

232

he was not hungry and for that matter, neither was she, but she expected a long restless night ahead and decided that they should both eat to sustain themselves.

Isak accepted the plate listlessly. They both bowed their heads in prayer as Isak included in the grace a few words for their daughter's safety. As they picked at their food, Marie spoke softly.

'This waiting is the worst thing. If only there was something we could do. Why hasn't that American phoned?'

'It could be that he's found something and he's trying to sort it out. Also remember that these cell phones go out of range in parts of the country.'

'You're pinning a lot of faith on just one person,' Marie replied.

At that moment, their landline started to ring. Marie rushed off to it and fumbled with the receiver before putting it to her ear.

'Marie Stein wat praat!' She said, trying to keep the quaver out of her voice.

'Hello Marie, Marius de Wet here!' Marius replied in Afrikaans. Before Marie could respond he spoke rapidly.

'Listen, we haven't found her yet and as I think you know, half the district's looking for her, but...'

'Give me some good news, please Marius?' Marie implored him.

There was a slight hesitation before Marius replied. 'I think you could call it good news. Don Watson, from Buffalo Hills Hotel, did a search of the resorts in the area. He came across a small picnic place. The guard at the gate says that a man and a woman answering to Elke and Justin's description, spent a few hours at the place and then left just before dark tonight. Their car was the same model he hired.'

'Elke, was she...?' Marie asked.

'She looked fine, didn't say anything, just looked straight ahead. Marie, she's alive - that's what counts!'

Marie started sobbing and was unable to respond. She put the phone down and tried to smile at Isak.

'She's been seen alive.'

She crossed over to Isak and hugged him with all her strength as if the intensity of her embrace could communicate the depth of her despair.

*

Justin finally found his voice. Bud's intrusion on the phone had shocked him into silence and virtual catatonia. He could not think what to do next. It was the last possible thing he could have imagined to have happen.

'What in the hell's Ed doin' at your place?' he croaked.

'Looking for you, seeing that your blundering efforts've made me your best advertised accomplice!'

233

Bud took a deep breath and snarled.

'What's it going to be? Will you make arrangements or do I shoot big brother here and now?'

'I'll call you back as soon as I've spoken to the States' Justin replied miserably.

The phone clicked off and Bud looked up at Ed.

'You'd better hope your crazy brother's still able to pull this off' Bud told him. 'Otherwise your visit to the McNeil ranch'll be a long one, like until they dig your bones up a hundred years from now!'

'We can do this another way' Ed replied, having spent the last couple of minutes trying to find an escape route.

'Forget about Justin. I'll arrange for a million to be paid to your lawyers before I sign over the shares to Justin.'

Bud smiled sardonically.

'Hey! You've given me a good idea. I'll take the million from you; and from Justin!'

'That wasn't the deal…' Ed began.

'Right. I just moved the goal posts.'

He turned to Simon. 'You'd better get going with the rhino.'

Bud took a bulky envelope from the inside pocket of his jacket and handed it to Simon.

'All the paperwork's signed and you'll find enough money there to start you off somewhere else. Thanks, my friend. You've been a great help to me!'

The two men shook hands. As he left the room Simon opened the flap of the envelope and was clearly impressed by the wad of notes he could see within. He looked around.

'Thanks, Boss. I think you better move as well.'

'I will, Simon. All organised. I'm flying out of here as soon as I've sorted out these jerks. Costa's collecting me in the chopper.'

Simon grinned, raised his hand in a mock salute and left the room.

*

It had taken Martin much longer to get the Brits Police loaded up and ready for a raid on Bud McNeil's ranch than he had anticipated. However, they were now speeding towards the ranch in a convoy. Martin drove his own SUV in front. Captain Kloppers in charge of the Police team sat next to him. Two Police vans with eighteen armed men followed directly behind them. Martin drove as fast as he dared but the vans following him were not exactly the Flying Squad and he was frustrated at having to stick to speeds of around 120 kph.

Martin filled the Captain in on the events of the last few days. He also explained that they would have to be careful when they reached the ranch. As far as he knew Ed would either be watching the ranch or perhaps somehow trying to bluff Bud McNeil. He certainly didn't want to get Ed shot in the process of trying to rescue him. The fact that he hadn't called again also indicated that he may have been captured by McNeil.

'What about the stolen platinum?' Captain Kloppers asked.

'Ed and the girl're our top priority. Then we'll see what we can find.'

The two men fell silent as they raced down the road anxiously counting the kilometres as they drew close to the ranch.

Justin called his lawyer in the US. He was lucky as the man was about to go out.

'Justin here, did you okay the two hundred and fifty thousand into McNeil's account?' he asked without preamble.

'All done, Mr Willjohn' the lawyer replied. 'How's it goin'?'

'Fine' Justin replied impatiently. 'Now I want you to transfer another seven hundred and fifty thousand. The original deal's on track again.'

'Er.' The lawyer's hesitation made Justin's stomach muscles tighten. There couldn't be a problem. He had plenty of assets. Elke watched him listlessly. She was propped up on the bed looking in better condition now that she had showered but nevertheless she was still exhausted and most of Justin's conversations on the phone had made little sense to her. She was horrified to hear Justin demand Ed's shares in exchange for her safety and her heart went out to her fiancée who had obviously not argued the point overmuch. It occurred to her that now was the time to try and escape again, but she wondered if she had the strength to do so.

Justin listened with growing horror as his lawyer explained that after he had transferred the quarter million dollars, his mother and the Board of Willjohn Industries had frozen his loan account until Justin returned home to explain his actions.

'They can't do that!' Justin stormed. 'It's my money!'

'Unfortunately they've found some fine print in your old man's will, which instructs them to withhold large withdrawals from your account without receiving a full and logical explanation as to why you need it and how it will be profitable for both you and for the company.'

Justin spent another five minutes exploring every possibility with his lawyer but drew a blank. Finally, in a fury, he rang off and called Ed's number again. This time the service provider announced that the number was not currently available. Justin had been lucky to get through the first time in that area. With shaking hands Justin checked Bud McNeil's number and dialled that instead.

Bud answered the call.

'Bud, it's Justin. The quarter mil's gone through as promised but I gotta get back home to justify further expenditure, which I can do easily enough, and if I've got Ed's shares I control the company and I'll demand it.'

Bud shook his head. 'Too complicated. Looks like your brother's outlived his usefulness. You might as well keep the girl; Ed won't have any need of her where he's going. Just watch your back, pal. When I'm settled in overseas, I'll be coming for you!'

Bud dropped the phone back on its cradle and turned to look at Ed. As he did so, he raised his automatic and pointed directly at Ed's heart.

'Your family's put a hold on your brother's accounts. Too bad. I could've used the extra cash but I'll make do without it. You guys're big trouble so I'm not going to take it any further.

His finger tightened on the trigger. Ed watched in horror as his life seemed to be about to come to an abrupt and ignominious end.

'Hey, hold it! I can make up the shortfall. Just let me call. I'm not the black sheep!'

Bud smiled, shook his head and pulled the trigger.

*

Justin stared at the telephone in shock. Bud had refused his offer and hung up on him. His only thought was that if he shot Ed, then Justin's leverage with the family would have irrevocably disappeared. His mother and Franklin had already put a hold on his money. He felt the world crashing around him. His already precarious hold on sanity was slipping away. He stood up and started trashing the room. He ripped the telephone from its cable and set it flying across the room to smash into the far wall.

He grabbed a side table, lifted it up and smashed it with all his strength against the television set. The glass front of the television shattered and a series of small electronic explosions occurred within the box behind the screen.

Elke was unsure whether he would turn his mad rage towards her next. She drew on her last reserves of strength to slide off the bed as Justin faced away from her. She crept towards his jacket which was hanging from the back of the door leading to the parking lot outside. Justin had earlier put the door keys in his jacket. She reached the jacket, delved into his pocket and withdrew the keys before Justin's attention turned back towards the bed. Even though he had already stepped into a hallucinatory world, where reality was beyond his grasp, Justin noticed that something, the creature that he had held captive, was gone!

He wheeled around looking frantically for his prey. She was at the door fumbling with the keys in the lock. With an animal howl of fury he leaped at her, hands outstretched, his carving knife forgotten. He knew he must silence the creature, stifle it stop it moving. Nothing must move around him ever again!

*

Martin and Captain Kloppers stopped at the gate to the McNeil ranch, leaped out of Martin's SUV and approached the guard house. The policeman already had his gun in his hand. He yelled at the startled security guard, who was already reaching for the internal phone which connected him to the ranch.

'Hold it! This is the Police. Don't contact anyone! Come out and open the gate!'

The guard complied slowly with the order as Martin fretted over every last second. He had a growing feeling they were already too late.

*

Bud looked at the crumpled body on the floor in front of him. Who was the American kidding, he wondered?

CHAPTER 39

Bud shook his head in bemusement as he quickly stepped over to a large chest of drawers against the wall. From the middle drawer Bud withdrew a pair of handcuffs he had bought after a gang of poachers had been caught on the ranch. He and his staff had had difficulty in restraining the poachers until the Police had arrived.

Bud rapidly returned to the centre of the room. Ed had not moved. He bent down and carefully clipped one end of the handcuffs to Ed's right hand. The big American lay face downwards on his left side. His body was limp, but he was a much heavier man than Bud, who had some difficulty in rolling him over onto his stomach. Once this was achieved, he managed to clip the second cuff around the left hand, all the time holding his gun at the ready. That achieved, he stood up and chuckled.

'Come on, Ed, you can't kid the kidder. My gun's loaded with blanks. What's your excuse for falling down?'

There was still no movement for a few moments. Then Ed, with difficulty, rolled back onto his left side and stared up at Bud. He was still adjusting to the fact that he was still alive.

'When you pulled the trigger, the gun went off and I tried to dodge the bullet, I suppose. I felt no impact, so I continued falling and decided to play dead.'

Bud nodded. 'Sounds reasonable but why didn't you try to take me when I was putting the 'cuffs on?'

Ed allowed himself a half grin.

'Now you tell me you were firing blanks I feel like an idiot, but lying there, I figured that you'd still be pointing the gun at me. I'd rather take my chances with these;' he moved his hands backwards to expose the cuffs, 'than have you shoot me again!'

Bud agreed 'Ja, you're right. Now I've got to decide what to do with you!'

Ed wriggled backwards with difficulty, trying to prop himself upright against the large sofa behind him. Bud put his gun down on a coffee table and helped to drag Ed to a more upright position, leaning against the sofa.

Ed thanked him curtly, then asked 'Why blanks?'

Bud replied 'Fair question; but if you tell anyone else, I'll really have to kill you. Trouble is, I'm not really a killer.'

Ed chuckled. 'McNeil must be Irish not Scots - that's the most Irish statement I've heard in a while!'

'Well, you know what I mean. Look I've got a hell of a reputation as a tough, ruthless gangster. If the other guys are scared of me, I've got a better chance of not being challenged. It's like the old bull elephant who has to be half dead before some young bull plucks up the courage to challenge him.'

Ed nodded tiredly. 'Fascinating. Where do we go from here? Remember my priority is to get my girl back.'

'Don't blame you there. That brother of yours is a real fruit cake.'

He paced up and down for a few moments before continuing.

'Look, I may not be a killer but I still look after number one.' He glanced at his watch. 'My chopper should arrive any moment. I'll leave you here. You'll be rescued in due course. The cops're bound to search this place eventually.'

'So, your *humane* approach isn't compromised by the thought of my starving to death if they don't arrive, or your staff deciding to kill me off?'

Bud sighed. 'Don't complicate my life, Ed. Tell you what. As soon as I'm out of the country, which should be in a couple of hours, I'll call in and tell the cops you're here. Fair enough?'

'I wouldn't necessarily employ you as a charity worker but I'll live with that. At least I hope I will.'

Bud moved his head in agreement, went back to the middle drawer of his chest of drawers and withdrew an empty ammunition clip for his gun plus a box of live bullets. He brought them over to the coffee table, unloaded the blank ammunition clip and started loading the empty clip with the real bullets. Ed watched him sardonically.

'You have a complicated morality, Bud,' Ed commented. 'Planning to change the habit of a lifetime?'

Bud looked at him. For the first time Ed could see that the little man was uncertain. He cleared his throat before replying.

'It occurred to me that I'd look pretty dumb if the cops do arrive before my chopper does and I try firing blanks at them. There are limits to anything y'know. I'm glad it's all over in many ways. I've lived a charmed life for years but luck was turning against me. I'm a careful gambler. When the dice're against you, take your winnings and leave.'

Bud loaded the last live bullet into the clip then looked up at Ed.

'Hey, seeing as we're being so civilised, like a drink?'

Ed inclined his head in agreement. Bud put the live clip down on the coffee table but was careful to take the gun with him as he went over to the sideboard to pour a couple of stiff whiskies.

*

Elke had the key in the lock and was starting to turn it when Justin crashed into her, howling like a crazed animal, with his outstretched hands groping for her throat. Justin was slightly built and about the same height as Elke but the intensity of his madness added a further impetus to his charge. Elke was knocked sideways, almost losing her balance altogether. She stepped backwards, desperately trying to avoid his outstretched hands, which had momentarily encircled her neck. As she back-pedalled, Justin's hands slipped away but he chased after her in a blind fury, now swinging his arms in an effort to knock her down.

Elke retreated further and further from the front door in her efforts to escape his clutches. Suddenly Justin leaped to one side and grabbed his carving knife, which he had left on a side table next to the bed. Elke could see that his blind rage was diminishing and was now replaced by a crafty look, as he took a firm grip on the knife and started to stalk her. He was careful to keep himself between her and the front door. Elke suddenly had an idea. She continued to retreat but now backed up towards an upright lightweight wooden chair against the wall close to the bathroom door. As soon as she was close enough, she reached out and grabbed the chair. Instead of using it as the shield as Justin half expected, Elke threw it as hard as she could at her attacker.

Her unexpected action surprised Justin. He ducked but the chair still caught him on the shoulder with one of its legs raking across his face. Elke did not wait to see what effect she had created but she leaped for the bathroom door, wrenched the key out from the outside of the door, where Justin had put it and dived inside the bathroom.

Once again, she fought to put a key in a lock before Justin could reach her. However, this time she was on the far side of the door. As her one hand fumbled to insert the key in the lock, her other hand gripped the door handle as hard as she could. She also leaned her body against the door and prayed that she could withstand any onslaught Justin might mount.

*

Bud put both glasses of Scotch on the coffee table, smiled at Ed and spoke gently.

'Sorry, but I'm a naturally suspicious kind of guy.'

He picked up the clip containing the live ammunition and slipped it into his gun. Then keeping the gun in one hand, he picked up one of the glasses and held it to Ed's lips for him to drink.

'Cheers' Bud murmured, as Ed gratefully sipped some of the fiery liquor.

Bud took the glass away, then picked up his own and raised it towards Ed in a cheers gesture, before taking a large swallow.

'Isn't this cosy?' Bud chuckled.

At that moment, a noise could be heard outside the room. Bud swore, dumped his glass back onto the coffee table, leaped up and in a swift movement put an arm around Ed's throat, with his other hand pressing the gun into Ed's temple.

The door to the sitting room burst open. Captain Kloppers and three policemen poured into the room, guns drawn and pointed at Bud.

'Drop your gun!' Kloppers yelled at Bud.

The little man gave a crooked grin.

'I don't think so. Ed and I'll be leaving in a moment, so let's not do anything foolish.'

As he spoke, the distant sound of an approaching chopper could be heard.

Captain Kloppers took a couple of steps forward. His gun was aimed at Bud's head.

'You don't stand a chance. We've got roadblocks in a ring around your ranch here. Be sensible!'

Bud could hear the welcoming sound of the chopper drawing closer.

'Tell me, Officer, how many men d'you have outside?'

Captain Kloppers could see no point in lying.

'Eighteen men. Every exit is closely guarded.'

'I'm sure it is. Now what I want you to do, is to tell every one of those men to come inside and join us here.'

Kloppers looked puzzled. 'But why?'

'Just do it!' Bud snarled.

He pressed the gun even more tightly into Ed's temple. He also increased pressure around Ed's throat, making the American retch and gasp for breath.

Kloppers had no way of knowing that Bud could be bluffing. He lifted up his two-way radio.

'Andre, bring all the men into the ranch house. Over.'

'Ja, Kaptein. There's a chopper coming in to land. Is it one of ours?'

Kloppers looked at Bud, who gave Ed another few moments of extreme pressure to his throat. Ed writhed as he fought for breath.

'Tell him you called for it' Bud rasped.

Kloppers nodded glumly and did as he was told.

Elke had the key halfway into the lock before there was a heavy thud on the far side of the door. Simultaneously Justin tried to turn the handle from the outside. Elke used her last reserves of strength and adrenaline to resist his attack. The key had slipped out of the keyhole. Fighting with everything she had, Elke pressed the door handle upwards. Despite her efforts Justin was beginning to turn the handle.

She finally slotted the key back into the lock. But just as she started to turn the key, Justin succeeded in turning the handle. Frantic, Elke put her shoulder to the door and tried to prevent Justin from opening it. Justin applied all his own waning strength to push the door open. It moved a couple of inches but Elke, with a supreme effort, managed to close it again. Once more she almost turned the key but was prevented in doing so by another fierce bombardment from Justin.

Elke could hear him sobbing and yelling on the other side of the door. 'I'll kill you. I'll kill you!'

Elke was a great believer that you could potentially do anything, if you could be confident enough in your own mind that you could do it. You had to prevent the sly voices in your head from saying 'No, not possible' or better still, keep the voices quiet altogether by the power of your certainty.

Knowing that this final effort could be literally life or death, she focused her entire being on keeping the door closed for the precious second it would take to turn the lock. An image of a smiling Ed swam into view. She knew in that instant that she could do it. There was a gap of about three inches. With horror Elke saw Justin's fingers groping through the gap. Without even thinking, Elke bent down and bit a couple of fingers hard. There was a scream from the other side of the door and the fingers disappeared. So did Justin's weight momentarily release from the door. Elke triumphantly slammed the door shut and turned the key. Elke slowly turned her back against the door and slid down onto the floor, shaking uncontrollably.

*

Bud pulled Ed up onto his feet as the rest of the Police entered the room, followed by an anxious-looking Martin.

Bud frog-marched Ed across the room, keeping a firm grip on his throat and the gun to his head. He reached a two-way radio attached to the wall then released his hold around Ed's throat without moving the gun from the young man's head, he warned

'Don't try anything, Ed. Stand dead still.'

As a precaution Bud kept Ed positioned between himself and the cops in case one of them wanted to play sniper.

'Is this a good time to test out your theories of non-violence?' Ed asked him.

'No, damn you!'

Bud's usual cool was rapidly deserting him. He operated the radio with one hand keeping a watchful eye on both Ed and the cops, who seemed to almost fill the other half of the room. They, in turn, watched carefully for the slightest opportunity to gun Bud down. Bud called the chopper on the radio.

'Costa. I've got company here. Remain in the air until you see me on the helipad. I'll have a hostage with me and don't worry if you see some cops. That's what the hostage is for. Over!'

'Hey! What's going on? I'm out of here!' Costa sounded terrified.

'You do that, and your family'll never get out of the Congo as promised. Up to you. Over.'

There was a silence then a burst of static before Costa spoke again.

'Roger that, but don't take long. This bird chews up fuel, remember.'

'Couple of minutes. Over and out.'

Bud put the radio down, immediately grabbing Ed around the throat again and hugging the American's body as close to him as he could. He also kept moving the two of them around on the theory that a moving target would be even more difficult to hit with accuracy. The police watched frustrated. It was clearly too dangerous to try a shot. One of the men looked at his Captain pleadingly, believing he could take Bud out. Kloppers shook his head. It wasn't worth the risk. Bud moved Ed into the middle of the room. He would have to cross over it in order to reach the front door.

'Sorry Pal, you're not rid of me yet. Anything you want to tell these guys about your fiancée before we take off?'

'Yeah' Ed replied. He briefly told Martin and the Police about Justin's phone call.

*

Justin hammered on the door but his efforts were futile.

'Elke open the door. We can work something out here!'

Elke could hear the fear and uncertainty in his voice. She stood up shakily, ignoring his entreaties and made her way to the small window over the toilet. It was far too small for her to climb through it, but the window opened easily enough. Elke took a deep breath of fresh air. It had never smelled as sweet before. She could sense freedom but it was not yet within her grasp. There was one more thing she had to do.

*

Bud's natural cockiness surfaced as he steered Ed towards door. He stopped in front of the coffee table, bent down swiftly and picked up his glass. He drained the last of the amber liquid.

'Hate to see a good Scotch go to waste,' he told everyone.

Before anyone could react, his arm returned around Ed's throat once more.

'I want you gentlemen to behave yourselves now. I'm leaving with my good friend, Ed. If I see any of you guys appear from the building, it'll be easy enough to shoot him and catch my chopper before you guys can catch me.'

He grinned at them.

'I made a long speech to Ed before you guys arrived about not being a killer at heart. I'm not, but an instinct of self-preservation can be a powerful overriding factor.'

At that moment Ed dropped his jaw and simultaneously pressed hard against Bud's forearm. He bent over with such rapidity that Bud did not have time or the ability to let go of his hostage's throat. Bud flew over Ed's shoulders and landed with a crash on the floor, but not before he had pulled the trigger of his gun for the second time that night!

*

Elke took a deep breath of the fresh air flowing through the bathroom window and started to scream as loudly as she could.

CHAPTER 40

Rob and Don sat in the bar of Buffalo Hills Hotel having a nightcap. It had been a long anxious day. There had been no further word on Ed, Justin or Elke since the earlier sighting at the picnic site some hours previous.

As the barman served them with coffee and liqueurs, he looked at his bosses anxiously.

'Any sign of Mr Willjohn, sir?'

'Which one?' Don responded gloomily.

'The nice one, sir.'

It had not escaped the staff's attention that Ed had been a model guest since his arrival. Justin had been unpredictable with the staff, charming one moment and in a towering rage the next – usually over some ridiculous or even imaginary fault. The hotel had always set extremely high standards of service in every department but it was a fact of life that a few guests would go out of their way to complain, no matter how good the service. It was rare, but it happened. Justin fell into this category, whereas his older brother had always been extremely appreciative of the caring approach shown to him. It was not just because he had become friendly with management either. Ed had noticed how all the guests, as well as casual visitors for tea and drinks or a meal, had felt equally welcome at Buffalo Hills. Ed had expressed these thoughts over a drink with Rob one evening and now the tall Manager frowned, as he replied to the barman.

'No sign yet, Johnny. We'll let you and the rest of the staff know as soon as we hear anything.'

Johnny thanked Rob and turned his attention to other customers. Don stirred his coffee as he thought through the unfolding drama.

'When did Martin discover Ed had gone off on his own to the McNeil ranch?'

'Nearly three hours ago,' Rob replied. 'Marius called me. Martin spoke to him as he was heading towards the ranch with the Brits Police.'

So both our young lovers're in real danger,'

Don raised his liqueur glass. 'Here's to Ed and Elke; may they both return safely!'

'I'll second that if I can only get a drink around here!'

Marius de Wet's voice spoke from behind them. Rob and Don turned around to greet him. Don turned back to call Johnny but the waiter had seen Marius and was already approaching with his usual glass of chilled dry white wine.

Marius had nothing more to add to what Rob and Don already knew. The three tried to discuss other matters, such as the composition of the latest Springbok Rugby team to tackle Wales that coming weekend. They also touched on Bafana Bafana, the South African soccer team at the World Cup, who had just earned a creditable draw with Paraguay in their opening match. However, the mood was not right and the normally ebullient trio soon subsided into desultory comments over their concerns for Ed and Elke.

*

Elke was not the sort of person who screamed. She was by nature a far more stoic, "stiff upper lip" type, who tried to conceal her innermost emotions. However, the events of the terrible day with Justin lent impetus to the release of emotion in a loud high-pitched scream, which must have reached virtually every corner of the motel and its surrounds.

After she had been screaming for a few seconds, there was a predictable crazed explosion from Justin. He also started yelling and beating upon the bathroom door. For the first time since her capture after the car crash, Elke felt that she was in control. The bathroom door was robust and Justin was very unlikely to break it down. This was not a Hollywood movie where both goodies and baddies smashed through doors with impunity. This was real life and mad Justin was far more likely to break his previously damaged collarbone or dislocate a shoulder. Elke's major worry at that moment was simply the question of whether or not people would respond to the increasing volume of noise coming from their chalet.

*

Bud had landed hard on the floor with the breath knocked out of him. Ed had also fallen with his hands cuffed behind his back but his natural athleticism had asserted itself. He rolled over onto one shoulder as he fell, then upon impact he thrust hard with his legs, increasing the roll in a direction away from the winded body of Bud.

After a brief moment's hesitation Captain Kloppers, followed by seemingly every cop in the room, rushed at Bud and fell on him. The little man had dropped his gun as he fell. One of the cops, feeling left out by the scrum of bodies around the platinum thief, dived for Bud's gun and picked it up.

Martin, realising that there were enough cops in the room to raid some Mafia hideaway, sensibly stood back as Bud was secured. He then stepped forward to help Ed to his feet. The American was unable to get up on his own with his hands still cuffed behind his back.

Martin looked at his friend with a mixture of relief and exasperation. 'You okay?'

Ed nodded slowly. As the tension ebbed away, he felt as though he could sleep for many hours, but thoughts of Elke's continued captivity flooded back and he was already planning what to do next when Martin spoke again.

'I don't know whether to call you a bloody fool or a hero,' he said. 'You were extremely lucky Bud didn't shoot you.'

The room suddenly went quiet as the policemen dragged an angry looking Bud to his feet. Captain Kloppers overheard what Martin was saying and nodded grimly.

'He's right sir, you could've been killed.'

Ed laughed unexpectedly.

'Sorry to disappoint you guys but I was in no real danger.'

'You were luckier than you think' Bud snarled. 'I don't normally miss and in your case, I should've plugged you!'

Ed smiled at him. 'You're saying that you only miss when you're shooting blanks. Right?'

Bud sighed resignedly.

'I never miss when I'm hunting game or target shooting. Like I told you I've never shot any humans.'

'So, what went wrong, Bud? Did you miss on purpose?'

Bud looked at him furiously.

'Go to hell, you bloody Yank, you've just ruined everything!'

Ed reached out for Bud's gun. The policeman holding it obligingly handed it over. Ed clicked the release and the ammunition clip fell into his hand. He held it up.

'Sorry Bud, you were shooting blanks again.'

'What?' Bud was incredulous. 'But I...'

'You thought you'd put in the live ammo but when you went over and poured us a drink, I managed to get my foot onto the table and push the clips around so that you reloaded the blanks. Sorry that your grand gesture of the drink was your downfall. The moral of the story, I guess is, don't drink on the job!'

At that moment the two-way radio squawked. Costa's voice came clearly over the speaker. 'Hey, Bud, hurry up pal, or I'll have to abort. I'm running out of fuel!'

Justin continued his futile attempt to break down the bathroom door as Elke kept up her screams. Justin dimly heard voices in the parking ground outside. It was clear that they were heading towards the chalet where he and Elke were between them making enough noise to waken a cemetery full of the dead!

Justin may have slipped over the fine dividing line between sanity and madness, but he had not lost his innate cunning. He stopped hammering on the bathroom door and made his way rapidly to the front door of the chalet. When it became apparent to him that people were standing on the far side of the door, he seized the initiative and opened it wide, staring out anxiously at three men who stood on the threshold looking back at him with concern. One of the men was the middle-aged owner of the motel. An African security guard armed with a truncheon and a young white man made up the trio.

'Thank God you've come!' Justin blurted out before the others could speak. 'There's a woman in my bathroom yelling like she's about to be murdered!'

The men looked at each other confused. Finally, the owner asked 'What's she doing in your bathroom?'

Justin tried a more aggressive tone.

'You tell me, pal. As you know I came here on my own. I was settling down for the night, suddenly this dame steps outta the bathroom.'

'You didn't know she was there?' the owner asked in disbelief.

'Hell, no. I guess she was reading a book in the tub or something. She was real quiet. Then she comes out, looks at me and yells for me to get outta *her* room. I told her it was mine.'

'Why's she still screaming?' the young man asked.

'Reckon she thought I was trying to rape her or something. I wanted to explain but she wasn't having any of it. She went back inside the bathroom and started hollering!'

The owner nodded. 'I'm sorry sir, it all sounds like a big mistake.'

He stepped forward, followed by the other two men. Justin moved aside and let them in.

As they headed for the bathroom Justin called out.

'I'll go wait in your Reception. I don't wanna tangle with that crazy chick again.'

The owner glanced back and nodded.

'I'll call you, sir. I'm really sorry.'

Justin gave a half wave and stepped out of the front door as the owner cautiously tapped on the bathroom door.

*

Captain Kloppers looked at Bud. 'I want you to tell your chopper pilot to land.'

'What's in it for me?' Bud queried.

Kloppers shrugged. 'No promises but any co-operation can be used in mitigation later.'

Bud shook his head in disagreement. 'Not good enough. I'd rather let him get away.'

Ed stepped forward and picked up the mike of the two-way radio. Once again, his ability to mimic voices came in handy.

'Coming out now, Costa. Don't worry if you see a few cops, I've still got my hostage.'

'Okay, but hurry' Costa replied.

Ed picked up the gun with blanks and handed it to Bud. He then turned to the Captain.

'Can you let me have a gun, please?'

The Policeman smiled and shook his head.

'Sorry, Mr Willjohn. But I like the idea.'

He turned to the younger of the other two white cops in the squad. 'Franz, kom.'

Despite Ed's protests, Franz was quickly installed as the hostage. He removed his Police jacket, put on Ed's parka and steered Bud out of the door with his own gun shoved into the little man's ribs. Ed was frustrated but appreciated the Police's professional approach to the trap he had devised for the chopper pilot.

Bud and Franz went out of the door close together, followed by the policemen who raced around in a wide circle, surrounding the chopper that was descending to land on Bud's helipad. Martin and Ed watched the scene play out from one of the wide windows of the ranch house. Kloppers was insistent that neither of the civilians should take any further part in the operation. It was like a scene from a movie.

Bud and Franz approached the chopper as it landed, ducking instinctively as they stepped beneath the whirling rotors. They entered the chopper together, seconds later a stream of Policemen surrounded it, with guns drawn.

*

The Motel's owner tapped again on the bathroom door before calling out.

'Lady, this is the Motel's owner. I think there's been a big misunderstanding.'

Elke stopped screaming as soon as she heard a different voice outside the door. She had no illusions that Justin would try to wriggle his way out of the situation. She came to the door and spoke in Afrikaans, praying that the man on the other side spoke the language.

'Meneer, the American doesn't speak the "taal" – tell me if he's holding you hostage? Just say yes or no'

The Motel owner was by now thoroughly confused but he responded with a firm 'No!'

Elke still held back. She had experienced enough trickery from Justin in one day to last a few lifetimes.

'Please lady open the door and we can quickly sort this out. It seems as though we've double-booked or something.'

Elke began to realise what Justin had done but surely, when she came out, his story would not... suddenly the penny dropped. Elke rapidly unlocked the door and opened it.

'Where is he?' Elke demanded.

The three men stared at her in confusion.

'The American said he'd wait for us in the Reception as soon as we've...'

Elke spoke firmly and distinctly. The authority in her voice was unmistakable.

'Listen. That man is a criminal. He abducted me this morning and now he's trying to...'

At that moment, Elke heard a car engine start up, followed by high revs and the squeal of rubber on the road as the vehicle took off at speed.

Elke rushed to the door and looked out. Justin's car was fast disappearing into the distance. Elke sighed. At least she was free. Suddenly, overcome with emotion, her voice cracking, Elke looked back at her liberators.

'Please call the Police.'

A wave of blackness suddenly enveloped her and she collapsed at the feet of the startled Motel owner.

*

Martin and Bud walked down to meet the Police returning with Bud and Costa in tow. Ed looked at Bud for a few moments.

'You're a strange guy, Bud, a kinda contradiction in terms. Animal lover, thief, pacifist, or so you say. A man of many parts.'

Bud shrugged and turned his head away without speaking. Ed looked at Captain Kloppers.

'Can you call the Police at the airport. The shipment of rhino should arrive there in a short while. There's a stash of our platinum in the cage.'

It felt good to identify with the mine again and to be recognised as being back on the side of the good guys!

Kloppers took the details and instructed one of his men to call the airport from the radio in the nearest Police car.

Ed's attention was rapidly turning back to Elke and her whereabouts. He grabbed Martin's arm.

'Listen, can we get back to the Hotel. I need to find out about Elke.'

The Policeman who had gone to radio, came running back. He was a slim African who gave a huge grin as he approached his Captain, Martin and Ed.

'Sir, they found the lady! She is okay!'

Ed felt the world spin around his head for an instant then with a rising sense of euphoria he grabbed the hands of every Policeman in sight, shook their hands enthusiastically and took off at a run towards his car with Martin in close pursuit.

*

Elke sat propped up in the bed, where not long before Justin had held her a terrified captive. She sipped a mug of steamy hot coffee and smiled at the Motel owner, Dawie Schutte and his wife Joanna who had come over to help her husband revive the beautiful young woman who had swooned at his feet. At least that was the way he would jokingly tell it for some time to come. Joanna knew Elke's parents slightly. As soon as she was fully conscious again, the phones started ringing, with the Motel owner on his cell phone to the Police and Elke on to her parents, followed immediately by a call to Marius to help her find out about Ed's situation.

All that had happened over an hour ago. The Police had asked her to remain where she was. Anyway, Elke was in no condition to go anywhere.

A doctor, who lived nearby, had come over and given her a thorough examination. The blow on the head from the car crash earlier in the day had possibly given her a mild concussion but otherwise, she was simply exhausted from her ordeal.

There was a gentle tap on the door. 'That'll be the Police,' Joanna said and went over to open the door. She was wrong. A dishevelled and worried looking young man stood in the doorway, staring anxiously into the room.

'Ed' she called out as he dashed forward and fell into her arms.

CHAPTER 41

As Justin drove away from the Motel he had been filled with rage and thoughts of revenge against his brother and the blonde bitch. Now two hours later, the young man was physically and mentally exhausted. As his adrenaline level had dropped so the rising tide of madness had receded somewhat.

Justin would never be described as normal and the events of the past few days had driven him to new levels of delusion and self-justification. However, he was at least thinking clearly enough to plan his escape. This was something he had not done earlier as the thought of failure had not occurred to him. Now he realised that the Police would be out in force looking for him. He was in a foreign country, his accent unmistakable and, unlike his brother, he had no skill with changing accents. He was under no illusion that Ed would provide a photo to the police and this would be widely distributed to the media.

He would be wanted on charges of aiding and abetting the theft of platinum as well as abducting Elke. No matter how much he would like to do terrible things to the two E's, his priority was to get out of the country.

Fortunately, he did not have a problem with money. Even though his mother and the board of Willjohn Industries had suspended his loan account he had been carefully salting away money into another account over the past couple of years. By his standards he was no longer rich but half a million dollars would tide him over, if he could only stay out of jail.

He was vaguely aware that the Botswana border was not far away, but he also knew that it would be the first place that the Police would expect him to head for – either that or Johannesburg International Airport. His crude recollection of the map of Africa was that Mozambique and Zimbabwe lay to the North and North East, with a little country called Swaziland somewhere in-between.

On his own, the situation looked helpless. He needed an ally. His half a million bucks represented something over four million rand and he could not believe that there was no one he could bribe to help him with that kind of money available. He grinned as he thought about Ed instituting a search worldwide for any other bank accounts in the name of Justin Willjohn. It was inconceivable that he would look for an account under the name of Per Ludorff. Justin had even bought a US passport under that name. It was based on the records of a young child born to Swedish immigrants. The boy had died at age 3 in Minneapolis. He would have been virtually the same age as Justin.

The younger Willjohn had bought the passport two years previously at a time when it seemed as though he would have had no chance of taking over Willjohn Industries. His intention was to defraud the corporation any way he could and stockpile assets under Per Ludorff's name. Then Ed had decided that he would not make a career out of the family conglomerate and the door had opened a crack.

Had Justin been able to discredit Ed sufficiently to obtain his shares or succeed in his later attempt to exchange the shares for Elke's freedom, the Per Ludorff passport and bank account would have become ancient history. Now it was his critical lifeline. His only concern was to change his appearance sufficiently so as not to look like Justin Willjohn but also to remain close enough to the likeness of his photo in the Per Ludorff passport. The more he had thought about it, the more impossible it became.

Justin was already on the road to Witbank, a town which lay en route to both Mozambique and Swaziland, when he realised that the smaller the towns, the less chance he had of finding what he needed, which was an expert passport forger. Such people existed in every country, he was sure. One just had to find them. He also remembered seeing a newspaper article about a Nigerian syndicate who had been arrested in Johannesburg after a Police raid which uncovered both drugs and hundreds of passports.

He realised that he was far more likely to find an underground connection in a city like Johannesburg than in some hick town in the country. At the next off-ramp he turned off resolutely, crossed over the motorway and headed back towards the metropolis. The dangers of remaining in South Africa would be offset by the advantages of having a new appearance and a new passport for one Per Ludorff.

*

Ed and Elke held each other in silence. The magical contact of each other's bodies infused new life and hope into two very tired people. Dawie and Joanna had tactfully left the room upon Ed's arrival

After a very long time, Ed loosened his hold on his fiancée and moved away sufficiently to have a good look at her. Despite her shower and the coffee, Elke still looked tired but even without make-up, her classic beauty was unmistakable. Ed wondered how he could be so lucky as to have found this angel. He also thought grimly of how close both of them had come to dying over the past few hours. However, here they were, miraculously together again.

There was a light tap on the door. Ed let go of Elke, swung his legs off the bed and went over to open the door. Dawie stood there smiling at him.

'I just wanted to know if my wife could make you something to eat. The kitchen's closed, but...'

Ed suddenly realised how ravenous he was.

'If you could organise some sandwiches and coffee, that'd be great. I don't think I can travel anywhere tonight. D'you have another room?' The Motel owner nodded. 'Not a problem. Shall I bring the food here?'

'Here, definitely!' Ed replied. 'This young lady and I have some more details to fill in.'

The Motel owner went off to organise food, his mind filled with pleasant thoughts of young love. In particular, in this age of almost non-existent morals, he was surprised, but delighted, that Ed had asked for a separate room. Now, there's a real gentleman, he thought, as he entered the main building in search of his wife.

*

Simon and the truck driver turned off into the Freight Section of Johannesburg International Airport. At the last moment, he and Bud had decided that Simon would accompany the Rhino on the flight instead of their usual handler. With the generous money Bud had given him, Simon was optimistic that he could disappear on the other side of the world and lie low for a while.

The truck approached the security check before being allowed into the freight loading area. All their papers were in order and Simon did not expect any problems. He realised that it was possible that things could have gone wrong at the ranch but he had great faith in Bud's ability to slip out of any difficult situation.

The security guard took the papers from the truck driver and examined them closely. Simon thought that the inspection was taking a long time. He experienced a sense of unease, but the man nodded finally and handed the papers back to the driver. The truck drove through the security point and headed for the unloading bays.

'Nice night for flying' he remarked to the driver as he looked up at the typically clear and star-filled Highveld winter sky.

*

Over sandwiches and coffee, Ed and Elke took it in turns to tell each other of their adventures since that time - a million years ago or perhaps just that morning - when they had both left the lawyer's office in Rustenburg. Before refreshments had arrived, they had spent some precious minutes simply holding hands, then kissing, before Ed had remembered that he owed some people a phone call, even though it was nearly midnight.

The first call had been to Isak and Marie Stein. They knew that Elke was safe but they had insisted upon being updated on Ed's situation as soon as there was any news. A sleepy Marie had answered. Ed spoke first.

'Sorry to wake you, Mrs Stein, but I believe you wanted to be told as soon as I appeared, or didn't, for that matter.'

Marie had given a half-hearted chuckle.

'I'm delighted that you're safe' she replied. 'We will need to talk, but certainly not tonight.'

'Agreed.'

Ed handed the phone over to Marie's daughter. The two women quickly decided that breakfast at the farm would be a good idea.

Ed had then called Sam, Buffalo Hills Hotel and Marius. After that he had called his mother in the US, firstly to say that he was safe and secondly to warn her and the Corporation that Justin was still on the loose. He had kept the conversation brief but had promised to call her again the following day, her time, to give her a full briefing on what had happened.

'Are you okay, honey?' she asked him anxiously.

'I'm fine, Mom, so is Elke, but I'm afraid we still have a serious problem with Justin. I'm too tired right now to go into details. Later!'

Once they had outlined their respective adventures, Elke struggled to keep her eyes open. Ed realised this, kissed her goodnight, and took his leave.

As he reached the door Elke called out softly 'Love you.'

He turned and blew a kiss at her.

'Love you too!'

As he closed the door, he felt decidedly shaky. He experienced a few pangs of regret that Elke and he would not be sharing a bed but consoled himself with the thought that even if they had, they would probably have fallen asleep before anything could have occurred!

*

At the loading bays Simon was surprised to see another game cage on top of the ramp, close to where they would reverse the truck.

He wondered whether there was another consignment of animals on the same flight. He hoped not because depending upon what animals were in the other cage, there could be problems. Simon had visions of his rhino battering at the sides of their cage, with a couple of lions growling from the other cage.

As they manoeuvred the truck to back its tail up against the ramp, he realised with surprise that the other cage was empty. He had no sooner wondered what an empty cage was doing at the loading section of the Freight Division when a Police Officer and three policemen stepped out of an office next to the ramp and walked up to him.

*

Justin entered the outskirts of Johannesburg at 1.45 in the morning. He stopped at an all-night garage, bought a couple of pies and asked where he could find an hotel He reasoned that although his real name and picture was already in the possession of all border posts and airports, it was unlikely, in fact impossible, for the authorities to have circulated his picture to every hotel. That would probably happen the following day when he expected to see his face smiling up at him in the morning papers.

The garage attendant told him that there was a small hotel for commercial travellers a couple of kilometres down the road. Justin drove on in search of the place. Like the other players in the drama, he was in fact reaching the limits of his endurance. He made himself yawn as much as he could so that his eyes would moisten momentarily and help him to keep focused on the road ahead.

Finally, Justin saw the hotel sign off to the left. He turned off the road into the driveway. It was a very small hotel but looked reasonably clean. At that point, the normally fastidious Justin would have settled for a dog kennel.

Wearily, he entered the front door of the hotel. A male night receptionist was dozing at the front desk. Justin consciously made an effort to contain his customary arrogance and gently rapped on the counter with his knuckles. The man woke with a start and reluctantly set about booking Justin in.

*

Marie Stein, with a rare show of emotion, hugged her daughter. She had gone out to meet the young couple as they approached the front entrance to the farmhouse. Ed stood quietly behind Elke and waited for mother and daughter to celebrate the moment. Marie turned to Ed. They stared deep into each other's eyes for a long moment and then, amazingly under the circumstances, Marie opened her arms to the young man.

Ed hugged her back. It was brief but it was significant. They still needed to talk but Ed read Marie's gesture as being more than conciliatory. It was more of an unspoken apology.

Isak waited for them on the stoep. The poor man looked sicker than ever, Ed thought sadly, as Elke moved forward and hugged her father. As Elke relinquished his arms, Ed stepped up and shook hands with Isak.

Over breakfast both Ed and Elke told a horrified Marie and Isak what had happened to them.

'The worst thing for me, was not knowing what had happened to Elke. It was worse still figuring it out that it was my own brother!'

Ed was unexpectedly overcome with emotion and bowed his head as Elke put a comforting hand on his arm.

*

Justin slept late. He showered and dressed in his dirty clothes from the previous day, thinking that his first priority was to buy more clothes, then to make contact with the underworld somehow.

Booking into the hotel the previous night had been simplicity itself. The night receptionist had barely glanced at Justin's fake passport. Checking out could be trickier, Justin thought. By now he was probably in the papers but he had taken the calculated risk of sleeping late rather than trying to slip out of the hotel early.

Justin need not have worried. A group of tourists were checking out as he approached the reception area. Justin paid his bill with cash and was once more almost unnoticed. Before leaving the hotel, Justin spoke to an attractive little brunette behind the reception desk.

'This is my first time in Johannesburg. Are there any areas I should avoid?'

The girl thought for a moment.

'Don't go near Hillbrow' she advised. 'It's a high crime area; and maybe the city centre, although that's not too bad. Just keep your eyes open.'

'Like any big city, I guess' Justin replied.

He thanked the girl and left the hotel, knowing that the place called Hillbrow could very well be the place to look for someone to help him with his passport as well as changing his appearance. Another thought occurred to him as he started his car. The Police would have his registration number. He let the car idle for a minute or so as he thought it through. In the end he decided to use the car a little while longer. As soon as he could, he would hire another vehicle in the name of Per Ludorff. He drove back to the nearby garage and asked the way to Hillbrow. The attendant shook his head gloomily.

'Not a good place, boss. What you want there?'

Justin forced a smile. What in the hell did it have to do with him?

'I know, I'm told it's a bad place but I'm a writer. I like to find the action and write about it.'

The African shrugged. 'Okay, boss.'

He gave Justin instructions. The fugitive was soon on his way to find himself some gangsters.

*

Simon was led out of the holding cell at Kempton Park, the nearest Police Station to the airport. His world had collapsed the previous night when the Police had supervised the transfer of the two rhino into the empty cage next to their parking bay. The Police had then quickly dismantled the corner posts of the original cage and retrieved the stolen platinum.

As Simon was removed to a Police van that was to take him to the nearby magistrate's court, he wondered what had happened to Bud and whether his former boss would be able to help him in any way. More than likely Bud was also behind bars, Simon thought.

At the Stein farm breakfast was over. Ed was beginning to relax for the first time in a long while. He still had to talk with Marie and Isak about marrying Elke but he felt that Marie's attitude had certainly improved. His thoughts were interrupted by his cell phone ringing. He picked it up and pressed the appropriate button.

'Ed Willjohn here.'

'Ed, it's Sam. The cops think they know where Justin's gone. They'll keep us informed of any developments.'

CHAPTER 42

Ed looked up at the Stein family from his cell phone.

'They've got a lead on Justin.'

Isak and Marie nodded understandingly. Elke's face revealed her immediate reaction to any reminder of her ordeal. Ed reached out to take her hand. She clasped it tightly then her face crumpled as she dissolved into tears. Ed spoke urgently into the phone.

'Sam, I'll call you back.'

He switched off the cell but by then Elke had pulled away, bolted from the table and rushed inside the house. Marie quietly stood up and followed her. Ed also stood uncertainly, not sure of his role in Elke's well-being whilst she was still at home and so many things between her and her parents were as yet unspoken.

'I think you should leave her be for a moment,' Isak's quiet voice intruded on his thoughts.

'Marie's good at these things. Elke's suffering from a delayed reaction - just give her some time.'

'Of course.' Ed stood awkwardly, not sure whether to remain at the farm or leave and speak with Elke later.

'Sit down, Ed,' the older man, sensing Ed's discomfort, spoke gently. 'Let's wait and see what Marie has to say.'

Ed nodded, suddenly feeling rather distressed himself. The enormity of what had happened was only now beginning to sink in with all of them. Ed could not help thinking about how he had caused nothing but turbulence in Elke's life since they had first met. He cleared his throat and tried to surreptitiously wipe a tear from his eye.

Isak missed nothing. He smiled gently.

'Listen, you've both had a terrible time and about now I expect that you're beginning to blame yourself for everything.'

Ed looked at the older man in surprise and nodded. He still did not trust himself to speak. Isak sighed and leaned back in his chair, stretching his fragile frame.

'If you look deep inside yourself and examine your motives for anything you may have done over the past few weeks and you can honestly say that you always acted with the best of intentions for all concerned, then don't beat yourself up over any of this.'

Ed felt the tears welling up again. This time, however, they were tears of relief that he should encounter such a wise person at this critical time. The fact that this old man was also Elke's father made it so much more remarkable. Ed had fleeting visions of his own father's gentle wisdom which he had been guided by until his father's death, which had left a huge gap in Ed's life. Now suddenly, here was this man, whose daughter could have died or been traumatised for life, who was reassuring him that he, and only he, could decide if blame were to be laid at his door. Ed finally found his voice.

'Thanks for that, sir' he answered. 'I can blame myself for using poor judgment over Justin's apparent stability, but I can honestly say that my intentions were always based on the greatest good for all.'

Ed looked over to the door where Elke had run inside the house.

'As you know I love your daughter more than anyone I have ever encountered in my fairly short life so far. I'm hoping that soon, real soon, your wife and I can have a serious chat and clear the air.'

'And put right some of the untruths that your brother managed to pass on to her?'

Ed nodded grimly. 'He's been doing this since we were kids. How could I not guess that he'd do it again? Any time he saw I had potential for happiness, he made it his mission to try and destroy it.'

'He must be a very unhappy young man' Isak responded. 'D'you have any idea what started it?'

'Who knows? One thing I've realised is that the more his family and friends try to be nice to him and boost his self esteem, the worse he bites back at us!'

Marie returned from inside the house as both men stared at her anxiously.

'She's fine. She just needed a good cry' Marie smiled fleetingly, 'and her mother's arms around her. Something that hasn't happened for a while!'

Marie sat down at the table and poured half a cup of strong black coffee into her mug. She offered the others a refill but both men declined.

Marie looked over at Ed.

'Elke asks you to excuse her. She wants to sleep some more and she'll phone you later.'

'Sure,' Ed replied and stood up immediately. 'I need to get to the mine, as soon I've gotten a change of clothing from the hotel. Thanks for a great breakfast and I can't tell you how relieved I am to see Elke safely back home.'

Ed shook hands with Isak. Marie accompanied him to his SUV. There was an awkward silence as they walked, then Marie spoke.

'Ed, I'm sorry we got off on the wrong foot. We must sit down soon and sort everything out.'

Ed looked at her. She still had most of the features that made her daughter such a beauty but her face was much thinner with unmistakable lines across her forehead and a suggestion of wrinkles on her neck and throat. There were also dark patches under her eyes. For an instant Ed had a clear insight into the terrible stresses this fine and proud woman must be undergoing.

'Just name the time, Mrs Stein. There's nothing more important in my life than Elke's happiness and secure future. You and your husband are part of that future as well as her present and past. So, let's clear out the cobwebs and take it from there.'

Marie nodded. Ed reached the car and opened the door.

'Just one thing I want to make clear before you go,' Marie said.

Ed turned back to face her. She was having difficulty with the words.

'I think you know now that Justin had me believe that you were without financial resources other than your job.'

She paused uncertainly. Ed let her find her way through the issue without interrupting. She finally continued.

'I think I must have come across as someone who was only concerned with Elke marrying money. Of course that would be nice, but I was mainly worried that you might have seen Elke and this farm as a way...'

Her voice trailed off as she realised how deep this conversation was probing into the relationship.

Ed smiled. 'I really understand. I've always seen you as a person who is fiercely concerned about your family's welfare. I really respect you for that, even though I was your prime target for a while, I guess!'

Marie suddenly looked years younger, as relief flooded through her. She knew it was going to work out now.

'Thanks, Ed. I don't think I deserve your forgiveness but I'll take it gladly.'

For the second time that morning they hugged each other briefly, before Ed climbed into his vehicle and drove away from the family who had become the centre of his universe.

*

Justin drove along the motorway heading towards Johannesburg's city centre. The petrol attendant had told him to look for the Harrow Road off-ramp then take the road up through "The Wilds," an open parkland with many species of indigenous African flora. He then took the left-hand fork leading up past St John's College, one of Johannesburg's leading private schools, before turning onto Harrow Road itself. As Justin had no clear idea of his actual destination in Hillbrow, the attendant had simply told him to make a right turn just after coming over the brow of the hill and in sight of a shabby residential tower called Ponte.

As Justin drove, he could not help but wonder how it was that he had been travelling through the city's affluent upmarket suburbs and yet he was heading for an area reputed to be the major crime centre in the region.

After he left St John's on his left, Justin noticed a rapid deterioration in the quality of his surroundings. He also observed more and more high-rise apartment blocks. Few of them had been painted in recent times and the depressing sight of washing hanging out to dry on many of the balconies brought home to him the rapid transition from obvious wealth to equally obvious poverty.

He also realised that he could drive around all morning without having the faintest idea of where he was going! Justin turned into Kotze Street in Hillbrow and from the amount of traffic and pedestrians, he figured that he was probably in the centre of the infamous suburb. He saw an open parking ground to his left and pulled in there, looking for a space as far away from the street as possible. He had no idea whether the South African Police were efficient or otherwise. He could not judge if it was time for him to dump the car, but one thing was clear, if he were to make contact with the local underworld, he would have to do so on foot.

*

Ed emerged from his room at Buffalo Hills Hotel, feeling much better after a shower and change of clothing. He could have easily slept for hours but there was far too much to do. On the way to the Hotel, Ed had called Sam back. His boss had told him about the lucky break in the pursuit of Justin.

A policeman in a patrol car in the Edenvale district was on the two-way radio and was taking down the details of Justin's hire car, when he noticed a vehicle, driven by a young male, which answered to the description just given to him. As he watched, it stopped at a garage on the other side of the road.

The policeman had asked his partner, who was driving, to stop. The traffic was particularly heavy at that moment. The suspect's car was already moving and the policeman realised that they would never make the turn onto the other side of the road, which had a concrete barrier down the middle of it. He had leaped out of the car and run across the busy main road. Cars squealed to a halt or skidded to avoid him as he frantically held out his hand for them to stop. He had been too late to catch the car, but he did see enough of the licence plate to know it was the elusive American. He had spoken to the petrol attendant who had confirmed Justin's description and had added that the man had asked the way to Hillbrow. This had surprised him as it was hardly the kind of place a foreigner would want to visit. The policeman had returned to his patrol car and a massive manhunt was now underway, to search Hillbrow from end to end.

*

Despite everything that Justin had done to Elke and to himself, Ed expressed a concern to Sam that his brother might resist arrest and be shot dead. Ed did not know how trigger-happy the South African cops were. Sam reassured him by saying that recent legislation had decreed that Police were not to shoot a suspect unless they could show that their own lives were in danger. South Africa's new Constitution was widely regarded as one of the most forward-thinking in the world, although Sam expressed some reservations.

'The only problem is that if human rights are extended to criminals as well, it can make it tough on the Police, but at least in Justin's case the chances are that they'll take him alive.'

Ed thanked Sam and said he would get to the office as soon as he could.

On his way out of the hotel, Ed stopped at the reception desk and asked for Rob. Both he and Don appeared and shook his hand boisterously.

'We've never lost a guest yet and we don't intend to do so now' Don joked.

'I hate to tell you, but my little brother could be your first casualty!' Ed responded grimly.

He quickly gave Rob and Don the latest news that Justin seemed to be heading for Hillbrow. Rob nodded thoughtfully.

'Makes sense. He's probably trying to connect up with someone who can smuggle him out of the country.'

Ed sighed. 'If I thought he'd stop messing with other people's lives, I'd buy him a ticket myself! The truth is, the guy's a danger to himself and the community. The sooner he's arrested the better.'

The other two nodded silently. Ed turned and headed for the front door.

'See you guys later.'

On his way to his SUV, Ed was greeted by Elliot Standen, the Hotel's Senior Director who had recently returned from long leave. After making sure that he was in one piece, Elliot suggested that Ed should join the management over dinner one evening that week and tell them the story of his adventures. Ed readily agreed. The hotel and its staff had been wonderful to him. The least he could do was to bring them up to date.

'Let's see if we can find Justin first' he added 'then the story will have some kind of closure.'

Justin walked along Kotze Street. He realised that there were virtually no white people on the streets but he was not subjected to curious stares, with the exception of some youths loitering and smoking pot on a street corner. They gave him a calculating stare. Justin thought wryly that his dirty clothing from his adventures on the previous day were an advantage. He was not an obvious mark for a pickpocket or a mugging. Nevertheless, he walked briskly past the youths, then saw a café up ahead, where a number of tables and chairs were spread out over the sidewalk.

Justin went straight to the café and took a seat at one of the outside tables. A tall, muscular African waiter approached him with a big smile. He placed a rather tired-looking menu in front of Justin, who waved it away.

'Just a strong black coffee.'

As the big man turned away Justin called out after him.

'Say, can you help me with some information?'

The waiter turned back to him.

'What do you want to know, sir?'

Justin did not have time to beat about the bush.

'I'm told that the Nigerians run the scene around here,' he began.

The waiter's pleasant features tightened perceptibly but Justin persevered.

'I need some help and I'm told...'

'Are you looking for girls, boys, stolen goods?' the waiter asked. He was no longer smiling.

Justin shrugged. 'Something like that, I guess. I'm told the Nigerians...'

The waiter moved closer and stood right over Justin, looming large and ominous in the young man's vision.

'Mister, I'm Nigerian! I work hard for an honest living. Not all Nigerians are like you say!'

'No, I'm sure you're right, I just...'

Justin realised that he had pressed a very sensitive button with the man. The waiter interrupted him with a yell.

'Take your dirty business somewhere else. Get out of here!'

Justin fled. The last thing he wanted was to attract attention. He suddenly felt very lost and alone. He headed instinctively back to his car. Hillbrow seemed to press in on him from every angle. The noisy crowd, hawkers yelling out their special deals, two taxi drivers arguing on the side of the street, music blaring from a dozen or more portable radios. Kwaito music and Rap echoed and reverberated through the concrete canyons. Justin started to run. He reached his car, opened the door and feverishly inserted the key in the ignition.

As he did so, two smartly dressed policemen appeared from around the back of a row of parked vehicles. They headed straight for him. With a little terrified moan of fear, he turned the ignition, banged the car into first gear and raced forward. The Police and the parking attendant tried to stop him, but Justin bore down on them at speed.

CHAPTER 43

There was very little space between the rows of parked cars, but Justin ignored this as his vehicle accelerated. The cops quickly realised that Justin was not going to stop for them and hastily leaped aside. One of them talked urgently into a walkie talkie as he scrambled between one of the rows of cars. Justin noticed this and wondered how close their reinforcements were. A moment later he found out that they were very close indeed.

Two Police cars converged on the entrance to the parking lot from either side. For an instant Justin considered bashing his way between the two vehicles as they stopped almost bumper to bumper with their hazard lights flashing.

He rejected the idea immediately and swung his car hard, across the face of the entrance, swerving right almost immediately into another pathway between the parked cars. He was now heading back in the direction from whence he had come.

The cops on the ground peered out from between the cars, yelling for him to stop. Justin had no intention of doing that. He had quickly returned to the manic state of the night before. In fact, he was almost euphoric and felt quite detached from his actions. The side of his car clipped the protruding bumper of a badly parked car. There was a metallic ripping sound and the steering wheel threatened to spin out of his hands.

Justin held on tightly and managed to prevent the vehicle from careering into the cars on the other side of the lane. There was no time to think. He could only react as each new obstacle presented itself. He was now rapidly running out of road. A ramshackle wooden shed loomed up straight ahead. One end of the shed was just visible on the left, with the bulk of the structure running away to the right. Justin took his foot off the pedal for a moment as he realised that he had reached the end of this particular road.

Then he saw that just behind the shed was another road which had been cordoned off from the parking lot by a wire fence. He had no means of knowing whether the fence ran behind the shed or ended as it reached the wooden structure. Almost gleefully Justin decided that it was the only option left open to him. He floored the pedal again and the vehicle raced the remaining few yards, heading straight for the shed.

*

Ed parked his SUV in his parking place at Premier Platinum. He was a little nervous. Even though the adventures of the past few days had ended with the successful retrieval of the second batch of stolen platinum, he was not sure how Management viewed the fact that Justin was his brother.

In his own mind, he had a number of things to be responsible for. He should have learned his lesson about Justin's instability long ago. Had he not been his brother, Ed had no doubt that he would have acted differently. His late father, who had been a powerful business tycoon, also had an Achilles heel with regard to Justin in some respects. Fortunately, he had had the good sense to keep him away from the business.

Their mother was, after all, a typical mother. She would always seek any possible redeeming features in her youngest son. However, Ed thought bitterly as he headed for his office, none of the above excuses the fact that I put a whole lot of really great people at risk, including my own fiancée. Would a firmer hand have worked with Justin? Should Ed have put him on the next plane back to the States?

Ed conjured up a picture of his younger brother, pale and listless, with one arm in a sling, arriving at the airport, having miraculously survived the destruction of New York's World Trade Center.

Some guys could have done it maybe, but I guess I'm just not tough enough, Ed said to himself as he waved at the receptionist rather gloomily and walked rapidly to his office. He did not want to speak to anyone for a while.

Ideally, he would have liked to pick up the threads of his work, attend to all the unanswered messages and sundry crises that had developed undoubtedly over the past four days. Only once that was finished would he feel up to facing Sam and Martin again. Ed was mildly surprised to see that the office block seemed virtually deserted. Normally there was a steady buzz of activity. Suits me just fine, he thought as he opened the door to his office.

Ed stepped inside and stared in disbelief at his desk. Neatly laid out on it was a complete cowboy outfit - a ten-gallon hat, shiny leather boots, with large heels and spurs. A gun belt, with two fancy looking guns protruding from the holsters, was hung over the back of a chair in front of the desk. Leather chaps, a mustard-coloured cravat – the only thing missing appeared to be a horse!

Ed's gloom lifted miraculously as he read the wording on a large card placed in the middle of his desk. 'Welcome back. When you're suitably dressed, please join me in my office. Sam.'

As he began to comply with the instructions, Ed realised that he had some true friends here. Friends for life who instinctively knew that he would arrive at the office with a terrible sense of anti-climax after his undeniable "cowboy" activities of the past few days!

Justin could not associate himself with his own actions as the wooden shed loomed up in front of him. He was definitely watching a movie and the camera was shooting the point of view of either Bruce Willis or Keanu Reeves. Justin loved this sort of movie, because no matter what happened, the good guys always crawled out unscathed from some place. And today, surely, he was one of the good guys!

The Police and a few amazed pedestrians watched horrified as Justin's car hit the shed at about seventy kilometres an hour. The wood was old and very dry.

The shed, or at least one end of it, literally disintegrated as the car ploughed through it. The ground in the parking lot was about a metre higher than the level of the road beyond the shed. Justin's car flew through the air for a short distance, shedding broken plants, paint cans, some old overalls and a host of smaller bric-a-brac it had collected on its path through the hut. Thankfully, there was no one inside the hut at the time.

The cops began to realise that their quarry was getting away when suddenly everything changed with a horrible finality.

A large truck, moving at speed down the street from the left, hit Justin's car at the very moment its wheels touched the ground. The truck driver did not even lift his foot off the accelerator before impact. The arrival of the medium sized car from literally nowhere would be an image the driver would carry with him for the rest of his life. The truck was a fully laden horse and trailer, probably weighing some twenty tons and travelling right on the legal limit of 60 kph in a built-up area.

By the time the truck had stopped, the remains of Justin's car were probably no more than half a metre high and were firmly wedged under the massive engine and gearbox of the horse. It was not Justin's day to be one of the good guys!

*

Ed tapped on the door of Sam's office. He looked as though he had just stepped off the set of a Western movie. He was almost sorry that the pearl handled revolvers they had found for him were just toy guns!

He opened the door and stepped through. His spurs jingled on his boots, and he adopted a proper gunslinger's feet apart stance, his hands prowling restlessly just above the butt of the revolvers. He saw Sam grinning at him from behind his desk.

'Wal howdy pard'ner!' he said in his now celebrated Texan twang.

The room exploded with laughter and applause from both sides of the door. The entire management and administrative team stood with glasses raised to Ed as he suddenly began to feel quite foolish in his cowboy attire.

Sam, glass in hand motioned for some quiet. He came around his desk as someone handed Ed a glass of champagne. The two men met in the middle of the room, clinked glasses, raised them in a cheers gesture.

'Welcome back, cowboy!'

The subsequent party did very little for Ed's good intentions to catch up on his work!

*

Rob Schutte was busy with the final preparations for a large conference at the hotel the following week. They had had a good year for conferences but this one was special. The large company concerned was a first-time client for the hotel, even though they had twice won the prestigious award for conference centre of the year. Rob, Don and Elliot were proud of their track record in respect of conferences. It was a major part of the hotel's business. However, competition had been fierce over the past few years and it had become necessary to seek ways of going that extra mile, every time a group of up to 120 delegates came to the hotel.

One of Buffalo Hills specialities was a leadership course. It had proved to be very popular with their clients. However, Rob was considering ways of adding even more to it when the phone rang. He picked up the receiver. 'Rob Schutte.'

'Mr Schutte, Ian Raper here. I'm the current President of S_2A_3, The Southern Africa Association for the Advancement of Science. We're talking to a number of key hotels and lodges around South Africa, with a view to offering them membership of our Heritage Association. This is an Association which combines a concern for both our historical and environmental heritage. In your region we feel that your hotel would be an ideal candidate for membership. May I come and see you?'

Rob wondered at the way in which things sometimes happened out of the blue, which fitted perfectly into what he was already thinking.

'Your timing's perfect, Mr Raper. I'm sitting here, looking ahead to where we need to go with our conferences as well as the hotel itself. The words environment and ecology are foremost in my mind, so yes, how about next Monday? Join me for lunch at the hotel?'

'Wonderful' Ian responded. 'I'll be there. I've been to your hotel a couple of times, so no need for directions. See you on Monday.'

As he put down the phone, Rob's mind was buzzing with ideas, but he realised that he should first understand more about this Heritage Association before he got too carried away. He had in fact heard of the rather strangely nicknamed S_2A_3 which he recalled had been formed at the turn of the Twentieth Century by the then Astronomer Royal, Sir David Gill. A later President of the Association had been one of South Africa's best known men of the mid-Twentieth Century, Jan Smuts who was at various times South African Prime Minister, a British Field Marshall in World War II, and a founder of the League of Nations. The S_2A_3 was formed to provide an umbrella body for all the sciences in South and later Southern Africa.

To be associated with it in any way would be a prestigious move for the hotel. He was flattered that Raper had approached them to represent their region. His pleasant thoughts were interrupted by another phone call. This time the news was not good.

'Mr Schutte, Captain Klopper here, Rustenburg Police. Your former guest, Mr Edward Willjohn's brother, was involved in a serious accident whilst evading arrest this morning.'

'I see' Rob replied, with mixed emotions. 'Is he -dead?'

'We expect so, sir. A truck drove over his car. The Fire Department and paramedics have been trying to extricate the car from under the truck. I don't think he could have survived. Tell me sir, is his brother at the hotel?'

'No, he insisted on going to his office at Premier Platinum, although we all thought he should rest.'

'Thanks, sir. We'll keep you informed. I'll call the mine now.'

Rob put down the phone and shook his head. He could not help thinking that it would be better for all concerned if the truck had achieved what the tragedy of September 11th in New York had failed to do.

*

Elke woke up with a start. It was not dark, but she judged from the light behind the curtains that it must be late in the afternoon. With a groan she turned to her alarm which she had set to give her two hours sleep. It had been turned off. She had no memory at all of hearing it earlier. She swung her legs over the edge of the bed, put her feet on the floor, stood up and nearly collapsed as a wave of giddiness overwhelmed her.

She sat down on the bed and waited for the awful feeling to pass. As she did so, there was a light tap on the door. Before she could answer, her mother opened the door and peered inside.

'What d'you think you're doing, young lady?' Marie asked sternly.

Elke tried to shake off the last vestiges of her giddiness.

'Sorry Mom, didn't even hear the alarm.'

'That's because I switched it off. You don't seriously think you were going to work today?'

Marie stared at her fondly. The events of the past couple of days had reawakened the maternal instincts that Marie had fought so hard to suppress ever since Isak had fallen ill, once she had needed to become the de facto "man" of the house.

Elke gave an embarrassed smile. 'That was my intention, Mom, but I'm feeling a bit dizzy.'

Marie shook her head.

'Why d'you have to inherit my stubbornness, girl? You had a nasty bang on the head, then that lunatic drags you around the countryside and you're surprised that you're a little dizzy?'

Elke nodded and with a grimace climbed back under the bedclothes. She put on a little girl's voice as she said 'Yes, Mommy.'

Marie shook her head. 'Listen, I'm serious now. You've probably got a mild concussion. You must rest. The doctor'll be here in half an hour.'

'Come on, Ma, I don't need...' Elke protested without conviction.

'Yes you do' Marie replied severely. 'When you're back on your feet, I've got a lot of work that needs to be done. I can't have you falling all over the place,'

She grinned, suddenly looking years younger for the first time in a long while.

'and you might break something!'

Elke smiled back wearily. She closed her eyes. A minute later Marie left the room, pleased to see that her daughter was fast asleep again.

*

Ed tried to keep his attention on the work in front of him. Sam, and to an extent Martin, had both handled many of the queries and requests that had been destined for Ed's desk, since the American's involvement with the platinum heist and its subsequent events. However, a number of matters still required Ed's attention.

Shortly after his welcome-back champagne toast had finished and he had changed back into his working clothes, Captain Kloppers had called with the news that Justin was almost certainly dead. Although it was just a formality, Ed had been totally distracted as he waited for the call confirming his brother's death.

It was so ironic that he had gone through the same terrible wait only a short few months before. Justin had escaped when thousands of others had perished. Now it was Justin and thankfully no one else in the wreck of the car.

The call made him jump, even though he had been waiting for it for some hours. In fact, he had begun to wonder why it had taken so long for the news to reach him.

He picked up the phone. His mind was quite blank. He had spent four or five hours reflecting on virtually every moment of his life and relationship with Justin. In a sense he was all thought out. Whatever will be, will be!

'Captain Kloppers here again Mr Willjohn.'

Ed kept his voice even. 'Yes, Captain.'

'Sir...'

The voice on the other side sounded very uncertain. Ed decided to help him.

'Just give it to me straight, Captain. I'm fully prepared.'

'Ja, thanks sir, but the point is, I don't know what to tell you!'

'Surely they've gotten to the car by now' Ed asked, confused.

'Yes sir. That's the point. There was no one inside the vehicle. We've searched everywhere in the vicinity but there's no sign of your brother!'

CHAPTER 44

'What're you saying?' Ed asked Captain Kloppers in astonishment.

'It doesn't look as though your brother was killed, sir, but it beats me how he got out of the car before it hit the truck!'

Ed had a sinking feeling. Little brother had seemingly pulled another rabbit out of the hat.

'Maybe he saw what was going to happen, opened the door and rolled out?'

Ed was still trying to digest the unexpected news when Captain Kloppers replied.

'Ja, I'm sure he must have done but there were probably ten or more people watching the incident. I don't understand why he wasn't seen.'

Ed could not offer any other theories. He thanked the Captain for keeping him posted and rang off. He sat at his desk for some minutes, not moving a muscle and staring blankly into space. The roller coaster ride of life with Justin was far from over.

*

Isak and Marie were sitting around a cosy log fire sipping a sherry before dinner, when the door opened and a sleepy-looking Elke entered the room.

'I was hoping you'd sleep right through.'

Elke smiled and went over to the Thermos flask of coffee which the Steins nearly always had available. She poured herself a mug.

'Sorry. Hope I won't be awake half the night now, but I've had a good rest and I'll be ready for work tomorrow.'

'You take as long as you need. There's no point in rushing back and then having to go off again in a couple of days!'

Elke took a seat near the fire and spent a few moments enjoying the ever-changing pattern of the flames which were steadily devouring the logs. Isak had a rule about log fires. He would only burn wood from exotic trees. There had been a grove of Eucalyptus gums, originally from

Australia, on the farm. Isak had steadily chopped them down and had planted indigenous trees in their place.

Elke looked at her parents affectionately.

'Thanks for your concern,' she said, 'but I'm fine, really. It was a terrible experience but I'm young, fit and no bones're broken. The worst thing I could do would be to mope around the house for days. Then I'd really go nuts!'

Both Marie and Isak nodded. Their daughter was mature enough not to be foolish about her health. There was a comfortable silence as Elke sipped her coffee. In fact, for the first time in months the three Steins were completely at ease with each other.

*

Bud McNeil stood at a counter as one of the Policemen put a cloth bag down in front of him. Bud lifted up the bag and carefully removed his personal possessions from it. A gold watch, an ostentatious diamond, a gold ring, a gold bracelet and his wallet, containing a few hundred rand, were all carefully checked in case of damage or loss. The bag emptied, he dropped it back on the counter and turned away without a further glance at the Policeman.

'You need to sign a receipt confirming that everything's in order.' The Policeman called out.

Bud turned back insolently, scribbled his signature and turned away muttering.

'You're telling me the cops could steal things?'

'No. We're just making sure that you don't accuse us if something were to disappear.'

Neither really believed the other as Bud walked out of the Charge Office to give Bonnie a welcoming hug. Bonnie had quickly organised bail which had been set at 250,000 rand, after lengthy wrangling. Captain Kloppers and the State Prosecutor had strenuously opposed bail, feeling certain that Bud would flee the country the moment he was out on bail.

The Magistrate had set bail at a level he believed would be a sufficient deterrent for anyone to forfeit such a large sum.

Earlier Bud had told Bonnie to also pay Simon's bail which was set at a much more modest 8,000 rand. The chopper pilot had already been released as the Prosecutor had realised that it could not be proven that Costa knew anything about Bud's criminal activity. Privately he was convinced that the young man knew exactly what was going on but trying to prove it was something else again!

As they drove away from the Police Station, Bud leaned back in his seat and closed his eyes. Bonnie was a good driver, and Bud was only too happy to be driven as he planned his next step.

Sam was apologetic but he needed to conclude the paperwork on the stolen platinum. Ed sat on the other side of Sam's desk, with Martin next to him as they completed the report which Sam would have to hand to the Police the following morning. Ed could hardly keep his eyes open but tried very hard not to show it. Sam however was an observant man and eventually caught Ed stifling a yawn.

'Sorry, we're almost finished, then I'm sending you back to the hotel with a driver,' he added.

Ed smiled in embarrassment. He was about to resist being driven when he realised just how tired he really was. He had not slept at all the night that he had gone looking for Martin and last night, it had been about three in the morning before he had fallen asleep in the little motel, only to be woken at 6.30 the following morning.

'Sorry, guys,' he told Sam and Martin, 'I'm not much good to man or beast right now.'

'Five minutes and we're done,' Sam replied briskly.

Ed stayed awake somehow and even managed to remember some important details for the mine's statement to the Police. As soon as it was done, he excused himself and went through to his own office where he tried to call his mother. They had spoken briefly from the motel the night before, but the facts were too confusing for Ed to be able to give her any details of the forty-eight-hour adventure.

As Ed dialled, he wondered what he could say to his mother about Justin. The phone was promptly answered by the Housekeeper.

'Hi Mrs Griffiths, is my mom available?'

There was a slight pause,

'Sorry, Mr Ed, your mother's gone away for a few days.'

'Gone away?'

Ed could hardly believe his ears. His mother had seldom left her house since his Dad had died but to leave now when her two boys had just been involved in a life or death adventure was incredible.

Mrs Griffiths continued.

'Your mother said if you called, I should tell you not to worry, everything's under control but there's something she has to do and she'll call you as soon as she's able to do so.'

Ed thanked her and put the phone down. He was too tired to even try and figure it out. He'd guessed he'd have to wait till she called.

There was a tap on the door. 'Come in' Ed called.

The door opened and the driver stood in the doorway.

'Your car's outside, sir' the driver, Absalom, told him.

I'll be right there,' Ed replied, suddenly glad he was being driven back to the hotel.

Justin could hardly believe he was alive. It was late at night. He lay on a bed in a seedy hotel in the heart of Hillbrow. He was badly bruised and scratched but miraculously he had received no serious injuries. When he had staggered into the hotel a few minutes earlier, the receptionist at even this low grade establishment, which was undoubtedly also a brothel, had been dubious about giving him a room. Justin had put cash on the table plus a generous tip for the receptionist before the man had shrugged and handed him a key.

Justin replayed his incredible escape over and over in his mind. A millisecond before his car had hit the old wooden hut in the parking ground he had seen a truck moving quite fast along the road on the far side of the hut. The truck was travelling from left to right and it did not take a rocket scientist to realise that Justin's car and the truck were on a collision course. As his car hit the hut, Justin had already thrust his driver's door open with his body half-way out of the car. The impact of the vehicle's bumper, radiator and bonnet striking the wood at speed, was enough to tear a gaping hole in the side of the hut. Nevertheless, the open door protruded far enough out from the side of the car to catch the splintering shards of wood as it passed through into the centre of the hut. The door slammed hard into Justin's torso as he began to fall out of the car.

He probably passed out for an instant as an excruciating pain shot through his body. Luckily for him the wood was already shattered and it was not like striking a solid object. The door, reacting to the growing pressure of Justin's falling body, sprang open again the moment the car had broken through into the void in the centre of the hut. With no further resistance, Justin tumbled out into the middle of the structure as the car ploughed onwards, hitting a collection of stored objects piled up against the far wall. The vehicle slowed noticeably but its momentum was such that it still broke through the far wall, bringing the roof down after it. What the horrified spectators saw was the car burst through the far side of the hut and land, as Justin had feared, directly in the path of the oncoming truck.

No one noticed that the car was driverless. The door had slammed shut in the second impact and it was less than a second before the huge truck struck the car and rolled right over it. Its lightweight metals crumpled into an unrecognisable heap beneath the awesome thrust of the twenty-ton vehicle.

The entire hut had collapsed in the wake of the car's impact. Justin was still stunned and was buried under a mass of broken timbers and corrugated iron roofing.

The luck of the devil applied here. Justin had ended up lying up against a packing case. As the rest of the hut had collapsed around him, a couple of planks and a sheet of corrugated iron had fallen on one end on the packing case, the other end on the floor, effectively creating a tiny cave of safety for Justin.

The moment the truck and car collided everyone's attention was focused on the mayhem in the street. By the time Justin's head had cleared and he had gingerly tested his limbs, there was no one in the vicinity of the hut. Justin could hear the rising babble of chatter and occasional shouts as a large crowd quickly gathered in the street.

Justin had managed to clear away a space on the end of his "cave" furthest from the street. He had cautiously peered out. There had been no one nearby. With growing confidence, he had started to climb out of the debris. Then he saw two men hurrying towards him but in a moment they had detoured towards the vehicle wrecks. They never saw him. Justin slipped away from the remains of the hut to the nearest row of parked cars. As soon as he had achieved this, he realised that he was actually going to escape!

Now, despite feeling as though he had just done twelve rounds with Mike Tyson in his prime, his mind raced as he cautiously sat up in the bed and began to plan his next move. There was no way he could sleep right away. To have escaped seemingly certain death as well as having evaded capture once again, propelled Justin's manic nature into a feeling of euphoria, despite his physical condition and the dirty dingy room he found himself in. He knew that it was only a matter of time before he would arise phoenix-like from the ashes of his defeat and soon crush his enemies forever!

*

Elke finished her coffee, hugged both her parents and excused herself. There was something she had to do before returning to her room. She put on a warm jacket and went outside to the stables where she checked on her special horse, Witblitz.

The animal whinnied as a dark silhouette approached in the moonlight. The horse immediately knew it was her and stamped excitedly in his stall. Elke reached out and caressed his forehead. Witblitz represented so much of her joyful childhood and teen years, before her Dad had begun to exhibit his first signs of heart disease. She caressed the beautiful animal and spoke softly to it. It was for her the best possible way of restoring her equilibrium. As much as she truly loved Ed, there were elements of her past that she would never relinquish. Witblitz was at the top of that list.

*

Despairing of sleep, Justin got up and showered in a terrible, dirty-looking bathroom. There was a cake of cheap soap and a threadbare but reasonably clean towel which encouraged him but the nozzle of the shower was rusty and he struggled with a pathetic stream of water that constantly varied in temperature. Nevertheless, he managed to clean himself reasonably well. He re-entered the room and gloomily eyed his dirty clothes thrown over a chair. Most definitely, he would have to buy new ones in the morning.

Elke returned to her room, undressed and slipped into bed. She was now beginning to acquire some peace of mind and the terrible mental images of her hours as Justin's hostage were slowly receding. However, there were still so many questions to be answered. Where was Justin? Would he try to destroy their lives again? Elke also knew that Ed and she needed to sit down and discuss their future. In the mêlée that had occupied her full attention over the past thirty-six hours or so, she had learned that her future husband was a multi-millionaire. Her first reaction was to be thoroughly intimidated. He must be used to moving in very sophisticated circles in the upper echelons of society; a little farm girl like her was surely just a convenient distraction until he was ready to return to the US?

Another voice within her told her that this was not so. Ed had shown great depths of emotion and love for her. He had confronted her mother when she was acting on Justin's misinformation. He had done many things that reassured her that he, unbelievably, did love her. But was he really serious about buying a farm and settling down in South Africa? It took Elke over an hour for exhaustion to overcome her jumbled thoughts but when she finally slept, it was the sleep of peace.

*

Ed awoke to the sound of Absalom calling him. 'Wake up, sir. We're at the hotel. Wake up please sir!'

Ed groggily opened his eyes. They were parked close to the reception area of Buffalo Hills Hotel. Ed thanked Absalom, stumbled out of the car and headed for the reception.

As he asked for his keys, Don approached him.

'Hi, cowboy!'

Word had obviously gotten around, he thought sleepily. He chuckled. 'Hi, Don.'

He took his keys from the receptionist and turning in the direction of his room.

'I know you're tired but can you spare Rob and I just two minutes in the bar?'

Ed could hardly stand up.

'Can't it wait till morning?' he replied, too tired to be polite.

'There's something you need to see' Don pressed him. 'You won't be disappointed - promise!'

Ed nodded and called out to Don as they headed towards the bar.

'If I fall asleep in mid-sentence...'

He got no further. As he entered the bar, next to Rob, he saw his mother waiting for him. Everyone had very broad smiles on their faces as Ed rushed forward to hug her.

CHAPTER 45

Ed could not believe that his mother was actually standing in front of him. In his mind, she was still on the other side of the world. Only as they chatted did he begin to realise that all she had had to do, was fly to New York from Minneapolis - a short hop, then take the considerably longer transatlantic flight on South African Airways to Johannesburg.

Just over a day later, here she was, and Ed was delighted. He had felt the burden of so many responsibilities on his young shoulders. Although he was not a person who constantly ran home to Mommy at the first sign of trouble, he valued her usually calm and well-reasoned counsel when they did get a chance to meet.

'This is the nicest surprise I've had in a while!'

They eventually stopped hugging and headed for a quiet corner where they could chat. Rob and Don smiled understandingly as Ed looked over his shoulder at them.

'Time to catch up' Rob called out. 'I'll send your mother's drink over.'

Ed nodded and made sure his mother was comfortably seated. His exhaustion had been replaced by a sudden burst of adrenaline energy, which he knew would only last a short while before he really had to get some sleep.

Jean Willjohn looked at Ed affectionately.

'I've just been hearing about your adventures from Rob and Don' she told him. 'I guess you're kinda wiped out but maybe we can spend a few minutes catching up?'

'Of course, Mom' Ed replied. 'You've got no idea how glad I am to see you!'

Ed spoke for a few minutes bringing his mother up to date on the situation. This had to include mention of Elke, her background and Ed's intention to marry her.

His mother was clearly taken aback by the sudden mention of a prospective daughter-in-law, but she knew that could wait. What was more immediate was the situation with Justin, as well as a need for him to be found before he did something even worse than he had already done.

'All I know is that Captain Kloppers, who's been a great help, has been told that Justin somehow escaped from his car before it was crushed by the truck.'

'Is there no doubt at all that he survived?' his mother asked.

Ed shrugged. 'If he couldn't be found at the scene of the accident, then we must presume that he was able to get away from there. I guess it's possible that he was badly hurt and could have gotten worse, or even died, someplace else, but I doubt it,' he concluded.

His mother's eyes started to glisten with tears at the thought of Justin lying dead somewhere. Both of them felt a sense of outrage over Justin's behaviour but neither of them wanted him dead.

*

Justin dressed and went downstairs. As he reached the reception desk an office door opened to his left. He caught a glimpse of a huge, flashily dressed African sitting behind a large desk, with all kinds of African curios and statuettes surrounding him. The man reeked of money and Justin doubted whether it would have been derived entirely from the run-down hotel they were in.

Feeling that his luck was definitely holding up well, Justin spoke to the receptionist. Last night's man had been replaced by a very attractive woman, who gave him a big smile.

'Hi, I was wondering, what's the name of the owner of the hotel?'

'We call him Mr T, sir. I can't pronounce his name - it's Nigerian.'

Justin decided that he had definitely died and gone to heaven without even the loss of his body!

Mr T, the owner of the dirty little Hillbrow hotel and brothel, peered through a one-way mirror at the reception area. The young white man standing there, waiting to see him looked familiar. Mr T had a good memory for sensational news. He had found that he could sometimes take advantage of situations, particularly if they appeared on his doorstep. The young receptionist was waiting patiently as Mr T went back to his desk, picked up that afternoon's Star newspaper and looked at a photo on the front page. The headlines screamed "American millionaire on the run in South Africa." The photo and the man outside were one and the same. Mr T smiled gleefully at his receptionist.

'Anna, tell him to come in.'

Justin was ushered into Mr T's sumptuous office. Mr T shook his hand and gestured to a comfortable-looking suite of armchairs away from his desk with a low coffee table from Mozambique, ornately carved from ebony.

'Coffee, something to drink?' Mr T queried.

Justin smiled wryly. 'Maybe a black coffee and some brandy. I need a wake-up shot!'

The receptionist nodded as Mr T looked at her. She then withdrew. 'And bring some sandwiches,' Mr T called out after her.

Justin thought fast. The big Nigerian was giving him the royal treatment. He did not look like a social worker or a philanthropist, so the odds were Mr T already knew who he was.

'What can I do for you, Mr Willjohn?' Mr T asked, confirming Justin's thought.

He sighed inwardly. Every time someone found out who he was, it cost him money. The tragedy was that right now, that commodity was very suddenly in short supply – at least in the quantities that Justin had been used to having available at the click of his fingers.

*

Bonnie drove Bud to the cottage at Kosmos above Hartbeestpoort Dam. They decided not to return to the ranch, where the Police would almost certainly be prowling around. It was quite possible that the cops would also have the ranch's phone tapped. Bud had registered the cottage in the name of an obscure company which would not easily be linked to him. He was confident that they would not know of its existence.

As Bonnie drove, Bud frequently looked back to see if they were being followed. On his instructions, Bonnie had taken a circuitous route and had doubled back a few times in order to throw anyone who may be following off their tail. The cops were clearly angry that Bud had made bail and they would be out to get him, any way they could.

Once inside the cottage, Bonnie poured Bud a drink and then bustled around in the kitchen, preparing a simple but delectable supper for the two of them.

Bud had been considering dozens of alternative plans during their drive to the cottage. He had been delighted to make bail but nevertheless the prospect of throwing away a cool quarter of a million rand did not sit well with him. On the other hand, he already had quite a substantial amount of money salted away in his Swiss bank account, and he was hopeful that he could sell most of his assets in South Africa in such a way that the courts would not be able to attach them.

It therefore made sense to jump bail and lose the 250,000 rand. He reminded himself that it was only about 62, 000 US dollars anyway!

Bonnie arrived with a simple meal of grilled chicken breasts, baby marrows, butternut, rice and a spicy sauce. She had opened a bottle of Backsberg Cabernet, one of Bud's favourite wines and set the tray down on the counter of the small wood-panelled bar in a corner of the sitting room.

Bud gratefully drained his first glass of wine with indecent haste, swallowed a couple of mouthfuls of the food, murmured appreciatively, burped, then raised his wine glass which had already been refilled by the ever-attentive Bonnie.

'Just what I needed, babe!'

He drank a toast to her. Then he spoke the words she had been waiting to hear for a very long time.

'Listen sweetheart, it's time you and I got hitched, but we'll have to live overseas.'

Bonnie's eyes filled with tears. Bud was a terrible rogue. A real rough diamond but he also had a great sense of humour and he lived life to the full. She knew that he had taken a bad knock over the foiled platinum deal. He was undoubtedly feeling lonely and vulnerable. Not the best way to cement a relationship but at her age, with the onset of some serious cellulite and a few extra lines around her neck and forehead, Bonnie knew that she would take any reasonable offer that came along before it was too late!

She was still a very sexy lady. With careful maintenance she would look good for some time to come but the signs of wear and tear were there. Even on a reduced fortune, Bud was still a good option. She leaned over and kissed him on the mouth then leaned back again to raise her glass in return.

'Here's to us, overseas!' She smiled at him.

Bud nodded. 'First thing we need is some new identities and new passports.'

The Bonnie and Bud's big adventure had just begun!

*

Elke woke up at her usual time of 5.30am and groaned. Her body felt as though she had aged fifty years in forty-eight hours. Mentally she was refreshed by her long sleep, so it was really a question of getting the suppleness into her body movements again. She dragged herself out of her bed and started to do some stretching exercises. After five minutes of pure agony she began to loosen up. Satisfied that she could now at least walk without looking like a cripple, she dashed into a scalding hot shower and finally emerged feeling close to normal once again.

Elke dressed in warm clothes and emerged from her room just as her mother was preparing to go out onto the lands. She looked at her daughter doubtfully.

'You should still be in bed.'

Elke chuckled. 'From being a hard taskmaster, you've turned into an old nursemaid, Ma!'

Marie shook her head gloomily.

'I just want you to be fit enough so that when I do push you, you won't have any excuses for not working hard. Come!'

Marie led the way out of the house. An icy blast hit them as they walked briskly towards Marie's bakkie.

The two women spent an hour or so checking on the fruit trees. There was some concern that the mid-winter frosts could do some damage. They were in a relatively frost-free area, but it had been a cold winter and Marie, the perfectionist, needed to be certain that her precious trees were unharmed.

Satisfied that they were untouched despite some evidence of frost where an opening in the hills above them allowed a freezing blast of air to cut a swathe across a corner of their orange grove, Marie turned away and began to go through a list of things she wanted Elke to buy at the Behrens supermarket that morning, when Elke's cell phone rang. It was barely seven o'clock. Mother and daughter looked at each other anxiously as Elke put the cell phone to her ear.

'Elke Stein wat praat' Elke said, speaking Afrikaans as the most probable language of her caller in that area.

Ed's American drawl came clearly over the instrument. 'Hi sweetheart, sorry to call so early. Did I wake you?'

'Ja, sure!' Elke responded in indignation. 'I left the house at six o'clock, so I expect that you're the lazy one around here!'

Ed laughed. 'Okay, you got me. Listen, d'you think your mother would give you time out to come and have breakfast with me. There's someone here I really need you to meet!'

Elke could not imagine who would be interesting or important enough for her to drive to the hotel for breakfast, but as long as Ed was there, she would share scrambled eggs with King Kong!

'Hang on' Elke said. She turned to her mother. 'Ma, Ed wants me to meet someone at the hotel. Can I take a couple of hours? I'll do the shopping straight afterwards, promise!'

Her mother looked at her sharply. The work-related tyrant rose in her for a moment before her face softened.

'Take your time. I still think you need to rest!'

'Thanks Ma,' Elke lifted the cell phone again. 'I'll be there in half an hour.'

'Great!' Ed clicked off, still leaving Elke in a mystery over the unnamed guest.

*

Bud and Bonnie rose early after a night of passion as they celebrated Bud's long-delayed proposal of marriage, helped by a bottle of Moët and Chandon. Bud was a bundle of nervous energy. He did not want to lose a moment now that he had decided on his course of action. Bonnie drove into Johannesburg, with Bud slumped against his passenger seat. His face was almost completely hidden beneath a jacket with its collar turned up, dark glasses, a cap and even a scarf round the lower part of his chin and mouth.

Bonnie had suggested that Bud was behaving exactly like someone who did not wish to be recognised, and that people would look at him more closely.

'Yeah' Bud had responded. 'But they still won't see who it is!'

Bonnie had given up and headed towards the suburb of Troyeville in the south of Johannesburg. Bud knew the whereabouts of the best forger of passports in the city. Bud had sent a number of his accomplices to the man over the past couple of years. Every one of them had successfully left the country without any trouble from the authorities.

They pulled up at the forger's house just after 8.30am. A woman was leaving the house with two small children in tow, heading for a nearby school. Bud told Bonnie to come inside with him. He had decided that he would stand a far better chance of slipping past the authorities as a married man with his wife accompanying him. The Police knew him as a bachelor.

Pedro, a small, stooped man in his late fifties, with white hair and thick spectacles, opened the door. Bud and he had never met face to face. The man looked at the couple with suspicion.

'Sorry to come to see you so early, Pedro, Bud McNeil, I've sent...'

'Oh ja!' Pedro looked relieved. 'Come in. It's too bloody cold out there. It's definitely not what I came to Africa for.'

Bud and Bonnie followed the man inside. Pedro led the way to an untidy office off the hallway and gestured to Bud and Bonnie to sit on some rickety chairs in front of his desk. Bud wondered why it was that people like Pedro, who made a very good living as a forger, should remain in his small house in a very unfashionable suburb.

Bud leaned over the desk as he squeezed past Bonnie, who had sat down in the first chair. As he did so, his eyes caught sign of an open passport. The familiar face of Justin Willjohn stared up at him. Bud grabbed the passport and looked at it in a fury.

Pedro stepped forward to try and take Justin's passport away from Bud, but the ex-platinum thief was too quick for him.

'My other work is none of your business!' Pedro said angrily.

He moved across and opened a drawer. Bud caught a glimpse of polished steel within it, which clearly indicated a firearm of some sort. Bud hastily put the passport back on the desk and backed off. He needed this man's co-operation.

'Hey, I'm sorry. You're quite right but I've been looking for that little bastard all over the place. When I saw his face…'

'You don't touch my things!' Pedro said. The gun never appeared but the drawer remained open.

Bud sat down and spread his hands wide.

'Look, Pedro, that was foolish of me but I got a shock when I saw that bloke's face. Do me a favour, I want passports for the two of us and I'll treble your fee if you tell me where I can find young Justin.'

Pedro considered Bud's request as he slowly sat down opposite them.

After meeting with Mr T and enjoying a large breakfast, Justin had returned to his room and had slept for a further two hours, hugely relieved after finding out that Mr T would, for a very large fee, take care of everything for him. Justin's passport was probably already in the hands of the forger. New clothing and pyjamas had just been delivered to Justin's room. He was beginning to unwind and was almost looking forward to the idea of his new life and persona as Per Ludorff. The new clothes fitted nicely. He put on his watch, picked up his wallet and headed out.

As he opened the door, he was stunned to see the angry face of Bud McNeil just a few inches away from his own, with his fist raised about to knock on the door!

CHAPTER 46

Justin backed up and tried to close his bedroom door in Bud McNeil's face, but the little man was too fast for him. Bud dropped his shoulder and charged the door before Justin could close it. Although he was taller and heavier than Bud, Justin lacked the other man's determination. He reeled back as the door flew open and Bud reached out to grip the youngster's throat with both hands. Justin flailed about with his arms but Bud easily evaded him and increased his pressure on the other's throat. Justin felt himself losing consciousness and his legs buckled.

Suddenly Bud let go. He turned, slammed the bedroom door shut then looked back at Justin who had slumped onto his bed fingering his throat.

'Now that I've got your attention, you little turd, you and I are going to have words!' Bud snarled.

*

Elke walked up to the reception desk of the hotel. A smiling receptionist told her that Mr Willjohn was expecting her, and would she join him in the restaurant? Elke entered the gracious mock Tudor room and looked around. She saw Ed sitting at a table with an elegant middle-aged woman.

Elke realised with a shock that it was probably his mother. There was a strong family resemblance and besides which, she could not think of anyone else that Ed would want her to meet for breakfast without any prior warning! Ed saw her immediately, stood up and strode over to greet her. The woman at the table gave her a polite smile.

Elke suddenly panicked. She had quickly changed out of her farm clothes after receiving Ed's invitation, but she was hardly a match for the understated, but evident designer, clothing his mother was wearing. Ed and Elke had a few seconds together before moving into earshot of the table.

'That's your mother, isn't it?' she asked.

Ed grinned. 'Do we look that much alike?'

'Ed, you should've warned me.' Elke murmured as they moved across to meet the matriarch of the Willjohn clan.

*

'How'd you find me?' Justin asked fearfully now that Bud seemed to have ended the violence for the time being. Bud grimaced and reached into a hip pocket of his jeans. He withdrew the passport photo of Justin that he had first seen in Pedro's house and thrust it at Justin, who looked at it in blank amazement.

'Where in the hell?' he began.

Bud laughed. 'It just so happens that you and I both need to leave the country without attracting any unwelcome attention. Unfortunately for you, you chose to get your new passport through Pedro, who is the best in the business by the way, unfortunate because Mr T and I have done a few deals together and Pedro has provided a number of my, er, associates with passports over the past few years.'

Justin looked up at Bud. He was still sitting on the edge of his bed recovering his equilibrium from the unexpected attack.

'What've you done with my passport?' he asked anxiously.

Bud smiled. 'Nothing. Pedro'll have your Per Ludorff documents ready by tomorrow, along with mine and Bonnie's. I've got Mr T arranging flights to Rio for the three of us.'

'Rio!' Justin exploded. 'I need to get back to the States!'

'And you will, but we need to get US visas and even with my connections I can't fiddle those in forty-eight hours.'

'I don't need a visa for the US,' Justin responded sullenly. He sensed what was coming.

'But we do and as we'll be travelling together...'

Bud let the words fade away as he smiled at the American.

'And how long will we be travelling together?' Justin asked.

Bud chuckled. 'For as long as it takes for you to repay me for destroying my business and my reputation!'

He spoke rather primly as though his reputation had been squeaky clean prior to meeting Justin.

Justin got off the bed gingerly and bent down to pick up his hotel keys, which had dropped onto the floor during Bud's initial onslaught. He straightened up and looked at Bud who returned his stare with a mischievous grin. However, the humour did not extend to Bud's eyes.

Justin shook his head. 'Won't do you any good. My money's gone. The family's stopped my loan account.'

'And you're down to the million bucks or so that you've salted away over the past couple of years. Come on, Justin, I know all the tricks. I

288

invented most of 'em and you're going to be my meal ticket for a while until I'm satisfied you've made up for your bloody stupidity.'

Justin looked down. His carefully stashed stockpile of reserve funds was going to disappear before he could do anything constructive with it.

He made one last attempt at bravado.

'And if I say go jump in a lake?'

'Then when I hand you over, the grateful authorities'll probably reduce my sentence to a point where it might be worth staying here,' he replied.

Justin had nothing more to say. As the two men prepared to leave the room Bud added a final warning.

'Don't get into a life of crime, pal, you haven't got the brains for it!'

*

Elke and Jean Willjohn shook hands. Ed's mother had a firm clasp but Elke still had to reduce her normally sturdy grip, for fear of hurting the older woman.

'How d'you do, Mrs Willjohn? I'm so pleased to meet you at last, but you've caught me completely unawares. Your son never told me...'

'I never told him either, dear. I arrived last night unannounced.'

After they had all helped themselves to the sumptuous breakfast buffet, Jean turned to Elke again.

'It seems as though we've surprised each other. Ed tells me that the two of you are engaged!'

Elke glanced at Ed in dismay. She was really being thrown in the deep end. She nodded.

'Yes. As Ed's probably told you, we've had some pretty exciting moments over the last week or so. I know he should have told you sooner, but it really wasn't that easy.'

Jean nodded sombrely. 'I haven't gotten the full story about Justin yet, but I understand that my younger son held you captive for a while.'

'Yes. He never really hurt me, but it was a frightening situation.'

Tears suddenly welled up in her eyes.

Jean's heart went out to this lovely young girl. Jean had experienced enough of her youngest son's malevolence to know that the experience must have been terrifying. For once her maternal instincts were replaced by repugnance for her son's deeds. She reached out unexpectedly and clasped the young woman's hand.

'I'm truly sorry that a son of mine should cause you such trauma,' she said.

Elke bowed her head, unable to speak for a moment, then regaining her self-control she looked up at her future mother-in-law.

'Whatever hurt Justin may have done, has been more than compensated for by Ed's concern. And love,' she added shyly.

Jean withdrew her hand and nodded. She sipped her coffee before continuing.

'Forgive me if I seem a little distant, my dear, but this has all been quite a surprise. Have the two of you had a chance to discuss when you plan to marry and, more importantly, where you want to live?'

There was an awkward silence then Ed responded.

'Mom, I'm sorry for the surprise but as Elke said we haven't had much time to think it through ourselves. Justin made sure of that!' Ed smiled affectionately at Elke. 'But make no mistake, we're very much in love and the adventures of the last few days have confirmed it a thousand times over. When I thought that I might not see Elke again, I nearly went nuts!'

Ed sighed as he recalled some of the terrible moments of the recent past. He then looked at his mother firmly.

'Mom, please just accept that we're seriously and totally in love with each other. We have discussed the future but it's early days. As you know I never wanted to take over Willjohn Industries and even with Justin out of that picture, I'm sorry, Mom, it just wouldn't work.'

Jean nodded. 'But that doesn't answer where you intend to live when you're married.'

Ed and Elke looked at each other. Everything was suddenly progressing at breakneck speed for the two of them, but Ed's mother's question was fair enough. It would clearly affect the three of them.

Ed cleared his throat.

'Look Mom, nothing's cast in stone but my contract's up with the mine in a few weeks. I can renew it but I'm not sure I want to.'

Ed leaned forward. His eyes sparkled as he began to discuss his ideas enthusiastically. Jean recognised the signs. Even as a small boy, Ed had always been very focused with his plans and ambitions. She also knew that once he had formulated a plan, it would be difficult, if not impossible, to dislodge him from his intended path. She also realised with a sense of foreboding that the plans were unlikely to include a return to the US any time soon.

*

Bud and a reluctant Justin joined Mr T in his office. Mr T's dollar signs were now tempered by the fact that Bud had now shoehorned in on the act. Although the new arrival was a small man, Mr T had already sensed the man's underlying propensity for violence. Had he known what Ed had discovered about Bud during their confrontation at the McNeil ranch, he would not have been so respectful. Bud intimidated people but was not himself a killer. However, it was quite probable that he had ordered a few hits in his time.

Bud had discovered in his youth that if he acted aggressively enough, people assumed he would stop at nothing. It was the typical façade of a bully, who were mostly cowards at heart. Bud had successfully bluffed his way through dozens of physical encounters. The very large and powerful Mr T had no intention of double-crossing Bud and the little man knew it. It boosted his considerable ego to see how easily he could intimidate others.

'How're we going with tickets for Rio?' Bud asked as Mr T ordered coffee for his guests.

'They'll be delivered this morning. You're all booked on the 9.00pm flight tomorrow.'

'Will the passports be ready in time?' Justin enquired anxiously.

Mr T nodded. 'Pedro just needs a new photo. I have an out-of-work television make-up artist coming around at noon. She'll give you a makeover and then we'll have all of you photographed. The photos will go to Pedro this afternoon and you'll have your passports by tomorrow lunchtime.'

Justin smiled weakly and nodded. He felt as though he was in the most expensive taxi in the world with the meter ticking steadily. Once he got to Rio he would have to give Bud and his girlfriend the slip. Otherwise he'd return to the States completely destitute.

He was certainly not the kind of guy who could just roll up his sleeves and start again.

'Some brandy in your coffee?' Mr T asked.

It was still morning and normally he would have refused.

'Why not?' He answered glumly.

*

Ed had hoped to leave the discussion about his future for another day but his mother had always been a direct, no-nonsense person and he realised that she would not be satisfied with vague answers.

'Look, it's early days but this is how we see it right now. Elke has grown up on a farm and if you recall I was always my happiest when we were on the ranch back home. She's also writing her doctorate in biology and she feels strongly about the steady erosion of all eco-systems around the planet. I agree with her.'

Jean looked at the young woman with growing respect. She was not just a rare beauty but obviously had brains as well. Ed continued.

'I read the other day that, at its present rate of pollution, planet Earth will not be able to sustain life in another 30 years! That's a truly frightening thought. Elke and I want to make a difference, no matter how small. I propose to buy a farm close to her parents' place and combine the two to produce organic uncontaminated crops for the region. Elke knows much more than I do about farming and she'll be a real crusader in favour of cleaning up the environment.'

Jean opened her mouth to speak but Ed forestalled her.

'Before you think you've lost a son, I can promise you that we'll visit you regularly, unless you choose to visit us first.'

There was a long silence as Jean digested this latest bombshell.

'Well, you've given me plenty to think about!'

Elke took this as a cue. She excused herself saying that she had to get back to work.

Ed looked at his watch. 'Yeah, I better make tracks for the mine.'

His mother shook her head firmly. 'I called your boss Sam last night. He and I agreed that you need another day or so to recover from your adventures. He also insisted that you show me around the area.'

Ed sighed. He could see that his life would not be his own for a day or two.

'You win Mom!'

He walked Elke to her car. She was quiet and thoughtful as they walked together.

Ed looked at her anxiously.

'Everything okay?'

Elke thought before replying.

'You've shocked your mother with your plans for the future. I just hope that she'll be able to come to terms with them.'

'Yeah,' Ed replied, 'but I tell you one thing, she likes you!'

Elke wasn't so sure, but she kept quiet. They kissed tenderly before Elke drove away.

*

Rob Schutte looked at his watch. He had a meeting due with Professor Ian Raper in ten minutes regarding the proposed Heritage Association. He looked at the paperwork on his desk. They had a large conference for WesBank, a major motor vehicle finance institution, starting that week.

Rob had briefed "Moose" their Leadership Trainer who had for some time provided excellent courses as an optional extra for any conference at the hotel. Moose seemed to be collecting nicknames. He had recently been told by the team leaders of a successful conference, that his name from henceforth would be "Renoster Speedcop." Renoster was the Afrikaans for rhino and Rob made a note to find out how the new nickname had emerged.

He made his way onto the patio. Ian had already arrived. They exchanged the usual pleasantries and were about to get into the details of the new Heritage Association when Ed and his mother walked past.

'I hope you had a good breakfast, Mrs Willjohn?' Rob called out.

Jean smiled. 'It was great, thanks.'

On an impulse Rob introduced the Professor to Ed and his mother and touched on the possibility of the hotel joining the newly formed

Heritage Association. Ed was immediately interested.

'I'd like to hear more about it some time,' he told Rob. 'Elke's deeply concerned about the environment. We'd like to see how we could help.'

Ian was delighted. 'I'd be happy to give Rob extra copies of the literature I'll be leaving for him.'

Ed and Ian exchanged business cards and promised to speak to each other again.

As they walked towards Ed's car to begin a tour of the district, Ed looked at his mother.

'Okay Mom, aside from your worries about my staying in South Africa, what're your first impressions of Elke?'

His mother replied quietly and rather sadly.

'I think she's a wonderful young girl, dear, but of course, she's all wrong for you!'

CHAPTER 47

Elke returned to the farm just after nine o'clock. Her mother was about to leave for Rustenburg but waited in her bakkie until Elke drew alongside in Isak's car, which she had borrowed for the day.

Elke gave her mother a wry smile.

'I suppose you want to know who it was that Ed wanted me to meet?' Her mother shrugged.

'Not necessarily. I just wanted to know if everything is all right. I understand that Justin's still on the loose, so until he's safely behind bars, I'll remain anxious about the two of you.'

Elke laughed, although she also had an uneasy feeling about Justin.

'Don't worry, I'll bet he's trying to get out of this country as fast as he can,' she replied. 'I very much doubt if we'll see him back here, anytime soon.'

As she finished her sentence, she had two distinctly separate thoughts. The first was a nagging doubt that they would ever be completely rid of Justin. The other thought was more whimsical. She had just used the American expression in her speech, "anytime soon," and it made her realise just how pervasive constant contact with Americans could be. There was something about their turn of phrase that was appealing and easy to imitate. The constant barrage of American television and movies had bred a generation of young South Africans of all colours who were beginning to replace the harsh cadences of the South African accent with a kind of mid-Atlantic twang. Certainly, American catch phrases like "no ways" and "later" were becoming more and more part of South African English.

Elke realised that when she was with Ed and possibly even in the few saner moments she'd had with Justin, she tended to dredge Americanisms from her sub-conscious and use them in her speech. Elke decided that she, an Afrikaans speaking girl of German descent, who now spoke

English with an American influence, was definitely in line for some kind of an identity crisis.

'So, who was it?' her mother asked.

Elke pulled her mind back to the present and sighed.

'You won't believe this, but Ed's mother arrived from the States last night,' she replied.

Her mother's consternation showed on her face.

'Magtig, but these Americans move fast, my girl! Is she out here to help plan the wedding because that's our...'

'Hold on, Ma!' Elke chuckled. 'You're way ahead of things. Jean Willjohn had no idea that we were even engaged. She knew nothing about my kidnapping or anything like that but as a typical mother she was worried, and I think she simply decided to come out and see what her two boys were up to.'

Marie shook her head in amazement.

'And when she heard that you two were engaged?'

Elke shrugged as she switched off the ignition of her Dad's car and got out to stand next to the driver's window of her mother's bakkie.

'I'm not sure, Ma. She's a very polite and gracious lady. She doesn't reveal her feelings, but I sensed that our engagement came as quite a shock.'

Marie nodded and in turn switched on the ignition of her bakkie.

'We'd better arrange a luncheon for her before she goes back then.'

Elke realised at that moment that her mother had completely bought into the idea of Ed and her as a couple. In fact, she was probably happier about it than her prospective American mother-in-law. She watched fondly as her mother drove off on her way into town.

*

Ed and his mother drove into the village of Kroondal and stopped off at the Otterman's delightful little coffee shop in the old mill. Over a cup of coffee Ed tried to get his mother to explain in more detail why she felt that Elke was all wrong for him.

Jean Willjohn brooded over this for some time before replying. 'What concerns me is that you come from very different worlds. What happens when you grow tired of living in Africa, as I'm sure you will? How will she react to relocating to the United States?'

'What makes you think that I'll get sick of living here?' Ed demanded. 'You've been in the country for, what, forty-eight hours?'

Jean Willjohn sipped her coffee reflectively. Ed was right, of course. It was far too soon for her to make any judgment about South Africa and the attractive rural area in which Ed was proposing to live.

If he came home, she realised that he would still not join Willjohn Industries. It was far more likely that he would want to develop the ranch.

Was there so much difference between his being two or ten thousand miles away from home? Would a four-hour plane flight make him that much more accessible than a twenty-hour journey?

So, was it the girl herself? Jean had no illusions about a mother's protective instincts over her children. Elke was a stunning beauty. Good grief, Jean thought, this is the country that has produced the actress Charlize Theron. Are all these Afrikaans girls such beauties? So, was it jealousy? Maybe, but it was also a concern about Ed and Elke's compatibility. Jean was an intelligent and perceptive woman who was also fully capable of critical self-analysis. Could she honestly judge the girl on the basis of a half hour meeting, when both she and Ed were recovering from a traumatic ordeal?'

Jean looked up at her son and spoke gently.

'You're right, son! I'm jumping to all kinds of conclusions here; both about the country and about the girl. Tell you what. You show me around. Take your time to explain why the place has such magic for you. Tell me more about Elke. I'd like to meet her again and her parents, I guess. I promise not to pre-judge the situation any more than I already have.'

Ed reached across and squeezed his mother's hand. 'Thanks, Mom. That's music to my ears. Let's get going now. My tour's a long one so we better stick to the schedule!'

On their way out of the coffee shop, they encountered Rolf Otterman. Ed greeted him and briefly introduced his mother. Since that early meeting with Rolf many months before, Ed had not really seen the man again but as he was going to be marrying into the Kroondal community, he felt he should make an effort to see more of these friendly rural folk who were a quaint mix of modern hi-tech skills and old world charm. Just like the American Midwest, was his last thought on the subject.

*

Bud and Bonnie relaxed over a good red wine, a 1988 Nederburg Cabernet Sauvignon, in a restaurant in Parktown, an upmarket suburb not far from the frenetic buzz of Hillbrow.

Johannesburg, just over a hundred years ago, was a desolate, windswept region of open grasslands at an altitude of over eighteen hundred metres. It could get comfortably warm in summer, but it was often bitterly cold in winter. When the mine dumps grew around the outskirts of the city, the harsh winds would blow the cyanide-laced dust across the streets and into the houses. For many years it was indeed an overgrown mining camp, with all the discomforts that implied.

In the 1950's and 60's more and more trees were planted in order to bring some greenery to the city and to protect its burgeoning population from the icy winter winds that blow from the distant Drakensberg mountains two hundred and fifty kilometres to the south of the city. When there's snow on the 'berg, Johannesburgers wrap up warmly.

Now, the city was one of the greenest in the world. Even in mid-winter a number of suburban restaurants watered their lawns and put tables and chairs outside in the relatively warm midday sun. The profusion of trees now protected the customers from the 'berg winds. A sunny day in winter could be a special time for Johannesburgers.

Bud and Bonnie had chosen the restaurant as part of a nostalgic last look around the city they would never see again. Bonnie had no regrets. She was leaving the country with her man and they were shortly to be married. In fact, their false passports would pre-empt the event. They were about to become Mr and Mrs John Cousins, courtesy of Pedro, the forger.

As they sipped their wine and casually looked through the luncheon menu, a stranger approached their table.

He was of medium height, slim, with black hair and a two-day stubble on his face.

He had slightly protuberant teeth and surprisingly rounded cheeks. For a moment Bud wondered if the man were a beggar but he was wearing an expensive casual shirt and colourful waistcoat.

The man stopped and stared hard at Bud.

'Excuse me for interrupting, sir;' the man spoke so softly that Bud could hardly hear what he was saying 'but I'm told that you're a well-known platinum dealer. Perhaps too well known!'

Bud went cold for an instant as he wondered what in the hell the guy was up to. Then he laughed. It was a good belly laugh, partly out of relief, and partly out of genuine amusement.

'Pretty good, pal!' he responded as Bonnie stared at the two men in confusion. Bud turned to Bonnie. 'Sweetheart, I'd like to introduce a good friend of mine - Per Ludorff!'

Bonnie looked at Justin in amazement. The transformation was quite remarkable. There was no resemblance to the old Justin other than that this new creation was about the same height and he still spoke with an American accent.

'Have to work on the voice, pal' Bud chuckled 'but otherwise, great! Sit down. We were waiting for you before we ordered.'

*

Ed and his mother, Jean, entered the parking grounds of the Sterkfontein Caves and the site of some of the most significant palaeontological discoveries in the world. He had driven Jean from Kroondal over the Olifantsnek Pass in the adjoining valley, which he had explained was still known as the Moot to the local Afrikaans families in the region. Ed had pointed out the area at the foothills of the spectacular cliffs, where the battle of Nooitgedacht had taken place during the Anglo-Boer War, with disastrous results for the over-confident British.

Instead of continuing down the valley to Hartbeespoort Dam, Ed had driven along the attractive winding road in a cleft between the next fold of mountains and into the tiny village of Magaliesburg. They had both been surprised and pleased to see that a Boys Town existed, deep in the hills of the region, giving the boys a beautiful environment in which to come to terms with whatever curve balls life had thrown at them.

Ed was struck, once again, by how many elements of South African life mirrored British or American culture. Boys Town, to an American, was exclusively Spencer Tracey country and the fact that the movement had travelled across the world to Africa, was a truly heart-warming sight for both Ed and his mother.

Offered a wide choice of places to visit, Jean had immediately pointed to the Sterkfontein Caves on the tourist map Ed had shown her. Jean was a keen amateur palaeontologist who had spent many weeks in the wilds of the American Midwest tracing early signs of Native American civilisations. To visit the site, where Dr Robert Broom had discovered "Mrs Ples," one of the most significant finds of the twentieth century, was an extraordinary opportunity for her.

She and Ed strolled over to the small museum next to the restaurant close to the actual diggings. Ed could sense his mother's excitement.

'Africa kinda gets under your skin, doesn't it?'

Ed opened the door of the museum and ushered his mother inside.

'Don't push your luck, Junior!'

The twinkle in her eyes belied any real irritation and hinted at her genuine involvement in an area which was now recognised as a cradle of civilisation.

*

Bonnie, Bud and Justin enjoyed a memorable lunch. For a while their differences were forgotten as Bud spoke enthusiastically about his few years on the game ranch, after he had made his money in the scrap metal business. Over coffee, Justin brought them abruptly back to the present.

'When do I get my passport?'

Bud's expression immediately hardened.

'Why? Thinking of going your own way?'

Before Justin could reply, Bud made his position very clear.

'This is how it works. I hand you your passport as we enter the check-in counter at the airport, not one second before. Got it?'

Justin lowered his eyes in the face of the little man's blazing intensity.

'Okay' he mumbled, 'but I've got a few things to do before we leave.

Will you pick me up from the hotel tomorrow or should I drive myself to the airport?'

'We'll pick you up' Bud replied firmly. 'Anyway, where'd you get wheels from? You need an ID to hire a car.'

'Mr T rented me one,' Justin responded. 'I'll be ready from 3pm tomorrow at the hotel.'

'Where're you going now?' Bud asked suspiciously. 'I don't want you to go fooling around and get caught. Hey, you're my meal ticket for the next few weeks!'

Justin nodded glumly, hoping that he was not going to be asked to pay for lunch. He stood up.

'I'll be careful.'

He was about to leave when Bud spoke again.

'Listen, Justin, or should I say, Per. Let's make one thing very clear. If you're not at the hotel at three, ready to leave with us for Rio, don't think you can just get another passport. Pedro and Mr T know the score and that you're coming with us. If you don't show, I can promise you the cops'll have a very detailed description of you as Per. Pedro won't make you a new passport. Mr T won't let his make-up lady give you another identity. They'll nail you, my friend, so you'd better be there!'

Justin nodded again looking downcast.

'Thanks for the lunch' he said and walked away.

Bonnie looked at Bud.

'Shouldn't you keep him under wraps?'

Bud shook his head. 'He hasn't got the guts to run from me.'

Bud leaned over and kissed Bonnie lustily on the mouth.

'Let's forget the kid. I could use some quiet time for the two of us together before we start on our travels.'

*

Justin pulled up at the security gate of Buffalo Hills Hotel. He looked at the guard, who would have recognised him as Justin Willjohn but who gave no sign of recognition of Justin's new persona as Per Ludorff.

'Hi, I'm a friend of Mr Ed Willjohn from America. D'you know if he's in?'

The guard shook his head. 'No, sir. Mr Willjohn, he go out.'

"Per" made a show of being irritated.

'Okay. I'd like to leave a message for him at reception. I'm staying at Sun City. He can call me there.'

The security guard nodded and Per drove through without further difficulty.

As far as he knew, his brother was still at work. Justin had no intention of testing his new disguise on Ed. He expected that his voice would give him away, although he had spent most of his journey to Buffalo Hills practising a deeper tone of voice. He had attempted an English accent, but even to his untrained ear it sounded terrible. No, he had to avoid people he knew really well at all costs.

Per parked his car. Making sure he had not been seen, he avoided the reception area and headed straight for Ed's room. He had already written Ed a note, which read 'You will deposit one million dollars in account number 458132 0689 of the Swiss Fidelity Bank in Zurich by noon tomorrow. If you do this, I swear that I will never bother you again. Your about to be ex-brother, JUSTIN.'

Justin checked once more to make sure that no-one was watching as he bent down and slid the envelope containing his note under Ed's door. He straightened up and turned towards the alleyway between Ed's room and another block of rooms. The alleyway led directly to the driveway and parking area.

As he did so, Per abruptly became Justin again. He stared in total disbelief as his mother walked down the alleyway towards him.

CHAPTER 48

Jean Willjohn was lost in thought. She was also slightly lost in reality. The events of the last few days had taken their toll. This normally calm and well organised woman, secure in her considerable wealth as well as her long established social circle amongst the elite of Minneapolis, was now completely distracted. She had turned down the alleyway between two blocks of rooms at Buffalo Hills Hotel and had suddenly gone blank as to how to reach the patio, where she and Ed planned to meet.

A young man approached her from the opposite direction. He was a plain-looking unexceptional sort of person. Nothing about his appearance triggered any kind of recognition in Jean's mind. Besides which, apart from being momentarily lost, her head was filled with the disappearance of her wayward son, Justin, as well as the impending and for her unwelcome, wedding of her other son, Ed. Even though she had told Ed that she had suspended judgment on the prospect of Elke as a daughter-in-law, she was fundamentally against it.

As Jean looked around, trying to get her bearings, she realised that she had no idea which way to turn. On an impulse she spoke to the young man who had by now almost drawn level with her.

'Excuse me, young man, can you tell me where the hotel's patio is?'

Justin, disguised as Per, nearly choked. His own mother had not recognised him, but he was certain his voice would be a dead give-away. Pitching his words as low as he could and introducing a rough edge to his voice he replied.

'Straight down and to the right, ma'am!'

Jean smiled in surprise. 'Hey, a fellow Statesider!'

Justin nodded and tried to move past her but she put out a hand.

'Jean Willjohn from Minneapolis. Are you staying here?'

Justin took her hand and shook it. The bizarre irony of the situation did not escape him. The name Per Ludorff was on his lips but at the last second he realised that it would be fatal to give that to her.

'Grant Johnson, New York' he croaked. 'I'm not staying here. I just came to deliver a message.'

As he said this, he could have bitten his tongue off. His mother and Ed would very likely put two and two together after Ed had received the demand note he had left under Ed's door.

'Pity.'

Jean figured that Ed should be exposed to as many Americans as possible in the hope he might be reminded of where his real roots lay.

'D'you have a few minutes to join us for a drink?' Jean asked. 'My son Ed'll be along right away. He's been working out here.'

Justin wondered how long the nightmare would last. He tried his poor imitation of an American bullfrog once more.

'Sorry a'am. You're very gracious but I need to get back to Johannesburg. Thanks anyway.'

Jean nodded regretfully. Justin managed to extricate himself and head for the car park. He had to restrain himself from running all the way to his car.

*

Elke arrived back at the farmhouse, before going into town to buy supplies for the following week. Her mother was still on the land, supervising the digging of a new irrigation furrow. As she entered the yard, she saw that they had a visitor. A gleaming black Mercedes Sports was parked in front of the house.

As she drew close to the stoep, she saw the familiar figure of Kurt von Wallenstein sitting with her father. Elke was pleased to see him as a friend, but she hoped that the man had finally accepted that he and Elke were not, nor ever had been, an item. The men turned towards her and stood up as Elke stepped onto the stoep.

She smiled. 'It's always presumed that women do all the skinnering but men don't do so badly in that department either.'

Kurt chuckled and her father gave a wan smile. Isak was not well. His heart was constantly giving him trouble and although he made light of it, Elke and Marie were becoming increasingly worried about him.

'Wie geht's?' Kurt asked Elke in German.

She replied in English, which was unusual for her.

'Fine thanks, Kurt, and yourself?'

'Apart from a broken heart,' he replied wryly 'I couldn't be better!'

'Good' Elke replied.

She genuinely liked the man. She just did not want to marry him.

'I came over to offer my congratulations,' Kurt continued. 'If you won't marry me and if you have to marry an uitlander, I can't think of a better choice!'

Elke laughed. That was probably the most endearing thing Kurt had ever said to her.

The three of them chatted amicably for a few minutes before Elke excused herself, saying that she needed to get to the store and back before the labour force went home. Kurt also said goodbye to Isak and walked with Elke to their respective cars. As they approached Elke's bakkie, Kurt predictably raised the issue of their relationship once again. In fairness it was a half-hearted effort, but Elke had to give him an A for perseverance.

'Elke' he began 'if you should ever have any doubts about Mr America or even get cold feet about getting married; I'm still here for you.'

Elke smiled. Kurt had chosen his words well. She did not feel offended. Impulsively she reached across and kissed him on the cheek.

'Thanks, Kurt. You're a real friend.'

*

Ed joined his mother on the hotel patio. He was still digesting the reality of Justin's hand-delivered note and demand for money. Ed was torn between ignoring the note completely and complying with the demand. After all, Justin was still his brother. Perhaps Justin had genuinely realised that he had lost his position in the family forever and would make a new life with the money. As Ed thought about this, he realised just how unlikely it was that Justin would ever overcome his all-consuming jealousy and leave the family alone.

'Mother calling planet Ed!' Jean said playfully.

Ed realised with a start that she had been talking to him.

'Sorry Mom,' he said sheepishly. 'Just got something on my mind.'

'So it seems' Jean smiled at him. 'Pity you weren't with me a moment ago. I just met another American here.'

'Oh! Staying at the hotel?'

'Said he was just delivering a message to one of the guests.'

Ed froze in his seat then groaned.

'Oh no, what did he look like?'

Ed stood up, already knowing the answer.

Jean shrugged. 'Kinda ordinary. Dark hair, slim, young, early twenties.'

'Blue eyes, a voice that could've been Justin's?' Ed asked harshly.

His mother stared at him aghast. 'Oh no!' she managed weakly.

Ed dashed towards the parking ground.

Jean remained seated. She tried to picture the young man. As she did so, she realised that he certainly could have been Justin in disguise. Come to think of it, there had been something remarkably familiar about his body language.

*

Justin drove at his usual breakneck speed heading towards the dam and subsequently Johannesburg. Once again, he realised that he had

303

the frightening habit of saying the first thing that came into his mind without considering the consequences. Ed only had to hear that an unknown American was delivering a message to one of the guests and he would immediately put two and two together. Justin pounded the steering wheel in frustration and nearly left the road from his efforts.

*

Ed returned to his mother on the patio only after he had had a futile conversation with Captain Kloppers. Ed had told him that Justin had just left the hotel and the policeman, reasonably enough, asked him what car Justin was driving and what did he look like now he was disguised. Ed had gloomily agreed that the chances of catching him were remote. He promised to get the best possible description his mother could give him. At least they could circulate that to airports and border posts, but Kloppers had gently advised Ed that they were not really any closer to catching Justin.

Ed sat down and asked the waiter for a coffee. Jean looked at him questioningly, but her son shook his head. Instead he pulled out Justin's note demanding the one million dollars.

Jean read it carefully then looked up at Ed.

'I think we should give it to him,' she said finally.

Ed sighed. The coffee arrived and he busied himself with sugar and milk, while he phrased his reply.

'I don't think so, Mom. Why do governments refuse to give in to kidnappers and blackmailers?'

Jean sighed and replied reluctantly.

'Because more people would do it, if they knew it was successful.'

Ed grimaced. 'That's only part of it. The person making the demand, in this case Justin, says he'll never bother us again. That's a load of hogwash. He's not gonna invest that money and live off the interest for the rest of his life. He's gonna live dangerously as he's always done. In a year, six months, maybe even next week, he'll be cleaned out and broke. Then he'll be back. You can bet on it, Mom. This is no way to solve the problem.'

'Maybe not,' replied Jean, with tears in her eyes. 'But he is my son and I can't just leave him to his own devices.'

Ed shook his head. 'That's exactly the problem. If you, or I for that matter, had the courage to cut him adrift, he would have a better chance of learning how to cope for himself.'

'Or get killed in some back alley,' Jean added tearfully.

Ed had to agree but refrained from commenting. A waiter approached the table. Ed looked up at him.

'Excuse me, sir. There's a phone call for you.'

Ed nodded then turned back to his mother.

'Think about it, Mom. It's a terrible decision. Either way we could play it wrong. I'll be right back.'

Ed followed the waiter into the foyer of the hotel where the receptionist pointed to a phone booth. Ed crossed over the hallway and picked up the phone.

'Willjohn!'

'I know it's a tough call' Justin's voice spoke to him, 'but I've just figured out an inducement.'

'I can't wait,' Ed replied dryly.

'What if I throw in Bud McNeil?' Justin asked

'Too late bro, he's already been arrested.'

'Yeah, but he's out on bail, and he's gonna skip the country. I can lead you to him, providing the money's deposited in my Swiss account by tomorrow morning.'

Ed asked, 'Why should I care if he gets away or not?'

He already knew the answer, but he played for time while he tried to work out his best options.

'Because you're the kinda Ivy League Mr Squeaky Clean that you are, pal. You know that Sam and Premier Platinum would hate for that little jerk to get away.'

Ed had to agree. Still he played for more time.

'Tell me, it was you speaking to Mom at the hotel, wasn't it?'

Justin laughed. 'Thought you'd figure it out. I bet Mom didn't realise until you told her?'

'No. Okay, suppose I give you the money, and I'm not saying I've agreed, how's this gonna work?'

*

Bud and Bonnie picked up Justin at the hotel as arranged. Bud was relieved to see him. Despite his threats, Bud realised that Justin was such a loose cannon that one could not rely on him to do anything right.

Justin, as Per Ludorff, was edgy but nevertheless was waiting downstairs for Bud. The two men shook hands with Mr T and thanked him for his help. As they climbed into Bud's vehicle Justin could not help asking if the other man had the passports.

Bud patted his jacket pocket. 'All safe and sound,' he responded.

Bonnie sat in the front seat, looking like a fading movie star. Her obvious good looks and liberal application of make-up did not appeal to Justin, but he greeted her civilly enough. In fact, both Justin and Bonnie shared an unspoken camaraderie since they were both, to a large extent, parasites orbiting around the dominating presence of the little big man, Bud McNeil.

As they drove to the airport, Bud was in an expansive mood.

'Jo'burg's been good to me,' he began, 'it's a city with a lot of character.

I don't think it's ever fully shaken off its roots as a mining camp. Did you know that it's the largest city in the world not built on the banks of a sizeable river?'

'I didn't know that' Bonnie chipped in. 'How did that happen?'

Bud shrugged. 'Must've been the gold. The mining took place on the gold reef, river or no river. The wealth was so enormous that the camp became a town and finally a city, despite the logistics of being some seventy kilometres from the Vaal River. Anyway, as from tonight that's no longer our problem, is it?'

He grinned at Bonnie who dutifully smiled back but Justin sensed that she was more emotionally distressed at leaving the world she knew so well, than either of the two men.

Bud drove carefully along the motorway towards Johannesburg International Airport. The last thing he wanted was to get stopped for speeding. They were on time, but Bud suddenly felt anxious about their impending departure. There were any number of things that could still go wrong. He glanced in his rear-view mirror at Justin. The young man was still edgy, but then he had always been neurotic, ever since Bud had first met him. For a moment he wondered whether the extra risks attached to taking Justin with them were worth it.

Bud reminded himself that the 250,000 rand bail he was about to forfeit was nothing in dollar terms, but he had every intention of bleeding Justin as dry as he could and preferably leaving him to stew in a Brazilian jail. He was guessing, but he suspected that Justin was still worth somewhere between a quarter and half a million dollars even after the Willjohn family had cut him adrift. Bud was determined to extract every cent he could. The little swine had cost him so much. Bud was not a forgiving man.

They drove into the International Airport's underground parking area and unloaded a surprisingly small amount of luggage. Bud and Bonnie had one suitcase each and Justin simply carried a large piece of hand luggage. For all of them, leaving South Africa forever was a new start, a new life. None of them needed or wanted any unnecessary old memories. The three of them lined up in the queue for the South African Airways flight to Rio. There were three or four people ahead of them. Justin turned to Bud.

'I need my passport please.'

Bud hesitated. 'Why bother. I'll hand them all in with the tickets. Once we've booked in, you'll get it. Okay?'

Justin shrugged and waited impatiently for the queue to diminish.

After seemingly hours, Bud stepped forward and presented the three tickets and their accompanying passports to the smiling SAA ground attendant. The luggage was clearly underweight, and formalities were quickly completed.

The young lady handed Bud the boarding passes, tickets and passports. Justin pointedly put his hand out to receive his papers. Bud hesitated for a long moment then shrugged.

'We're going straight through pal, so don't try anything!'

Justin smiled his notoriously dangerous smile.

'Why should I? I've always wanted to enjoy the pleasures of Rio.'

At that moment a number of plain-clothed policemen descended upon the trio. A protesting Bud and Bonnie were taken off together, whilst Justin was escorted away by two young men, one of whom was Kurt von Wallenstein.

CHAPTER 49

'What have I done wrong?' Bud whined as the Policeman led Bonnie and him away.

Captain Nhlope in charge of the Police team responded with a wry smile.

'I think you know very well, sir. You are out on bail and you have been apprehended in the process of boarding an aircraft to take you out of the country.'

Bud tried a long shot. 'Nonsense. We were just seeing our friend Per Ludorff onto the plane.'

As soon as the Police had approached them Bud had tried to hide the passports and tickets. The sharp-eyed Captain did not buy it for a moment.

'Sir, will you empty your pockets please?'

Bonnie started to weep. Bud gave her a hard warning glance. She tried to contain herself, which resulted in her making some pathetic snuffling and choking sounds. Bud tried outrage.

'Who the hell d'you think you are?' he stormed. 'You haven't shown me a search warrant!'

Captain Nhlope kept his patience. He was used to hearing almost every imaginable excuse and justification. He produced an arrest warrant.

'Sir, we can do this back at the Police Station or we can do it now. If you have no passport or tickets, I will take your explanation for being here more seriously.'

Bud shrugged. He was beaten and he knew it. Without further protest he pulled his own passport and ticket out of the breast pocket of his jacket, managing to leave Bonnie's passport in his pocket. The Captain took the documents and studied them. Unfortunately, Bud had pulled out Bonnie's ticket along with his passport.

Nhlope raised an eyebrow.

'It seems as though the lady was planning to travel as well. I need her passport too.'

Bud reluctantly withdrew the remaining passport. He reached across and squeezed Bonnie's arm.

'Sorry girl,' he muttered.

Bonnie was crying openly now. She nodded mutely. Bud turned back to the Policeman.

'What's happened to our friend, Per?' he asked.

'Mr Willjohn is being taken to Rustenburg, where he will be held until his trial,' the Captain replied.

Bud sighed. His last bargaining chip was gone. He had hoped to give up Justin in exchange for some possible reduction in his sentence. Now it seemed as though they were both in deep trouble, with poor Bonnie unwittingly drawn into it all.

*

As Kurt drove Justin, alias Per, away from the airport, the young American sat sullenly in the back seat. As part of his deal with Ed, he had agreed to give up Bud, the forger Pedro and Mr T. The brothers had agreed that Justin would be seen to be arrested as well, in case Bud decided to revenge himself upon Justin. This way, it was hoped, Bud would assume that Justin was also under arrest.

The deal Ed had struck with Captain Kloppers was a tough one, for Justin. In exchange for turning state witness, he would have to attend a Criminal Rehabilitation Centre that had recently been opened in Tshwane (the new name for Pretoria).

After the trials of Bud, the forger and Mr T, Justin would then be deported without an option of ever returning to South Africa. What the family did with him thereafter was entirely their business. Kloppers had strongly advised against giving Justin any large sums of money. He had suggested that the most they should consider was a small monthly allowance. Kloppers had added that if it were his brother, he would not even give him that. It was safe to assume that the youngster would have salted away a substantial amount of money during his two years of employment with Willjohn Industries.

Justin looked at Kurt. 'Which Police Station are you attached to?' he asked.

Kurt, who had agreed to help Elke and Ed, for whom he had a grudging respect, did not realise that Justin would believe him to be a real cop. However, when Justin made this assumption, he decided to turn the screws even tighter upon the young man. Elke's story of her kidnapping had enraged the aristocratic German. He felt that Ed's deal with Kloppers was unreasonably lenient and here was a chance at least to intimidate Justin.

'I'm based in Rustenburg' Kurt replied, thinking that it was partially true. His extensive farms and other land holdings were all in the Rustenburg and Kroondal districts.

'So, what do we do now?' Justin asked.

'I'm taking you back to Rustenburg. I'm going to find the coldest, darkest cell in the prison, put you inside, then throw away the key,' Kurt replied.

Justin swivelled around in his seat and stared at Kurt.

'No ways. That wasn't the deal, pal! You're to take me to Buffalo Hills Hotel. I've gotta meeting with Ed and my mother. Captain Kloppers told Ed...'

Kurt held up a hand for silence.

'Listen here you little jerk. If I had my way, I would've shot you at the airport for attempting to escape.'

'But I...'

'But nothing. I'd like to have shot you anyway. I still might. What you did to Elke...'

'So, you know her' Justin began.

'She's well known and well-loved in the community. So, when you hurt her, you hurt all of us. I'm also part of the Kroondal German Community. We're all loyal South Africans but we also have a special bond. If I dropped you off in Kroondal's main street and told people who you were, you'd be beaten to pulp in ten seconds.'

'But the deal is that I'm turning State witness. I've got to do some kinda rehab, I appear as witness in the trial then I'm outta here!'

Kurt nodded. 'That's what you were told. The reality may well be rather different.'

'I've been double-crossed!' Justin wailed.

He glanced at Kurt again. He was probably twice his size and looked very fit indeed. Strangely he saw no firearm and nor had Kurt put handcuffs on him. To Justin's convoluted mind, this seemed to confirm that Kurt was tempting him to try and escape so that the big man could indeed beat him to a pulp.

Their car was already on the off-ramp of the freeway leading up to the Nichol Highway and Fourways. As they stopped at the lights before the highway, Kurt looked at his prisoner and spoke softly.

'Try it, my friend. Open the door and start running. Let's see how far you get.'

Kurt realised that Justin really believed him. He momentarily wondered whether he shouldn't hop over to Hollywood one of these days. He'd make one hell of an actor!

*

Sam Mohale took time out of his busy schedule to drive over to Buffalo Hills and have coffee with Ed and his mother. Although it was after working hours, Sam still had a pile of papers on his desk, but he really wanted to meet Ed's mother. He also wanted to put Ed at ease about his few days away from the office.

As the introductions were completed and they settled into their chairs on the patio, Ed began with an apology.

'Sam, I'm sorry I'm taking this time off. I know that you and my mother kinda did a deal on the phone, but if you need me back right away...'

Sam laughed. 'What do I say to that? If I say I don't need you, you'll think that you haven't made a contribution to the mine, which you certainly have. If I say we can't cope, you'll be in your office before your mother and I have finished our coffee. So, what do I say?'

His eyes twinkled as he said it. Jean Willjohn laughed.

'I think you have a diplomat for a boss, son.'

Ed nodded. His mother was right. In the eight years since the end of the Apartheid era, people like Sam were in positions of power and influence all over South Africa. Ed's year in South Africa had led him to the conclusion that the transition from White power to Black power could not have been easy for either side. Sadly, several Africans had been given important positions in large companies, but they did not have the qualifications to fulfil the demands of their role. There were exceptions however and Sam was one of them. In addition to an excellent education, he was one of those rare people who managed to create a climate in his vicinity where everyone looked right past any potential colour issues and just saw a good man, a strong leader and someone who truly understood the industry in which he had worked for so many years.

Ed took it one step further. He saw a good friend, with whom he had shared a few adventures over the past few weeks. He threw up his hands in surrender.

'Okay, so I'll mosey along on Monday and try to remember what it's like to be in the mining industry.'

The others laughed but Ed felt a pang as he knew that at the end of his contract, he would not want to renew it. As soon as he and Elke were married, he wanted to implement his plans to expand the Stein farm. He would then start to learn more about farming.

His time with Premier Mine had been a wonderful experience but he was equally excited about the prospect of farming, especially with Elke at his side. He also hoped that he would be able to take some time to return to the family's Wyoming Ranch and introduce Elke to the lifestyle of cattle ranching in one of the most beautiful states in the US. Ideally, he hoped to be able to spend a few months every year in Wyoming with the Stein fruit farms as his main base of operations. He resolved to discuss his plans fully with Sam the following week.

Ed then updated Sam on his deal with Justin. Sam nodded and sighed.

'I can see that it's difficult for a brother to put a sibling in jail but for what it's worth, I believe it's where he belongs.'

Jean's eyes filled with tears.

'You're probably right. If I thought that he would stand any chance of rehabilitation in jail, I'd be the first to support it. Nothing against your jails as such, Mr Mohale. This would apply equally almost anywhere in the world right now.'

Sam nodded. 'I understand. I really hope you can rehabilitate him. He certainly comes across as a charming young man. Since Ed and he came over to our house for dinner, my wife still cannot believe that he's responsible for all the mayhem.'

'That's a large part of the problem. If he were mean and hateful all the time, I guess we'd be able to accept it more easily, particularly Mom here.'

As they were chatting, Elke arrived. She greeted everyone and then asked if she could have a quick word with Ed. The two of them strolled across the lawn in front of the patio.

'Problems?' Ed asked her anxiously.

The events of the last week had left them both feeling totally paranoid. Elke shook her head and smiled her glorious smile. Ed felt his spirits rise. Elke had had so little to smile about recently. It was a joyous moment for both of them. Before she could speak further, Ed took her hand and stared at her intently.

'D'you have any notion of how much I love you?'

Elke shook her head. They embraced impulsively in full sight of Jean and Sam who tried to continue a polite conversation but were both distracted by the young couple's obvious intensity of feelings for each other. Sam spoke first.

'I hope you approve of their engagement, Mrs Willjohn?'

Jean looked at him. Her eyes were troubled.

'How would you feel, Mr Mohale, if your one child were no more than a deranged criminal causing havoc in everyone's lives. Then the other is an outstanding young man, but who has no interest in his hometown or the huge business my late husband built up for his children?'

Sam thought about it as Ed and Elke continued to hold hands and chat together animatedly.

'Hmm, you were kind enough to call me a diplomat a moment ago. Right now, I want to be undiplomatic and speak my mind. Is that all right with you?'

Jean raised an eyebrow then nodded.

'You've no idea how much I'd value an honest, no-holds-barred opinion right now!'

Sam sighed gently. 'I come from a culture based on respect and obedience for one's elders. Sadly, that culture in its contact with er so-called Western value systems, has not fared well. Nevertheless, I was brought up to respect my father's views at all times.'

He grinned briefly.

'Notice I said father. We come from a patriarchal society. I happily include respect for my mother as well. Anyway, I also think this is a two-way street. I believe a parent should also respect a mature child's needs and ambitions if that child has a proven record of being responsible. Unfortunately, you seem to have two extremes here. Justin clearly still needs parental guidance and, yes, discipline.'

Sam could see that Jean was following him attentively. He just hoped he could deliver the best possible advice.

'In Ed's case, he's a young man deeply in love but such is his high level of responsibility, as I've seen often enough in his work, that I am convinced he will want to do his best to include both you and Elke in his life. Even if there are logistical problems, he won't shirk his responsibilities there either. He loves Elke and I know he has grown to love this country, for all its faults. He also loves you. That's obvious enough. Personally, I would respect his ideas and his decisions.'

As he finished speaking Ed and Elke kissed briefly. Elke headed back towards her car and Ed returned towards the table. Jean had barely retained her composure. She impulsively reached out and put a soft hand on the African's arm.

'Thank you, Mr, no, let me call you Sam. And I'm Jean. You've helped me enormously.'

Her voice fell away as Ed returned to the table with a grin.

'Boy, it doesn't take long for you guys to get into an exchange of opinions over my future!'

Everyone laughed. Ed added that Elke had come to invite Jean and him to lunch on Sunday. She had been embarrassed to do it in front of Sam, in case he felt left out, but it was necessarily a family affair. He looked at Sam.

'Elke insists that we make a time to have you your wife over, real soon.'

Sam smiled at his friend and responded with his tongue firmly in his cheek.

'Apart from the obvious racist implications, I completely accept your explanation.'

Ed looked at his mother who had reacted with surprise to Sam's comment.

'Don't worry Mom. Folks here're inclined to tease each other over issues which would've been unthinkable a few years ago. It's pretty healthy, I guess.'

Sam had left the hotel by the time Kurt arrived with a tearful Justin in tow. Justin had removed his false teeth and the tiny pads which had made his cheeks fuller. Despite his dyed hair, he now looked recognisable as Justin Willjohn once again. As soon as he saw his mother, he rushed forward and ran into her arms, sobbing bitterly.

Kurt and Ed exchanged looks. Ed held out his hand.

'Thanks, Kurt. I owe you one.'

Kurt grimaced. 'I hope you won't be too upset at what I've done.'

He explained that he had made Justin believe that the deal wasn't happening and that he was still going to jail. Kurt had allowed Justin to persuade him to let the young man see his mother and brother before being taken to the lock-up.

Ed nodded thoughtfully. 'How'd he take it?'

Kurt looked in the direction of Justin and Jean, who were talking together softly. Justin was still distraught.

'I can't conceive of giving your brother any sympathy after what he did to Elke. I understand he's your brother, but...' Kurt let the words hang in the air.

Ed remained lost in thought for some moments then said.

'So, you gave him something to think about. That's good, Kurt. I accept that you and everyone else think we're being too soft on the kid, but look at what it's been doin' to my mother!'

'I understand, Ed. I'm not trying to be critical here. I thought I'd inflict just a little mental torture, which I, as an outsider, was only too happy to do. I hope you don't think I overstepped the mark?'

Ed shrugged. 'Even if you did, he deserves it. The problem is that the moment the pressure's off, he thinks he can get away with everything again. It's a hell of a situation, we'll see if this rehab place helps, but I won't hold my breath.'

Justin finished chatting to his mother and reluctantly turned towards Ed. He looked at his brother with undisguised hatred.

'Why did I believe you'd keep your word. You've wanted to destroy me ever since we were kids. I guess nothing's changed, has it?'

Kurt, standing next to Ed, realised that he had probably driven the brothers even further apart, which was certainly not his intention. He turned to Ed.

'Maybe it's time to tell your brother the truth. Will you see that he gets to the rehab centre?'

'Yes of course.'

'I'll be on my way then.'

Ed shook hands with Kurt, knowing that he had another good friend in the district. As he left, Justin turned to Ed surprised.

'Hey what happened to my torturer? Thought he was taking me to the Rustenburg jail.'

Ed grinned.

'Slight change of plans little brother. Count yourself very, very lucky!'

CHAPTER 50

Ed and Jean drove out of Buffalo Hills Hotel's driveway and headed for the Stein Farm. Jean was looking supremely elegant as usual and Ed had a momentary pang about this. Isak and Marie were typical farm folk. Both were well-educated and they came from well-known families in the district. However, they had few social airs and graces, which was something that delighted Ed. Despite his upbringing in a family of enormous wealth, attending the best schools and colleges, Ed had always been taught by his late father that people in all strata of society, were after all, just people.

When Ed was about twelve years old, he had come home in tears one day after school. By the time his Dad had come home, he had locked himself in his room, brooding over the events that had caused his grief. Jean, who was already used to Justin's endless tantrums, had been disturbed to see her elder son had been so badly upset by something he was unwilling to talk about. It was out of character for Ed to behave like that.

His father had asked if he could come in. Ed had opened the door. His father had entered and sat on the end of the bed. He had waited quietly, pensively until Ed had finally blurted out that some of the boys at school had called him a filthy snob. Ed's father had shaken his head and sighed.

'From what I've observed of you, son, that's the last thing you should be accused of.'

He had studied Ed carefully then continued.

'Hey, d'you know what a snob is?'

Ed had hung his head.

'The guys say that snobs live in big houses, take money from the poor and think they're gods!'

His father had laughed bitterly.

'That's the price you pay for success, son. Anytime you do something better than the other guys, or they think you have more money, a few

316

jerks are gonna get very jealous and call you names. You can take it as a kinda compliment. It shows that you're doin' something well enough for those guys to notice you and want to say something to put you down.'

'It's just not fair.'

'Of course not. In addition to our position of affluence, you're also a great athlete. Your grades're good. You've just become a perfect target, pal.'

Ed had asked tearfully if he should then stop winning? His father had replied sternly.

'Never, ever be ashamed of winning or being the best, son, but equally don't make a big deal about it.'

'I never have Dad. I've looked to see if I've been boasting or showing off. I'm certain I haven't.'

His Dad had sighed.

'It doesn't stop them from inventing something unfortunately.'

His father had crossed over to Ed and given him a comforting hug.

'And by the way, the word snob was coined in England in the days of the so-called ladies and gentlemen, the aristocracy and so on. The definition of a snob is *one who apes gentility*. In plain English, that means someone who imitates the gentlemen of this world. The idea being that if you're already a gentleman, you can't be a snob. It's only the would-be gentlemen who can hold that title. So, it's a case of the pot calling the kettle black. They're jealous of your success and your family status, which I guess here in the US of A is the equivalent of what the English would have called gentry – wealthy gentlemen.'

His father had stood up and ushered his son out of the bedroom. As they made their way downstairs, his father had a final word on the subject.

'I'm proud of you, son. Just try to be a regular guy. You come from a wealthy family but that should never give you the right to feel superior. Succeed on your own terms. Use your wealth wisely, help others where you can, which doesn't mean free hand-outs. It means help others to succeed as well, and as for those kids who called you a snob, don't show that it hurt you. Just ignore them, pal.'

His father had clapped Ed on the shoulder and as they had entered the dining room for dinner, the subject was closed. Ed had never forgotten his father's words. Now, as they drove towards the home of the woman he loved, Ed wondered whether his family's wealth would be an asset, or another barrier, in the weeks to come.

*

Justin had been deposited in a modest but comfortable little residential hotel in the suburbs of Pretoria and he was going nuts! His rehab programme was only due to start the following Monday and he still had half a day and night in which to mull over his fate.

As he walked down the road in search of the nearest pub, he reviewed the events of the last couple of days with displeasure. His brother Ed and his mother had placed him fairly and squarely between a rock and a hard place.

Ed had explained that Justin's position was that of an informal parole, without having gone through the courts. The deal he had been offered was specific. If he went through the Criminal Rehabilitation Programme, the family would pay him five thousand dollars a month for two years. If he did not get into any more trouble with the family or with anyone else for that matter, during that time, he would receive half a million dollars. If after a further three years, he would be seen to have been completely rehabilitated, he would receive a further half million. The downside was, he thought gloomily, that if I step out of line for an instant, the family will withdraw the money; and if I'm still in South Africa the Police will press charges for kidnapping, platinum theft and a host of misdemeanours, which could put me away for a considerable length of time.

On the face of it, Justin had no choice but to walk the old straight and narrow, but the young man's mind did not necessarily work that way.

Deep in thought, Justin strolled along one of Pretoria's many leafy avenues, which would in a few weeks' time with the advent of spring, burst into the glorious blues and reds of jacaranda trees and hibiscus blossoms. Either I forget about revenge for a long time, take the money and get on with a more modest life than I had ever planned for, he thought, or I say the hell with it and nail Ed finally for all the injustices he's put upon me over the years. Heads he wins, tails I lose, Justin thought sourly as he entered the Keg & something-or-other, in search of enough alcohol to dull his senses for another day.

*

As Ed drove along the winding driveway of the Stein farm, he asked his mother about something he had begun to realise was central to his planning for the immediate future.

'Mom, how much longer can you stay in South Africa?' he queried.

Jean put a hand up to head to smooth a couple of stray hairs back into place as she considered her reply.

'I don't really know' she said. 'I guess I don't have anything too vital back home. There're a couple of charity dinners I should be attending but they'll survive without me, even though they'll miss my check book.' Jean looked at Ed circumspectly. 'Why d'you ask?'

The farmhouse appeared around the corner and Ed cursed himself for leaving this conversation so late.

'Mom, we're nearly there, so I can't go into it now but I'm trying to plan my future here. You, the Steins, particularly Elke, are all essential parts of my future. Even Justin, I suppose. I just wanted to get a sense of what could be achieved without causing major upsets one way or the other.'

His mother smiled at him.

'When you try to rush a conversation, your normally sensible remarks emerge as gobbledy-gook, son. Let's see what happens here, shall we?'

As Ed drew up in front of the farmhouse, Elke, looking like a movie starlet in a modern Western, stepped out of the house and headed towards them. She wore a simple but elegant silk shirt and light mustard tapered trousers, with a multi-coloured scarf which contrasted nicely with the rest of the outfit.

Ed fell in love all over again. There was no sign of the tired and bruised prisoner of a few days ago, nor of the no-nonsense farmer who had breakfasted with them at the hotel. Ed realised with rising excitement that Elke had intuitively recognized that she must match his mother's elegance. In his admittedly biased view, she had not just matched Jean but had, in fact, surpassed her.

As they disembarked, Elke went around to his mother and gave her a hand getting out of the SUV. Ed joined them and Elke gave him a quick embrace and kiss, which was again correctly judged. Too much affection would have embarrassed his mother. Too little would have devastated him!

*

Justin ordered a bottle of Nederburg Baronne. It was a 1995, which the young waiter, who was a Hotel School student, was anxious to tell him was not a classic year but Nederburg wines never lowered their standards to any extent.

'In fact, sir' the young man continued 'South African wines don't suffer from huge variations in vintages as do many of the European wines. Our climatic conditions produce consistently good wines.'

Justin nodded impatiently. 'Yeah, yeah, bring me a mushroom burger and a side of salad.' He was intent on getting seriously drunk and did not need to be confused with the details.

As the young man walked away disappointed that his new-found knowledge had fallen on fallow ground, Justin could not help but admire the youth's excellent physique and crop of blonde curly hair. Justin was still not prepared to confront his occasional confusion over his sexual preferences and set about reducing the quantity of wine left in the bottle in front of him, as he forced himself to return to the decision he must make – rehabilitation or revenge!

*

Jean, Ed and Elke moved onto the patio, where Isak had stood up slowly to greet them. He had been seated in his favourite comfortable chair facing out onto the lands, which were just beginning to show some response to the earliest days of spring.

The parched yellows and leafless trees were interspersed with small patches of new green and framed, from the land's edge upwards, with the bright but faded blue of the African sky, with occasional wisps of cloud acting as advance scouts for larger masses of cumulus somewhere not far below the horizon.

Isak wore his usual Sunday suit, an old but impeccable piece of cloth which would have cost him dearly some thirty years previous. He shook hands with Jean and suggested that they all move across to the dining table, set out further down the patio.

'My wife is just checking on the food and will be out in a moment.'

He guided Jean to a place to the right of his seat at the head of the table.

Elke winked at Ed, who grinned back. This was their very own theatre of family drama unfolding in front of them. In their hearts they both hoped for a positive outcome but equally in both Ed and Elke's minds, their future was together, with or without their respective parents' blessing.

Elke stepped forward to offer Jean a drink. The older woman nodded thoughtfully.

'Do you have a gin and tonic?'

'Certainly' Elke replied. 'Pa?'

Isak grimaced. 'I'll have a small sherry, skatjie.'

Ed opted to have sherry as well. He had found that South African sherries, even though the Europeans had stopped them from using the word sherry, were excellent.

Marie appeared wearing the mildly harassed appearance of any housewife intent upon producing a culinary masterpiece. She was not as elegantly turned out as Elke, but she had certainly taken the trouble to wear a sensible blouse and jacket, instead of her usual severely practical farmer's jeans and shirt. Ed felt quite emotional about the whole thing. Only a few short days ago, he and Marie had been fighting angrily over her daughter's future. Then having overcome that hurdle, Marie had unreservedly made every effort to welcome Ed's mother in a manner that was calculated to make the best possible impression upon the wealthy American socialite.

His mother, Ed noticed, was visibly relaxing in the ambience of the old-world charm of the place and Isak in particular was working his magic. There had been a tense moment when Jean and Marie shook hands and stared deep into each other's eyes as though trying to assess each other's reading of the situation. Jean then did something Ed had not seen her do in many years. She impulsively leaned forward and hugged the other woman. A spark of friendship was ignited, Elke thought excitedly. Her spirits rose as she went to fetch the drinks.

Justin quickly worked his way into his third glass of wine. It was a superb bottle, regardless of any vintage nonsense. The hamburger arrived, smothered in mushroom sauce and supported by a pile of freshly fried chips. The hamburgers in Africa are as good as they get, he thought benignly. The wine had lifted his spirits and he was close to a decision. As usual with Justin, it was based on his lifelong determination to have his cake and eat it!

*

The food was outstanding. Ed told Marie sincerely that if she ever tired of farming, she should consider opening a country restaurant. He would personally be happy to grow fat and useless as her major customer. Everyone laughed and Ed risked a sidelong glance at his mother. She was clearly enjoying herself and had obviously been impressed by the sophisticated level of conversation held around the table.

Ed had discovered some time before that whereas Americans knew extraordinarily little about South Africa, the reverse was not true. Isak in particular was current on the trials and tribulations of the Bush administration, the woes of the huge US corporations and their not so creative accounting, as well as his own thoughts on bin Laden, the Middle East and the chances of another war with Iraq.

Elke tried to veer away from politics by discussing the imminent Summit for Sustainable Development to be held in Johannesburg, with an expected sixty thousand visitors from around the world. Jean finally looked around the table and exclaimed

'Hey! I'm not too sure who's meant to be the country bumpkins around here! You folks're so well informed on world affairs that I confess I'm kinda outta my depth!' The others laughed.

Isak leaned across to Ed and murmured 'Ed, could we have a quiet chat for a moment?'

The two men excused themselves and went into Isak's study. As they walked together, Ed noted that Isak was slowing down more and more every time he revisited the farm. Isak wasted no time in getting to the point as they sat down on worn but comfortable leather upholstered chairs in the study.

'Ed, I think you and I understand each other well.'

Ed nodded, fearful of what the older man was about to tell him.

'I'd like to thank you for your support when things looked pretty bad.'

Isak nodded and sighed.

'I'm afraid they don't look too much better now' he said. 'Not from my side, anyway.'

Isak leaned forward and spoke quietly but with great intensity.

'Listen Ed. I haven't told my family yet but I was at the doctor this week.'

For a moment his voice faltered but then he continued imparting his personal sense of urgency to Ed.

'They tell me I've got six months. They've advised against any of those major ops like triple by-pass or even a heart transplant. They say the rest of the body's not in good shape either.'

Ed stared at Isak in shock. He knew how devastating this news would be for Elke and Marie. At least, he consoled himself, the financial side would be taken care of. The Stein farm as well as another nearby farm Ed had already enquired about would make a fine economically viable combination. However, he had really looked forward to sharing this new adventure with Isak, who was becoming more of a father figure to him every time they met.

Isak continued. 'Death doesn't frighten me too much but leaving the family behind does.'

He paused again, seeking the right words.

'Look, it's obvious to anyone that Elke and you are very much in love. You know what would make this old man really happy?'

Not so old, Ed thought, but he nodded again, not trusting his voice. He would really miss Isak when and if it happened.

'If you and Elke were to get married soon, and I thought that, as your mother is in the country...' He let the thought hang.

Ed cleared his throat. 'First of all, I won't accept that your condition is beyond hope. We'll discuss that later but for now, in answer to your question, you and I are totally on the same wavelength. The sooner I marry Elke, the better. I do want my mother to be here for that and I've already established that she doesn't have any serious reasons for not staying here for a while longer. I just need her blessing, that's all.'

Isak smiled. 'Then let's go and work on that!'

They stood up. Isak thrust out his hand. He had a firm grip still, which Ed returned with feeling. They returned to the ladies, intent upon concluding a deal that was so close to both their hearts.

*

Justin was feeling very mellow indeed. The bottle would squeeze just one more glass of wine and there were plenty more bottles available in the cellar. A glorious young redhead had arrived with a group of friends and was eyeing him appreciatively. Justin had decided to do the rehab while he plotted his revenge. For the moment all was good in his world and he hoped that would also be calamitous for Ed's future!

CHAPTER 51

When Ed and Isak returned to the patio, Elke was in the kitchen making the coffee. Jean and Marie were engrossed in the serious matter of comparing America's hominy grits with South Africa's mealie pap.

'Not that I've prepared it myself,' Jean said, 'but we have friends in Lexington, Kentucky who own one of the biggest stud farms in America.'

'On the week of the Kentucky Derby,'

Jean pronounced the word "derr-bee," which was the American way, instead of the English perversity of pronouncing it "daa-bee."

'Which is the biggest horse race in the US. The major breeders throw crazy parties. Each one tries to outdo the other in ostentation. One lady hires the tents of a three-ring circus every year, plus a separate restaurant for each with about five different bands. Totally over the top - the Big Top maybe.'

Marie grimaced.

'Do they get any work done on the farms?'

'Some of them make millions from breeding racehorses. In fairness they do work hard to keep their bloodstock in top condition, but I have to admit they do throw their money around. Another family once indulged in their eighteen-year-old daughter's whims by converting their charming nineteenth century Kentucky mansion into a Japanese tea house, but then served cold and tasteless Chinese food.'

'Mom' Ed cut in with a grin, 'what in the hell's all this to do with hominy grits?'

Jean smiled back at him unabashed.

'I'm getting there, honey.' she replied.

Ed was delighted to see that his mother was sufficiently relaxed to start in on her own stories, but the trick was to keep her on the track of what she was trying to say.

'Our friends went the traditional route and provided long established Kentucky dishes, such as Kentucky ham, fried chicken, all kinds of vegetables and salads as well as,' she glanced at Ed triumphantly 'hominy grits!'

Ed nodded indulgently as Elke arrived back on the patio with a tray of cups and pots of filter coffee.

'Yeah, yeah, but you forgot to include the guest of honour Olivia Newton John, who arrived by helicopter as week-end guest of the lady Governor of Kentucky. Very traditional scene that was!'

As the others laughed Ed added 'and you forgot to mention that the best party thrown that year was by a South African couple who had just bought a ranch in the district, Ron and Myrna Rosen, originally from Johannesburg, I believe!'

His mother looked at him in amazement.

'Son, you were about eight years old. How'd you remember all that?'

Ed shrugged. 'You've told the story often enough, but the Rosen's I remember because we were invited there. It was the best food I've ever eaten. Myrna wrote cookery books as a hobby but boy, she knew how to put her theory into practice!'

Over coffee, Ed deemed that the ice had been sufficiently broken to embark on the most important speech of his young life. He tapped a spoon on the side of his cup and stood up. Elke looked at him expectantly, her eyes shining. Marie and Isak glanced at each other and looked up at Ed, knowing that his words would probably change their lives and that of their daughter forever. Jean studied her coffee cup. She was very troubled about the speed with which Ed was trying to move events along.

'First I'd like to thank Marie and Elke for a lunch that rates right up there with my first South African cooked meal in Kentucky. I'd also like to thank Isak and Marie for so graciously agreeing to my betrothal to Elke.'

Ed looked at his mother.

'Mom, if you still have reservations about our marriage, I respect that, but I intend to change your mind.' He laughed. 'Just consider that Marie wanted to strangle me up until a week or so ago, courtesy of Willjohn Junior.'

Jean finally looked up at her son. Her eyes were troubled.

'Ed, before you say anything else, let me qualify my reservations.'

The patio became very silent as Jean considered what she was about to say.

'Elke, you've quickly shown me that you're a delightful, intelligent young woman. Your parents, in just an hour or so, have reminded me just how much we city folk have totally lost, in terms of family and spiritual values. Isak and Marie, you have welcomed me into your home, and I have felt just that – at home – for the first time in some years.'

She looked around at all of them. Ed was very tense but the Stein family were listening and absorbing everything she had to say. Marie, in particular, Jean sensed, was relating, as one mother to another, to her describing as honestly as she knew how, the way she felt.

'I have no problem with these two wonderful young people getting married,' she continued 'but I do have a serious problem with the timing of it.'

She turned towards her son.

'Ed, you have admitted that you and Elke have spent very little quality time together - largely through no fault of your own.'

Jean grimaced as she thought of the havoc created by Justin.

'I have a problem adjusting to the idea that my one son, who has proven to be a wonderfully balanced individual, wants to live some ten thousand miles from home. His future children and my grandchildren to be...'

Elke smiled, mildly embarrassed.

'...will grow up a very long way from one of their grandparents.'

Ed opened his mouth to reply but Jean held up her hand. She was not finished yet.

'And perhaps the biggest problem which confronts all of us is my other son Justin!'

There was an uneasy silence as the others digested this thought. Jean sighed.

'Whatever you and Elke decide, son, I'll respect it but if you would consider waiting six months, you'll make this potential grandma a happy lady.'

The silence continued. Ed could not resist an anguished glance at Isak. The man, who had just told Ed that he had only six months to live, had his eyes closed, his lips pursed but he was also nodding in agreement with Jean's words.

*

'So, where're you from?' the cute redhead asked Justin.

It had been ridiculously easy. All Justin had done was to exchange a few smiles with the girl and she had left her group to come over to sit with Justin. Since he was now openly Justin again, he had gone to a hairdressing salon and had them return his hair to a semblance of his former blonde self. He could always return to his other persona, he reasoned, but why look very plain when the real Justin certainly caught people's attention.

'I'm from Minneapolis' Justin replied, 'but I spend most of my time in New York!'

The girl's eyes danced with excitement. 'New York, New York!' she sighed. 'I've always wanted to go there; that and LA!'

As they chatted, Justin established that her name was Corinne and she was an art student. She was slim and nearly as tall as him with a gloriously unusual elfin face framed by lustrous dark red hair. She was very friendly, almost over-friendly.

Justin had always been complicated about women. He liked to feel in control but Corinne was very assertive. She had no problem with exuding an aura of both sensuality and hunger that Justin found slightly intimidating. However, after nearly a bottle and half of wine he pushed his misgivings away. Besides, he was in for a few lonely weeks if he stuck with the Rehab Programme, so he resolved to let the little adventure with the girl in front of him play out any way she wanted.

Ed was distraught. He loved his mother very much but he had also grown very close to the entire Stein family. Even Marie, once Justin's malicious rumours had been dispelled, had warmed to him and was emerging as a strong woman of great integrity. She would undoubtedly be devastated by Isak's passing but she would pick up the pieces and continue her life.

His love for Elke was uncomplicated. She was simply the most beautiful person, both physically and spiritually, that he had ever met. His love for her was non-negotiable even though he had felt like one of the team of the television series "Survivors" ever since the two of them had met. It had been a non-stop frantic scramble to avert disaster. Even now, as Elke and he were finally about to spend more time together, he was faced by the terrible "Sophie's choice" between respecting his mother's or Isak's wishes. If he waited six months before he married Elke, Isak would probably be dead. If he married Elke right away, he might spoil his best chance of getting his mother's full agreement to the marriage.

*

Justin had fumbled around his immediate problem, which was how to get Corinne into bed. He clearly could not risk smuggling her into the modest accommodation organised for him by the Rehab Centre. He had been told that once the Programme started he would not have a social life until he was finished. To have a girl in his bed on the first night was not the best way in which to become a model student, which is what he had decided to become – outwardly, that is!

'So where are you staying?'

Corinne had asked him directly, after he had embarked upon a rambling story about getting to know the people and not staying in the five star hotels which the rest of his family insisted upon.

'Some little bed and breakfast joint' Justin replied 'which is a prob...'

'We'd better go back to my place then!' Corinne said matter-of-factly as she drained her glass and stood up. 'Let's go!' she added.

Justin followed her unsteadily as she waved cheerily to the crowd with whom she had arrived. Corinne's friends waved back with a couple of the young men in the party making some loud and suggestive comments as she stepped past them. She ignored them and looked back at Justin, then took his hand firmly as they stepped through the front door. With her other hand she pointed to a colourful Volkswagen Beetle, painted with bright red and yellow flowers.

Justin wryly wondered whether he could have found anyone more different than the luscious but untouchable Greek girl Persephone. Corinne seemed to be intent on getting him into bed as fast as she could. As he eased himself into the psychedelic but incredible battered old Beetle, Justin reflected on how his life was a roller coaster of ups and downs. And it was only three o'clock in the afternoon!

*

Ed felt like a man on a tightrope. There was no room for compromise, and he could certainly not reveal Isak's terrible secret. He wished that he had not decided to try to settle the wedding arrangements there and then, but he could hardly pull back now.

'Mom' he began 'I really understand what you've said and nothing would give me greater pleasure than to arrange everything so that all of us're happy about...'

He noticed that Isak was looking increasingly agitated. The poor man must be feeling terrible about this, he thought.

Isak spoke out unexpectedly.

'Edward, your mother has some very real concerns. I think you should consider her request.'

Jean looked at the proud man and smiled gratefully without any idea of how great a sacrifice he was proposing.

Ed felt grief rising up in his throat. Isak was trying to put Jean's wishes before his own but it was a sacrifice that Ed suddenly could not tolerate.

'No, Mom' Ed spoke sharply, in fact much more severely than he intended.

Jean looked at Ed in surprise. There was a sudden edge to his voice that she had never heard before.

'Look, you and I enjoy a really great mother/son relationship. I think you know that I would never hurt you if I could possibly avoid it. Nor do I normally withhold anything from you.'

He paused as he gathered the strength to ask a vital question.

'I want you to respect my judgment and not question it, this one time in my life. Will you do that for me, Mom? It's more important than you'll ever know!'

Jean felt a moment's anger that Ed should put her in such a spot in front of virtual strangers. However, she also knew that Ed was an extremely level-headed person who would never behave this way without a good reason. Jean also wondered whether his love for the girl was such that he simply could not wait to have her as his bride. Again, she decided that it would not be in his nature to be that selfish.

Jean sighed reluctantly.

'I'll go with whatever you decide, just as long as these good folk agree too.'

She looked at Marie and Elke who both nodded their assent.

Isak had his eyes closed again and seemed to be dozing. Jean decided not to disturb him, having been told by Ed that the man had heart problems.

Ed took a deep breath and ploughed on.

'Thanks Mom, I really appreciate that. Someday...'

He glanced at Isak again but the older man remained motionless with his eyes still closed. The hell with it, Ed decided. He had made his decision. There was no time now for excuses or justifications.

'Okay. Elke and I would like to be married in three weeks' time. This is only a suggestion, but Elke and I thought that we should get married in the church in Kroondal and then, unless you'd rather have the reception here on the farm, we thought it would be appropriate to have it at Buffalo Hills. If Isak were in good health I would expect it to be here but I think that we can take a lot of the hassles out of the event by having professionals do the whole thing.'

Jean opened her mouth to speak but Ed gently cut in again.

'Sorry Mom, just let me finish, then we can get everyone's input.'

So far so good, he thought. No explosions of outrage from either side. If I pull this off, they should send me to the Middle East as a negotiator, he thought with grim humour.

'Okay then, we would like to honeymoon in the US and by the way, before anyone says anything, I'll accept that Isak and Marie will arrange for the wedding and the reception but I insist that I pick up the tab for the honeymoon.'

'We're not without resources, Edward,' Isak spoke stiffly.

Ed looked at him.

'I know that, sir, but honeymooning in the US will give my family the opportunity to meet Elke as well as show my bride, my roots. If the rand weren't so weak against the dollar, I would never have suggested that I paid, but it'd be crazy not to use dollars.'

Isak seemed to be mollified by Ed's rationale.

'Then while we're talking money, my good friend Marius de Wet has been helping me with some enquiries. There's a very interesting farm for sale, just about five kilometres away from here. As I think you all know I won't be renewing my contract with Premier Platinum, even though it's been a great experience.'

Elke hung on every word. They had had only the briefest opportunity to discuss their future, but Elke trusted his judgment completely.

'I've always wanted to farm, long before I came to South Africa and fell in love with this area and its people' he continued. 'Elke's beginning to turn me into a serious conservationist and we both believe that farming with eco-friendly methods is the way to go.'

Ed looked directly at Marie and then Isak.

'And with your permission, we'd like to begin to take an interest in the management of this farm as well as our own. It will also give me the opportunity to learn from you both. I don't kid myself I can just buy some land and be a farmer. Fact is, I plan to do some agricultural courses as well but with the combined skills of the Stein family backing us up, I guess we'll make good.'

There was a long thoughtful silence.

Ed concluded by saying. 'Now that I've set the cat firmly amongst the pigeons, I'll throw the meeting open for debate!'

The silence continued but to Ed's relief it was not an oppressive silence. It was rather a time to digest his plans, which would have such far-reaching effects on all of them. Ed had not considered it necessary to add that he certainly would have the funds to back up his plans, but this did not mean that he would not want to make the farming project totally viable.

*

Corinne looked at the sleeping American with satisfaction. They had made love, then Justin had passed out from all the wine he had drunk. He was a lousy lover, she decided, but if he could open the door for her to get into America, it was worth any sacrifice it might take. She was not overly promiscuous but when she went for something, she would stop at nothing. With a reasonably handsome and very wealthy American in her bed, how could she possibly go wrong?

CHAPTER 52

The sun was sliding quickly below the horizon. Its blood red orb shimmered and distorted around the edges as a thin line of cloud began to blush with the sun's fleeting caresses.

Ed and Elke stood silently arm in arm watching the magical moment from the top of the cliffs overlooking the southern boundary of the Stein farm. Witblitz, Elke's magnificent horse, quietly nibbled at patches of new grass emerging in advance of spring's glorious time of growth and renewal. Ed's horse, a powerful chestnut, grazed nearby.

It had been a frantic three weeks since the two families had lunched together. It was one thing to say, "let's get married right away." It was another thing altogether to do justice to the occasion. The days had passed in a blur. If Ed and Elke had felt that their time together was too brief before they had set the date, it had been just as bad since that time.

As things finally started to come together, Ed had grabbed Elke that afternoon and spoken to her firmly.

'Time out, lady! Your dress is finished, the cake's ordered, the guests are all invited, the church is booked, Buffalo Hills is excelling itself in arranging the reception and so I have a unique idea!'

Elke had looked at him quizzically.

'If you're going to suggest we just elope instead,' she grinned 'I'm almost ready to agree! But then I have realised that weddings are mostly about family and friends. It's our final sacrifice to them!'

Ed had laughed. 'Yeah, too right, but I'm told that once it's under way, we might get to enjoy it too!'

'You think? That gives me some hope.'

Elke's eyes twinkled. Thankfully, they both shared a good sense of humour. Still chuckling Ed had shaken his head.

'Sorry, no elopement. Your Dad would never forgive me. I just want a couple of hours alone with you. I have this quaint idea that we should get to know each other before the event.'

Elke had gazed at him solemnly, taking in every detail of his ruggedly handsome face.

'My man' she'd replied softly 'I feel I've known you for an eternity and longer. But it's a great idea. I'll get the horses.'

They had ridden up the slopes to Elke's favourite spot in the whole world. In the event, they had said very little. It was a powerful element of their relationship that they were both completely comfortable with companionable silences.

The sun disappeared on its endless circular quest to illuminate its small patch of the universe. Ed turned towards Elke. She responded immediately, sliding inside his enfolding arms and tilting her face upwards to meet the urgent softness of his lips. Finally, they pulled apart before their rising passion threatened to pre-empt the consummation of their nuptials the day after tomorrow.

As the two horses descended sure-footedly along the path towards the farmhouse, Elke, who was leading, turned in her saddle and called out.

'I hope you won't get too drunk tonight!'

'Why not?' He replied teasingly. 'I'm getting the perfect bachelor party, some forty yards from my bedroom! Isn't that a licence to get as drunk as a skunk?'

Ed laughed as Elke looked at him worriedly.

'Don't worry, babe. I've made it very clear to Jacob and Sam that I'd rather enjoy the evening with my friends than be carried to my room in a state of oblivion. They've promised not to overdo it.'

Elke smiled and turned back to watch the trail ahead as the abrupt and unforgiving African twilight rapidly gave way to the warm blanket of an early spring night.

'I've briefed them very thoroughly as well.'

Her voice carried clearly in the evening stillness.

'They understand that they'll have me to deal with, if you're not in good shape for Saturday!'

'So, nothing can possibly go wrong!'

As they saw the lights of the farmhouse flicker in the darkness, Ed had only one real worry. As usual, it revolved around Justin. Jean had insisted that his nemesis and younger brother attend the wedding. Ed had reluctantly agreed that Justin could be at the Church but had added that there was no ways Justin would be allowed into the reception. It was non-negotiable. Even though the Rehab Centre had sent glowing reports on Justin's progress, Ed knew that every time people started to tell him that Justin was doing well, that was the time to be worried, very worried!

Justin left Corinne's apartment and hurried back to his modest but comfortable room at the residential hotel. He had quickly discovered that his Rehab supervisors rewarded good behaviour generously and stomped hard on any attempt to break the rules. The advance warning about no social life during the course was not strictly true but he had had to become the star of the course to be given time off.

Even then, all privileges would be revoked if he were even a minute late. The hotel's receptionist had to check his arrival time every night he was allowed out, which amounted to a maximum of three times a week. Under different circumstances, Justin would not have lasted five minutes on the Rehab course, nor would he have maintained his relationship with the randy and demanding Corinne, unless it suited his plans. It had been a terrible three weeks for Justin in many ways but the end of it was in sight and he had achieved virtually all his objectives over that period.

Today, the Principal of the Rehab group had finally given his permission for Justin to attend the wedding with the proviso that Justin be back at his hotel at the normal curfew hour. Despite three weeks of growing frustration Justin was now certain that all his arrangements were in place. The day after tomorrow would be the culmination of it all, with Corinne playing an unwitting key role in his elaborate scheme.

*

The bar was packed. Rob had organised that the bachelor party would occupy the area furthest from the entrance to the bar which led into the Hotel's reception area.

Ed, after some deliberation, decided that he would only drink Scotch. He knew he would quickly get drunk on wine, which was his preferred drink. Beer was too filling and so he went for what was considered the cleanest drink available.

He had also, upon advice, taken a couple of teaspoons of olive oil which was said to cover the lining of his stomach. Despite all his precautions Ed was determined not to exceed more than four or five drinks but he had no illusions that as the evening progressed it would be tougher and tougher to resist the well-meaning and boisterous insistence that he have another drink.

To Ed's delight, Isak had arrived early and had one of the farm's African drivers standing by to take him home as soon as he began to feel too tired. His future father-in-law was deep in conversation with Franklin de Vos, President of Willjohn Industries, who had flown in the previous day along with Grant Weston and Eddie Ho-Lin, two buddies of Ed's from his college years. Ed's friends from the Hotel and the valley were also there in full force. Rob, Don and Elliot from the hotel, Marius de Wet, Errol Saperstein and Kurt von Wallenstein representing the farmers and then Sam Mohale and Martin Gericke from the mine were all there to toast Ed on his way to his new life as a married South African farmer. Captain Kloppers popped in briefly wish Ed well. He was off duty and was happy to accept a beer or two.

'It's interesting that you should also have a Dutch surname' Ed heard Isak say to Franklin.

He didn't hear the response as he moved past them to greet the newly arrived Johann Kloppers. He suddenly remembered, with a shock, that his plans for tracing the origin of his family name had been forcibly set aside by the series of adventures that had been instigated by Justin. Perhaps there would be some opportunity during their honeymoon, Ed thought. He and Elke had agreed that if they were to start a new farming venture, it would take most of their time and attention for the next year or so. Ed was also mindful of the fact that Isak had only been given six months to live - not that he was able to tell Elke. All things considered; he had persuaded Elke that they should take a two-month honeymoon on the premise that it may be some years before they could get away again.

Their route was to be elastic in places. They would spend the first night at the Michaelangelo Hotel in Sandton then fly down to Cape Town for a week where Elke would show him South Africa's crown jewel of tourist destinations.

'Of course, you've been spoiled by spending time in the Magaliesberg' she had teased 'but I still think you'll like Cape Town!'

At the end of that week they would then fly from Cape Town to Atlanta, Georgia. Ed had suggested flying to various parts of the US, but Elke had insisted firmly that if they were to see the great land mass of North America, she would prefer to drive. Ed realised ruefully that, as an American, the possibility of not flying everywhere had not occurred to him.

Now he realised that it could be a great idea to include Las Cruces, New Mexico in their itinerary, where hopefully Jannie and Marlene Pretorius would continue to help him in his quest to see if he was actually related to the famous General Ben Viljoen.

His thoughts were interrupted by a hearty thump on the back from Grant Weston. His former College buddy had put on weight from his football playing days when he had been a trim and muscular 230 pounds. Today he was closer to 260 but his 6 foot 8-inch frame carried it well. Ed nearly collapsed from the well-meaning blow. He turned around trying not to look as though a few vertebrae had been crushed and forced a smile. Grant had always been too rough and tough, but he had a heart of gold.

'Say buddy, the guys here' he waved vaguely at Marius and Kurt who grinned back him 'they been tellin' me that our football's for sissies.

Out here they say they play Rugby without any body-protection and I wouldn't last five minutes!'

Ed assured him that he would survive anything short of an atomic bomb on his head but the couple of International Rugby matches he had watched did lend some credibility to the South Africans' claims.

'Tell you what. Ask them this.' He leaned forward and whispered in Grant's ear as the big man obligingly bent down until Ed was at least within range.

Grant nodded blankly then turned back to Kurt and Marius with the question.

'Ed says I should ask you guys who won the Tri Nations?'

The two South Africans looked suitable chastened. New Zealand's All Blacks team, named after their traditional black jerseys, had comfortably beaten the South African Springboks.

Ed went over to join Sam and his other American, or more accurately Chinese-American pal, Eddie Ho-Lin. It was definitely going to be a long night!

*

Justin had not trusted Corinne's Beetle to make the journey from Pretoria to the Church at Kroondal and had paid for a hire car, which he had prudently put in Corinne's name.

They were both appropriately dressed for the wedding. Corinne wore a flamboyant, but less revealing than usual, cocktail dress and Justin had bought a dark suit for the occasion. At least his stashed funds overseas were in dollars and he did not have to worry over much about his expenses in South Africa. Nevertheless, he would be delighted to see the back of the country, which along with his brother's mean-spirited efforts had combined to almost ruin his life.

That was about to change forever, he thought, as they passed a sign saying "Kroondal 10 kilometres." Taking Corinne on board had been a calculated risk. If Justin thought he were manipulative, he was an amateur compared to the pixie-faced redhead. Justin had quickly discovered that she was utterly single-minded and had no compunction about using anyone in the process. Corinne wanted to live and paint in the US. She had sold a couple of paintings to visiting Americans and they had assured her that she would do well in the US.

However, she had been refused a visa to the US a couple of times on the basis that as a young single woman without a substantial income, she was a definite risk in the eyes of the American authorities. They were right. She would do almost anything to get herself a green card. Justin worried over the deal but felt he had no choice. Corinne had undertaken to get him out of South Africa without having to go through passport controls. In exchange, they would get married in Botswana, then return to the States. Corinne made it clear that she had no wish to remain married to Justin.

She found him selfish, moody, and a lousy lover. She also sensed an underlying threat of violence in the way he sometimes stared at her. Nor did she believe a word about his rambling story of how he was a Consultant at the Criminal Rehab Clinic, but he was in fact working undercover because of his crime-busting activities in the US.

He also claimed that his brother Ed was linked to some platinum smuggling syndicate and had put a contract on his head. When Corinne had asked why it was so important to attend the wedding, Justin had said simply that he needed to give Ed a sign that he would not be intimidated. He also wanted to see his mother again before he returned under deep cover to the US.

Corinne was certain that the young American was seriously deluded and possibly insane, but she had complete confidence in her own ability to remain in control of the situation. Once they were safely in the US and she was Mrs Willjohn, she would worry about getting rid of him.

As they found parking outside the Lutheran Church where his brother and that snivelling bitch Elke were to be married, he realised that it was going to be a big wedding. He was momentarily sorry that he had been told bluntly by Ed that they were not welcome at the reception afterwards. He would have loved to have flaunted the glamorous Corinne but then again, he intended that they would be long gone by the time the reception was fully under way.

Justin entered the church with Corinne on his arm. The soft tones of the organ playing some appropriate Handel was in stark contrast with the immediate angry looks he received from some of the wedding guests who knew him or had heard of his abduction of Elke.

Two places had been reserved for him and Corinne next to his mother in the front row. Justin was shocked to see Franklin and two of Ed's closest cronies from College. Franklin nodded curtly as he edged past him to his seat. Corinne sensibly tried to keep a low profile. She sensed the undertow of animosity against Justin and wondered what the man she was about to marry had done to rouse such open dislike.

As they settled down in their seats, a grim-faced Kurt crossed over to where they were sitting. He leaned forward and spoke softly to Justin.

'I don't like your being here, but your mother insisted. I'm watching you, pal. One step out of place, and wedding or no wedding, I take you straight to the Rustenburg Police, who can't wait to get their hands on you!'

Justin smiled his deadly sweet smile.

'I'm nearly through the Rehab, Kurt. It's a wonderful course and I'm really pleased you recommended it. It's certainly changed my life!'

Kurt looked at him sharply, nodded and moved back to the other side of the aisle where he sat down close to Marie Stein.

Justin glanced at Corinne who was smiling at him sardonically. Had she overheard? Justin realised at that moment that it did not really matter. They were each on their own agenda. As long as they were useful to each other, there would be no betrayal but there would soon come a time, Justin realised, when he would have to get rid of this redhead from hell, forever! Meanwhile, it was time to concentrate on his revenge.

Ed stared out over the congregation. The church was packed. The Stein's were a much-loved family in the Kroondal community. He already recognised a number of familiar faces, such as the Ottermans, in addition to his own particular circle of friends. Over the next year or two he was certain that he would get to know many more members of the close-knit community who were there to see Elke marry the Uitlander. He made a vow there and then to make every effort to become part of the community.

Choosing a best man had been a nightmare. At first, he had thought about asking Grant or possibly Eddie to stand up for him, but in truth, over the past year he had grown very close to a number of people from the valley and its environs. He had approached Marius who had diplomatically suggested that he would rather be there for him in the role of more of a father figure.

In the end Ed had asked Sam Mohale. His now former boss had been very moved by the request and had gladly agreed. Ed glanced across at the dignified and statesmanlike African, who misunderstanding the glance, grinned and reached into his pocket to withdraw the wedding rings. Ed nodded slightly and Sam put the rings back in his pocket as the first bars of the Wedding March announced the arrival of the bride. Ed looked up and focused on the extraordinarily beautiful young angel in white who now entered the church on Isak's arm.

Ed had fantasised over this moment and had spent much time over the past few days staring at the rare beauty who was about to become his wife. He was nevertheless quite unprepared for Elke's glowing radiance, enhanced by the lovely wedding gown which Marie and she had commissioned from Peter Soldatos, one of South Africa's top couturiers. Two little flower girls who were distant cousins and Elke's best friend from Pretoria University, made up the entourage.

Elke stepped slowly forward, with her father, Isak, bravely erect and proud beside her.

Ed had never really had any doubts about his bride-to-be but as she stepped slowly towards him, Ed's heart was filled with an almost unbearable joy.

It was this picture of her that he would remember for the rest of his life.

*

Justin drove into the entrance of Buffalo Hills Hotel well ahead of the rest of the wedding guests whom he had left milling around outside the church. He had driven at his usual breakneck pace along the country roads to the hotel. Corinne enquired mildly why they were going to the hotel when they would not be attending the reception. Justin smiled at her.

'Just want to leave Ed a message on his car.'

He picked up an aerosol can of shaving cream and waved it at her.

'Besides, no wedding's complete without an appropriate present.'

He glanced over his shoulder at the gift-wrapped parcel on the back seat. Corinne had seen it earlier and wondered what kind of gift one would give to a hated brother.

'What did you get them?'

'I had to think hard about it, but I've found something for them I doubt that they'll ever forget!'

He refused to be drawn further into a discussion on the subject. Corinne was not really interested anyway.

Asking Corinne to remain in the car, Justin slipped out of the driver's seat, opened the rear door of the car and leaned in to pick up the gift. He had arranged the wrapping in such a way that he could slip his hand inside the package, which he did, making a rapid adjustment to something inside it. He carried the gift and his can of shaving cream over to Ed and Elke's car. Some work had already been done on the vehicle which Ed had hired to take them to Johannesburg after the reception. A couple of lines of shaving cream already adorned the vehicle, as well as an incredible old boot, tied to the car by a piece of string, which someone must have rescued from an old suitcase probably dating back to the Anglo-Boer War.

No one was around, but in the distance Justin heard the sound of a number of cars approaching the hotel. He had very little time and he hoped against hope that the car would be unlocked. It was.

Justin rapidly opened the rear door and shoved his wedding gift under the driver's seat. He straightened up and closed the door just as the first cars entered the hotel and drove into the parking ground close to Ed's car. Justin waved in a vague sort of way, not knowing who was in the approaching cars. He took his shaving cream can out of a side pocket and sprayed the words "May the only hard feelings be yours. Love Justin," on the rear windows of the car. Putting the can back in his pocket he sauntered off back to his own car, as Marius, his wife and Kurt

337

got out of their respective cars and stared at the young man who had caused such havoc over the past few weeks.

They strolled over to Ed's car and looked around it as well as giving a cursory glance inside it. The wedding gift was completely out of sight. Kurt shrugged as he saw Justin's message.

'Crude, but typical' he murmured.

They headed towards the reception which was to be held in one of the conference rooms. As they entered the beautifully decorated room, festooned with flowers and silk drapes, Marius still had a puzzled frown on his face.

Justin and Corinne drove up to the twin-engined Beachcraft plane waiting for them at a deserted airstrip on a farm some twenty kilometres from Buffalo Hills Hotel. Justin had been unusually chatty on the way to the plane, which Corinne had arranged for them. Justin's money had easily persuaded the young pilot who regularly flew tourists into remote parts of Botswana's Okavango swamps, to take Corinne as a genuine registered passenger.

The pilot would land on another deserted air strip a few kilometres outside the country's capital, Gaberone, unload Justin and then quickly fly on to the Gaberone airport, where he would leave Corinne. She would go through customs and immigration then book into a hotel in Gaberone. Justin would be delivered to Gaberone the following day by a local farmer who was pleased to receive some dollars for his participation in the scheme. Corinne and Justin had already been married in Pretoria the previous week. The following day they would make their way to Zimbabwe or Zambia, then to the UK and finally the US.

In fact, Justin was in no hurry to return to the US once he had left Africa. He would see what would happen once the wedding present he had placed in Ed's car had taken its effect. He had every intention of finding a new passport in Europe and he would probably have to rid himself of Corinne somewhere along the line.

Meanwhile he chatted to her at length about his unhappy childhood and Ed's unwillingness to ever let him express himself. Big brother was always the successful one. Little brother had to always settle for second place. Corinne switched off as he rambled on. She doubted whether much of what Justin was saying was true. One look at Ed at the church had made her realise that she had definitely ended up with the runt of the litter.

Justin and Corinne boarded the plan. In a few minutes they were on their way towards the border with Botswana.

Justin was delighted that it had been so simple. The bomb was timed to go off in three hours. He had been assured by one of the friendly hotel receptionists earlier that week that Ed and Elke were due to leave the

Reception promptly at 8.30pm in order to arrive at the Michaelangelo Hotel by 10pm. According to Justin's calculations the bomb should go off somewhere around the time that the new Mr and Mrs Willjohn would be driving around the side of Hartbeespoort Dam.

A young man whom he had befriended at the Rehab Centre and whom he had identified as least likely to finish the course, had happily put Justin in touch with criminal elements in Pretoria. For an exorbitant price Justin had purchased five sticks of dynamite and an excellent timing device which had arrived in a cardboard box.

He and Corinne would already be over the border and safe by the time the bomb exploded. Revenge would be sweet, and he would finally be rid of the one person who had always gotten the better of him. Justin did not really think in terms of consequences, as his earlier adventures had proved. He lived in an eternal madness of the present, which he twisted to suit his own realities. Tomorrow was far too far away to worry about.

As they flew towards the border Justin became increasingly garrulous. For the first time Corinne began to doubt whether she could really maintain control of the unstable young American who was her passport to the United States, her distorted version of the fabled Shangri-La.

*

The wedding reception was everything that such a happy event should be. Marius was Master of Ceremonies and made hilarious introductions to the main speakers. Sam, as Best Man, added a further dimension with his blend of dry humour as well as some sound advice for the couple which had been handed down over the generations by a succession of African elders. It was a recipe, he assured them with a straight face, for a happy marriage and at least ten healthy young children.

An emotional Ed responded to all the speeches.

'My friends, I came here a year ago not knowing what to expect. I saw it as a brief overseas adventure that I would recall from time to time as I paged through an old photo album, but I did not expect to find a completely new meaning to life, which occurred the evening I looked across a crowded restaurant and saw a young woman who literally took my breath away.'

Ed paused and smiled at Kurt.

'I'm also delighted that her date for that evening, Kurt here, has been forgiving enough to be here tonight and I am honoured to include him amongst my growing circle of really good friends.'

Ed looked down at his new wife beside him.

'Elke and I are looking forward to making our future in the Kroondal district. I shall always remember my first home right here at Buffalo Hills. I look forward to popping in regularly to see Rob, Don and Elliot who have excelled themselves here tonight with this magnificent wedding reception.'

As Ed spoke, warmly thanking everyone who had contributed towards the wedding, he did not see Marius slip quietly from the room. Despite the warmth and hilarity of the event Marius had spent much of the evening worrying over a mental picture of Justin at Ed's car. On the face of it, a final defiant message from the disturbed youngster was no more or less than what everyone could have expected, but he felt that there was something more. Marius replayed and replayed the scene in his mind.

Justin with a can of shaving cream was writing a message on the back of Ed's car. He then headed back to his car and left the hotel. No! As Marius had turned into the parking ground, he had seen something else. Yes, that was it! Justin had slammed the back door of Ed's car shut before going to the rear window and spraying his message on it. The car park was close to the Conference Centre. He knew that as soon as Ed finished the speech, he and Elke would dance the first waltz, cut the cake, say goodbye to everyone and leave.

Marius hurried over to Ed's car. He tried the back door. It was locked. He moved forward and tried the driver's door. It was also locked. At that moment the security guard from the gate came up to him. He knew Marius well.

'Good evening, Mr de Wet. How are you?'

'I'm well, thanks Joshua. D'you know who has the keys to Mr Willjohn's car? I just need to check something.'

Joshua smiled and withdrew the key from his pocket.

'Do you want to leave a message inside the car?'

Marius shook his head.

'No Joshua, I just need to check and see if someone else has already done so!'

*

Ed came out of the luxurious bathroom of the Michaelangelo's bridal suite. Elke was sitting in the bed, wearing a cream coloured negligee, and looking, as all brides should, a little eager, a little shy and very, very much in love!

As Ed stepped forward to join his wife in bed, he remembered fleetingly that his great friend Marius had told him to call in the following morning. There was an urgent matter that could wait that night but no longer than that. He urged Ed not to forget to call. Ed took another step forward and all thoughts of phone calls, messages and urgencies were the very last thing on his mind as Elke and he embraced, gently at first, but with growing passion as they began to experience a oneness that neither of them could have ever imagined!

oOo

GLOSSARY

Afrikaans - An official language of South Africa, spoken by around 6 million people as their first language. Derived from the form of Dutch brought by settlers to the Cape in 17th century.

Bakkie - A pick - up truck in South Africa. A light delivery van.

Big five - Lion, leopard, rhinocerous, elephant and African buffalo. A term coined by big - game hunters.

Boer - Dutch word for farmer.

Boer War - First - 20 December 1880 - 23 March 1881.

Boer War - Second - 11 October 1899 - 31 May 1902.

Boma - A livestock enclosure in central and southern Africa.

Buck - Impala.

Burg - Castle or fortress in German. In South Africa a town or city.

Casevac Chopper - Casualty Evacuation Helicopter, a military term for the emergency evacuation of casualties from a combat zone.

Chivas Regal - A blended Scotch whisky produced by Chivas Brothers, part of Pernod Ricard, in Speyside, Scotland.

"Clements se Slag" - Afrikaans for "Beating Clements."

Coloured - A person of mixed race.

Dagga - Afrikaans for cannabis.

Dassie - Rock rabbit.

Dronkie - A drunkard, South African slang.

Hick town - An insulting way of referring to a small town in the countryside that is not deemed to be very sophisticated.

Horse and trailer - A truck and trailer.

Jalopy - An old car in a dilapidated condition.

Kloof - Afrikaans for gorge.

Koeksisters - Afrikaner Confectionary made from fried dough infused with syrup or honey.

Kroondal - Village in the North West Province with a large German speaking community.

Kudu - African antelope with a grey/brown coat, white vertical stripes and the male has long spiral horns.

Kwaito - Music genre that emerged in Johannesburg during the 1990s. It is a variant of house music featuring the use of African sounds and samples.

Lekker - Afrikaans for good.

Loerie - South African bird. There are 2 main groups - arboreal species with mainly green plumage and crimson wings and the the species that mostly inhabits the savanna areas with a plain grey plumage.

Lucerne - Alfalfa.

Magtig - Afrikaans for "Oh Lord" or "Heavens above." Literally "mighty."

Mealie pap - Corn or maize based dish.

Melktert - Afrikaner egg custard tart.

Meneer - Afrikaans for Sir.

Moenie worrie nie - Afrikaans for "don't panic," "don't worry."

Moot, the - The Dutch word Moot means Moat in English and refers to the wide valley which separates the Magaliesberg and the Daspoortrand.

Mopane worm - A large edible caterpillar that primarily feeds on Mopane trees.

Moroko - African spinach.

Mrs Ples - The popular nickname for the most complete skull of an Australopithecus africanus ever found in South Africa.

Oom - Afrikaans for Uncle.

Palace of the Lost City - Hotel complex set on the high ground at Sun City.

Palooka - A stupid, clumsy or uncouth person.

Pressed ceiling - In the USA known as tin ceilings. Extruded patterned sheets of metal used as a cheaper alternative to patterned plaster ceilings.

Quartzite - An extremely compact, hard, granular rock consisting essentially of quartz.

Scorched-earth policy - A military strategy that aims to destroy anything that might be useful to the enemy.

Shebeen - An informal licensed drinking place in a township.

Skatjie - Afrikaans for "darling."

Skinnering - Gossiping - South African slang.

Stoep - In South Africa a verandah in front of a house.

Stope - An excavation in a mine or quarry in the form of a step or notch.

Sun City - A casino and resort complex in the North West Province of South Africa.

Taal - Afrikaans for "language."

Tsotsi taal - A gangster language from the urban townships

Tswana - A member of a southern African people living in Botswana, South Africa and neighbouring areas or their language.

Tukkies - Nickname for the University of Pretoria.

Uitlander - Afrikaans for "foreigner."

Unisa - UNISA, one of the largest correspondence university systems in the world, based in Pretoria.

Vrou - Afrikaans for "woman" or "wife," from the Dutch.

Wat praat - Afrikaans for "speaking" - literally "what talks."

Wie geht's - German - "How are you?"

Witblitz - White Lightning, also the name of a potent alcoholic homebrew made in the Cape Province.

Zulu - A member of a South African people traditionally living mainly in Kwazulu-Natal province. Also the name of their language.

MAP

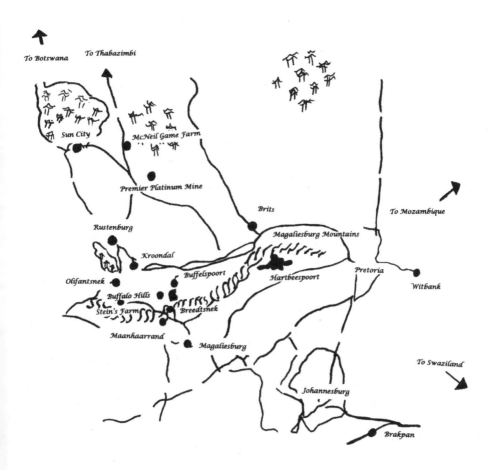

ABOUT THE AUTHOR

Chris has spent his working life in the film and television industry, starting with the BBC in London, then ATV in Birmingham, where he was the youngest Studio Manager in Britain.

Later, in South Africa, he wrote and directed film and TV commercials and had four South African entries at the Cannes Advertising Festival. Chris wrote, directed and produced documentaries, eight of which won international awards.

He then concentrated on writing screenplays and had five feature films and seven television series screened. He is currently obtaining finance for an action adventure feature film that he has written and is co-producing.

https://www.pagodatreebooks.com
https://twitter.com/BooksPagoda
https://www.facebook.com/profile.php?id=100008582913719

ALSO BY CHRIS DRESSER

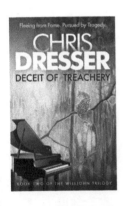

Deceit of Treachery, Coming October 2021

After his wife's brutal murder, a famous concert pianist escapes to South Africa. Will the Russian Mafia catch up with him and silence him for good?

Marc Breton flees England to live a solitary existence in Buffalo Hills Hotel, but he meets a beautiful Spanish artist, Luiza Esterillo. Will he find solace for his grief in the burgeoning love of this young woman? Or will he lead her into deadly danger?

Deceit of Treachery is the second book in the Willjohn series of thriller mysteries. Chris Dresser's love of South Africa shines through in this story of grief, love and treachery.